D1381242

The
ORCHID SHROUD

ALSO BY MICHELLE WAN

Deadly Slipper

DOUBLEDAY CANADA

The
ORCHID SHROUD

A Novel of Death in the Dordogne

MICHELLE WAN

Copyright © 2006 Michelle Wan

All Rights Reserved. The use of any part of this publication, reproduced, transmitted in
any form or by any means electronic, mechanical, photocopying, recording or otherwise,
or stored in a retrieval system without the prior written consent of the publisher—or,
in the case of photocopying or other reprographic copying, a license from the Canadian
Copyright Licensing Agency—is an infringement of the copyright law.

Doubleday Canada and colophon are trademarks.

Library and Archives Canada Cataloguing in Publication applied for.

ISBN-13: 978-0-385-66119-5
ISBN-10: 0-385-66119-3

BOOK DESIGN BY DEBORAH KERNER / DANCING BEARS DESIGN

This is a work of fiction. Names, characters, businesses, organizations,
places, events, and incidents either are the product of the author's imagination
or are used fictitiously. Any resemblance to actual persons, living or dead,
events, or locales is entirely coincidental.

Printed and bound in the USA

Published in Canada by
Doubleday Canada, a division of
Random House of Canada Limited

Visit Random House of Canada Limited's website: www.randomhouse.ca

10 9 8 7 6 5 4 3 2 1

TO ORCHID-LOVERS EVERYWHERE.

AND TO MARG, JENNY, AND ANNE,

VERY IMPORTANT PEOPLE.

ACKNOWLEDGMENTS

This book drew on the help, kindness, and encouragement of many people. I thank them all. Special acknowledgment is owing, however, to certain individuals. In France, *un grand merci* to: Bob and Mary Woodman, Michel and Marie-Sylvie Renard, Marie-Léontine Carcenac, Ginette and Louis Ducourtioux, Bruno Dalle, Patrick Lemesle, Marie-Pierre Kachintzeff, and Garry Watt for their friendship, wonderful food experiences, and for helping me to get the language right and understand so many things about life in the Dordogne. I am also grateful to Nicole Levy for her assistance with things legal and notarial; Charles Amiguet for information on hunting; and Didier Ribeyrol for input on the French Gendarmerie. I would be remiss if I did not single out, among the above-mentioned, Patrick for his invaluable guidance on police procedures; and Marie-Pierre, Garry, and Michel and for their kindness and generosity in helping me to nail down facts and fine-tune details. My gratitude to all of you.

Closer to home, I wish to thank Allan Anderson for his botanical expertise and for helping me to find places where Canadian Slipper Orchids grow; Margaret MacKinnon, David Antscherl, and my husband, Tim, for their critical review of the draft; Frances and Bill Hanna not only for their wise input and support, but for naming this book; and my sister, Grace, whose encouragement and wonderful house inspire me.

I also used a number of botanical, nonfiction, and other

resources in researching this novel. In particular, I wish to recognize the scholarship of the following authors: Phillip Cribb (*The Genus Cypripedium*); Alec M. Pridgeon, Phillip J. Cribb, Mark W. Chase, and Finn N. Rasmussen (*Genera Orchidacearum, Volume I*); Holger Perner (personal communications); Pierre Delforge (*Orchids of Britain and Europe*); Mark Kurlansky (*Salt, A World History*); Mark Girouard (*Life in the French Country House*); Michel Louis (*La bête du Gévaudan*); and Calude Seignolle (*Contes du Périgord*). Any distortions or errors that may have occurred in making the leap from fact to fiction are mine.

As always I end with deepest thanks to Tim, the love of my life and friend of the path, who goes with me every step of the way.

This work of fiction takes place in the Dordogne (dor-DOHN-yuh), a *département* in southwestern France where the wooded countryside in spring rings with the cuckoo's call and where wild orchids still bloom. The characters in this book are entirely fictitious, and invented places jostle with real ones. The Sigoulane Valley and the places in and around it are imaginary. The orchids, with the exception of one, exist and are endangered. Please respect them and their habitat. Above all, rejoice in their beauty.

The
ORCHID SHROUD

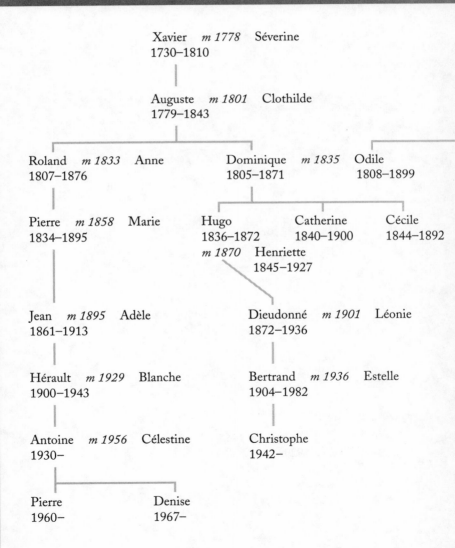

DE BONFOND and VERDIER
FAMILY TREES

(only main bloodline individuals and dates shown)

DE BONFOND FAMILY

Xavier   *m 1778*   Séverine
1730–1810

Auguste   *m 1801*   Clothilde
1779–1843

Roland   *m 1833*   Anne
1807–1876

Dominique   *m 1835*   Odile
1805–1871   1808–1899

Pierre   *m 1858*   Marie
1834–1895

Hugo   Catherine   Cécile
1836–1872   1840–1900   1844–1892
m 1870   Henriette
1845–1927

Jean   *m 1895*   Adèle
1861–1913

Dieudonné   *m 1901*   Léonie
1872–1936

Hérault   *m 1929*   Blanche
1900–1943

Bertrand   *m 1936*   Estelle
1904–1982

Antoine   *m 1956*   Célestine
1930–

Christophe
1942–

Pierre   Denise
1960–   1967–

Albin   *m 1770*   Catherine
1736–1798

Guillaume   *m 1801*   Eliane
1773–1840

Raymond   *m 1835*   Bernadette
1807–1883

Bernard   *m 1862*   Albertine   Eloïse
1837–1902   1843–1910

Albert   *m 1894*   Marie-Claude
1867–1915

Guillaume   *m 1925*   Sylvie
1897–1943

Michel   *m 1953*   Lucie
1929–

Guy   *m 1979*   Mariette
1954–

The man in the greasy beret dropped his burden to the ground. He glanced over his shoulder. As usual, he, André Piquet, was up to no good. Nothing serious, mind. Just the kind of routine skulduggery that the Piquets, a noted clan of *tricheurs*, generally practiced.

With a quick slash of his hunting knife, André severed the cord that secured the mouth of the sack. It sagged, spewing some of its contents over the damp litter of pine needles and last year's fallen leaves. Sheathing the knife, he upended the sack. Smelly kitchen peelings mixed with dried maize tumbled to the ground.

Baiting *sangliers*, the tough wild pigs that hunters in the Dordogne prized above all game, was frowned on as unsportsmanlike, not to say damned sneaky. The idea was that the *sangliers*, which roamed freely through the deep valleys and dense forests of this region of southwestern France, became accustomed to feeding at the baiting stations, with the result that, when the hunting season opened, *voilà*, you had a ready population of pigs in place for the kill. If you were quick off the mark, you could bring down an animal or two before anyone got wind of what you'd been up to. It was the Piquets' guiding principle. Do it the easy way, secretly and fast, and your neighbor would never be the wiser. Also, it meant not having to share out your kill, taken on the quiet like that, with other hunters and local residents.

As he rolled up the sack and stuffed it under his jacket, André heard a sound. He looked about him. The woods in early evening were chill and gloomy. It occurred to him that everything was uncommonly still. Normally starlings and crows made a racket around this time. Suddenly he felt a little nervous. Was someone spying on him? Or maybe it was the speed with which the darkness was moving in.

Again, his ears caught the noise, a kind of scraping that was not the drilling of a woodpecker, or the creaking of branches in the wind. It seemed to be coming from somewhere to his right. Now curiosity vied with caution. Treading softly, he pushed through the thick undergrowth in the direction of the noise. He parted a curtain of pine branches and stepped into a small clearing. What he saw outraged him: a juvenile boar, freshly killed by the look of it. It lay head-on to him, one of its underdeveloped tusks driven into the dark, rough earth.

"*Putain!*" André, thrust suddenly onto the unaccustomed moral high ground, gave vent to his disgust. Baiting pigs was one thing, but hunting out of season, especially if someone beat you to it, really went against the grain. Funny, though, he hadn't heard a shot. And there did seem to be an awful lot of blood about. The ground all around was churned up and soaked with it.

Then he realized that the wild pig had not been shot. Drawing closer, he saw that it had been brought down by something that had slashed its haunches, severing the hindquarter tendons to disable it before going in for the kill. Feeding had already begun, for the belly had been partly torn open, the slippery guts spilling out. André whistled through a gap in his stained front teeth. Whatever it was had to be big. A boar, even young, was a tough adversary for most dogs. Maybe a pack of dogs? he wondered. He hunkered down for a closer look, balancing on the balls of his feet.

It was then that the long gray form came on him, hitting him from behind with tremendous force. He sprawled forward, driven face-down into the blood-wet earth. He felt a visceral shock as something ripped deep into the flesh of his shoulder.

"Nom de dieu!" André shrieked. A hunter, he knew the ferocity of the wounded boar, the dangerous valor of the stag at bay. Never had he encountered anything like the savagery of this attack. Desperately he rolled over, shielding his face and throat with one hand while attempting to free his knife from its sheath with the other. He stood no chance against it. With a snarl conceived in hell, the creature came in for the kill.

1

The first shattering blow echoed down the line of empty rooms. The big man stepped back, raised the iron mallet again. It struck home with another sickening thud.

Christophe de Bonfond recoiled at the first hit, turned away at the second. His normally cheerful face was pale.

"Je ne peux pas . . ." he murmured to his companion. "I can't. It really is too much."

"Then don't," Mara Dunn responded in French, drawing him away by the arm. She was a small, slim woman, forty-something, dressed in jeans and a T-shirt that read in English: *Outside of a dog a man's best friend is a book. Inside of a dog it is very dark.* This was attributed to Groucho Marx. Her head was topped with short-cropped hair. She had dark eyes, straight brows, and a decisive chin. Her expression, normally vivid, was at the moment tightly composed. Why had he insisted on being there? She said in an even tone that belied her exasperation, "We'll leave them to it, shall we?"

The little man nodded, shuddering as the steady, awful cadence of blows continued. In his haste to be gone, he pulled free of her and scuttled through a doorway leading into a small antechamber that gave access to the stairs.

"Smokey," Mara called over her shoulder, "I'll be down on the terrace with Monsieur de Bonfond if you and Theo need anything."

Aristophanes Serafim, otherwise known as Smokey the Greek

because he was from Thessalonika and a chain smoker, paused in the middle of his swing. A limp Gitane clung like a tubular growth to his lower lip. His sweat-stained T-shirt was stretched over a barrel chest and a large belly.

"What would we need?" He spoke French with an accent as thick as feta cheese. The blunt head of the mallet completed its arc. A large sheet of plaster crashed down around him in a cloud of dust, exposing roughly dressed stone that had not seen the light of day for more than a hundred years. Smokey's younger brother, Theo, equally big, sledgehammer in hand, stepped up to inspect the damage.

"Well, just in case." Mara's eyes lingered anxiously on the pair. She had not worked with the brothers before and was not reassured by what she had seen so far. Their setup had been casual at best; the necessary precision of the task they were undertaking seemed beyond their comprehension. "Please try to take things down as carefully as possible." She glanced up. "You're sure of the bracing?" Her greatest fear was the roof collapsing.

Both men regarded her with indifference. The Serafims were good at demolishing walls but didn't seem to care much what else came down with them.

The terrace ran across the back of the main part of the house, overlooking an expanse of geometrically clipped yews and boxwood: an eighteenth-century garden done in the Italian manner, for all that this was twenty-first-century southwestern France. In fact, everything about Aurillac Manor placed it more in the past than in the present. It was a large U-shaped structure, consisting of an original central block with wings, added on at later times, extending backward to enclose part of the garden. Built of local stone and along traditional lines, with Early Renaissance and Baroque touches, the overall effect was charming if slightly quirky.

She stood beside Christophe at the terrace's edge. Below them played an eighteenth-century stone fountain in the shape of a leaping dolphin. Its nose, chipped off at the tip by some past violence, pointed like a crooked finger at a door giving access to the south wing. Water dribbled from the dolphin's mouth into a handsome but rather scummy pool. Aurillac's grounds staff was down to one old man and a girl. If asked, Christophe would have complained of the difficulty of getting good help.

"Silly of me, I know." His brown eyes were unhappy. He was a small, round person in his early sixties, immaculately dressed in fawn-colored trousers and a summer jacket of slightly darker hue. His sparse, graying hair was neatly slicked back; his features were soft and rosy. He resembled, Mara thought, one of those nice pink marzipan pigs displayed in the windows of the better confectionary shops. Except for his expression. Confectionary pigs smiled.

"It—it's too much like living flesh . . ." Christophe managed to sound both apologetic and petulant at the same time. The flesh of the de Bonfonds was what he meant, overlying the brittle bones of old money, the stiffened sinews of class and privilege dating back centuries, embodied in a house.

"You wanted a gallery," Mara reasoned with him. "You can't have it without knocking out walls." A naturally quick, impatient person, she had learned the necessity of coaxing clients along. The demolition stage was never easy. People had a hard time seeing past the rubble.

It had been Christophe's idea to convert the entire upper floor of the north wing into an elevated gallery. The *galérie* was a popular feature of grand French country residences in the sixteenth and seventeenth centuries. Initially a broad corridor linking parts of a house, it had evolved its own specialized function as an elegant walkway, a place for meditation and indoor exercise, a showcase for displaying family treasures and works of art. According to

Christophe, the fact that Aurillac Manor lacked a *galérie* was not because it wasn't grand enough but simply owing to pure bad planning.

"You see," he had explained when Julian had brought Mara out three months earlier, "Aurillac, or at least the central block, will be five hundred years old next year. The *galérie* is my birthday present to the house, you might say, and the perfect architectural complement to a little book I'm writing on the history of my family." One had to take his use of "little" as an intended understatement, for the draft was said to run to over four hundred pages. "The de Bonfonds were ennobled, you know, by King Louis XV in recognition of invaluable services rendered to the crown. In fact, our family motto, 'Blood And My Right,' was suggested by the King himself, who intended it to refer to the rights and privileges conferred by our ancient bloodline. Rather like the British Royal Family's 'God And My Right,' except that the Brits"—here he had giggled—"recognize a higher power."

The book, in turn, was intended to mark the quarter-century anniversary of Christophe's small, elite publishing house, Editions Arobas. It was great fun, he said, everything coming together all at once like that. Christophe, who seemed to have pots of money, had glowed with excitement.

"Can you do it?" he had asked Mara earnestly as they strolled through the series of gloomy rooms making up the north wing. "Julian told me how good you are. I did talk to an architect, you know, but I didn't like him. A dreadful man with dirty fingernails, *pas sympathique du tout.*"

"I expect he mentioned these are all load-bearing walls?" Mara, a French Canadian interior designer with an eye for old houses, had seen many misguided renovations since setting up shop in the Dordogne eight years ago. "You can't just knock them out. They hold up your roof." She had spoken coolly, but excitement had surged through her like a drug. The wing, built before communicating corridors came into fashion, consisted of three large rooms, one giving onto another by way of smaller, interspersing antechambers. That meant breaking down five dividing walls in addition to the portion of the old exterior east wall where the wing had been joined on, thereby extending the gallery all the way to the front of the house. The creative use of space was her métier, and her mind leaped ahead to all the possibilities.

In the end Mara had worked out a plan (with another architect, who had clean nails and who was more *sympathique*) for converting the internal walls into a series of weight-bearing arches. The structural integrity would be ensured, and Christophe would have the sense and functionality of continuous space. She also planned to cut away the window embrasures at forty-five-degree angles to increase the illumination. It was Mara's most important commission ever and a challenging project. Christophe was proving to be a grit-your-teeth client. Changing his mind. Fretting. (What if the structure was damaged? What if the gallery was not, after all, to his liking?) And now not being able to stomach the violence of the hammer's blow.

"Look." Once again she took him by the arm, turning him firmly from the dribbling fountain that was beginning to wear on her nerves. "Stop worrying. This is just the messy part. Think about the finished product. You'll love it. Family portraits on the walls, statues in the alcoves. The private space of a gentleman, for pleasure and contemplation." She threw out the line like a sop.

Christophe brightened. "Of course. You're right, as ever. I'm so glad Julian introduced me to you. I simply could not have entrusted the work to someone who didn't understand my feelings." He allowed himself to be led away. A moment later he glanced slyly at Mara and shook his head. "Although what l'Adorée will say to all of this I really dread to think."

"Who"—Mara's back went rigid as she braced herself for another complication—"is l'Adorée?"

"The Adored One, my great-grandmother, so named because my great-grandfather loved her passionately. Theirs was the romance of the century." He gave her an impish grin. "Her spirit still walks, did you know?"

"Formidable." Mara laughed gustily. A ghost she could deal with, and Christophe's sense of humor seemed to have returned. In a good mood, the man was tremendously likable, which made his sulks and moments of unhappiness all the more affecting.

"Her name was Henriette Bertillon," he went on. "She was a great beauty and a wonderful soprano. Apparently she was plucked out of a convent school where her pure voice soared over the cloister"—Christophe's hand spiraled up in a simulation of soaring—"and thrust onto the stage of the Paris Opéra. My great-grandfather Hugo heard her sing and fell madly in love with her. They married, and when she became ill with tuberculosis, he brought her here to the family country estate to recuperate. Come. I'll show you her room."

He steered Mara toward a door at the south end of the terrace. It opened directly into a lovely chamber, the walls of which were covered in cream-colored *boiserie* inset with lozenges of painted fruit and flowers. True, the paint was chipped and faded, but the effect was charming all the same. In an alcove, Mara spotted a *bonheur-du-jour,* a delicate lady's writing desk with a raised back, that she would have given an arm to acquire.

"As you can see," said Christophe, "it's been converted from a bedroom to a sitting room—*le petit salon,* my parents called it. I'm told l'Adorée loved this room because it opened right onto the terrace and garden. I always thought she died young. However, the fellow I hired to do the background research for my book tells me she lived well into old age."

"And her spirit?"

"Temperamental. Dear me. My housekeeper, whose parents

worked in the house in my parents' and grandparents' time, claims she once caused dinner plates to fly—"

"Arrh," a voice grated hoarsely behind them.

They turned. It was Theo Serafim, standing in the open doorway. He was covered in a fine layer of plaster dust. He carried his mallet as nonchalantly as a tack hammer. Dark runnels of sweat scored his cheeks.

"Oui?" Mara drew straight, black brows together, the knot in her stomach that she was coming to associate with the Serafims pulling tight.

"Smokey says you want the stones numbered." Theo's accent was even thicker than his brother's.

"Exactly." She let her breath out slowly. "Left to right, top to bottom, while they're still in place. Monsieur de Bonfond wants to keep the stones, and he wants them ordered. I explained everything to Smokey yesterday. You have a problem?"

"Arrh. It's just that it's a double wall, and we're working at it on both sides, like."

She waited distrustfully.

He scratched his head, releasing a cloud of particles into the air. "So how do you want them numbered? The side he's on, or the side I'm on? Left to right his side is right to left my—"

"Christophe," said Mara in as even a tone as she could manage, "will you excuse me a moment?"

2

The object that Henriette de Bonfond, née Bertillon, had caused to fly was not a dinner plate but a goodly-sized crystal ball. She had two strong arms, and the orb she had flung from the terrace had crashed into the nose of a fishlike creature that rose out of the fountain below her, carrying away with it a large chip of stone before disappearing with a satisfying splash into the murky depths of the basin. She had chosen the crystal ball because it appeared to be a valued family posses-sion, occupying pride of place on a plinth in the main reception room. She had intended simply to hurl it into the pool. That it had damaged the fountain en route was better still.

Henriette's fury was occasioned by her impossible situation. She had given up the lively salons of Paris for a promised life of ease and comfort. Not that she had expected Hugo's family to receive her well. At least, not at first. She brought neither money nor property into the match. Beauty, wit, and intelligence were her entire dowry. However, at Aurillac she had found a penny-pinching austerity beyond imagin-ing and a degree of ill-will that chilled her to the bone. Hugo, now that he had bedded her, did nothing to defend her. Instead, he went hunt-ing every day, returning in the evening smelling of horses and wet leaves and stained with the blood of his kill. She was left to the com-pany of his odious mother, his great lump of a sister, and his gouty fa-ther, who leered horribly at her from the fireside armchair to which he was confined.

A survivor, Henriette had instantly picked out Hugo's mother as her principal adversary. Odile de Bonfond was a thin, grim woman with a mouth like an iron trap. Henriette astutely sized her up as harder and more grasping than a bordel *keeper and more preposterously puffed up about her station in life than the most arrogant Parisian lackey. Odile was also cruel and clever. Henriette found herself the target of daily acts of malice. The fare at Aurillac consisted mainly of game brought down by Hugo, who had a bloodlust for the hunt. When they had a* civet *of hare, it was Henriette who was somehow and inexplicably served the head. She was kept short of candles, perhaps in the hope that she would trip on the stairs and break her neck. She was sure that the servants had been instructed to ignore her orders. Only one, a new girl named Marie, showed herself kindly toward the newcomer. Between mistress and maid a certain sympathy had sprung up.*

As Henriette watched the ripples in the pond die away, she knew it would be a fight to the finish. She was confident enough of her skills to feel that in time she would more than better her new sister and father-in-law. She was not so sure about Odile.

3

Business was a word-of-mouth affair, Julian Wood reckoned happily. Or, as the locals put it, *de bouche à l'oreille*, from mouth to ear. He was a tall, lean man, topping fifty, with a long face, a badly trimmed mustache and beard, and unruly, grizzled hair. He stood a moment, looking across the Sigoulane Valley, a broad sunlit depression on the north shore of the Dordogne River. Trellised vines filled the valley floor. Rows of them spilled up the gently sloping western flank to join a pure, blue sky. Julian hooked his thumbs into his jeans pockets and breathed deeply. It was a glorious morning, the kind of weather he had left England for nearly three decades ago. The kind of weather that kept him rooted in the Dordogne.

It was simple. Julian had introduced Mara to his good friend Christophe de Bonfond, which had led to her securing the renovation of Aurillac Manor. Christophe, in turn, had set Julian up with his cousin Antoine de Bonfond, an uncomplicated man of the soil whose large, upright figure belied his seventy-odd years. With the result that Julian was now coming away from the prestigious Coteaux de Bonfond winery with a fat contract in his pocket. Or as good as, for the deal with Antoine had been concluded with a handshake and the prospect of landscaping the new sales pavilion, destined to receive the delegations of buyers and busloads of tourists who were the foundation of the winery sales. That was how things worked in the Dordogne, and just in time, too, from Julian's perspective. His bank account had been running desperately lean of late. Whistling an off-key rendition of "Money Makes the World Go Round," he hopped into his battered Peugeot van, keyed the ignition, and drove off.

Good old Christophe. He thought again with gratitude of their odd friendship, formed twenty-three years ago, during a back-breaking and often hysterical attempt to restore the Italianate format of Aurillac's gardens. Julian did the spadework, and there had been a lot of it, for everything had been allowed to run wild; Christophe had the hysterics; and the project was eventually abandoned half finished. Shortly after that, Christophe had published Julian's book on wildflowers of the Dordogne when no one else would touch it. The work, originally planned in picture-book format, had been converted by a bright junior editor to a bilingual botanical guide. At first Christophe had balked. It was not the thing that small, select Editions Arobas did. But the idea had proven so successful that Arobas was now set to publish Julian's *Wild Orchids of the Dordogne* as a companion edition. Julian, who wanted nothing more than to garden and pursue his orchidological passions, was actually in danger of becoming an established author.

Julian's relationship with Mara, more dizzying, went back not quite fourteen months. At the thought of her, he left off whistling and rubbed his beard reflectively. Like a man unable to trust a run of luck, he didn't entirely believe that Mara had come into his life. One disastrous marriage long ago and subsequent unsatisfactory relationships had left him doubting. The two of them were so different. She was high-energy and driven. He was content to go, slowly, with the flow. She was an interior designer, constantly interfering with the natural scatter of things. He was an outdoors kind of person who, for the most part, took life as it came. She did not share his floral enthusiasms.

Well, opposites attracted, he acknowledged as he downshifted into a turn. Although it could also be the typical story of two expatriates thrown together in a country where you were always to some degree an outsider, and where existence ran according to an often elegantly unfathomable logic. Nothing new there. Lust? Definitely. But there was more to it than that, he felt. Something—he chewed his bottom lip, thinking of fitting similes—like a taut piece of elastic between them that held him fast (but that could also fling him back nastily, if the other end were let go). Nevertheless, there she was, causing him to experience a sense of glad anticipation he had not known for years.

Julian slowed as he approached the turnoff for Aurillac, which stood high on a ridge on the east side of the valley. Christophe was laying on drinks and lunch that day, "to commemorate the breaking of stone." Julian glanced at his watch. Just gone half ten. He supposed he could turn up early to see how the demolition was progressing, but he'd only get in the way. Mara at a work site, he knew from experience, could be cranky. On the other hand, he had plenty of time to run out to Malpech and back, rounding out what was already shaping up to be a perfect day. He gunned the engine and drove straight on.

His way ran south out of the valley along a road that cut through the immaculately groomed vines of Coteaux de Bonfond, fifty hectares planted in Merlot and Cabernet Sauvignon grapes with smaller cultivars of Malbec. The valley held the sun like a bowl. This, combined with its sheltered position and peculiar gravelly soils, resulted in an annual production of twenty-four hundred hectoliters of wine, a portion of which went into the making of one of the finest, if not *the* finest, Bergerac reds. Julian had done his homework. The winery star was its Domaine de la Source, a splendid, full-bodied wine that took its name from a spring that poured out of a hillside above the winery in the forested north end of the valley. In fact, the landscaping plan he had proposed cleverly centered on a water feature, modeled on that spring. Again, he had done his homework.

As he neared the valley head, he passed Antoine's house—Les

Chardonnerets, it was called—an imposing structure that rode like a stone ship in a sea of vines. Beyond it, the order of Coteaux de Bonfond gave way to the sketchier plantations and cottages of smaller growers. At the village of Sigoulane, a cluster of steeply roofed buildings fashioned from the warm yellow limestone of the region, he found himself at the river. He rumbled across the old stone bridge and turned east, following a network of minor roads that wound between rumpled hills and past fields of young wheat ablaze with spring poppies. Iris Potter had left a message on his phone the evening before: she needed to talk to him about a sketch she was preparing for a section of his book, and could he drop by at his earliest?

The new book was Julian's magnum opus. It contained lovingly annotated photographs of every species of wild, terrestrial orchid native to the Dordogne. There were dozens of them: Lady Orchids in their spotted purple skirts; Military Orchids standing to attention like diminutive soldiers; pale, fleshy Bird's-nests; braided Lady's-tresses; Man, Pyramidal, Lizard, Butterfly, and Monkey Orchids. There were also the many kinds of *Dactylorhiza*, and the cunning genus of *Ophrys* that mimicked the insect pollinators they sought to attract. He had spent years charting and photographing these flowers and knew them like old friends. Each spring he returned to woodlands, meadows, and bogs to visit his favorite colonies, or searched anxiously for individual plants whose fate he feared for. And each year he found that the orchids were fewer in number as their habitat was gradually encroached on or destroyed.

One flower, in particular, haunted his waking hours. An unknown Lady's Slipper which he had never seen in real life and of which he had only one very bad photograph and no information. He had given a copy of the photo to Iris to draw, hoping that her artist's eye could render whole something that for him was frustratingly incomplete. He was itching to see what progress she had made on it. He was less enthusiastic about running into Iris's tem-

peramental paramour, Géraud Laval. Géraud was also a keen orchidologist and Julian's nemesis in all things botanical, especially
where this Mystery Orchid was concerned.

*A*h. *C'est vous,*" Géraud barked as he opened the door to Julian.
"What do you want?" A retired pharmacist, he was a short,
bald, goblinesque man with wiry tufts of hair sprouting from both
ears. Julian, who could only guess at Géraud's age, believed grimly
that he would never die.

"Don't be rude, Joujou." Iris, a dumpy little figure in a paint-
stained smock, pushed forward to pull Julian inside. "He's here to
see me." She raised a weathered face to exchange pecks with Julian, one per cheek—the number varied, depending on where in
France you were. A Brit expatriate and longtime Dordogne resident, Iris dabbled in sentimental watercolors for a living but could
turn out surprisingly accurate botanical drawings when called on.
"And, no, he doesn't want to see your latest hybrid." She steered
Julian away from the glassed-in plant room attached to the rear of
the house. The space there was crammed with tropical orchids, an
exotic display of showy colors and bizarre forms, unlike the more
modest terrestrial varieties that Julian preferred.

Undeterred, Géraud shouted, "*Kingianum* cross. Got it for an
obscene price from a whore of a breeder who literally *stole* it from
someone else." Géraud's passion was possessing and breeding tree-
dwelling epiphytes, although he also maintained a vast collection
of terrestrials that he had pirated from elsewhere and planted in
his back garden. Géraud was notoriously unfussy about how he acquired things.

Iris said earnestly, "Listen, Julian, I need to talk to you. That
photo you gave me—"

"I know," he apologized. "It's dreadful. The film, as I told you,
was damaged. Unfortunately, it's all I have to go on."

"Ha!" roared Géraud, trailing after them. "You're mad. Putting that thing in your book, pretending it's an unknown species of *Cypripedium*."

"What's wrong with that?" Julian fought to keep his cool. "I'm treating it as an uncertain sighting."

"Based on a dog's breakfast of a photograph. You know as well as I do there's only one native species of Lady's Slipper in Western Europe, *Cypripedium calceolus*, which doesn't grow in these parts and never looked like that."

"Oh, you're just jealous. Admit it. You're hoping as much as I am that this flower really exists. You're afraid I'll claim it first. You can't stand the thought that someone else might get credit for discovering a rare—"

"Discover?" Géraud almost shrieked. "Discover? What have you discovered? Where's your proof?"

"Don't worry," Julian yelled back. "I'll find it. And you don't fool me. You're beating the bushes for it, too. I've seen you skulking around Les Colombes."

"Stop it." Iris intervened physically between the two men. "Géraud, go away. I mean it. Go away. Julian and I need to talk."

"You're chasing a phantom," her volatile consort cried, stalking off. "Don't say I didn't warn you."

Iris pushed Julian down the hall into her studio and slammed the door.

"Look. I've done your color sketch. But I want you to know I honestly couldn't make anything of the whatsit, the labellum, from the photo." She handed him her drawing. It depicted a flower rising from a single stem. Two long, blackish-purple lateral petals spiraled fantastically away from a large middle petal that was only partially sketched in.

"But you've left most of it blank," Julian cried.

Iris shoved wisps of graying hair out of very blue, ingenuous eyes. "What else could I do? I mean, you want this to be accurate, don't you? Here." She unpinned a much-handled print copy from a corkboard and held it beside the drawing. A dark stain ran through the middle of the image. She tapped the spot. "You tell me."

"I did. The labellum is a shoe-shaped pouch with an opening at the top where insect pollinators enter. You know the legend. Venus lost her slipper, it changed into a flower, hence the name."

Iris said flatly, "I don't see it."

"Trust me. And anyway, you can take a little artistic license, can't you?"

"But what? Fat and bulbous? Long and thin? It's like one of those dot-to-dot drawings children do, except the dots are missing. Anything I put in would be pure guesswork."

Julian stared glumly at Iris's sketch. She was right, of course. He was asking her to make a drawing of something that had to be at least partly imagined. And yet this orchid had once grown on the grounds of the château of Les Colombes, no more than a few kilometers from where they stood. Twenty years ago, Mara's twin sister had found and photographed it. The badly stained print she had left behind was Julian's only evidence of its existence. Unfortunately, Bedie Dunn was in no position to describe it or guide him to it. She was dead.

"What about Jeanne de Sauvignac? Have you tried asking her?" Iris referred to the only other person who might be able to help him.

He shook his head. "No good. I tried, but she's genuinely round the twist. I doubt she knows what day it is, let alone where Bedie's orchid might have grown."

Iris sighed. "Poor thing. Of course, she never was exactly right, was she? She's back at Les Colombes now, did you know? A nurse goes in daily, but I hear that Rocher woman is more or less looking after things. In fact," Iris said grimly, "the villagers say she and that ghastly son of hers are practically living at the château."

"Vrac?" Julian conjured up a hulking form and a frightening face with a vacant, although at times cunning, look. Together, Vrac and his mother, la Binette Rocher, made an intimidating pair.

"Mmm. I ran into la Binette selling her ewe's cheese at the market in Brames last week and ventured to ask how Jeanne was. The woman told me quite rudely that it was none of my onions. One shudders to think . . ."

Julian did shudder. Although it was equally possible that the Rochers, in their way, were doing a passable job as caretakers for the elderly woman. The de Sauvignacs of Les Colombes had always stood as *seigneurs* to the Rochers, Jeanne was a de Sauvignac, if only by marriage, and the Dordogne was a region where old loyalties held.

Iris returned to her sketch. "I have another problem. I don't know what to do with these things that look like petals but aren't. I mean, orchids have three petals and three other thingummies, don't they?"

"Sepals," corrected Julian. "A dorsal sepal on top and two side sepals. They lie behind the petals and wrap around the flower while it's in bud. And, yes, orchids normally have three of them. But the morphology of *Cypripediaceae* is different. In Slipper Orchids, the two side sepals are mostly or completely fused into a single synsepal. Sorry. I should have explained."

"Bother," said Iris. "So how should I do it?"

Julian considered. "If you rotate the drawing to give a three-quarters view, you can show it as one broad synsepal hanging down behind the labellum."

"Right. Give me a day or two. I'll call you when it's ready."

"Bless you, Iris."

"Bless yourself. You'll need it when Géraud gets through with you. He's determined to expose you as a fraud, you know."

Julian did know.

Julian drove west, retracing his path toward Sigoulane. The church bells were ringing out noon as he rattled through the village, its houses still and sleepy in the midday sun. He was hungry. Fighting with Géraud always gave him an appetite.

Julian reached Aurillac Manor by way of a road that ran up from the valley bottom and along the crest of the escarpment. The road eventually dwindled to a narrow lane bordered by ancient chestnuts before ending, almost without warning, in the graveled forecourt of the house. He parked there, ran up the steps to the massive front door, and rang a brass-plated doorbell.

It was a long time before the housekeeper, Thérèse, appeared. She was a tiny person with a deeply creased face topped by a wispy knot of white hair. She wore a flowered apron over a dark dress that hung to mid-calf. Her feet were clad in stout black leather lace-up shoes. She could have been seventy or a hundred. She belonged to that race of Périgordines who lived long lives and who, from a certain age onward, scarcely seemed to change.

"Ah, Monsieur Wood," she cried, letting him in. The name came out as "Vood." "They're waiting for you out back."

He pecked her dried-apple cheeks and handed her a bottle of champagne. "Put that on ice, will you? And this"—a bag of almonds coated in raspberry liqueur and chocolate—"is for you."

"Coucougnettes!" The old woman beamed with pleasure at the sight of her favorite confection. *"Mais, c'est très gentil."*

He took himself through to the terrace. A table, bearing monogrammed silver and an impressive array of glasses, had been placed in the shade of an orange-and-white-striped awning. Christophe rose to clasp Julian's hand.

"Eh bien, mon ami. Ça va? Cousin Antoine came through?"

"He did. But he wants the rock garden done, including a water feature, in time for their marketing launch next month. I'm going to have to work miracles."

"That's why I recommended you." Christophe's expression was smug.

"Well done." Mara grinned and half rose from her chair to exchange kisses, her eyes conveying a welcome and something like relief at Julian's appearance. "Christophe's been telling me about his great-grandmother."

"I was just saying"—Christophe waved a hand—"that the poet Aristide Ladurie once described her as 'walking by day in a cloud of gold'—reference to her hair, of course—'and charming the night with *Myosotis* eyes.'"

"Forget-me-not," Julian translated, sitting down.

"She throws plates," Mara muttered.

Christophe assumed an air of mock self-reproach. "Alas, I have rather monopolized Mara's attention with tales of ectoplasms. When she should have been seeing to those dreadful vandals upstairs."

Julian murmured in her left ear, "Wouldn't mind doing some monopolizing myself." His nose brushed her hair, catching her intimate smell of sandalwood. Her special throaty laughter filled his ear. She kicked him under the table. "Ow!"

"Don't scoff, my friend." Christophe wagged a pudgy finger. "All old houses have their phenomena. Ask Thérèse if you don't believe me."

The housekeeper had appeared with a frosty bottle of champagne in an ice bucket. It was not the bottle he had brought, Julian noticed, but one bearing a far superior label that Christophe must have had at the ready.

"Tell them about the Wailing Ghost, Thérèse," Christophe urged.

"I will not," the old woman cried indignantly. "It's not a thing to talk about."

"Oh, pooh." The little man took the bottle from the bucket, worked the cork out smoothly, and tipped the frothing champagne quickly into crystal flutes. "It's supposed to be an ill omen. Thérèse has heard it many times."

"I have heard it twice. Each time before a death."

"She used to frighten me into good behavior with it when I was a boy. *Santé.*" He raised his glass to Mara and Julian, who returned the toast. "Said it lived in the cupboard under the stairs."

"That was the cat." The old woman fixed her employer with a stern eye. "And it was you who locked it in there. You shouldn't laugh at evil. Bad things happen. Look at that scoundrel Piquet. Always up to no good. The devil claims his own in the end."

"Dreadful incident down in Colline Basse." Christophe shuddered around a swallow of champagne. He plugged the bottle with a silver stopper to conserve the bubbles. "A few weeks ago. You must have heard about it."

Everyone had. The media had been full of it. A *sanglier*-baiter had been killed by some kind of wild animal that had fed on him and left the remains for carrion-eaters to finish off. Local villagers, hunters, and gendarmes from the canton, in collaboration with the responsible office of the Ministry of Ecology, had been beating the woods for the thing ever since. But it was cunning, whatever it was, eluding the best-organized *battues.*

"They said it was a feral dog or a rogue wolf protecting its kill," said Mara. "I hope to god they catch it."

"Couldn't have been a wolf," said Julian. "There aren't any in the Dordogne."

"It was no dog or wolf," Thérèse muttered.

"What was it, then?" Julian asked sardonically. "A *loup-garou?*"

The housekeeper glared at him. "Werewolves exist. They have lived in this valley for centuries. Haven't you heard of the Sigoulane Beast?"

"*Balivernes,*" Christophe declared promptly. "Old wives' tales."

"*Ah eh?* Then what about the *maquisard sans tête?* Something tore *his* head off."

Christophe looked annoyed. In response to Julian and Mara's questioning glance, he said, "It was during the war. My gardener Didier and my cousin Antoine found a body—a Resistance fighter, it was thought—in the woods below the house. They brought it up in a wheelbarrow. I was too young to know anything about it, but it must have been awful for Antoine, who was just a kid himself then. The man had been decapitated. They never found the head. The Germans did it, of course. Although a few superstitious ones"—a resentful glance in Thérèse's direction—"put it about that the Sigoulane Beast was responsible."

"It was. If you don't believe me, ask Didier. He knows a lot more than you think." Thérèse swept the tray up and marched away.

"Now I've upset her," their host laughed nervously. "She's been cranky all morning. Finds all this tearing down of walls as disturbing as I, no doubt—"

There was a shuffling noise behind them. It was both Serafims this time, without their hammers. By now they were so thickly coated in plaster dust that it was difficult to tell them apart. They conferred uneasily between them as to who would speak.

"Can we talk to you a minute?" Smokey took the lead, addressing Mara through lips that were startlingly red against the chalky mask of his face. For once he was without a cigarette. His dark eyes, fringed with white eyelashes, were almost alarming.

"What now?" Mara said, feeling her stomach contract again.

"Problem. With the wall. It's a double wall, like, with a gap in the middle."

"I know that. It's the old exterior wall, where the wing was joined to the main building."

The stonemason considered this for a moment. "Maybe you'd better come."

"Now? Look, if it's rubble fill, you'll just have to dig it out—"

"Not that," said Smokey ominously.

"Well, what, for heaven's sake?"

Smokey the Greek gave her a long, complex look. "You'll see soon enough."

They followed the brothers at a trot across the terrace, Mara, Julian, and Christophe wheezing breathlessly in the rear. They continued in that order through a door and up the narrow stone staircase servicing the north wing, coming into the antechamber that led into the large room at the front of the house where Smokey had been working.

The scene there was disastrous. Dust roiled in the air. The floor, protected somewhat haphazardly by plastic sheeting, was littered with shards of plaster. Stones, presumably numbered, were piled near a window outside which the brothers had erected a beam and pulley for lowering debris to the ground. Heavy wooden braces shored up the ceiling just above the area of work. The east wall of the room had been partially breached. Smokey and Theo stepped up to the ragged hole they had made.

"In there," said Smokey, standing aside, like an unhappy showman presenting the climax of an act he did not like.

Mara peered into the dark cavity.

"What is it?" Julian breathed over her shoulder. "Family treasure?"

"There's something down there." Christophe's voice rang with boyish excitement. "Some kind of a package." He turned to Smokey. "Well, get it out, man! Let's have a look."

Smokey did not comply. His expression, as best as could be determined, was sullen. Silently, he handed Mara a flashlight. She trained the beam on the object. They all stared down at it.

"It looks—my god!" Christophe reeled back, hand pressed to his mouth.

Mara gasped and felt Julian stiffen beside her.

The small form lay face up, swaddled in some kind of cloth. The darkened flesh had collapsed and dried about the little skull.

The nose was a shrunken button. The eyes, fallen into their sockets, were covered with withered flaps of skin. The child, for it was a human baby, had been placed with its arms outside the covering and crossed upon its breast. Stiffly the tiny, clawlike hands clutched a rosary, as if in suspended prayer.

The discovery itself was shocking enough. However, one detail hit Mara hard: the child's lower jaw was jammed sideways, dragging the lips apart. As she stared at it, she felt certain that this infant had struggled, had protested death with all the small strength it had possessed. Rudely illuminated, the black, disturbing crater of the mouth seemed to shatter the stillness of the room with its unuttered cry.

4

B ut why?" Christophe cried. "Why the police?" He sat in a chintz-covered armchair, brown eyes sweeping from face to face. "Why not just a priest? I really think a priest would be much more appropriate."

They were in Thérèse's parlor, adjoining the kitchen. The room bore her mark—white lace curtains, not a speck of dust, a threadbare carpet worn as much by cleaning as by use, old furniture polished to a mellow glow and smelling of beeswax.

"Use sense," Thérèse snapped. She stood at a table, pouring brandy. She had been told about the baby, although she had refused to view it. Her hand shook. Liquid slopped onto the tabletop. She wiped it up with her apron. "Here. Drink this." She thrust a glass at her employer, served Mara, Julian, and lastly herself. "It's what comes of laughing at evil," she scolded them all. "God save us." Her voice broke.

Julian saw that she was close to tears. He put his glass down and guided her to a chair. The old woman huddled there, looking suddenly very frail.

Christophe returned to his main theme. "I don't see why we can't just leave it where it is. Seal it back up. I mean"—the pink had returned to his cheeks; he had regained some of his bounce—"it's not as if this were a . . . a recent event. Look, the main part of the house was built in 1505. The north wing was added in 1642. That—*thing*—could have been in the wall for centuries."

Julian scratched his head thoughtfully. "Or put there more recently."

"But it's clearly," Christophe almost shouted, "an *old* baby. You can tell from its appearance. Thérèse, what do you know about it?"

The old woman goggled at him. "Me? *Mon dieu*. It's not my bastard!"

"For heaven's sake," shrilled Christophe. "I mean, you've lived here all your life. So did your parents. Surely you must have heard something."

"I've never had time for gossip," Thérèse told him with a lift of her bony chin. "All I can say is, it's somebody's illegitimate kid. Whoever it was had to get rid of it."

Mara went a little pale. "Are you saying someone buried a live baby in a wall?"

"Of course not," the housekeeper muttered sulkily. "They would have killed it first."

"I should never have let myself be talked into this insane renovation," Christophe moaned, rocking to and fro. "Knocking down walls. See where it's gotten me! Mara, you must get hold of those men. Your wreckers. Tell them to hold their tongues. At least until we figure out how to deal with this horrible situation. If need be, I'll make it worth their while to keep quiet."

"I expect it's too late." Mara ignored his implication of blame and glanced out a window giving onto the forecourt. The Serafims had gone. They had left without a backward glance, slamming the doors of their battered truck and shooting away in a spurt of gravel. "They've probably spread the story everywhere by now."

"Oh my god," Christophe wailed as the reality broke on him. "I'm about to publish a luxury quarto edition, Garamond type, calf-bound, on the glorious history of the de Bonfonds. We are one of the first families of the land, representing generations of achievement and unstained family honor. And now a dead baby turns up to be explained. Do you have any idea how embarrassing this is to me?"

"Oh, come on, Christophe," Julian objected. "You're exaggerating."

"Exaggerating! This thing is a corpse, literally, at the de Bonfond banquet. You seem to forget that my book is not only intended to honor the long line of de Bonfonds before me, it also commemorates the quarter-century anniversary of Editions Arobas and the impeccable standards Arobas represents. The proofs are nearly ready, and suddenly I have a cadaver to account for. Can't you see the position this puts me in? Moreover, for your information, small publishing houses like mine are struggling to stay alive. It's only my personal fortune that's been keeping things afloat. I don't necessarily expect the history of the de Bonfonds to cover costs, but I can't afford to be a laughingstock. This could ruin me. It could bring Arobas to its knees."

"Surely it's not as bad as that," Julian laughed uneasily. "Is it?" It occurred to him that perhaps the fate of his own *Wild Orchids of the Dordogne* also hung in the balance.

"It will be once the word gets out. *Arobas Anniversary Release Stifled at Birth. De Bonfond History Hides Skeleton in Closet.* Headlines like that can be extremely damaging."

No one spoke for a moment.

"Loulou," Mara said suddenly.

"Eh?" said Christophe.

"Loulou La Pouge. He's a friend. Used to work with the Police Judiciaire in Périgueux. I'll give him a call. He'll know how to handle this."

Dead, you say?" the ex-cop's voice boomed cheerfully into Mara's ear.

She replied, "Very. It's probably been in there for a long time, and it looks like a very young baby."

"Hmm. Born out of wedlock and murdered at birth, the body concealed in a wall. Infanticides. Always nasty affairs."

"Loulou," Mara pleaded, "we need your help. We called you because Christophe doesn't want a lot of publicity. He's desperate to keep a lid on things."

"I can imagine," said Loulou. "Well, tell him it will probably be entirely straightforward. The gendarmes will come, do their thing, and *ça y est*. If the body is as old as you think, there'll be the routine follow-up, more for the sake of form than anything. After all, the perpetrator will be long dead. A headline in *Sud Ouest*, some local curiosity perhaps. But that's all."

"Good," said Mara.

"Although"—Loulou seemed to reconsider—"we must take into account that it's getting on for summer, and the media are usually hungry for news. This could be just the kind of thing they'd sensationalize. Ridiculous, but there you are." He went on with growing enthusiasm, "Moreover, if this proves to be a more *recent* murder, then that's a different matter entirely. A full police investigation will be required, the baby's identity will certainly have to be established, so a search will be done—church registries, birth records, even the national archives—and everyone who had access to the house for the past so many years will have to be found and interrogated. I expect Child Welfare will also want to be involved. The case will probably make headlines everywhere, and so forth."

"Er, yes." Mara glanced over her shoulder at Christophe, who sat sunk in the armchair staring at his feet. She cupped her hand over the phone and hissed, "Look, Loulou, I'm quite sure this death goes back a long way, and I'm asking you as a personal favor to do everything possible to make sure the matter is handled discreetly. It would make things easier all around."

"What? Oh. Do what I can," Loulou promised happily. "Always glad to help."

Within an hour, a lone officer from the Gendarmerie in Brames arrived, which was unusual because gendarmes always worked in pairs. Somehow neither Mara nor Julian was surprised that he was closely followed by Loulou. The two men, who appeared to know one another, got out of their cars, conferred briefly, and then walked together across the forecourt. Or, rather, Loulou led the way with the young gendarme seemingly in tow.

Julian, Mara, and Christophe hurried out to meet them.

"Alors, mes amis," Loulou hailed Mara and Julian. He was tubby and bald with a shining, cherubic face. Gravely he pumped Christophe's hand. *"Quelle mauvaise affaire!* But never mind. The lad here will take care of everything. Had to come on his own, and you're lucky they could spare him. Everyone's out beating the woods for this killer dog, or wolf, or whatever it is. It was spotted last night near Petit Tournant. Killed a sheep. I'm here informally, of course."

The lad was Sergeant Laurent Naudet, a gangling young man with a round face, sympathetic eyes, and big ears. His uniform seemed too large for him through the body and too short in the arms. "Really, Uncle, this is highly irregular," he started to object, but Loulou thumped him soundly on the back.

"Don't worry, lad. I'll let you do your job. I'm just an old man along for the ride." To the others he explained proprietarily, "My niece's boy." To Christophe he said, "And don't you worry. Had a little talk with his commanding officer, Adjudant Compagnon. Know him well. Good man. Although he was just a bit touchy at first, my being ex-PJ and all. They're sensitive about things like that." Loulou referred to the double structure of the French police system, the Gendarmerie Nationale, which was organized along military lines and reported to the Ministry of Defense and had under its jurisdiction small towns and rural areas; and the Police

Judiciare, which policed larger centers and reported to the Ministry of the Interior. Ideally, the two branches, although quite separate, worked together when required, but there was a natural competitiveness between them in matters of turf and the solving of crimes. Loulou, with his Police Judiciaire links, was clearly stepping over the line. In fact, as a retired PJ with no official status, he had no business there at all. Not that this deterred him in the least. He squinted up at the imposing façade of Aurillac Manor with the air of a connoisseur.

"Scene of the crime, eh?" he chortled.

Christophe went pale. Just then Thérèse shouted down from the front door that he was wanted on the telephone.

Christophe said to Mara, "Take them up, will you? I'll be along shortly. And Mara"—his voice dropped to a murmur—"use the servants' stairs." He hurried into the house.

As Christophe had requested, she took them around the north wing to the back of the house, up the staircase leading to the antechamber, and into the room where Smokey had revealed his find. Everything seemed strangely hushed. The dust had settled. With its rubble-strewn floor and piles of stone blocks, the place had the timeless air of an abandoned archeological site.

Mara pointed to the partially demolished wall. "It's in there."

Naudet stuck his head into the cavity.

Loulou pulled him back. "You'll need this, I think." He produced a flashlight from a capacious trouser pocket. "A good cop is always prepared."

Laurent Naudet made a gesture of despair and went quite red.

With the aid of the flashlight they looked down on the dead child. It had been placed in a scooped-out cavity under one of a series of bondstones that served to tie the two faces of the wall together. The Serafims, in breaking through the wall, had taken out each course of stones, starting at the top and working down on their respective sides, clearing away the riprap fill as they went. At a point about a meter and a half from the floor, they had lifted out a bondstone and made their startling discovery.

The body, preserved by the cold, airless environment of the wall, lay covered in dust and surrounded by rubble. Viewing it a second time, Mara noted that the baby's wrapping was of faded blue silk, fringed with tassels of darker blue. As the beam of light played over dried flesh the color of tea, she saw a quiff of bleached-out hair, shrunken arms dressed in fine cotton sleeves trimmed with lace. A cross of filigreed silver attached to a rosary of ivory and amber beads had slipped down along the baby's side. Some-one had loved this child enough to lay it out with care and commit its soul to God before closing it up in its rough, inhospitable tomb. Inevitably, her eye was drawn to the terrible void of the mouth. The natural result of the collapse of flesh in death, she told herself firmly. But she found she had to turn away, her ears once again assailed by a soundless, deafening cry.

Perhaps the others heard it, too. Loulou, for once, was silent. Julian looked somber. Young Naudet stared, deeply disturbed. At this point Christophe burst into the room.

"You won't believe this." His small, pale hands fluttered up around his face like panicked moths. "The press have already got wind of the story. That was them on the phone. I've put them off for now, but it won't be long before the dam breaks."

"What did you tell them?" asked Julian.

"I told them . . ." Christophe gulped. "I told them it was a cat."

"Un chat?" marveled Loulou. "How?"

"It was the only thing I could think of. I said it was a cat that the workmen had mistaken for a . . . for a . . ."

"Never mind," said Mara. "Sergeant Naudet, how quickly do you think this matter can be taken care of?"

"Well." The gendarme pushed his *képi* back on his head. "For now, my instructions are to secure and guard the site and take down preliminary information. The Procurer's Office in Périgueux as well as the Criminal Brigade Team will have to be informed. They'll come out to do their stuff. Then the body will be sent for examination to determine the cause of death. If it turns out a crime has been committed—"

"All that?" broke in Christophe. "It hardly seems worth it."

"Yes, well, it's not up to me, I'm afraid." Naudet returned the flashlight to his uncle and took out a notebook and a pencil. "Who exactly was it who found the, um, cadaver?"

"My workmen," Mara answered. "Theocritus and Aristophanes Serafim."

"And what time was that?"

"A little past noon," said Julian. "I remember hearing the church bells."

"The time of discovery is hardly relevant," Loulou pointed out, "since the poor thing's obviously been in there for a number of years."

"Uncle, please. Anyone else present at the time?"

"Apart from my workmen? The three of us."

"Your names, please?"

He scribbled the information in his notebook.

"No one else on the premises?"

This time Christophe responded. "My housekeeper, Thérèse Tardieux. And Didier Pujol, my gardener. He lives in, at the back of the property. Sometimes Didier's granddaughter Stéphanie comes over to help him. I don't know if she was here today."

"So there were a number of people about?"

"Yes, but none of *us* had anything to do with this," Christophe objected.

Naudet considered this. "I suppose not." He tugged one of his oversized ears.

"You might ask if anything was disturbed," prompted his uncle.

"Nothing," Mara cut in, taking pity on the young man. "The

baby is exactly as we found it. Of course, the workmen might have moved something while they were prying out the header. It's rough work, breaking down a wall, and they wouldn't have been particularly careful. I can give you their number, and you can check with them, but I think they stopped as soon as they saw what was in there."

Naudet wrote this down and closed his notebook. He fiddled with his cell phone but was unable to pick up a signal in an environment with meter-thick walls. He said as sternly as circumstances would allow, "I have to go outside. Please don't touch anything."

He headed for the stairs just as Thérèse reappeared.

"You're wanted on the telephone," she said grimly to Christophe.

"Oh, *mon dieu,* not another journalist. Tell them I'm not home. No, wait. Tell them . . ." The little man hurried after her. His voice, querulous, trailed away.

Loulou turned a twinkling but slightly malicious eye on Mara and Julian. *"Eh bien.* Once more you find yourselves in an interesting situation." He was alluding to the circumstances under which they had originally met, when Mara had come to him for help in tracing her missing sister.

"It's not *our* situation," Julian protested. "I doubt if it's anyone's. Alive, that is."

"Well, you're right on that score at least. That baby's been there for some time. And murdered, from the look of it."

Julian objected, "You don't know that. You sound just like Thérèse."

"Tenez, the face is squashed."

"It's dried out."

Loulou shrugged. "The *médecin légiste* will confirm my suspicions. Lamartine. Good man. I've worked with him. Babies' bones are very fragile. Any pressure would have resulted in telltale fractures."

"Thérèse thinks it might have belonged to one of the house-maids," said Mara.

"Ha. Put in the family way by one of the undergardeners. The question is, how did she get the baby in there? It's not that easy to punch a hole in a stone wall, you know."

Mara did know. "It's actually not that hard. These walls are drystone construction. It would have required a bit of work to pry the first stone loose, but once that was done, the others would have come away relatively easily. Not a large hole would have been needed. And then the stones could have been simply pushed back into place."

Julian scratched his beard. "Or else the baby could have been put there at the time of the original construction. Or when the north wing was added. When did Christophe say, 1642?"

Mara nodded. "Although, when the wing was added, they would have built onto the existing structure. They wouldn't have had to tear down the old wall."

Loulou was still developing his idea. "But if she did break into the wall, she would still have needed help in patching the hole back up. That's where the undergardener lover came in, I expect. Although it would be better if he were a stonemason."

"There's just one thing," Mara said thoughtfully. She took the flashlight from Loulou and trained it once again on the small form. "The baby's dress. Finely woven cotton. The sleeves are edged in lace. The cloth it's wrapped in looks like silk. And the rosary. Amber, ivory, and wrought silver. A little too good to have belonged to a servant girl, don't you think?"

"Hmm. A lady of the house, then?" Loulou peered over her left shoulder. "Yes, you're right. Definitely someone in the family."

Julian said glumly, "Christophe's not going to like this." He, too, approached the breach to look again at the diminutive corpse.

"Naturally," Loulou confirmed cheerfully. "Who wants a murderer in the family?"

Julian shook his head. "It's more than that. This house, the de Bonfond name, mean a lot to him. He was telling me only a few days ago that the family belongs to the old aristocracy, with a title going back to the reign of Louis-the-something, I forget which. This baby comes as a personal affront, not only to him, but to every de Bonfond before him."

He was about to turn away when something caught his eye. He stiffened.

"Mara," he said, "shine the light over there, will you?"

"Where?"

"There." He directed her hand, then impatiently snatched the flashlight from her. "My god!"

"But, I don't—"

"There." He pointed with a shaking finger. "Can't you see it?"

"See what, *mon ami?*" Loulou pressed forward as well. *"Tenez,* you really mustn't touch—"

But Julian had already reached into the cavity and was feverishly freeing the end of the blue silk covering which had been tucked around the baby's feet, revealing the top of an embroidered flower. Julian flicked it sharply to free it of a heavy coating of dust. The colors were faded, but the shape was unmistakable. It was a botanically accurate rendering of an orchid. A dark-purple sepal arched hoodlike over a bulbous slipper finely stitched in pinkish thread. The labellum was flanked by a pair of long, narrow, spiraled petals, also worked in purple. Julian caught his breath in disbelief. It was his orchid, a flower of almost sinister beauty, the one in the photograph, dots joined up, rendered whole.

"Cypripedium incognitum," he gasped. It was the name he had given it. His head felt light. "Mara, this is the orchid Bedie found. The one I've been searching for."

Mara stared at him, then back at the embroidery. "Impossible," she said.

Loulou coughed. "A coincidental resemblance."

"No." Julian shook his head emphatically. "No coincidence. It matches in every respect." Feverishly he pulled the tail of the baby's wrapping completely free and laid it out flat, exposing a slender stalk rising out of a sheathing of three lanceolate leaves worked in different shades of green. Loulou was too dumbfounded to object.

"The detail is astounding, down to the veining of the labellum. I now know what this flower looks like in its entirety. This is better than any photograph." Reverently, he traced the slightly raised stitchery with a trembling forefinger. "It's probably even to scale—" His hand froze.

"What is it?" Mara cried.

"The ventral sepal"—his voice was filled with disbelief—"is separated."

"My friend," interrupted Loulou, "what are you talking about?"

"I'm talking," said Julian energetically, "about these." He indicated two petal-like shapes hanging down on either side of the slipper. "This is bloody astounding." Seeing their baffled faces, he explained, "There are around a hundred and twenty species of Slipper Orchids in the world. The count varies. As far as I know, in all cases but two the lateral sepals are fused as one into what's called a synsepal. I was explaining this to Iris just this morning. This flower is another exception. You can see here the lateral sepals are clearly separate."

"Is this important?" Mara asked.

"It could be very important," Julian assured her. "First, Western Europe has only one Slipper Orchid, the Yellow Lady's Slipper. *Cypripedium incognitum* could represent not only a second species but a rare example of an evolutionary departure from normal Slipper Orchid morphology."

He stood for a moment, as if in a trance, then stirred. "You know, up to now I've gone on searching for my Mystery Lady's Slipper because, well, everyone has his passion, and this orchid is mine. To be honest, I dreamed of setting the botanical world on its ear one day by presenting my Mystery Orchid as an entirely new species of *Cypripedium*. But deep down, even though I've devoted a section to it in my book, I've always been prepared to treat it as a one-off genetic quirk. I mean, all I've had to go on was a badly stained photo that left a lot to be imagined." His eyes were drawn back to the embroidery. "This changes everything. The flower your sister photographed twenty years ago wasn't just some isolated mutant, Mara. This embroidery proves that it's an actual, distinct species with a living track record." He turned to face her, breathing heavily. "You understand what this means to me, don't you?"

"Yes," she said. She did understand, but at the moment she could not share in his exultation. She left him to walk to the windows, where she stood staring into the brash, relentless sunshine that dressed the remainder of the day. She, who had spent so many years reorganizing living space, had never thought of it as enclosing death. Now she wondered if death had some kind of special affinity to her. She thought she had said goodbye to it when she had buried her sister's remains. Now she saw that death had simply been biding its time, waiting for her to break down a wall. How long, she wondered, had the child lain there, uttering its endless wail, wrapped in its shroud of blue?

5

"Blue doesn't suit you," Henriette said to her sister-in-law.

Cécile de Bonfond, *a large, ungainly woman, reddened to the roots of her ginger-colored hair, clutched the azure silk shawl more tightly about her thick, sloping shoulders, and looked helplessly around the crowded room.*

The occasion was an afternoon reception. Aurillac's grand salon, normally kept closed, had been thrown open in honor of Hugo and Henriette. The pair had been wed in Paris in August, and the reception was the least effort that Odile de Bonfond could get away with. Her bitter inclination was to refuse to acknowledge the marriage altogether, but outward appearances had to be satisfied.

The notaire *Maître Caillaud and his wife were early arrivals, followed after an interval by Hugo's uncle Roland and his bony wife, Anne. Then old Abbé Fortin, who sat in a window embrasure, soaking up what warmth he could from the autumn sunshine and toothlessly gumming biscuits dipped in wine. Eventually, the salon filled up with the area's most prominent* hobereaux, *local gentry, all avid with curiosity about the new bride. Henriette, Parisian to her fingertips, viewed them with a critical eye. The men wore rusty black suits twenty years behind the fashion; indeed, one fat gentleman was stuffed into a moth-eaten velveteen jacket that made him look laughably like an out-of-work actor. The women were even worse, presenting an uninteresting assortment of frumpy crinolines such as shopgirls in the Faubourg Saint-Antoine would not have deigned to wear to an evening's cheap entertainment.*

Henriette was dressed in an off-the-shoulder gown of robin's-egg-blue tulle edged with satin ruchings and tied off at the waist by an indigo sash. She stood out like a flower among cabbages. She had been at Aurillac four weeks, and this was her first formal presentation to Sigoulane society, if one could call it that. It had taken that much time for her mother-in-law to invent a vague but respectable bourgeois background for her.

Nevertheless, the women of the party, with unerring flair, quickly sensed that something was not quite right about the newcomer. They pressed her hand, murmured compliments, commented on the weather, and withdrew to nibble cake and consider this creature whose flashing eyes, bold manners, and cut of dress seemed so unsuitable to the company. The men mainly stared hard at her daring décolletage, the like of which no one this deep in the country had ever seen.

Hugo, so lately besotted, regarded his wife complacently. For him she was acquired property that had already lost much of its allure. A large, heavy-featured man, he stood for a while at her side, receiving the good wishes of the guests with evident boredom. As soon as he could, he moved to the punch bowl and a group of men who were talking animatedly about the recent kill of a sanglier, *a young sow that the dogs had seized by the nose and ears. The men had let the dogs have their sport with it before dispatching it with their knives. Hugo's cold blue eyes glittered at the account.*

For a moment, Henriette was left alone. Unperturbed, she quickly sized up her situation. The women had gathered in a knot to gaze at her, like cattle, from the other side of the room. She stared back. With a smile and a swish of her gown, she turned her charms on the nonhunting male guests, flirting cleverly with Maître Caillaud and Monsieur Velveteen Jacket, conquering utterly the pompous headmaster of the Lycée Saint-Anselm in Brames, and enraging the wives.

Hugo's father, Dominique, was confined to a sofa throughout the event, his gouty foot propped up on a padded tabouret. He was an older, more dissipated version of his son, a fleshy man with pale-blue bulging eyes draped by loose curtains of flesh and a speckled scalp patchily covered in reddish hair. Irritably he waved aside the ministrations of his manservant and called instead for his daughter-in-law. She came to him very prettily, bringing him a forbidden cup of mulled spiced wine and stooping to change the position of his leg. How meekly she bent her head to him as he clutched her arm to draw her close.

"What's that damned son of mine been up to, eh?" He ogled her through a blast of unwholesome breath. "Pretty filly like you, should've filled your belly by now." His fat fingers fumbled to pinch her bottom through the folds of her gown.

How she smiled as she hissed into his ear: "Touch me again, you filthy old goat, and I'll tell the world what goes on in this family, which would shock the devil himself. I have found out many of your nasty secrets, you know, and I will air them in such a way that even you will not be able to hold your nose against the stench."

Dominique blenched, not just because his new daughter-in-law had contrived to knock his bad foot sharply as she pulled away. He had that afternoon spent an unpleasant hour closeted with Maître Caillaud. The notaire *had purposely come in advance of the other guests in order to converse seriously with Dominique, man to man. The squire's way with every willing wench in the valley, and particularly the heavy expenditures constantly required for the upkeep of a changing tableau of mistresses in Bordeaux and Toulouse, were threatening to empty the de Bonfond coffers. Parcels of land had been quietly sold to support his excesses. It had to stop. Dominique was not a man with an easy conscience, and Henriette's threat had hit him in a vulnerable spot.*

From her post at the other end of the chilly salon, Odile noted the brief but telling exchange between her husband and her daughter-in-law. Odile knew about the mistresses.

Cécile, Hugo's youngest sister, also watched Henriette. Cécile despised Henriette because her mother did, but she also envied her sister-in-law with a kind of lugubrious wistfulness born of the knowledge that, apart from a single dalliance, she had never been and never would be admired by any man. A moment later, Henriette was at her side. Flustered, Cécile turned away: she had been instructed by Maman not to speak to the Parisian trollop. That was when Henriette had said—almost gaily, as if imparting the latest gossip—"Blue doesn't suit you." And that was when Cécile's face had reddened to match the roots of her unfortunate hair.

"Women with your kind of complexion should stick to brown," Henriette instructed in a high, clear voice, giving Cécile to understand with no uncertainty that the shimmering, sky-blue shawl made a mockery of her red skin and freckles and that her best dress of drab olive silk would not do. But the shawl was the only pretty thing she had. Trimmed with tassels of darker blue and nicely embroidered, it would have complemented Henriette's gown admirably.

"You can't have it," Cécile said with childish directness. She was twenty-six, more at home with horses than with people, and unskilled in conversation. Words tumbled out of her like rocks—rough, unformed, and heavy.

"Ma chère," Henriette replied coolly, "I wish nothing of yours. I say this only for your own good. No doubt, living like savages as you people do, you have no concept of fashion. You look a fright."

Cécile's blush was now spreading in ugly splotches down her neck. She stared miserably at Henriette, tears forming in her pale, rather protuberant eyes. "I hate you," she cried hoarsely, to the consternation of those about her.

"I know," Henriette said with a smile.

6

A male baby, European type, six to eight weeks old." Loulou, who had his contacts in forensics, gave them advance information from the *médecin légiste*'s report. "But *how* it died, *mes amis,* that is the interesting part."

Mara and Julian exchanged glances. They were sitting after hours at the Chez Nous bistro in Grissac with friends and owners, Mado and Paul Brieux. The usual crowd of diners had gone, but the small *resto*, which served some of the best food in the region, still seemed crowded. That was because, in addition to the humans, three dogs were milling about. One of them was Julian's rangy mutt, Bismuth. The second was Mara's Jazz, a powerful tan-and-white animal of pit-bull extraction. The third was the local bitch, a handsome black-and-white short-haired pointer named Edith.

"Was it what everyone's been saying?" Mado, a statuesque redhead with golden eyes, asked. The story on the mummified child had broken with the force of a summer storm. For want of a name, the media had dubbed it Baby Blue, after the color of its wrapping. Another baby, the Brieux' five-month-old offspring, Eddie, gurgled sleepily on his mother's lap.

"They're saying," Paul put in, "the kid was throttled." He was a big man with forearms the size of Parma hams. It was hard to believe he had the lightest touch with pastry in the region.

Loulou dipped his head from side to side. "Death was not"—

he probed the interior of his mouth delicately with a toothpick, seeking remnant shreds of Mado's lamb ragout—"due to natural causes. Of course, I never thought it was." His round face had the smug, glossy look of an egg pudding. The freckles on his scalp resembled raisins.

"Well, get on with it." Julian found the ex-cop's well-known fondness for keeping an audience dangling very irritating.

Loulou put the toothpick down. "According to Lamartine, X-rays of the skull turned up a number of things." He held up one, two, and three fingers in turn. "*Primo,* dislocation of the mandible. *Secundo,* massive crushing of the nasal bones. *Tertio,* cracking and displacement of the maxillae. Not throttled. Smothered. Pressure was applied directly downward and with far more force than was necessary with an infant of that age. As if"—he tugged pensively at the wattle under his chin—"whoever had done it had been in a towering rage."

"*Mon dieu,*" whispered Mado, drawing her son tightly to her.

"Postpartum depression." Paul rocked back in his chair. "Mother off her head, kid screaming all the time, pillow over the face."

They all fell silent, contemplating the scene.

Then Paul asked, "How did it come to be mummified?"

"Oh, it can happen, given cool, dry conditions." Loulou reached across to share out the remains of a bottle of red—a Coteaux de Bonfond Domaine de la Source 1998, as it happened. "There are many examples of naturally occurring mummies in crypts, for example. And a wall's not so different. But one thing Lamartine said, it was a healthy baby, well fed."

Mado looked surprised. "How could he know that?" She shifted Eddie in her arms.

"Because there was evidence of saponification." Loulou scooted his bottom forward in his chair, the better to deliver his information. "That only happens with fat corpses, you see. The fat mixes with water to produce fatty acids that draw the moisture out. The dehydration slows down bacterial growth and the body is preserved. Now, the baby's fattest parts—its stomach, buttocks, and thighs—were literally turned into a waxy substance like soap. The upper parts of the body were more vulnerable and simply dried out. It was a good thing Lamartine had the X-ray evidence to go on. Otherwise, he would have had to rehydrate the body before he could have examined it."

There was another silence while his audience took this in.

Julian cleared his throat. "Any idea when it died?"

"I'm coming to that. Lamartine puts it certainly after 1860 and provisionally as late as the outbreak of war in 1914."

"That's a fifty-four-year span," Julian complained.

"*Bien*, with mummies it's hard to be precise. In fact, the science and tech lads had to rely on the baby's trappings to pin things down. It was wrapped in a woman's shawl. Silk. French manufacture, probably Lyon, factory-produced in bolts throughout the latter half of the nineteenth century and sold by the measure through the better shops in Paris and places like Tours and Bordeaux. However, one of the threads used in the embroidery was colored with a synthetic dye that came into use in France only after 1860. So that establishes the anchor date. The outside date of 1914 was based on the style of the child's clothing and the material, a kind of Egyptian cotton generally not available in France after Egypt became a British protectorate. As for the embroidery itself, done by hand to suit the customer, or, because many women did embroidery in those days, even by the wearer herself."

"But who she was remains the big question," muttered Julian darkly. Absently, he tossed bits of bread to the dogs.

Mado pointed out, "Anyway, the shawl could have lain around for years before being used as a shroud. What's going to happen with the body?"

"It'll be released to Christophe for burial," Loulou told them. "Eventually."

Mara, whose thoughts had been elsewhere, stirred. "Julian's taking care of the arrangements," she said.

"You?" Mado's leonine eyes widened as she swung about on him. She shoved him with a sandaled foot. "Why you? You're not a member of the family. You're not even Catholic."

Mara, who saw the shove, and who half suspected Julian of nursing an old crush on Mado and Mado of encouraging it, said wearily, "You may as well tell them, Julian." And when he shot her an annoyed look, she shrugged. "He's doing it for the shawl. The embroidery on it is of an orchid that's the same as the one Bedie photographed. Christophe said he could have the shawl, as long as the police don't need it as evidence, if he took on the funeral arrangements."

"Why is it," Julian cried out indignantly, "that nothing around here can be kept secret?"

Paul said with a small explosion of breath, *"Bigre!* I don't believe it. You're still after that crazy flower?" The Brieux knew all about Julian's elusive Lady's Slipper. *"T'es fou."* The restaurateur tapped the side of his head.

"Of course I'm after it," retorted Julian testily. "It's the botanical mystery of the century. How do you expect me *not* to be after it? It's as if someone were reaching out of the past to give me a vital clue."

"How the devil are you going to trace an orchid from a bit of embroidery?" Paul waved his arms.

"Why not? If someone embroidered it, they had to see the original growing somewhere."

"They could have imagined it."

"No, they couldn't. It's too precise structurally. It's a botanically accurate reproduction. In fact, it's better than Bedie's photo because it's complete."

"So what?" Paul challenged, banging the table with the flat of his hand. "You're still left with the problem of finding the thing.

That shawl could've been embroidered—what?—over a hundred and forty years ago."

"Ah"—Julian shook a finger in Paul's face—"but you're overlooking one important fact. That shawl is associated with Aurillac Manor. That's my starting point."

"Starting point? *Nom de dieu,* that's where it ended up. You have no idea where it came from, and that's what counts. All this for a flower?"

Julian scowled stubbornly. "Not just any flower. Look, how can I make you understand? The discovery of a new species of wild orchid is an important event in the botanical world. The *rediscovery* of an ancient European orchid lost to modern science, especially one as morphologically rare as this one—well, it's like finding Atlantis. You simply have no idea what this could mean. To me. To every living orchidologist." Julian broke off. Paul, Mado, and Loulou were looking unconvinced. Mara's expression was carefully neutral. Julian folded his arms across his chest and slumped down disgustedly in his chair.

"Just promise me one thing. Don't tell Géraud."

"Of course not," murmured Mado, making a mouth at her son. "Why don't I feel reassured?"

On their way out of the bistro, Julian said to Mara, "Sometimes I find Paul can be incredibly dense." He added hopefully, "Your place or mine?"

She did not answer. He took that to mean his place. Since he had come on foot, his cottage being only a short walk from Grissac, he climbed into her car. Bismuth and Jazz jumped into the back, while the pointer bitch, Edith, disdaining a lift, trotted off on business of her own. Mara started up and backed onto the road.

"Well, at least I know the shawl was made and embroidered in France," he sighed, "instead of on the other side of the world in China and imported here. But I was hoping Loulou could get a bit more out of forensics than that. Not that I expected them to turn up anything on the habitat of *Cypripedium incognitum,* of course." He knew from Bedie's photograph that the orchid had once grown somewhere on the grounds of Les Colombes. The shawl now gave Aurillac Manor as a second point of reference. That was valuable. However, he still had no information on the specific conditions under which the plant grew, which was what he really needed if he was going to find it. "So I'm stuck making a lot of guesses. Do I assume my Mystery Orchid behaves like the European Lady's Slipper?" *Cypripedium calceolus* liked cool shade and alkaline soil and attracted a specific pollinator, a bee called *Andrena.* He tugged his beard. "I mean, what if *incognitum* needs deeper shade or a wetter environment? Also, it looks like a whacking great flower, bigger than *calceolus* and with an even larger pouch. So does it attract a larger insect, or a wider range of insects? What?"

He turned the possibilities over in his head as Mara drove out of the sleeping village.

"You know," he said eventually, "at bottom, everything about orchids boils down to sex. In fact, the ancient Greeks considered the orchid as a symbol of sexuality. The word *orchis* means—"

"Balls," Mara cut in dryly. "*Orchis* means balls. Because orchid roots look like testicles. Géraud told me."

"Oh." They were now bumping down a gravel road, past farms where only occasional lights showed, or here or there the blue glow of a television in an unshuttered window. "Well, did he tell you that orchids are some of the most ingenious plants in the world when it comes to reproduction?"

"We didn't get that far."

"Then he missed the most important part." Julian waved his hands enthusiastically. "They go to incredible lengths to attract pollinators. Some orchids put out a scent like rotting meat to lure a certain kind of fly. Others produce a fermented nectar that gets visiting insects drunk in order to increase the chance of cross-pollination. Others have evolved physically to resemble the pollinators they want to attract. Take the Fly Orchid. Its labellum looks like a certain kind of female wasp, even down to the development of pseudo wings and eyes—" He broke off to glance at Mara. She drove, staring straight ahead. "The—er—male wasp tries to mate with it," he finished lamely, "gets covered in pollen, and then goes off to try it on with another Fly Orchid, which it pollinates in the process." It was hard to read her expression in the dark.

A minute later, Mara pulled up in front of his cottage. He reached across to stroke her cheek. "I've been looking forward to this all week," he said, really meaning it. "Time with you." She was unresponsive, and he found it necessary to explain, "Us alone. Coming in?"

She seemed to struggle out of a reflective mood. "Sorry, Julian. Not tonight."

"Oh? Something wrong?"

If there was, she clearly didn't want to go into it. "I'm just beat," she said. "Rain check?"

"Okay. If that's what you want." He paused, then added, "I suppose I could do with an early night myself." Stuffing down his disappointment, he tried at least for a lingering kiss.

She pecked him briefly. "I'll call you."

Julian stood with Bismuth at the roadside, watching her car disappear into the night, feeling stunned. Friday-night dinners at Chez Nous, weekends together, lovemaking, it was the rhythm that he measured his life against nowadays. He sensed that her leavetaking had been more cool than tired. Things had been running along so well. Now he wondered uneasily if Mara was going off him. His throat constricted with a feeling of dismay as the vision of a piece of elastic, suddenly gone limp, free-floated before his eyes.

For Mara, one of the things that was wrong was Baby Blue. The little corpse haunted the corners of her mind, demanding—what? Justice? Retribution? Truth? Because someone in the past had got away with murder. Later that night, she tried to spell out her feelings in an e-mail to her best friend, Patsy Reicher. Once resident in the Dordogne, now returned to her native New York, freckle-faced, gum-chewing Patsy was a psychoanalyst, erstwhile sculptor, and Mara's personal touchstone.

> *. . . I suppose we'll never know who killed him. But what bothers me even more, Patsy, is everyone's attitude towards this baby. We all call him "it" for a start. Christophe treats "it" like an unwanted parcel that he'd like to return to sender because he's so frantic about protecting his precious family name. Loulou, with his flair for crime, seems delighted that "it" was smothered—with unnecessary violence. Mado and Paul are shocked, probably because they're thinking how awful it would be if the same thing happened to their own son. As for Julian . . .*

That was the other thing that was wrong: Julian. His obsession with orchids. *Cypripedium incognitum* filled his vision, sucked up all his passion. It also made him shockingly callous. He didn't seem to care that Baby Blue had once had a life, albeit short, that the child had struggled vainly to live against a stronger force intent on ending his existence.

> *. . . What can I say other than for Julian Baby Blue seems to be nothing more than a lucky break in the hunt for his damned Lady's Slipper? . . .*

There was also the fact that she was grappling with the realization that they had been stalled in the same routine for months.

Dinners at Chez Nous, weekend sex, no commitment. Mara felt that love affairs, like water, ought to have a natural flow. She wanted things to move on. Where their relationship was concerned, Julian seemed perfectly happy to turn in the eddy of indecision, going nowhere. Only *Cypripedium incognitum* galvanized him. To put it simply, she felt sidelined. It was silly and demeaning to be jealous of a flower, but Mara, who found herself unexpectedly drawn to this eccentric, earnest, single-minded man, was.

. . . As for me, I'm no better. All I can think of right now is finding another stonemason to work at Aurillac. If Christophe cancels this project, I'm cooked because I turned away all other work to concentrate on giving the silly twit his gallery in time for the launch of his history of the effing glorious de Bonfonds. It seems crazy that no one really seems to care that a healthy infant boy had the life crushed out of him. Has the world gone mad? Write soon. Send sanity.
Mara.<

7

·

SATURDAY MORNING, 1 MAY

Sergeant Laurent Naudet cared. He was a pleasant young man who took his job seriously. It bothered him that the case on Baby Blue, now that the cause of death had been determined, seemed headed for the inactive files. No one wanted to waste time, especially with a killer animal on the loose, investigating a crime going back god knew how many decades. He felt that the murdered child deserved better than that. The Sigoulane Valley was part of his beat, and so, even though he had no further business at the manor, he decided to return there on his own time, at least to have another look at the room where the dead baby had been found. What he was doing was strictly against the rules, but, he rationalized, so far everything having to do with the case ran counter to regulations.

At the moment, he was zipping along on the pride of his life, a classic Kawasaki KZ1 that he had bought five years ago as a wreck, therefore cheaply, but still for far more than he could afford. Bit by bit he had painstakingly restored it. All legs and arms, he crouched atop the bike, resembling a large, rapidly moving mantis. His black helmet and the dark wrap-around glasses he wore to keep the wind out of his eyes enhanced the image. His heart swelled with satisfaction as the retooled 900cc engine easily took the steep climb up Aurillac Ridge. Now he entered the long, tree-lined lane leading to the house.

He drew within sight of it just as a red BMW pulled in ahead of him into the graveled forecourt. Another car, a green Renault with a dog in it, was already parked there in the shade.

"*Hé!*" An old man in dungarees came trotting around a corner of the house. He brandished a pitchfork at the BMW. The driver, a toothy man with slicked-back hair, put his head out the window. There were other people in the car. Laurent slowed and veered onto the verge of the lane. He pulled off his helmet but kept the bike idling, balanced between his legs.

"*Filez!*" Didier yelled, stabbing at the air. "Get lost!"

The driver ignored the threat. "Say, old fellow, is it true they've uncovered a whole crypt of bodies in there?"

"You're trespassing," shouted Didier. "Fsst! Move it or I'll call the cops."

The driver laughed at the gardener's ineffectual jabs.

"He said beat it." A strapping lass with big arms and muddy knees appeared from another direction. She wore shorts, a tank top, and ankle boots and carried a bucket.

"Don't get your knickers in a knot," said the toothy driver. He swung his door open and got out. "I'll give you twenty euros—Hey!" The contents of the bucket—a soggy mixture of coffee grounds, vegetable peelings, and fish bones—hit him in the face.

"Now shove off, you ghouls!" shouted Didier's granddaughter, Stéphanie. She grabbed the pitchfork from her grandfather, who stood by cackling, and prodded the intruder with authority. "Unless you want to wear this up your backside."

There was a moment of shouting and arm-waving before the driver stumbled back into his car. The BMW shot forward, swung around, and roared away down the lane, nearly clipping Laurent's bike in passing.

"You, too!" Stéphanie yelled, striding toward him. "Push off."

"I'm a cop." Laurent switched off his engine, hung his helmet on a handlebar, and dug into his pants pocket. "Laurent Naudet, Sergeant."

"You don't look like one." She barely glanced at his identification. "Anyway, he's not seeing people." The young woman was tall, although still a good head shorter than he. Her fair skin was covered in a dusting of freckles, and she wore her maize-yellow hair in two short braids. Her legs were as stout as a rugby-player's. Laurent admired the way her knees locked, showing the muscle definition of her thighs.

"I don't need to bother him. Monsieur de Bonfond, that is. I just wanted to have another look at the room where the baby was found."

Stéphanie wheeled around to her grandfather. "Says he's a cop."

"I *am* a cop," Laurent insisted firmly. "I'm the one who came out on Wednesday."

But she had walked away and was conferring with the old man. Laurent stamped down the bike's *kick* and went after her.

"Okay." She gave him an unfriendly head-to-toe with wary blue eyes. "I'll take you up. But make it fast. Some of us have work to do." She did not bother with the servants' stairs but led him, almost at a jog, across the forecourt and up the steps to the big front entrance.

"What's your name?" Laurent asked, following in her train.

"Stéphanie," she said without turning around.

They crossed an echoing vestibule. Laurent had an impression of tall paneled doors and a large expanse of black and white tiles. He knew that a sharp cop would be soaking up every detail, checking for clues. Somehow, his vision remained glued to his guide's solid posterior as it bobbed, roughly at eye level, up the grand stone staircase ahead of him.

Someone else was already up there. It was the woman he had questioned the other day, the one who had been hired to tear down the walls. She wore the same jeans and T-shirt (he didn't know English, but he recognized the words "book" and "dog") as on the day he had met her. Laurent experienced a momentary alarm, thinking that she and her men had resumed work. But she was alone, standing in the middle of the litter of stones and broken plaster, gazing at the wrecked wall. She turned at their approach.

"Madame Dunn. What are you doing here?" Laurent addressed her severely. This was mainly to impress the girl in pigtails at his side, but he then ruined the impression by coming forward to shake Mara's hand. His few years chasing criminals had not yet stripped him of his innate courtesy. He would have shaken hands with anyone he was not actually about to arrest.

Mara said, "Just looking. I didn't touch anything, if that's what you're worried about." Her eyes strayed thoughtfully to the wall, and then returned to him. "I was just trying to imagine how it must have been . . . for the baby . . ."

Laurent nodded, feeling an immediate sympathy. He was there for the same reason. Even Stéphanie looked sobered. The three of them gazed wordlessly at the dark cavity.

After a moment Laurent asked, "Why were you tearing it down?"

"What? Oh, you mean the wall." Mara explained about the elevated gallery.

"Daft, silly idea if you ask me," said Stéphanie. "Look, if you don't mind—"

"Don't go. I mean, not just yet." The gendarme faced her with an earnest pleading. "It-it's just that I might need to ask you a few questions."

Stéphanie stayed but found it necessary to stare hard at her muddy boots.

Laurent went back to his study of the wall. "What I don't understand is, why put the baby in there? Wouldn't it have been easier just to bury it in the woods?"

"That's a dumb question," muttered Stéphanie. "Whoever it was wouldn't have wanted to be seen carrying a dead baby through the house, would they?"

"If I needed to hide something in a hurry, breaking a hole in a stone wall wouldn't be the first thing I'd try."

She tossed her braids. "All you'd need is a crowbar."

"Better a cold chisel," said Mara, and went on to talk about drystone construction.

Laurent scratched his head, looking around him at the rubble-strewn space. "What would this room have been used for?"

Mara considered. It was a corner room, the end chamber of the central block of the manor. Its windows faced west, with a view of the forecourt, and north, looking out over a small orchard at the side of the house. She said, "I never saw it furnished, but it's a big room, so it could have been put to a lot of uses over the years. At a guess I'd say a bedroom."

"There was a bed in it," Stéphanie confirmed. "With a canopy thing. I remember seeing it when I was a kid. And a great monster of an armoire."

"A bedroom." Laurent's eyebrows rose. "Any idea whose?"

"How should I know? Anyway, a wall has two sides, in case you've forgotten. The kid could have been put in from the little room next door just as well."

The gendarme gave Stéphanie a look of such intense admiration that she turned quite pink. He asked Mara, "Your workmen didn't notice by any chance which side of the wall had been tampered with?" It was a question no one had thought of.

Mara said that she doubted it. Smokey and Theo had worked simultaneously on both faces of the double-coursed wall, sledge-hammering away the plaster coating and prizing out the stones. They weren't particularly observant fellows, and by the time they had found the baby, any evidence would certainly have been destroyed. Anyway, the room next door, being smaller and giving onto the stairs, had probably served as an antechamber or a cabinet of some sort, offering less privacy for digging holes in walls than a bedchamber.

Laurent turned back to Stéphanie. "You said there was furniture in here. Where is it now?"

The young woman shrugged. "There's a whole lot of stuff downstairs."

They clattered down the stairs. The two rooms immediately below were crammed with tables, chairs, commodes, chiffoniers, lamps, and carpets rolled up and standing on end. There were several beds, their faded canopies piled up in the middle of the mattresses, and three armoires lined up against a wall. Stéphanie, however, could not remember which bed and which armoire had been in the upstairs corner room. She stood around for a minute or two and then, with a shy, troubled glance at the gendarme, who seemed now to have forgotten her presence, left them.

Laurent looked at the beds. Then he looked at the armoires. He approached the first and opened it. It was empty. He studied the interior. He had trouble closing the door again because it had come slightly askew on its hinges. The second was redolent of the smell of naphthalene and full of women's clothing of another era. He shoved aside beaded dresses and jackets with moth-eaten fur collars and peered inside.

The double doors of the third armoire swung apart with a grating noise. The space within was half filled with blankets. He pulled them out. Something about the back of this armoire caught his attention. It was a typical construction of loose panels slotted into a grooved retaining frame. The panel of the right-hand section had been broken and lodged imperfectly back into place. Leaning in, Laurent peered at it closely. He bent down and ran the nail of his forefinger along the bottom groove of the frame.

He stood up. "I think that's how they did it," he said with satisfaction. His nail had scooped up a small quantity of pale, gritty dust.

Mara put her head inside the armoire, too. "I see what you mean," she said after a moment. "You think this thing stood in front of the spot where the baby was put in the wall?"

He nodded. "They forced the panel out. That would have let them work at the wall bit by bit through the back of the armoire, pulling the stones out to make the hole. This thing is big enough to have hidden everything. Then, after they stuck the baby in, all they had to do was shove the stones back in place, jam the panel into the frame again, and close the doors."

Mara agreed. "No one would have known. They didn't even have to do a very good job with the panel. And later, when the walls were plastered over, all trace of the break would have been covered up."

They were silent for a moment. Then Laurent said, "It changes everything, of course."

"How do you mean?" asked Mara.

The gendarme replied in his sternest tone, "The kid wasn't just smothered and then put in the wall. Someone planned to kill this baby. And they had its tomb ready well in advance."

Thérèse found her staring in stupefaction at Laurent. Mara had accepted that the child had been murdered. However, that its death had been carefully planned and preparations for its entombment made in advance came as a shock.

Laurent addressed the housekeeper. "Madame Tardieux. Do you know which room this armoire came out of?"

Thérèse looked suspiciously at the piece of furniture and then at him. "It's about that kid, isn't it. Why can't you leave it alone?" But she told him grudgingly, "Upstairs corner bedroom."

"You're sure?"

"I've worked in this house all my life. Of course I'm sure."

"Okay," said the gendarme. "Do you know who had that bedroom?"

Vous êtes fou, non?" Thérèse tapped the side of her head vigorously with a bony finger. "Do you have any idea how many generations of de Bonfonds have lived here? Anyway, this part of the house hasn't been used in my lifetime. It's damp because of the northern exposure, and the chimneys are all blocked up. Even in my parents' day, the family all had their rooms in the south wing. And it's no good pestering him with your questions because he's not talking to anyone. Except you." The housekeeper thrust her chin at Mara. "He wants to see you. And he's not in a very good mood."

What?" shouted Mara. "Talk to who? I can't hear you. Christophe, will you open this door?" She turned to Thérèse. "This is ridiculous. Have him get hold of me when he feels like coming out."

The door jerked open just wide enough for Mara to see Christophe's nose and one bloodshot, angry eye. "Why should I? Why should I come out? Do you realize they're saying someone in the family whelped a bastard? Or that a de Bonfond got a servant girl with child and had it sealed up in a wall? There are those who delight in tearing down the de Bonfond name, those wretched Verdiers not the least."

"It's true," Thérèse informed Mara. "They're cousins through the female line. They hate the family because all the money's on this side. They're putting it about that old crimes will out, and until someone is punished, bad luck will visit the valley."

"Pure superstition," hissed Christophe. "And spite. Guy and that odious wife of his rang up to say how terribly sorry they were. But I could hear the triumph in their voices. I'm not taking any more calls. Thérèse. Baby Blue, pah! I'll give them Baby Blue."

"All right," said Thérèse. "No more calls." She left them.

Mara was beginning to lose her temper. "Look, Christophe. You wanted to see me. I'm here. Get on with it."

"I told you. Jean-Claude Fournier. Lives in Tirac. Number's in the book. He's the historian-genealogist fellow who helped me with the research for my book. Knows as much about the family as anyone. Tell him I have another commission for him. He'll like that because he knows I pay well and he's usually short of cash. Tell him I want him to find out who this wretched baby belonged to and above all to clear the de Bonfond name!"

"Why can't you talk to him yourself? Why involve me?"

"Have you found another team of stonemasons to finish tearing down my walls?"

"No, but—"

"Then you haven't anything better to do, have you? I want him to start immediately. Thérèse can let him into the library whenever he likes. He's not to remove any material, mind, but he has free run of the archives. I don't care how he does it, just prove this infernal infant has nothing to do with me. And, Mara, he has one week to come up with something. Otherwise, I know him, he'll take his sweet time."

"And what if he doesn't? What if this Jean-Claude Fournier finds that Baby Blue was a de Bonfond after all?"

"Impossible," snapped Christophe. "He wouldn't dare. He owes me. Arobas published his book on the Resistance. And his nonsense on fairy tales, silly drivel dressed up as social analysis. Did it as a favor to him. No one else would touch it, frankly. You might remind him of that."

"I'll do no such thing," Mara snapped back, but Christophe was detailing further instructions that included daily progress reports. She was about to send him to the devil when she remembered that he had given her a hefty advance. Moreover, it was true, work was at a standstill. In fact, she had little better to do.

Christophe paced his bedroom, a large, old-fashioned chamber that he had occupied since boyhood. With the heavy curtains drawn, the room was dark and cavelike, filled with shadowy shapes of furniture, bulky as boulders. Christophe, as he moved from wall to wall, had the air of a trapped animal.

Once again he stopped to stare at his reflection in an ornately framed mirror. The glass was crackled with age, distorting his features. He brought his face close to it, peering anxiously. There was no doubt about it. His left eye, the one he had not shown Mara, had a definite yellowish cast. Its shape had changed. Normally round, it seemed pulled cunningly aslant. The skin of his face felt stretched and painful. A whimper of despair filled his throat as he backed away from the mirror. *Mon dieu,* he thought. Not this again. Then he looked down at his hands.

8

Mara left Aurillac, grumbling loudly that Christophe was not her sole client. For want of anything better to do, she went to see the only other client that she had active at the moment: Prudence Chang.

"If you're here to see how things are coming, they're not," Prudence said as she opened her door to Mara and Jazz. "The fellow you sent out the other day spent half the morning looking at my walls. Didn't do a lick of work. I haven't seen him since."

Prudence, a glamorous Chinese American ex–advertising executive from L.A., spent part of the year in a restored farmhouse not far from Mara's own place. Most of the renovation of the farmhouse had been (badly) done by somebody else. The selective conversion back to its original state, such as stripping off cheap, ugly walling to reveal the original creamy limestone, was being organized by Mara.

"Oh?" Mara murmured, thinking with despair that this was one more thing going off the rails.

"You look awful." Prudence tickled the top of Jazz's head with a perfectly manicured fingernail while taking in Mara's rumpled appearance with critical, slim-line eyes. Prudence wore designer clothes even in the country and never had a hair out of place.

"It's Christophe," Mara complained. "He really is impossible." She elaborated on her grievances as she trailed Prudence into the kitchen, where she was given the choice of coffee or iced tea. Mara accepted iced tea. She needed to cool down.

"He acts like a spoiled baby. And he's autocratic as hell." Now she followed Prudence back into the front room. She flung herself onto a plaid settee, one of a pair.

Prudence arranged her Calvin Klein shirtdress before sitting down more gracefully on the other. "That's because he's a de Bonfond. The family's rich as Croesus. He's an only child, inherited all kinds of real estate in Bordeaux. And his cousin Antoine—he's the Coteaux de Bonfond man—practically owns the Sigoulane Valley. Would own it all, if it weren't for a few ragtag winegrowers who won't sell out." Prudence knew a surprising amount about almost everyone.

"The nerve of him sending me to run his errands," Mara fumed. "He wants me to commission someone to prove Baby Blue has nothing to do with his family."

"Oh, that's because one of his cousins, Guy Verdier, is trying to cash in on the publicity by offering to sell the dirt on the de Bonfonds to the media. He's a—what do you call them?—*avocat.* Lawyer. So I suppose he'd know how to avoid being sued for libel. Lawyers are generally good at that sort of thing. His father, Michel Verdier, is one of the winegrowers who won't sell out to Antoine. There's no love lost between the families. Maybe this is Christophe's way of doing damage control."

"Well, I damn well feel like telling him he can get hold of this Fournier fellow himself, especially since he fully intends to suborn the results."

"Jean-Claude Fournier?"

"I suppose you know him, too?"

"I've met him." Prudence toyed with a carved amber bracelet. "Drop-dead gorgeous and *très charmant.* Kisses your hand up to the armpit if you let him. He's a practicing genealogist and a cultural historian, or so he calls himself. Writes things. That's one of his." She waved at a large book on the coffee table: *Le Visage de la Résistance en Dordogne (The Face of the Resistance in the Dordogne).*

"And that's another"—a smaller volume entitled *Contes folkloriques de la Dordogne (Folktales of the Dordogne)*. "Borrow them if you like. He spoke once at the Dordogne Women's Society meeting. I never really figured out exactly on *what*, but it was all very interesting. I keep telling you, Mara, you really should join."

"What, to get my armpit kissed?"

"Or any other body part. Speaking of which, how are you and Julian getting on?"

"Oh," said Mara evasively. "We've both been pretty busy. He's landscaping Coteaux de Bonfond, and as you know I'm renovating Christophe's house."

"You're supposed to be renovating mine. You need a kick in the pants. You and Julian, I mean. You're right for each other, you know. So when are you going to get it together?"

"We are. We do. Most weekends."

"That sounds really thrilling," Prudence said with patent insincerity. "You two remind me of a couple I used to know. They dated for years, even lived together on and off, but never got out of the starting gate. In the end he drifted off to Hawaii with someone half his age to raise macadamia nuts, and she set up her own software business in Anaheim."

"And the moral is?"

"You tell me."

Mara sighed. "The trouble is, Julian might be just as happy doing that. Raising macadamia nuts. If he weren't so busy looking for orchids."

"So that's where it's at, is it?"

In truth, Mara did not know where it was at, except that their parting the night before had not forecast romantic success. He had asked her to stay. She had turned him down. If he had pressed her, maybe she would have told him what was on her mind. They could have talked things out. But it hadn't happened like that. Were they, like Prudence's friends, fated to go their separate ways, he to his botanical pursuits, she, endlessly, to renovating other people's bathrooms? Her last sight of Julian had been in her rearview mirror, as she left him standing by the roadside outside his house: a tall, indistinct form, lonely in the darkness. The thought of him like that made her swallow hard.

Prudence, who had been studying Mara, broke the silence. "Tell you what. You read Jean-Claude's *Contes folkloriques*. It's full of tales of folks who make pacts with the devil. You could try selling your soul to Satan in return for Julian's love."

"No thanks."

"Oh, it's not as bad as it sounds," Prudence reassured her cheerfully. "Around here, people always get the better of the devil, poor dope. Typical Périgordine cunning."

Mara sat up in bed, pillows stacked behind her, drinking fruit juice straight from the container and squinting through a pair of newly prescribed varifocal glasses, which meant that she couldn't see anything properly, near or far. *Le Visage de la Résistance en Dordogne* was balanced on her knees. It was a photo-documentation of the local Resistance effort against the Germans in the years 1940–1944. She was surprised, given Prudence's description of the author, to find it a serious, well-assembled work.

An hour later, she got up, dumped her juice carton, punched her pillows into shape, resettled, and opened *Contes folkloriques de la Dordogne*. This was a collection of stories, interlarded with the author's comments. One, a tale told by a farmer from Liorac, was described as part of an oral tradition still very much alive in the region and representative of the typical werewolf "encounter" tale:

A farmer coming home from a housewarming late at night was walking along the bank of a stream. The moon was full, and he could see almost as well as in bright daylight. He saw a strange man on the other side of the stream, bathing in the water. When the strange man realized he had been observed, he transformed into an enormous wolf. The terrified farmer fell on his knees and prayed to the Virgin Mary. When he opened his eyes, the werewolf had vanished.

"Would've done better to swear off drink," Mara muttered to Jazz, who lay snoring at her feet. She read on:

. . . If we accept that all legends have their roots in the reality of a people, we must ask why the Sigoulane Valley offers such a particularly rich store of werewolf stories. Perhaps this is partly explained by the fact that in times past wolves roamed freely in the forests surrounding the valley. However, it is also possible that the tales took their origin from a series of gruesome deaths that occurred in the last quarter of the 1700s and again in the middle of the 1800s. Eyewitnesses claimed that a wolflike creature able to walk upright like a man was responsible for the killings. Fact or fantasy? There are many who believe the Sigoulane Beast, as it came to be called, was no figment of the popular imagination . . .

Mara was growing sleepy. The books gave her a curious picture of the man she had been instructed to meet: the competent historical documentarian sat oddly with the legitimizer of werewolf stories. She yawned. *Folktales* soon joined *The Face of the Resistance* on the floor.

9

Jean-Claude Fournier was slim, mid-thirties, and movie-star handsome. He had an aquiline nose, bright-yellow hair parted in the middle above a high forehead, and disturbing gray eyes, the kind that, because of their clarity, seemed to look right into you. His eyes at the moment were piercing Mara with a teasing discernment that made her thoroughly uncomfortable.

"*Mais oui,*" he said, smiling. He sat next to her on a velvet settee, watching her with interest. His hand on the cushion between them was nicely manicured. Incongruously, the strong, long fingers were sprinkled with dark hairs. "I put together an enormous amount of information on the de Bonfonds for Christophe over the past two years. Genealogical research is one of the things I do."

Very profitably, Mara thought, from the look of him and his elegant, almost *bijou,* environment. His house was a beautifully restored eighteenth-century cottage. A large back terrace offered a panoramic view of forested hills and valleys. It was cantilevered over a ravine which, she was informed, served as a run for deer, *sangliers,* and foxes.

"Then you'll take it on?"

"*C'est logique.* Although my notes are all at Aurillac. Christophe insisted on it, but as long as I can access them there should be no trouble." He paused thoughtfully. "A most interesting commission."

He had served her a peach wine apéritif, lightly brushing her fingers as he gave her the glass. In her nervousness, she had gulped down the contents.

"Another?" he suggested.

"What? No. *Merci.*" She focused on a Louis XVI armchair. She also noticed a collection of pentagrams, a phrenological skull, a crystal orb, a plaster hand, and wondered if, in addition to hair-coloring, Jean-Claude dabbled in the occult. "You do understand that Christophe wants the work done as quickly as possible, and quietly? He said absolute discretion."

"That goes without saying. May I call you Mara?"

"Of course."

"And you must call me Jean-Claude." He exuded a subtle scent of aftershave that somehow matched his Nile-green shirt. "I'm fascinated by your accent. Where did you learn your French?"

She laughed outright. "I'm French Canadian. From Montreal. We drawl and flatten our vowels and say things like '*y faire des gnangnangnan,*' meaning to talk stupid, and '*il tombe des clous*'—it's raining nails—but it's our way of speaking, and we hold to it."

"But your name. Dunn is not a French name."

"My father's Scottish."

"And Maman?"

"*Québécoise.* What we call *pure laine.* Dyed-in-the-wool."

"*Formidable,*" he breathed and leaned in.

Mara returned to her commission. "Christophe believes the baby was the illegitimate child of one of the servants. I don't need to tell you that he would be highly gratified if that's what you in fact discover."

"Understandably." His gaze lingered on her. "It would be easier for all concerned. Although," he added after a pause, "improbable."

It was what she already knew: the child's trappings really were too grand for the bastard of a servant. She sighed. "I suppose that leaves the family."

Jean-Claude refilled Mara's glass anyway. He did it in such a way that she was barely aware of it. "Unfortunately, yes. In fact, during the period in question—1860 to 1914, I believe the newspaper said—the de Bonfond family had several unmarried females of childbearing age living in Aurillac Manor."

"Why focus on unmarried women?"

Jean-Claude smiled, a not altogether pleasant smile. "Because a child for any one of them would have meant a bastard and social stigma. Sufficient motive perhaps to suppress the unfortunate infant's existence? Whereas the married women of the family could have simply passed the baby off as a legitimate son."

She took a deep breath and said, "All the same, I believe Christophe wants to know the truth." It was a lie, of course. The only one who wanted the truth was Mara herself. Christophe fully expected Jean-Claude to cooperate, in return for a handsome fee, by producing a plausible explanation for Baby Blue that left the family honor unsullied.

Jean-Claude cocked an eyebrow. "Are you sure?"

"Yes." She downed the second drink as quickly as she had the first. "He—er—thinks the only way to put an end to the gossip and the bad press is to identify Baby Blue and release the story himself. In a controlled way, of course. But he's in a hurry. Apparently some people named Verdier are trying to profit from the circumstances by selling the dirt on the de Bonfonds to the media."

Jean-Claude nodded. "Michel Verdier and his son, Guy. Cousins on Christophe's great-great-grandmother's side, if my memory serves me right. What about Antoine and his family? They're de Bonfonds as well. What do they say?"

"I don't know. I'm here representing only Christophe. And, oh, Christophe also said that if the Verdiers try to contact you, you're to let me know. He was very insistent that you remember at all times that you're working for him and no one else, particularly anyone who might try to . . . let's say, co-opt your services."

"Naturally," Jean-Claude murmured.

"When can you begin?"

"Right away."

"*Formidable*. I'll tell Christophe—"

"It will allow me to get to know you all the sooner." He smiled suggestively.

"I'm here strictly as a go-between, Jean-Claude," Mara said coolly. Prudence had called him *très charmant*, and he was. Mara's ex-husband, Hal, a talented architect with a drinking problem and a skyscraper ego, had also been *charmant*. Since Hal, she had steered clear of the type. Jean-Claude was also, she figured, a good ten years younger than she. Her few experiences with younger men had only made her feel old. "I think it will be better if we keep to business."

"But you're Christophe's representative," he argued reasonably. "Isn't it normal that I should want to know with whom I'm dealing?" His clear gray eyes locked on hers in an amused challenge. "Come. You're not married. At least"—his glance swept her left hand—"you don't wear an *alliance*. Do you have a friend who would object?"

"Yes," said Mara, thinking of Julian. "No." And wondered which it was.

10

Julian had risen to another glorious day, but his morning was quickly turning into a waking nightmare. His interview with Antoine de Bonfond the previous Wednesday had gone extremely well. Too well, perhaps, because it had set him up to believe that the landscaping of the sales pavilion would run smoothly.

The pavilion, an octagonal structure of glass and stone, had been built directly onto the old *chai*. The *chai*, where the wine was processed, aged, and bottled, had also been expanded. The conjunction allowed visitors to pass from reception straight into the areas where the art of winemaking would be explained and where they would hear the history of Coteaux de Bonfond and be impressed by the blend of tradition (hand-picking of choice grapes) and modern technology (the state-of-the-art methods of wineprocessing, the new stainless-steel vats) before returning to the pavilion and the object of it all: the point of sale. Julian's role was to do something with the space fronting the pavilion and surrounding the parking area. From what he could tell, it was practically solid limestone. Had it not been, he was sure that Antoine would have planted it with vines rather than waste good land, for everywhere else the rows of vines came right up to the buildings. In addition to the centerpiece water feature, Julian had proposed an informal rock garden. It was the only thing that could be done with the difficult piece of ground he had to work with.

"Excellent," Antoine had said. "Do it." A decisive man, he had spent a lifetime developing a modest winery into one of the leading *vignobles* of the Bergerac zone. Having mastered his calling, he seemed to be willing to let others get on with theirs if he thought they knew what they were doing.

Not so his son. Pierre was a pudgy individual approaching middle age. His black eyebrows grew together over small, mean eyes. He also had a way of breathing in through his mouth and out his nose with a minute, whistling sound that Julian found intensely annoying. Unfortunately, now that the preliminaries were over, it looked as if Pierre was the person Julian was going to have to work with. Unlike Antoine, Pierre had a slow, distrustful way about him and a strong preference for what he called *le parking* over vegetation. Julian found this strange in a man who derived his living from the soil. Until he learned that Pierre dealt strictly with the winery accounts.

"What's wrong with just gravel?" Pierre complained.

"It's boring."

"What does that matter?"

That was how they started off. Pierre proved, as the morning wore on, indifferent to the vibrant vista of form and color that Julian proposed and positively hostile to the anticipated cost of the project. He sat opposite Julian at a table in one corner of the new pavilion, wheezing in and out and taking a sadistic pleasure in crossing out whole sections of the landscaping plan that Julian had worked hours on and that now lay in tatters, so to speak, between them.

"This goes," Pierre said peremptorily, tapping the spot where the water feature was to be.

Julian started out of his chair. "But it's the centerpiece of the whole thing. Your father specifically agreed on a natural rock waterfall as a kind of signature piece for your Domaine de la Source. It's your leading label, after all—"

"Julian, Julian"—Pierre raised a hand—"I'm afraid you're going to have to get one thing through your head. You're dealing with me. Now, if Papa wants this waterfall, I'm willing to consider it, but first *you're* going to have to convince *me* that it's worth the additional expense."

Julian subsided, simmering. He thought he would much rather be dealing with Pierre's sister, Denise, a tall, sleek woman whom he had seen passing back and forth. She handled, he gathered, public relations and marketing.

"Giving you grief, is he?" she interceded at one point as she breezed by on her way to a display area she was setting up, showing the history of Coteaux de Bonfond. She took in at a glance Julian and the plan Julian was trying to defend.

"Get lost, Denise," said her brother.

"Get stuffed," she retorted over her shoulder. She, like her brother, was dark, but in a polished, glamorous way. There was also something very tough about her. "I want something better than a car park, Pierre, and you'd better see I get it. We haven't spent a fortune on this building to slap asphalt around it."

Work on the interior of the pavilion was still going on around them. Carpenters were finishing the area that was to be the site of tasting events. Denise seemed to be able to oversee the men, do her own job, and find time to antagonize her brother without breaking stride.

A moment later, she was back and leaning seductively over Julian.

"Don't let the little *crotte* talk you out of a thing," she urged. The frown lines on her carefully made-up face were more deeply grooved than the laugh lines. "I'll back you with Papa. I want this place absolutely outstanding for my marketing launch next month. Look at it this way: if you shoot your budget, Big Brother here will merely blow a valve. If I'm not happy with your landscaping, I'll have your hide. Take your choice."

"Denise," her brother yelled. He threw down his pencil and lurched to his feet. He looked like a man trying to swallow a hedgehog. "Piss off! I mean it."

"Yes, darling." She mouthed him a kiss and sashayed away.

Unfortunately for Julian, this interchange put the Crotte (the epithet, which meant "turd," was going to stick, as far as Julian was concerned) in a foul temper.

"I can't work under these conditions," Pierre shouted to no one in particular, revealing a wet, purple expanse of gums that Julian, despite his dislike of the man, found momentarily fascinating. The carpenters paused to look their way. "See me Friday—no, not Friday—next week. And you'd better have a scaled-down plan and a reasonable budget or the whole things is off."

"I'd like to point out," Julian argued hotly, "that your father approved this plan. His only requirement was that the work be completed by June. I have very little time to work with as it is. Delaying until next week is going to seriously jeopardize—"

"I don't give a damn," Pierre snarled, showing more mouth lining. "He's turned the whole thing over to me, and you do what I say, when I say, or you can take your shovel—"

"My, my, sweetums," murmured Denise on her way past again. She was carrying stacks of brochures this time. "Tossing your weight around? Don't give yourself a hernia."

Pierre leaned forward threateningly on his fists. "Haven't you anything better to do?"

Julian rolled up his plan and walked swiftly out of the pavilion.

He sat fuming in his van and wondering if his fight with Pierre was going to bring on another of his stress headaches. Thumpers, he called them. He had expected to spend the better part of the day at Coteaux de Bonfond doing preliminaries for the project. Now, as he gunned the engine and drove off, Julian wasn't even sure if there was going to be a project. Or if he wanted any part of it. By the time he reached the main road, however, his blood pressure had eased and the thumper seemed less of a threat.

Cooling down, Julian realized that the Crotte had simply been feeling his own importance. And his sister had taken immense pleasure in goading him. He wondered about Denise. There was something restless and predatory about her, a kind of hipless, reptilian allure. He remembered the quick tap-tapping of her sharp heels as she strode back and forth across the wooden pavilion floor, her narrow face, her large, black, malicious eyes. A vivid, disturbing woman. He wondered briefly if she could be an ally. On reflection, he decided that it would be like bedding down with a cobra.

It was a little past one. Nothing for him to do but go home, have a bite, and spend the rest of the day revising the plan. Trim a little here, a bit there, reduce the bottom line. Something to placate Pierre. Anything so he could get on with the work. It was early May, and he would have to go like the clappers to get everything ready in time for Denise's marketing launch.

He drove out of the valley, again taking by preference the network of small roads that linked the villages, hamlets, and farms of the Dordogne. About him spread a peaceful landscape of planted fields, market gardens of broad beans and artichokes, and grassy meadows where blond cows grazed. A lone tractor worked its way over the brow of a distant hill. As he took the turnoff toward home, he rolled down the window to smell the last of the lilacs, sweet on the wind. In the village of Grissac, climbing roses were coming into bloom against old stone walls. The roofs of the houses, steeply pitched and hipped, created their own peculiarly Périgordine outline against the cloudless sky.

Bismuth emerged from the bushes just as Julian pulled up alongside his cottage. Julian liked dogs, but had his doubts about this one. He had originally named the animal Rugby, in honor of his favorite sport, but later renamed him Bismuth (pronounced

"Beez-mute" in French) because the dog had so often caused Julian to reach for an antacid. Julian's grievances against his dog were many: he was ungainly, with a rangy body, large feet, and a bony tail; in puppyhood he had soiled every carpet in the house, gnawed the bindings off books (he liked the glue), and destroyed Julian's favorite hiking boots; finally, the beast wore an air of constant, timid apology ("hang-dog" suited him well), as if he knew he was destined always to be in the wrong, at least where his master was concerned, and this served only to make Julian feel guilty. Besides, Bismuth still chewed things. It was unfortunate from Julian's viewpoint that Bismuth could not be got rid of. He was the gift of a neighboring goat-farmer who owned Bismuth's mother, Edith. And his sire was Mara's own dog, Jazz. It was a situation typical of life in the Dordogne, Julian thought resignedly. Everyone was related, things were inextricably intertwined, and the consequences of acting badly were endless.

Bismuth looked doubtfully at Julian, sensing that his owner was not in a good mood.

"You might at least have got lunch ready," Julian growled as they went in. His cottage was a low, square stone structure with a leaky roof. Its best features were a spacious kitchen with a flagstone floor and a front room with a fireplace that sometimes did not smoke. The rest of the rooms were dim and poky. A general air of disorder bespoke its owner's untidy habits.

Julian rummaged around in the shelves and found a tin of cassoulet. He cranked it open, scooped the contents into a bowl, and heated it on high for four minutes in the microwave. He dumped the bean-and-meat mixture onto a plate. Bismuth watched him longingly. Julian tried to ignore him, but a long line of drool was now dropping from the corner of the dog's mouth onto the floor.

"For Christ's sake." Julian gave in irritably and scraped a portion of his meal into Bismuth's bowl. The food was gone before Julian had even seated himself.

After lunch, Julian realized that he did not feel at all like dealing with the Coteaux de Bonfond landscaping plan. He decided instead to call on Iris. He had purposely put off seeing her until he knew how the media would treat Baby Blue, or, more precisely, the child's accoutrements. To his relief, attention had been focused entirely on the baby, with only passing mention of the rosary and the shawl, and little or no reference to the embroidered orchid motif. He felt safe going back with the sketch of *Cypripedium incognitum* and advising her how to complete it without giving anything away to Géraud. He was surprised, when he came out of the house, to find that clouds were banking up in the northwest. The smell of rain hung heavy in the air. Before he even reached the main road, fat droplets were spattering his windshield. By the time he reached Malpech, rain was sheeting across the fields.

Iris received him cheerfully as usual and gave him a towel to dry off with—he'd had to gallop through the downpour from his car to the house. Géraud for a change was in surprisingly good humor. The drawback to this, however, was that Iris did not shoo him away, and though Géraud did not sit down with them in the front room, he hung about, fiddling with this and that.

"Don't let me stop you," he said blandly. "I'm just puttering."

"The slipper is larger than you have it." Julian peered at Iris's new sketch, which she had put before him on the coffee table. He was uncomfortably aware of his botanical nemesis hovering in the background. "And strongly veined. You have the color about right, but the veining needs to be more pronounced, a kind of reddish maroon."

This produced a soft snort from Géraud.

"Honestly, you must have X-ray vision," Iris marveled, "because I looked at that photo until my eyes hurt, and I really couldn't make anything of it."

"Yes. Well, I viewed it again under—er—ultra-high magnification and—er—made a few extrapolations." It wasn't exactly a lie.

He had looked at the print through a magnifying glass, but that had only increased the blurring of the flower without providing more information.

"And there's one other thing." Julian stopped, wishing desperately that Géraud would vanish.

"Yes?"

"The bottom sepals. In the sketch you have them joined."

"You told me to."

"I know, but I've revised my opinion. I believe now that they should be shown as—er—separated."

"What?" Géraud exploded, giving up all pretense of being otherwise engaged. "You're mad. Every species of *Cypripedium* except *arietinum* and *plectrochilum*"—Géraud insisted on taxonomical names—"has the ventral sepals united mostly or all the way to the tip."

"This one is different."

Géraud surged forward. "Then it's a case of peloria, anomalous reversion to the norm."

"No, it's not," Julian said stubbornly. His hunch was that the embroidery had been modeled on a typical plant rather than that the embroiderer had purposely depicted an aberration. He appealed to the woman. "Look, Iris, I'd like you to draw them as separate, hanging down one on either side of the labellum."

Iris shook her head. "Julian, the lower half of the flower is mostly obliterated by that streak running across the photo. Even ultra-high magnification can't show you something that isn't there."

"Ha! You see?" Géraud crowed. "Even she won't go along with this poppycock."

Julian rose to go. "Trust me. I know what I'm talking about."

All at once, Géraud was suspicious. His nostrils flared as if he had caught a telltale odor. "You're awfully sure of yourself all of a sudden. What's going on? Have you found out something? Why the mystery?"

"Will you do it for me, Iris?" Julian pleaded.

"If you're sure, *chéri*," she sighed.

He gave her a kiss on her weathered cheek.

"This whole thing's a monstrous scam," roared Géraud, trailing him to the door. "Your publisher should be told what you're trying to do. You won't get away with it. Don't forget, claiming credit for a new species involves more than a trumped-up sketch. You have to photograph the plant *in situ*, you have to dry-press a specimen, present an authentic—*authentic,* mind you—botanical drawing, and you have to publish your find. The only thing you won't have difficulty with is naming it, since I'm sure you intend to call it *Cypripedium woodianum.* Ha! You'll never get away with it. You'll be a laughingstock. Don't say I didn't warn you."

With Géraud's abuse ringing in his ears, Julian almost ran from the house.

11

MONDAY AFTERNOON, 3 MAY

Give him his due, Jean-Claude was prompt with his results. But, then, he already knew a lot about the family. He proposed a rendezvous at five o'clock at Aurillac Manor. His research notes were there, plus other material and family artifacts that Mara might find interesting.

Mara arrived twenty minutes late. Thérèse met her at the door: Christophe was still keeping to his room, and Monsieur Fournier was waiting for her in the library. She left Mara to find her own way to the large, handsome chamber on the ground floor.

"Ah, Mara." Jean-Claude strode forward to meet her, taking her hand and brushing the back of it with his lips. He did not, however, venture any farther than her wrist. She caught again the musky whiff of his cologne. He was dressed this time in shades of cream that emphasized his buttercup-yellow hair. His burgundy loafers sported overlying brass G's for buckles. Mara, who had spent the afternoon prospecting a work site, wore jeans, sneakers, and a T-shirt that read: *I Blow Raspberries on My Dog's Stomach. Do You?*

"I hope you approve." Jean-Claude waved a hand about him. "We're well chaperoned." The walls were hung with stern-looking ancestral portraits. His assurance was at odds with the fact that he still held her hand.

"Good," she said, disengaging herself and ignoring the ever-present tease in his voice. "What do you have for me?"

"It depends on how much you want to know."

"I have the basic facts. They're an old, titled family. The house goes back to the early 1500s and Christophe's great-grandmother was a celebrated soprano."

"Hmm. Yes. Well. Perhaps we'd better begin at the beginning, or as close to it as I can get. Let's start with the family motto, shall we?"

He took her elbow lightly and guided her to a massive fireplace at one end of the room. Four words were carved into the high front of the marble mantelpiece.

"*Sang E Mon Drech,*" Mara read aloud, puzzling over the familiar and yet unfamiliar letter combinations. "What is this? Occitan?" She referred to the old tongue of the region, more closely related to Catalan than to French, which still survived in many parts of southern France.

"Quite right. 'Blood And My Right,'" he translated. "In French, it would be *Sang Et Mon Droit.*"

"Oh yes." Mara recalled Christophe's bragging rights. "Something about the privileges conferred by bloodline."

Jean-Claude said dryly, "Something like that. At any rate, it suggests an old family of noble lineage, does it not? Which brings us to the family tree."

He now steered her toward a large library table in the middle of the room. An ornately lettered parchment covered the tabletop, protected by a sheet of beveled glass. It showed generations of de Bonfonds going back to the tenth century.

"Looks terribly old," she murmured, squinting at the faded, ancient script.

Jean-Claude laughed outright. "It's terribly"—he lowered his voice—"bogus. In fact, the earliest entry I could verify is here." He tapped a spot three-quarters of the way down the chart. "Xavier, Christophe's four-times-great-grandfather, 1730–1810, a man with a reputation for violence. He whipped a servant almost to death for spilling a flagon of wine. In the end, he was killed by his own dog. That's him over there."

He walked her over to the life-sized portrait of a man, done in middle age and compellingly posed in a dark cape with a touch of scarlet at the collar. Mara stared at a gaunt face with a big jaw, long nose, and ginger-colored hair and eyebrows that ran together above pale, protuberant eyes. Beside him stood a large, unfriendly-looking dog. The artist had rendered man and beast in such a way that their two bodies almost blended. One of the man's powerful hands grasped the dog's collar, as if restraining the animal. Maybe it was the one who had turned on its master. The other hand held an opened scroll. Stepping closer, she saw the family motto repeated, with a slight variation of spelling, on the scroll.

"He was titled," said her guide. "Le Baron de Bonfond. On paper, anyway."

"On paper? What are you saying?"

Jean-Claude laughed again. "Pure fabrication. I suspect a twist of his real surname, Lebrun, to which I have found reference, suggesting that our so-called Baron started out life as plain old Mr. Brown. He took the name 'Bonfond' from an upstream relative, inserted a 'de,' cleverly converted 'Lebrun,' to 'le Baron,' arrived newly made in the Dordogne, and married well. Interestingly, Bonfond was also the family name of Xavier's wife, Séverine, to whom he was distantly related. An insignificant little thing"—the genealogist waved at a bland, featureless face captured in a small oval frame—"who died in childbirth. Her branch of the family were Huguenots, wealthy but nonaristocratic."

Mara turned to him, dismayed. "Are you saying there's *no* title in Christophe's family at all, not even on the distaff side?"

"Exactly. Moreover, far from being a baron, our Xavier actually belonged to a much-hated class of men, the *gabelous*, salt-tax collectors—don't tell Christophe I told you. Although he seems to have used his position to do very nicely for himself, thank you."

"Salt?" Mara was incredulous. Was this the invaluable service rendered to the crown that Christophe had spoken of?

"Indeed. *La gabelle* was one of the most hated taxes in French history. In fact, it was one of the causes of the Revolution. The rich were exempt, of course, so the poor carried the load. Smuggling salt from regions where the tax was lower to high-tax areas was a profitable enterprise. That's where the *gabelous* came in. It was their job to enforce the tax and hunt down violators, and they were merciless. They raided homes, sent innocent people to prison, and lined their pockets with bribes. They were also notorious for carrying out body searches of women." Here Jean-Claude smirked. "Women were very much engaged in petty smuggling, you see. The *faux cul*—more delicately put, false fanny—was a favorite hiding place for contraband salt."

"And this house?" Mara asked, her faith in Christophe's account of his family collapsing like a mudslide in rain. "I understood it to be in the family for five hundred years."

"Séverine's, not Monsieur Xavier's. In fact, although he made himself out to be a son of the Dordogne, it seems our fake baron came from Le Gévaudan, a dirt-poor region at the edge of the Massif Central. Beyond that and his profession as a *gabelou*, I could find little about his background. Shall we move on?"

His arm pressed her forward toward more de Bonfond men. "This one's Auguste, Séverine and Xavier's son, and Auguste's sons, Dominique and Roland. Dominique was Christophe's great-great-grandfather, while Roland was the great-great-grandfather of Christophe's cousin Antoine, whom you may know. Roland founded the Coteaux de Bonfond winery, although Antoine expanded it to its present dimensions." Jean-Claude guided Mara farther down the wall. "Here we have Dominique's son Hugo, Christophe's great-grandfather." Mara saw in the latter a large, aggressive-looking man with the family eyes, nose, and jaw. "Hugo was a great hunter."

Jean-Claude's fingers had somehow come to rest lightly on Mara's shoulder. She stepped away, going over to inspect a smaller portrait hanging next to that of Hugo, a woman in blue with a mass of honey-colored hair. The females of the family, Mara decided, seemed to have been accorded considerably less canvas than their men. This one, however, merited life-sized rendering.

"Henriette," Jean-Claude identified. "Hugo's wife and Christophe's great-grandmother."

"The Adored One," Mara recalled. L'Adorée. Also the Walker and Plate-Thrower. She was indeed a beauty, but with a determined set to the mouth that confirmed her potential to make a troublesome ghost.

Jean-Claude shook his head. "Again, we have a play on names. The epithet was actually 'la Dorée.' The Golden One."

"Oh. Because of her hair?"

"Because of her cupidity. When Hugo met her she was a sharp little Parisian courtesan with a passable voice and a driving lust for money. Her father was a drunken stonemason who broke his back rolling off a roof, so young Henriette became the family breadwinner. Her main claim to fame was a magnificent bosom. It was said that she charged by the breast, so that her other nickname was 'One or Two?' Christophe believes she sang at the Opéra, but that would have been unlikely because it was still being built when Hugo wedded and then bedded her. Oh yes, she was no fool. She made him wait for it." Jean-Claude sounded almost disapproving.

"Of course," he went on, "Henriette didn't exactly embark on a sea of roses. She married a de Bonfond, for what it was worth, but she had to contend with a lecherous father-in-law, a husband with a reputation for slitting the throats of game he brought down and drinking their blood while they were still alive, and a virago of a mother-in-law." He pointed to another painting. It was a seated portrait of an older woman dressed in black. A narrow face with pale, close-set eyes scowled down on Mara above a rigid lace fichu. "Odile de Bonfond, née Verdier, wife of Dominique, and reputedly the very soul of avarice. She married into the family in 1835, on the strength of a considerable settlement. The deal was that Hugo would marry one of his Verdier cousins, thereby integrating the family fortunes and saving the Verdiers' bacon because Odile's dowry ruined them. Henriette spoiled all that."

Mara noticed that the dreadful Odile had been painted clutching a cloth purse. Perhaps the artist had a sense of humor. Or irony.

Jean-Claude continued. "Odile de Bonfond doted on her son and loathed la Blonde Horizontale, as she called her daughter-in-law, which we can take as a reference to how Henriette made her living. Dominique, on the other hand, undoubtedly relished having a pretty woman about the house, so the family dynamics must have been quite interesting. However, he died not long after la Dorée came to Aurillac. Just in time, too. His excesses were eating into the estate. Then Hugo died shortly after from a fall from his horse. His saddle girth snapped. Henriette lived to eighty-two, well into the twentieth century."

"Poor Christophe," Mara murmured, recalling his boyish enthusiasm over the love story of the century. "But"—she experienced a sudden stab of annoyance—"does he *know* all this?" Had he been lying to her all the time, was what she really wanted to ask.

Jean-Claude pursed his lips. "If you mean, did he invent the public persona of the de Bonfonds to hide their less than illustrious past, no. All of the misrepresentations I mentioned were established well before him. It's likely that Xavier was responsible for most of them, including the fake family tree that purports to go back to the Crusades but which, as I said, dates no further back than Xavier himself."

"But you told Christophe, didn't you? You told him what you found out."

Jean-Claude gave an eloquent shrug. "I tried. He had hysterics when I debunked a seventeenth-century claim to an episcopal branch of the family. After that he refused to let me remove so much as a note scribbled on the back of an envelope from the premises. I found it easier simply to give him the results of my research and let him do what he wanted with it. However, I think he must have known something was not quite right, at least where the baronetcy was concerned, because subsequent males after Xavier never used it, and Christophe himself has never attempted to claim it."

"But the book he's writing on the history of the de Bonfonds—?"

"Will no doubt be a highly sanitized version of the truth."

Mara groaned audibly.

Jean-Claude looked amused. "So. Where was I? Hugo and Henriette had one offspring, Christophe's grandfather, Dieudonné. He was born in 1872, just before Hugo's death. That's him as a child, done by Archambault, quite a well-known artist in his day."

Mara saw a portrait of a boy of perhaps seven or eight with dark hair and eyes and a round, impertinent face. "And later"—Jean-Claude led her to another section of wall, where canvas gave way to photographs, paint to sepia tones—"in middle age."

The impertinence had now mellowed into complacency: a heavy-set gentleman, posed with his hands on his knees, the broad face riding above a stiff wingtip collar. In feature and expression, he was a cruder, more vigorous version of Christophe.

"Dieudonné saved the day for the de Bonfonds because Dominique really had left the estate in a bad way, and Hugo, if he had lived, would probably have finished the family off. However, young Dieudonné was a terribly clever chap who invented a revolutionary inking technique on which he built a very successful printing business. He married well, Léonie Boursicaut, from an important Bordeaux family. They had a son, Bertrand, Christophe's father, who further filled the family coffers by marrying into the wealthy Pommarel family. And a daughter, Amélie, who died young of influenza."

The later generations of de Bonfonds, caught in various attitudes by the photographer's lens, gazed down at Mara. It seemed to her that prosperity had improved the family features. Gone was the earlier glare of greed and raw ambition. In its place a smug and more subtle acquisitiveness, the rounded look of people who were sure of their importance and their position in the world. She said as much. "I mean, they don't lunge out at you like they do in the paintings. They sit back and let the camera come to them. See for yourself."

Her guide looked surprised. He scanned the array of faces for a long moment.

She shook her head impatiently. "Jean-Claude, this is all very interesting, but nothing you've said gets us any further ahead with identifying Baby Blue. You've mainly talked about the men. It's the women we should be concentrating on, isn't it? You said that between 1860 and 1914 there were several females of childbearing age living at Aurillac. Tell me about them."

His hands went up. "Of course. My apologies. I only wanted to provide you with the, shall we say, necessary background for understanding the family we're dealing with." He smoothed back his golden hair. "Well, of the women, you've met Henriette. Then there was Eloïse Verdier, Odile's niece. She stayed at Aurillac between 1865 and 1870—through Odile's connivance, so she and Hugo could make a match of it—but moved back to her family's home after he married Henriette. Eloïse got over her disappointment and lived out her life as a spinster devoted to good works. There's no likeness of her here, but no doubt she was appropriately pious-looking. Then"—Jean-Claude stopped before a head-and-shoulders portrait of an anemic female with an otherworldly expression—"we have Catherine, the eldest of Odile and Dominique's daughters. She joined a convent at the age of twenty-four. Daughters often took the veil in those days, whether they wanted to or not, because dowries were expensive and the upkeep of unmarried females a drain on family coffers. Mind you, the family had to make a one-time endowment to the convent, but it probably worked out cheaper for them in the end because it was in exchange for Catherine's renouncing all inheritance rights."

They stepped up to the next painting: a large, plain female dressed in an unflattering shade of green and uncomfortably posed with a pug in her lap.

"This one's Cécile, Hugo's youngest sister. Hard to say which is uglier, isn't it, the woman or the dog? She, too, planned to take the veil, but nothing ever came of it. And finally"—moving on to a photograph of a plump, placid-looking woman—"Dieudonné's wife, Léonie, who came to Aurillac when she married into the family in 1901."

Mara gazed about her. "Which one?" she wondered aloud.

Jean-Claude nodded. "Indeed. Which one? Léonie I think we can discount. First, she simply doesn't seem the type, but also because, as I said, a bastard would have been much less of a problem for a married woman, who could pass it off as her husband's child."

"Henriette was married," Mara interposed, "but you said she was widowed early. A bastard could have been an embarrassment for her, too. Or did she remarry?"

"No, and for good reason, although I'm sure she didn't want for suitors. Her difficulty was that Hugo left her an annuity, not only contingent on her producing a surviving male heir, but requiring her to remain in a state of exemplary widowhood if she wanted to continue to touch her *rente*. Maybe she took a lover who put her in an embarrassing way, but I somehow doubt it, first because Maman Odile would have had her out on the street *tout de suite* for breach of contract, and second because I suspect Henriette's real passion was always money. In any case, she proved herself to be a very able administrator of her young son's estate."

"That leaves Catherine, Eloïse, and Cécile."

"Exactly. Now, Catherine is a definite candidate. Did she have a true calling, or was she confined to a nunnery because she was delivered of an illegitimate son? It's what they did in those days, you know. As for Eloïse, she came to Aurillac when she was twenty-two and stayed there five years. While cozying up to Hugo, did she curdle the cream by getting pregnant by the stable lad? If so, I wouldn't be surprised if the entire Verdier clan conspired to help her get rid of the baby. A lot was at stake for them."

Mara nodded.

"But for my money, the most interesting candidate is Cécile. Why? Because she offers us the most concrete possibilities and provides us with the most information. She kept a diary of sorts between 1861 and 1871, an absolute gold mine for someone like me and the source of most of my personal information on the family. In it she refers to a liaison with a certain captain in the Imperial Army—we're talking about Napoleon III now—whom she met in Paris."

He took her to a large, glass-fronted cabinet. It contained, Jean-Claude said, the de Bonfond family papers as well as all his research notes. One shelf was given over to Cécile's diary, organized by date in cardboard folders, secured at the corners by elastic loops. He pulled out the folder for the year 1870.

"I offer you excerpts that support my hypothesis. These relate to the summer when Cécile met her army captain. I had the unenviable task of putting her ramblings into some kind of order when I took on Christophe's book project. No easy job, since there were major gaps, and most of her entries weren't dated. Her handwriting was also awful."

He opened the folder and paged through a stack of loose sheets covered in ill-formed writing.

"I'll spare you the details of Cécile's more graphic entries, but here, for example, she refers to what we can only take as a sexual encounter." He read aloud: " *La nuit il me vient surnoisement.*' "

" 'He comes to me stealthily in the night,' " Mara murmured to herself.

"It's undated, and she doesn't mention names, but it sounds very much like a tryst with her army captain, doesn't it?" He sifted through more pages. "And again: *'Il me vient, toujours surnoisement, avec son regard bleu qui me transperce jusqu'aux entrailles.'* "

Mara's eyes rolled at the congested prose: "He comes to me, always stealthily, with his blue gaze that pierces me to the entrails." Cécile must have been a reader of romance novels.

"However, nothing came of the affair." Jean-Claude put the papers away and snapped the elastics in place. "The family intervened, and poor Cécile was forced to give her lover up. The fellow was probably just a common adventurer looking for an advantageous alliance anyway. In any case, he was cut down in the Franco-Prussian War only months later."

Mara guessed, "So she woke up one day to learn not only that her lover was dead, but that she was carrying his baby?"

Jean-Claude nodded. "Significantly, it's at this point that she first mentions following her sister into the Abbaye des Eaux. She didn't, in the end, but remained at Aurillac, growing ill, old, and mad."

"And you think she killed her child?"

"Et voilà. Or possibly the matter was decided for her."

Mara blinked. "You mean by someone in the family?" Then she recalled that Baby Blue had been smothered with unnecessary violence. "As if in a towering rage," Loulou had said. As if someone had wanted to crush the very life out of an unwanted bastard. She pictured the infant torn from Cécile's arms, stifled before the mother's horrified eyes, imagined the woman's screams. Had Cécile recovered the broken body of her baby, wrapped it lovingly in a shawl, and enclosed it in the wall?

"Merde," said Mara. It was all so sordid. An affair, a bastard, the swift dispatch of an inconvenient piece of humanity, probably engineered by the family. And definitely a de Bonfond. Bleakly Mara watched as Jean-Claude closed up the glass-fronted case. How

was she going to report this to Christophe? At the moment, she was glad that he was incommunicado.

Jean-Claude shrugged. "Of course, this is all conjecture. There's no definite proof, except perhaps one or two vague references I found in letters written by Eloïse to Cécile. Eloïse, by the way, is the great-great-aunt of Christophe's and Antoine's cousin Michel, who represents the Verdier side of the family."

"Christophe doesn't want you talking to them," Mara reminded him quickly.

"Don't I know it? When I was researching the de Bonfond family's history, I suggested accessing the Verdier archives, to fill in the blanks, so to speak. Christophe nearly had a seizure." Jean-Claude paused thoughtfully. "Come to think of it, this may be the source of the information Michel—or more likely his son, Guy—wants to sell to the media."

She sighed. "So, in addition to Baby Blue being Cécile's bastard, Christophe's family tree is a complete charade. Xavier invented a fake set of antecedents and a baronetcy to cover up the fact that he was a *gabelou* and, who knows, probably made up the family motto as well."

"That, too. Very likely."

"Almost certainly," said Mara. "Because he couldn't even get it right. It's carved into the mantelpiece as *Sang E Mon Drech*, and appears in his portrait as *Sang Es Mon Drech.*"

Jean-Claude stiffened. "Show me," he said.

She did, pointing out the errant "s" that appeared in the painted scroll but was missing in the carved version.

He peered long at the faded cursive lettering. "Blood Is My Right." He shrugged. "Old documents are full of orthographic errors. Cécile, for one, was a dreadful speller."

"Although there's a difference, isn't there?" She was not going to let him slide away from the fact that he had failed to spot the inconsistency. "Blood *And* My Right. Blood *Is* My Right. So which is it?"

Jean-Claude stepped back to gaze thoughtfully up at the fraudulent baron.

"I honestly don't know," he said. He looked troubled and, for the first time, completely thrown off his stride.

12

The early-morning air was still and chill. According to local wisdom, the risk of frost would persist until Les Saints de Glace, around the middle of the month. People did not plant their kitchen gardens before then. From where Julian stood on a rocky outcropping high on Aurillac Ridge, he had an unobstructed panorama of the Sigoulane Valley and, farther to the south, glinting in the cold, champagne light, the river. The Dordogne, tumbling out of the crystalline highlands of the Massif Central, was broad and peaceful in this stretch, swinging lazily between tree-lined banks and limestone cliffs, offering habitat for pike and perch, roach and bream, and good fishing for herons. Immediately below and behind him, forests cloaked the heavily folded earth.

Julian lingered a moment longer, taking in the view. This was his favorite time of day. Admittedly, he preferred to enjoy it clutching a mug of hot, sweet tea while appreciating a different scene: his own bit of land, where pink valerian bloomed on the stone wall dividing his property from that of Madame Léon; where the dew lay silvery on the tussocky grass; where the bottom of his garden was a cloud of cherry blossoms, and the old fig tree by his kitchen door was beginning to set hard little nuggets of fruit among broad, lobate leaves.

But he was driven by the imperative of his orchid. Ever since he had discovered the embroidery, he had been rising at the first sliver of dawn to conduct a fevered but methodical search of Aurillac Ridge. He had but a few precious days to devote to this activity before work on the pavilion kicked in. If it kicked in. He had not yet completed a revised plan, or, more to the point, a new budget for Pierre. The orchid, for the moment, was his top priority.

His reasoning went like this: The embroiderer had seen the flower and stitched its likeness on the shawl. This woman—he assumed it was a woman—was associated with Aurillac. Therefore, she must have seen the orchid somewhere in the vicinity of the manor. Given the roughness of the terrain, and wearing whatever females wore in those days, she would most likely have stuck to places where she could walk easily. Thus, he had already gone over the grounds immediately surrounding the manor and was now exploring the intricate network of paths radiating out through the extensive woodlands surrounding the property. In the back of Julian's mind, Paul's objection to the shawl's provenance lurked like a tiger: "That's where it ended up. You have no idea where it came from." Julian preferred to ignore the disheartening possibilities.

He sighed, gave a hitch to his backpack, and headed down a narrow trail overgrown with grass and bordered with cowslips. Orchid-hunting was a lonely, quirky occupation. Julian thought of famous orchid-hunters of the past: Rumphius, who went blind in the Moluccas; Skinner, who spent over three decades wandering in forests before dying of yellow fever; Cuming, who discovered more than thirty new orchid species; and Lobb, who brought home the magnificent *Vanda coerulea,* although he left his leg in the Philippines. There were many others, odd, elusive men every one of them, who disappeared for years into far, tropical jungles, some never to return. He wondered if he was going the same way, albeit closer to home and in less strenuous circumstances. Mara, he suspected, thought him obsessive. Maybe Linnaeus had had a point when he asked "whether men are in their right minds who so desperately risk life and everything else through their love of collecting plants."

As he walked, he was rewarded by occasional sprigs of Green-winged and tiny Burnt-tip Orchids growing along the borders of the trail. These were some of the earlier species to show themselves. Soon Lady Orchids, long-leafed *Cephalanthera*, deep-throated *Serapias*, and stately *Limodorum* would come into bloom. Their succession was as much a part of his internal rhythm as was the flow of seasons to the farmer, the rise and fall of tides to the fisherman, the wheeling of constellations to the astronomer.

Bismuth appeared suddenly from the undergrowth. His paws, snout, and the tips of his long, floppy ears were covered in mud. The dog looked doubtfully at his master.

"Grubbing again?" Julian growled. The dog came to him, tail thumping rapidly between his hind legs. "Oh, come on, then," Julian conceded and gave Bismuth a grudging scratch on the head. Bismuth, overjoyed, rolled over on his back.

Something else stirred in the bushes. Christophe's gardener stepped onto the trail. Stooped and thin, he resembled an elderly crane. His clothes, hanging loosely from his frame, resembling bedraggled feathers, added to the impression.

"Ah, Didier."

"Good dog, that," said Didier, as Bismuth righted himself and went over to investigate the old man's boots. "Don't hold much with them myself, but this one's got a nose. Make a good truffler. What're you doing here?" The gardener's inquiry was not rude, simply to the point.

"Well . . ." Julian was momentarily distracted by the idea of Bismuth's being good for anything. He decided to enlist the old man's help. "I'm looking for something." He dug out a copy of Iris's sketch of *Cypripedium incognitum* from his backpack and held it forth. "This. Have you ever seen anything like it?"

The gardener took the drawing from Julian and held it close and then at arm's length. He tipped his head this way and that and sucked his teeth. "Not sure," he said finally and gave the drawing back. "Although that might be the thing the old ones called *Sabot du Diable.*"

Julian's heart leaped in his chest. "*Sabot du*—Devil's Clog? What did it look like, this Devil's Clog? Where did it grow? Can you show it to me?"

Didier scratched his jaw. "That was long ago. Before my time. Doubt if you'll come across it around here anymore."

"Why not? What happened to it?"

"Folks used to dig it up wherever they found it."

Julian gasped with an almost physical pain. "Dug—it—up? Good god, why?"

"Don't know exactly. Planted *aconit* in its place."

"*Aconit?*" Julian was baffled. "You're saying people around here destroyed Devil's Clog and planted *aconit?*"

Didier shrugged. The conversation, which was becoming repetitive, ceased to interest him. He turned to move down the trail.

"Wait a minute." Julian hurried after him. "So *aconit* now grows wherever Devil's Clog used to be?"

Didier shrugged again. "Maybe. Maybe not. Stuff grows wild anyway."

"But why would they have done that? Plant *aconit,* that is?"

Didier gave him something that passed for a grin. "You're the know-it-all. You figure it out."

Julian rifled his brain. Aconite. Monkshood. He knew very little about the plant, apart from the fact that all parts of it were extremely poisonous.

"Hang on, Didier," he called, just as the old man was about to vanish into the trees. "Are there any of these old ones still around who might know anything about this Devil's Clog?"

The gardener chuckled. "Worms. All gone to worms."

"Well, is there anything else you can tell me? It's important that I find it."

"Oh." Didier glanced back over his shoulder. "I can tell you lots of things. It's up to you to ask the right questions."

Julian sat sunk in his favorite armchair. He had spent the rest of the day prowling the northwest sector of Aurillac Ridge, scanning the paths, detouring into clearings, and poking around in grassy patches. He saw orchids, but not his orchid. He was still reeling from the possibility that the local population had ripped up *Cypripedium incognitum* and replaced it with Monkshood. He wondered if Didier had got it right. He had pursued the gardener with more questions, got some interesting bits of local lore, but nothing more on Devil's Clog. Toward the end of the afternoon, a heavy downpour had forced him to abandon his search. On returning to his cottage, he had put in a few hours redoing the Coteaux de Bonfond landscaping plan, trimming bits to reduce the bottom line. Julian was prepared, if Pierre still didn't like it, to dump the project and let the Crotte face Denise's wrath. Dinner had been a plain omelette, which he had shared with Bismuth. The dog routinely ate kibble or canned food, whichever was available (sometimes both), plus a good portion of Julian's own meals, and yet remained as skinny as a whippet.

Julian sighed, worked his way farther down into the armchair, crossed his arms behind his head, and stared up at a familiar stain in the ceiling. Every time it rained, he remembered that he should climb up on the roof to see where the water was coming in. He wondered what Mara was doing. Their parting on Friday night had left him feeling cut adrift. Bound to happen sooner or later, the glass-half-empty side of him argued, as he contemplated the prospect of yet another relationship coming unraveled. Julian's affective career had started with an early, brief, and deeply wounding marriage to a woman who was as unfaithful as she was beautiful, and had bumped along over the years with others, none of whom had chosen to stay. Nevertheless, despite an acquired pessimism, his glass-half-full side *had* nursed seedling hopes of this one.

Meantime, the rain continued to drum drearily overhead. Maybe, he thought sadly, it would be better to stick to orchids. If Didier's old ones had dug up Devil's Clog wherever they found it, didn't that suggest the plant was fairly widespread? So, if Devil's Clog was the same thing as *Cypripedium incognitum,* that meant there had to be—at one time anyway—a population of the orchids large enough to attract attention. The thought made him sit up straight. Bismuth, seeing movement, was instantly at his side. When Julian remained frozen in that posture, the dog planted his head on Julian's thigh. Absently, Julian plucked at the silky ears, enjoying the feel of them sliding through his fingers.

But why the hell rip it out? he wondered. What was it about Devil's Clog that made it so noxious? He had read that many species of Lady's Slipper gave people a contact dermatitis, like poison ivy, which would have been as good a reason as any for getting rid of it. Or maybe it was toxic to grazing animals. But, then, why replace it with another poisonous plant? Whatever the reason—he scratched Bismuth's neck; the dog groaned with pleasure and presented his rump—it now only made sense to include Monkshood in his scan in the hope that the Devil's Clog that had once grown in its place had not been completely wiped out. Not entirely a long shot, and besides, Monkshood, a leggy plant with rather sinister-looking purple blossoms, was a lot easier to spot than a single, low-standing flower. A distant, persistent sound, vaguely familiar, brought him to. It was his phone. He reached for it.

"*Oui? Allo?*"

"*C'est moi, Thérèse.*" The housekeeper's voice was strident. "Do you know where he is?"

"Who? Christophe? No. Why?"

"Well, then," Thérèse concluded bleakly, "he's disappeared. Didier hasn't seen him. Neither has Madame Dunn. Antoine doesn't know where he is. Nor any of the people at Arobas. You were my last hope."

"How do you mean, disappeared?"

"Not here. Vanished. I took him his breakfast tray this morning. His room was a mess, sheets dragged onto the floor, shoes here and there. He was gone."

"About time, too. This business of shutting himself up in his room was getting ridiculous."

"But he hasn't come back. Not for lunch. Or dinner. He always eats at eight. It's gone half past. It's not like him."

Julian laughed. "He'll return. When he gets hungry enough."

"Well, I don't like it. Something bad is going to happen. I can feel it in my bones."

"Oh, come on, Thérèse. There's nothing to worry about. Christophe is just—well—being Christophe."

"Think what you like. You didn't hear it. I did." The old woman mumbled something that Julian did not quite catch.

"What did you say?"

"I said," the housekeeper shouted into his ear, "it woke me out of my sleep last night. The Wailing Ghost. It always cries before a death."

At about the same time on Tuesday evening, Madame Clémentine Dupuy of Les Ronces, situated at the north end of the Sigoulane Valley, heard a disturbance among her chickens.

"It's that *maudit* fox again," she called to her daughter-in-law, Chantal, eight months pregnant, and went for the shotgun. Her son, Daniel, a fertilizer salesman, was not at home. No matter, this time she'd have the vermin. She pulled on a pair of rubber clogs—the rain had stopped, but the short stretch between the *poulailler* and the farmhouse was muddy—and rushed out. She glanced up at the sky, low and bulging with clouds. More rain was on its way. The light was going fast, but Madame Dupuy could still see well enough to make her way at a trot down the little path leading to the henhouse. As she approached it, she was confronted by a sight that made her exclaim with anger. The gate to the enclosure had been torn from its hinges, and chickens were running loose everywhere. A scattering of feathers patterned the grass and clung to the gooseberry bushes that grew against the fence. A sudden breeze caused a host of feathers to rise up, almost playfully, in the air. Then she saw what lay on the ground: hens—how many she couldn't say—*mon dieu!*—it looked like an abattoir. Heads were strewn about, separated from partly eaten bodies.

Shock and fury seized Madame Dupuy, then common sense. A country woman, she had never known a fox to create this kind of carnage. Whatever had done this had killed first out of sheer savagery before settling down to its meal. With a pang, she spotted the limp body of her prize rooster, Hercule. It lay headless and eviscerated, its once-handsome plumage muddy and caked with blood.

Her hand was on the gatepost when she smelled something that triggered a warning in her brain: a feral odor—not the musky scent of a fox, but something stronger, more unwholesome—that told her just in time not to enter the enclosure. She stood for a few seconds, uncertain what to do. Then she heard it, moving about in the shadows behind the henhouse. Fear gripped the old woman, but she raised the shotgun and held her ground.

"Come out of there," she whispered into the gathering darkness. Taking a deep breath and with more authority, she cried out, "God preserve me, whatever you are, come out!"

She never had the chance to fire before the long gray form was on her. She let out a terrified yell and continued yelling as the thing struck her frontally, biting and snapping and driving her sprawling onto her back. She had the presence of mind, however, to grip the shotgun by butt and barrel and hold it before her like a quarterstaff. It was the only thing that kept the attacker from her throat. Then, as suddenly as it had erupted, the creature was gone.

Chantal, alerted by the screams, found her mother-in-law on the ground, sobbing with terror and bleeding from the face and arms. She helped the older woman up. Chantal stared about her in horror at the torn chicken carcasses. Madame Dupuy, coming to her senses and still clutching the shotgun, shrieked, "For god's sake, run! Get inside the house!"

The two women ran, holding on to each other, down the path. In the house, they rushed around shuttering and locking doors and windows. Chantal called the Gendarmerie in Brames. Words tumbled out of her so incoherently that the duty sergeant had difficulty understanding her.

"It's out there," she screamed. *"Pour l'amour de dieu,* get here fast."* She felt her first contractions as she hung up. Clutching her stomach, she dragged her husband's shotgun into the kitchen, where her mother-in-law, in shock, had collapsed onto the daybed. With a moan of pain, Chantal lowered herself to the floor, back to the wall, the weapon in readiness across her outstretched legs.

13

Julian appeared at the winery early, prepared to show the Crotte that he meant business. Not only did he have a revised plan, this time he was accompanied by his sometime assistant, Bernard, a young man with huge arms and thighs. No more haggling. They were there to break ground.

They found things in an uproar. Someone had hurled a small boulder through one of the big windows of the pavilion. The words *Assassins, Voleurs,* and even *Loups-garous* had been crudely scrawled in orange spray paint across the side of the building.

Julian braked the van and climbed out. "Wait here, will you, Bernard?"

"Sure." Bernard grinned, dug out his cigarettes, and settled back to read the morning paper. *Butchery at Les Ronces!* The headline marched blackly across the front page. *What Stalks the Sigoulane Valley?* In answer to the question, Clémentine Dupuy made this brief statement from her hospital bed: The creature that had savaged her chickens and attacked her was some kind of huge, hairy beast. It also smelled like the devil himself. Her life had been spared only because the thing had taken off at her daughter-in-law's approach. It was Madame Dupuy's belief that pregnant women have a kind of positive power that evil things cannot abide.

A knot of people—locals, Julian guessed—milled about the entrance to the pavilion. A winery worker appeared to be exchanging insults with the crowd while sweeping up broken glass. He punctuated his words with thrusts of his broom, to which the crowd responded with shouts and catcalls. The mood reminded Julian of a stew afloat with unknown ingredients, coming to the boil.

Off to one side, a wiry old fellow in dungarees, a plaid shirt, and a floppy black beret was having a separate, energetic conversation with Antoine. Denise, off to another side, was engaged in an exchange of her own with a stout man in a suit and a bosomy brunette. Or, rather, the couple talked while Denise looked as if she were being assailed by an unpleasant smell. Then another worker appeared in the frame of the broken window and began banging the remaining glass out with a hammer. Shards flew everywhere. The man with the broom threw up his arms and began to yell. The crowd jeered. Antoine also threw up his arms and strode into the pavilion. The man in the black beret shouted after him, "This won't end here. Don't say I didn't warn you," shoved his hands in his pockets, and strolled away.

Denise spotted Julian and immediately detached herself from the couple.

"Bit over the top, isn't it?" he said as she joined him, indicating the grafitti. "Why werewolves? Or assassins and thieves, for that matter?"

Denise's upper lip twisted in a sneer. "The good people of Sigoulane like to cover all the bases. They're blaming us for that kid's murder—"

"Baby Blue? How?"

"We're de Bonfonds, don't forget. And something hit a henhouse in Les Ronces last night and attacked the owner. The locals are saying Baby Blue has unleashed bad luck in the valley and we're to blame."

"Old crimes will out," the bosomy brunette called out, loudly enough for all to hear.

The man in the suit said smugly, "What she means is that we're naturally concerned—"

"Concerned!" Denise's dark eyes sparked dangerously as she swung about on him. "Gloating becomes you, Guy. It gives you that full-up, baby-go-potty look. And it's Christophe's damned crime, in case you forget. Go plague him."

"That's no way—" The brunette pushed forward, but Guy pulled her back.

"Mariette and I have expressed our solidarity—"

"*Mon cul,*" Denise said sweetly, referring to a part of the anatomy that well-brought-up French women did not mention. She turned away sharply, pulling Julian with her out of range of their hearing.

"Where is he?" she hissed.

"Who?"

"Don't play dumb. Christophe! Thérèse says he's gone missing."

"Ah," said Julian. "I don't know."

Denise gave him a skeptical glare. "I could kill that calf's head for bringing this down on me."

"Oh, be fair, Denise," Julian defended his friend. "He hardly did it on purpose."

"But he's not here to take the heat, is he? Look at this shit. The press are all over it. I had a *con* of a reporter from *Sud Ouest* out first thing this morning. How do I feel about having an infanticide in the family? Do I think Baby Blue has anything to do with the thing that's prowling the valley? Some of the local growers are saying this year's harvest will be blighted because of us. And to top it off, that puke-making Guy Verdier and his tart of a wife are hanging around, shaking their heads, and maundering on about the good name of the family. All I need!"

At that moment, Denise's cell phone rang. She slapped it to her ear, listened, and stalked off in another direction, waving her free hand. Guy and Mariette stood by looking huffy for a moment. Then, with a resentful glance at Julian, they left. The crowd hung around talking and gesticulating until Antoine came out again and bellowed for them to get back to their jobs, those who worked there, or to get lost, those who did not.

Events had not improved Pierre's temper.

"This fountain thing still goes," the brother pronounced with vicious satisfaction. He was seated at his table in the pavilion, having peered at the new plan and Julian's reduced budget. "In fact, in light of present circumstances"—he craned about to squint at the broken window—"I'm inclined to scrap this whole land-scaping thing."

"In light of present circumstances," Denise mimicked him, punching viciously at her cell-phone keypad on her way past. "You'd do better to pull your brains up from around your ankles and realize that we have to make everything look extra good, and that includes the damned water feature. I've just talked with Papa, Julian. He says do it. Everything. And don't mind old Mouth-Breather here. He's too busy peering up his backside to see day-light."

Julian's landscaping operations consisted of a front end and a butt end. Julian did the front end—the client relations, garden de-sign, stock purchasing, plus a fair amount of the actual digging, planting, mulching, and so on. The butt end was borne by Bernard. As needed, and when he wasn't having a smoke or scratching his crotch, the slow, easy-going youth served as Julian's heavy equipment. He made a good bulldozer and an equally effec-tive power digger. Bernard was the grandson of Madame Léon, the sweet old thing whose walnut orchard adjoined Julian's bit of land.

It was now four hours after the scene at the pavilion. Julian had made his point with Pierre, and work had finally begun. At the mo-ment, Bernard was strolling behind a rototiller that coughed out blue fumes as it churned up the area fronting the pavilion. He guided the machine casually, aiming it more or less at a piece of string that Julian had extended between two stakes. When he reached the string, he tipped the rototiller back, pivoted it around, and walked it in the reverse direction, trailing a pale wake of stones.

The sun overhead was hot. Bernard completed a couple more turns and throttled down. The machine shuddered to a halt. Scratching his stomach, he gazed around. Julian was now over in the car-park area, doing more things with stakes and string. Bernard walked down to Julian's van, raising a meaty arm in passing.

"Oi! Lunch." From the back of the van he dragged out a battered tin box the size of a small foot locker. Granny Léon made Bernard's lunches. On mornings when Bernard worked with him, Julian first picked up the box from Madame Léon next door, after which he went to get Bernard, who lived with his girlfriend, a paramedic who did not make lunches, in a neighboring village. Every evening, Julian returned the box empty. It was a service that he was happy to provide, since Madame Léon always included enough food for five. Bernard flipped open the foot locker and poked around in its contents. Ham sandwiches. Hard-boiled eggs. Fruit. Cheese. Flan.

At this point, a dusty, yellow Twingo that Bernard recognized as the winery runabout came speeding up the dirt lane connecting the pavilion with the road below. It braked hard alongside them. The driver was the dark-haired woman Bernard had seen going in and out of the pavilion earlier in the day. Good-looking *nana*. A bit on the stringy side for his taste, though, and a mouth like a sewer, forever effing this and effing that. The workmen around the place seemed scared to death of her.

"Hello," she called to Julian, ignoring Bernard. "Get in. I brought a picnic. Pâté de foie gras. Crab mousse. Champagne."

At Julian's questioning glance, Bernard grinned again and gave a thumbs-up.

"Why not?" said Julian and climbed in the car.

The Twingo swung about and shot off, racing down the lane back to the road. Bernard watched the car cut across the valley. He walked to the rear of the van and pulled the doors open. He set his lunch box on the van floor, hopped his bottom up beside it, and sat there, legs dangling out the back. So much the better, he thought, pulling out a sandwich as thick as a brick. All the more for him.

The road ran through the middle of the vineyard. Denise turned off it onto a dirt track that wound up the face of a hill. They parked in a grove of chestnuts at the top. From there, they had a wide-angle view of the valley: sunshine and rows of vines radiating away in all directions.

"Well, this is great," Julian said enthusiastically. He watched in fascination as she spread a checkered tablecloth on the grass and unpacked their meal, including the pâté and the crab mousse that she had promised. Her movements were quick. Her head, as she turned this way and that, reminded him somehow of a crow, sleek, black, and acquisitive. She wore a skimpy red elasticized top that molded to her hard little breasts, a short tight black skirt, and yellow canvas shoes.

She jerked her chin at the cold chest. "You can do the champagne."

Obediently, he applied himself to working the cork out of the bottle and tipping the foaming contents into the flutes she provided.

"*Tchin-tchin,*" he toasted her. They touched glasses. "Any idea who vandalized the pavilion?"

She took a gulp and frowned. "I'm sure Michel and his toad of a son were behind it. They generally are when there's trouble."

"Who are they?"

"You saw the son. Guy Verdier. My cousin. Oozy little *con*. His father, Michel, was hanging around somewhere, old guy in a black beret. He owns the vineyard next to us. Papa's been trying to buy him out for years because we want to expand, but he won't sell. It's the Verdiers' way of getting their own back."

"Did you report it to the police?"

"*A quoi bon?* It wouldn't discourage the next jerk with a grudge and an aerosol can." She snapped off plastic container lids. "The Sigoulanese are long on grudges. Help yourself."

He chewed an olive, tossed away the pit, and dug into the mousse with a spoon. It was light and creamy and flecked with pinkish shreds of crab meat.

"Against the de Bonfonds? What's their problem?"

Denise fixed him with a long, unfathomable gaze. It was, he thought, the first time he'd seen her motionless. Her eyes were large, curiously flat, and almost lidless. Julian felt disconcertingly like a rabbit being mesmerized by a snake. Then she shrugged, drained her glass, and held it out to Julian for a refill.

"Disputes over land." Kicking off her shoes, Denise stretched out well-muscled but shapely legs. "And our success. They take the work we offer and hate us for it. You tell me." She tore off a piece of baguette, loaded it with a heavy daub of rich pâté that was already beginning to sweat with the warmth of the day, and fell to eating, hungrily but with no apparent enjoyment. All business, Julian summed her up. He began to wonder what this outing was about.

She waved a knife at the surrounding landscape. "The de Bonfonds have had vineyards here since the 1800s. We've been hit by phylloxera, frost, drought, and war. We've lost most of our vines at one time or other. In 1980, Papa tore everything out and replanted with imported rootstock. 'It's my legacy to both of you,' he said. It took us fifteen hard years to re-establish, but we succeeded. That's what the other growers won't forgive."

"This is about jealousy?"

"Why not? All of them still work the land like they did in the Middle Ages. None of them, including Michel, has ever gone beyond producing for the local market and their own consumption, while we've turned Coteaux de Bonfond into a prestige winery with its own *appellation*. We're the sole producers of Domaine de la Source. Our 2000 *grande cuvée* won a *médaille d'or* in Paris. Most of the people in the valley, the Verdiers more than any, would love to see us cut down to size. Michel's usually behind most of the labor problems we routinely have. Steals our workers, says we treat them badly. Of course, that didn't stop him, when he heard we were expanding our facilities, from organizing the other growers in the valley to propose that we build on enough capacity to handle their production as well. We have our own *chai*, you see, but they don't. They have to take their grapes to Bergerac for processing. They said they'd pay us for our services but we—*we*, mind you—were supposed to lay out the capital cost. Papa told them to get lost. And now Christophe's damned bastard is giving them their chance to do their worst."

She stretched out full-length on her side, facing him, leaning on her elbow. Her dark hair fell seductively over her cheek. Julian found himself concentrating on her right breast, pushed up against her arm into an appealing mound of flesh.

"Look, Julian, we all know he's done a bunk because he's terrified of the media. Come on. I really need to know where he's hiding."

So this was what the charade with food and drink was all about. She hadn't believed him when he told her he didn't know, and she thought she could worm the information out of him with a *déjeuner sur l'herbe*. Julian felt slightly irritated and not a little let down. Figuratively he kicked himself for wanting to believe that the picnic, this tête-à-tête, was somehow about him. He held up both hands. "Sorry. I told you. I haven't a clue. Anyway, why are you so keen to have him back?"

"You can ask?" Denise left off being seductive and sat bolt upright, stiff with anger. "The media are all over *me* like flies on meat because they can't stick into *him*. I want him back to deal with it. After all, it's his house, his baby, his problem."

"Then leave it to him."

"Leave it to him!" She fairly spat the words out. "In case you didn't know, Christophe is a genius at ducking trouble. He plays the charming old-world *aristo* when really he's a spoiled, crazy old *con* who dabbles in publishing, who's never had to do a real day's work in his sod-all lazy life, and whose only reason for existence is to spend the fortune his parents left him. You think he's going to come out of hiding voluntarily to deal with Baby Blue?"

Julian was a little shaken by her vehemence. He had never thought of his friend in this light. He supposed in some respects she might be right.

"Okay." He tried to shrug it off. "You got a stone through a window and some spray paint because the villagers don't like you. But Baby Blue is hardly going to affect your sale of wine."

She flashed him a poisonous smile. "That's where you're wrong, sweetums. The media adore the idea that someone in the family was a child-killer. They love the broken glass, the graffiti, the animosity between honest villagers and nasty *seigneurs*. Worst of all, they're repeating the predictions of a poor harvest, linking it to the feral-dog attacks and some kind of curse Baby Blue is supposed to have unleashed in the valley. All this at a time when I'm trying to profile our label."

Julian rallied. "It's even worse for Christophe. He's somehow got to account for a murdered child in his glorious history of the de Bonfonds."

She gave a shout of scornful laughter. "If anybody even reads the dead-in-the-water drivel Cousin Christophe publishes."

Julian took great personal exception to her "dead-in-the-water drivel."

"You're overreacting," he replied coldly. "After all, it's people like Perry Pufnel, not Baby Blue, you've got to worry about. Pufnel's ratings are what sell your wine, and he goes by what he tastes, not what he hears."

"*Des conneries!*" She fairly crackled. "Bergerac sits in the shadow of Bordeaux, not because our wines aren't *grand cru*, but because Bordeaux is what people recognize, and that includes *monstres sacrés* like Pufnel. We're new kids on the block, as far as he's concerned. Eighty-four lousy points he gave us this year, and this year's vintage is as good as or better than our gold-medalist!" She stabbed a knife into a slab of pâté with a viciousness that made him blink. Even Julian, who had only a vague understanding of the point ratings of wines, supposed that this was less than Coteaux de Bonfond Domaine de la Source deserved. Perhaps Denise's concerns were justified after all.

"I say screw the lot of them." She looked murderous. "The French wine industry is going down the toilet anyway. We're being out-marketed and underpriced by New World wines. Well, Coteaux de Bonfond isn't getting flushed with the rest of them. If marketing is about brand recognition and giving consumers what they want, that's what we'll do. Right now, we depend on local consumption. In five years, I want us in every top restaurant from New York to Hong Kong. This isn't just about a new pavilion and your landscaping, Julian. This is about shaping our product to international tastes."

Julian thought about Antoine de Bonfond. A genius winemaker, but a man with soil under his fingernails. "What does your father think of all this?"

Denise shrugged. "As long as quality isn't compromised, Papa has no problem. Always provided," she added darkly, "the effort pays for itself."

"And will it?"

"It has to. We've invested everything we've got in remaking

Coteaux de Bonfond. If replanting was phase one, going international is phase two. And if Cousin Christophe spoils it for me"—she paused, breathing hard—"I'll have his entrails."

Abruptly, she turned to look out over the valley. Julian studied her curiously. From some angles she looked hard and haggard. How old was she? Late thirties? Early forties? From others, she appeared vulnerable and just a little bit scared. In that moment, Julian felt he understood her. She cared passionately about the winery, the success of Domaine de la Source. Her father had spent a lifetime building the label, and she was prepared to take on the world to sell the name. He wondered if she had much of a life outside the business. He already knew from Christophe that both she and Pierre still lived at home in the big family house at the edge of the winery. Neither was married. Where Pierre was concerned, it figured. Who would want him? But Denise? She was stunning, electric, intensely sexy. Also rude and undoubtedly ruthless, but Julian suspected she could be very nice when she wanted. Then he recalled the dynamics between brother and sister and wondered if they behaved as nastily to each other in private as they did in public. Was there a mother? Maybe they fought over Antoine's favor and who would eventually control the winery. For a moment he almost felt sorry for the Mouth-Breather.

Mara was feeling guilty and irritated. Guilty because Julian had sounded hurt when they had last parted. Irritated with herself for feeling guilty.

"It's not like there's any commitment between us," she complained aloud to Jazz as she drove out of Bergerac. She'd had a fairly successful morning, procuring an old set of cupboards that, with some retouching, would do fabulously for one client, and lining up another stonemason to finish off Christophe's project. The only trouble was, the man couldn't start until next month.

"Nor is there likely to be, the way we're going," she added grimly. Jazz sat in the passenger seat, enjoying the scenery, perfectly unconcerned.

She made the decision to swing north toward Sigoulane on the spur of the moment. She would stop by to see how Julian's work at Coteaux de Bonfond was going, suggest dinner that evening, his choice of restaurant, her treat. Eating out was a necessity rather than an option. Mara, although she did many things well, was an awful cook.

Sigoulane Village was drowsy with midday heat. In the little square, a dog slept in a narrow strip of shade at the base of a monument honoring Sigoulane's heroes of the Resistance. Mara drove through the village, past the smallholdings of local growers, and into the expansive terrain of Coteaux de Bonfond. Across the valley, the new pavilion, an imposing structure of glass and stone, winked in the sun. She turned off the main road toward it and pulled up in front of the entrance, where a man was replacing a window and someone else was scrubbing down one of the exterior walls.

Bernard appeared from the side of the building. Mara knew Bernard as Julian's helper, but mainly in another capacity, when he served with surprising agility as *garçon* on busy weekends at Chez Nous. She got out of her car.

"*Ça va, Bernard?*"

"*Salut.*" He shook her hand and waggled a finger at Jazz.

"Julian around?"

"Sure." Bernard gazed around him, as if this would produce his *patron*. "Thing is"—the young man clawed in a leisurely fashion at his right armpit—"he was. But he went off a couple of hours ago. With her." He jerked his chin, signifying a spot somewhere to the north.

Mara frowned. "Her? Who?"

"Her of the winery. Denise. Brought a picnic, she did. Foie gras, crab mousse, champagne. Sexy chick," he added as an afterthought.

"Oh," said Mara, as a yellow car came racing up from the main road. It came to a rocking halt near them. A slim, dark-haired woman jumped out on one side, Julian the other.

"Ah, Mara," Julian called, looking surprised and uncomfortable. "Er—meet Denise. Denise, Mara Dunn. She's doing Christophe's—"

"I know, sweetums," Denise broke in, sizing Mara up. With a slow smile and great deliberation, she turned to Julian.

"Lovely afternoon, *chéri*," she murmured softly but loudly enough for Mara to hear. "Let's do it again sometime soon." Then she embraced him with a display of intimacy that made Mara instantly reconsider her offer of dinner. Before Julian could free himself from Denise's stranglehold, Mara was back in her car and roaring away in a cloud of dust.

14

That night a wolf expert was interviewed on the eight o'clock news. Professor Lise Voisin had studied wolves for thirty years and headed a group of wolf rights activists known as Le Cri Sauvage, Call of the Wild. She was a grizzled woman past middle age with a long, deeply lined face, rather resembling a wolf herself. The male interviewer, a popular television personality with large white teeth and a widow's peak, addressed his broadcast audience:

"In four short weeks, the Sigoulane Valley, a normally peaceful wine-growing area in the Bergerac zone, has been transformed into an epicenter of terror. There has been one death and now a serious mauling, to say nothing of loss of livestock and family pets, by some kind of dangerous predator. People who have seen it describe it as an enormous wolf, a very large dog, or"—pause for effect—"something worse. Ask the most recent victim, Madame Clémentine Dupuy of Les Ronces, who was attacked outside her home last night, and she might tell you it was a creature from hell. Professor Voisin, what do you think of the suggestion that this thing is some kind of unknown or even supernatural beast?"

VOISIN: "Utter nonsense. The bite marks are definitely that of a very large canid."

INTERVIEWER: "In your opinion, could a wolf be behind these attacks?"

VOISIN: "That, too, is highly unlikely. First, there are no wolves in the

Dordogne. In fact, there are pitifully few wolves left in France. Those that survive are confined to the eastern alpine arc of the country. Second, the behavior is uncharacteristic. Whatever it is clearly has no fear of humans. Wolves tend to shun humans. They rarely attack people. I'd say it's more likely a vicious dog that someone has let run wild. Every year, as you know, dogs all over France are abandoned by their owners. Left to fend for themselves, some of them turn feral. It's shameful for a nation of supposed dog-lovers."

INTERVIEWER: "However, many people are convinced that a giant rogue wolf has somehow strayed or perhaps was even brought into the region. Couldn't this be the case?"

VOISIN: "If some fool has trapped and released a wild wolf in the area, it was a criminally irresponsible thing to do. Wolves are social animals. They live and hunt in small family units. A wolf alone and out of its territory would be under a great deal of stress. I know that a man has been killed and a woman badly bitten, but I point out that neither of these incidents was an outright attack. In both the Piquet and Dupuy cases, the animal was defending its kill. Because we don't know what we're dealing with, my association is joining together with other groups to protest the uninformed slaughter of this animal. We want the government to stand behind its agreements to protect large, native predators, at least until we find out what it is."

INTERVIEWER *(showing his famous toothy smile)*: "But this thing, whatever it is, has proven itself to be extremely dangerous. It's a man-killer. The local population is terrified. Do you honestly think people are going to listen to you? Wouldn't it make more sense to shoot first and ask questions later?"

VOISIN: "First of all, it's an exaggeration to say that people are terrified. In fact, most people are treating this with a great deal of common sense. Residents in the affected area are keeping their dogs locked up, they're not wandering alone at night in the woods, and for the most part they're going about their business as normal. Secondly, we must remember that wild wolves are on the verge of extinction in France.

Moreover, they're protected by French law and international agreements, namely the Habitats Directive and the Berne Convention. I know the Ministry of Ecology and Sustainable Development has authorized the killing of this animal. But I say that we must take this case, serious though it is, as a warning to ourselves and treat it intelligently and—yes—compassionately. The conditions of the attacks have been created by us—"

INTERVIEWER *(a look of heavy skepticism opening out on more teeth)*: "Oh, come, now, professor—"

VOISIN: "I say again, created by us." (Camera quickly zooms in for a head shot, capturing green, close-set eyes.) "We are destroying the habitat of wolves and all wild things just as surely as we're destroying our own, to our peril. There is a mystic link between wolves and humans. All of us have something of the wolf in us. We, like they, are social animals. We, like they, live by the law of the pack. And we, like they, are carnivorous predators. I say from the heart that the wolf is the symbol of all truly wild things in France. It is imperative that we learn to live in harmony with them. Our own survival is at stake. On the day when the last wolf in this country is destroyed, something deep within us will die as well."

Her delivery was so moving that the interviewer, normally never at a loss for words, was momentarily stunned into silence.

15

Julian did not have to put two sixes together to come up with twelve: Mara's abrupt departure from the pavilion had a lot to do with Denise. Why the hell did Mara have to turn up just at that moment? And Denise, of course, had intentionally made things worse. What was her—Denise's—game, anyway? That it was a game, he had no doubt. He recalled the look of malicious amusement in her eyes as Mara had sped away down the lane. If he hadn't been afraid of appearing ridiculous, he would have run after the car. He had phoned Mara that evening but only got her *répondeur*. He left a message: "Dinner Friday?"

Now, engaged in damage control, he reached across the table and took her hand.

"Listen, Mara. I know what it must have looked like, but I swear to you Denise arranged that picnic only in order to pump me about Christophe. For god's sake, the woman practically threw herself at me." Their conversation was taking place against the low-key sounds of cutlery, the genteel buzz of well-heeled diners. The restaurant, a posh establishment high on a bluff overlooking the river, made a change from Chez Nous.

Something in Mara's expression demanded elaboration.

"She's terribly manipulative," he added. He was astounded. He had never thought of Mara as the jealous type. And over such a little thing. He didn't know whether to be worried or pleased. A different approach was needed, he decided.

"Mara." He leaned forward to capture both hands. "Forget

Denise. Let's talk about us. We haven't seen much of each other lately. I mean, not since last Friday."

Mara's nostrils flared slightly. "That's because we normally only meet on Fridays."

"Well, yes." He had to let her hands go because a waiter had appeared with their starters: a pâté of quail on chopped aspic for her; hot lobster ravioli, the house speciality, for him. He took up fork and knife, grateful for the time to think. "That's something I wanted to talk to you about. Most weeks it's dinner at Chez Nous, weekends at my place or yours. Well, I think it's just not good enough." He managed to make it sound like a long-standing, bitter complaint. Three hot-air balloons drifted slowly past the restaurant windows, like a Technicolor dream.

"Oh? What, then? Picnics on the grass? Champagne? Foie gras?"

"Good god, no. Far from it. Not at all." Floundering, he concentrated on his food. By the time their dishes had been cleared away, he realized that he needed to up the stakes.

"What I'm trying to say is, we've been seeing each other for over a year now. And I thought . . . I want . . ." He stopped. What did he want? Sex with her was good. When he could get it. Was he asking for more? It would be nice. Quite suddenly he realized that what he really wanted was more of *her*. More of her quirky, go-for-it presence in his life. More—he was amazed to find himself thinking it—commitment. It was a word he thought he'd left behind him. The problem was, how to put it to her.

Two waiters approached, pushing a trolley with their main courses. Again thankful for the diversion, Julian watched them go about their work. They assembled the plates swiftly, expertly, announcing them as they set them in place in the manner of an important personal introduction: *"Pour madame, les ris de veau à la périgourdine."* Braised sweetbreads in a handsome copper dish, with an accompanying flat-edged spoon, designed for scooping up the rich Madeira sauce. Unfortunately, the spoon was fashioned for right-handers. Mara was left-handed. *"Et pour monsieur, la truite au bleu garnie."* Trout (that had been swimming in its tank minutes ago, before the chef had knocked it on the head), quickly cooked and simply served, dressed in butter and parsley. *"Voilà, et bonne continuation!"* They were gone.

Julian cleared his throat. "It's just that it occurred to me that maybe our relationship should move on a bit."

Mara paused, fork halfway to her mouth. "How?"

He took a deep breath. "Something a bit more permanent?"

She stared at him doubtfully. He had obviously been to a barber. His normally overlong hair was cut short, and his beard and mustache were neatly trimmed. She took a bite of sweetbreads topped with truffles and said, oblivious of the flavors cascading around her tongue, "What exactly do you mean?"

Hadn't he just said it, or was she being purposely obtuse? He found himself taking another deep breath. "Well, I just think we ought to know where we're going. I mean, where do you want to be five years from now? Where do I want to be?" He had read somewhere that this was a good way of putting it. It wasn't. It sounded like something he had read somewhere. He paused self-consciously.

His words should have filled Mara with a sudden gladness. His brown, melancholy eyes fixed on her in earnest interrogation. He had not spoken of orchids all evening. No longer turning in circles, going nowhere, Julian had come very much to the point. Why, then, did his question now engender a certain amount of panic in her? Could it be that she felt safe going forward only as long as he held back?

"Julian, is this some kind of marriage proposal?"

He seemed for a moment to have difficulty swallowing and appeared to be working something around in his mouth.

"Because, if it is, I have to tell you I'm not sure I want to go down that road again." She said it gently. Once with Hal was enough.

He pulled a small white bone from his mouth. "I'm with you there."

"But, yes," Mara went on, "if you want, we could talk about . . . like you said, something more permanent." The option of her house or his, with socks everywhere and inadequate heating, rose before her. "That is, if you're really serious."

"I am. Very." He spoke firmly, but there was a fugitive look in his eye.

In that moment, Mara experienced a letting go that brought a great understanding and a rush of tenderness for them both. Julian talked very little about his past, but she knew that he, like she, had sustained a lot of private pain. He was a sweet man and a simple man. Sweet, simple people tended to be terribly complex. He was reaching out, tentatively, ineptly, not because he loved her madly but because he cared enough not to want to lose her. Just as she cared enough about him to be unreasonably angry over finding him with Denise, which made her simple and complicated as well. Either way, fear of loss was a shaky footing to build on. "We're good friends, Julian," she said finally, and this time she was the one who reached for his hands. "Right now, that's good enough for me. Really, there's no hurry, is there?"

"No," he said. "Of course there isn't." Unlike the trout he was deboning, Julian was astonished to find himself off the hook and swimming free. The feeling left him feeling flat and a little at a loss.

The rest of the evening went well. Mara forgave Julian his wayward picnic with Denise and related Jean-Claude's shocking revelations about Christophe's pedigree. Over a selection of cheeses, they laughed at the genealogist's ineffectual attempts at seduction. Julian was very interested in Jean-Claude's theory that Cécile was Baby Blue's mother.

"Can you ask him if she did needlework? That would clinch it. I figure she saw the flower, was impressed by it, and embroidered a copy of it on her shawl. The fact that she got the details so exactly suggests that she knew the flower well, so she must have seen it more than once."

"Or else she picked it," said Mara, "and used it as a live model."

"Hmm," said Julian, sobered by the thought. Had the stupid woman destroyed the last living representative of the plant? No, that couldn't be. Mara's sister had come along a century or so later and photographed another exactly like it.

Julian then told Mara about his ongoing search for the mystery *Cypripedium*. He continued to spend every free moment combing the area around Aurillac but had seen nothing remotely resembling a Slipper Orchid.

"However, I have a new lead. According to Didier, a plant called Devil's Clog used to grow around there. He thinks it might be the same thing as *Cypripedium incognitum*. Unfortunately, for some reason the locals dug it up wherever they found it and planted Aconite—Monkshood—in its place. I'm praying that a few representatives of Devil's Clog survived. It's possible, you know." He gazed around him restlessly. Orchids had a limited blooming period, and if he didn't find it soon, he'd have to wait until next year. He shook his head and shared with Mara the ironic observation that the only person who took his quest seriously (apart from her, of course) was someone he didn't even like: Géraud Laval.

"Honestly, if he weren't so grabby, if I knew I could trust him, we could section off the terrain and search it together. It would go twice as fast." He said it with less vehemence than he might have because his attention was momentarily distracted by the arrival of dessert, a dense, dark wedge of chocolate gâteau topped with crème fraîche for him, a frothy sabayon for Mara.

"Why not give it a try anyway?" Mara suggested. "Or," she added slyly, "don't you want to share the glory?"

"It's not that," Julian replied earnestly. "If the bugger found it, he'd dig it up. He's notorious for that. And he, more than anyone, should know better. You can't just 'transplant' an orchid like you can a tulip, Mara. They're extremely habitat-sensitive, and they grow where they grow because of the presence of certain kinds of fungi that they depend on for food, especially in the early stage. It's a kind of *danse macabre*"—here he interlocked his fingers in a digital struggle that involved the noisy popping of joints—"where the fungus tries to parasitize the young orchid. But the orchid baby, because it takes several years before it's able to put out leaves to photosynthesize food for itself, tries to eat the fungus. Eventually, if the plant survives the fungal attacks, the two continue a long-term mycorrhizal relationship, with each trying to cannibalize the other and succeeding well enough to get what each needs but not enough to kill the other off."

"Like an old married couple," Mara mused.

"Sort of. Anyway, instead of gathering the seeds and growing them *in vitro* on agar jelly, Géraud just digs up the plant plus a huge ball of the surrounding soil, destroying whatever else is trying to grow there, which is often another orchid."

"He said he only digs plants up when they're at risk, like on a construction site." Mara did not particularly like Géraud, either, but found that Julian's sense of rivalry with the man often marred his judgment.

"Bollocks. He's absolutely wanton. His only objective is to add to his collection. Sometimes it works for him, but mostly the plants die. It's a pity, because orchids develop very slowly and take years to bloom. So, by the time he's dug up an orchid in flower, it might have been five or ten years in the making. The bastard's destroyed countless orchids this way. As far as endangered species are concerned, he's an out-and-out menace." Julian, breathing hard, tore angrily at a piece of bread.

Mara put her fork down. "I could help you," she said. She had done orchid searches with him before and knew better than anyone what they were looking for.

Julian's head shot up. "You mean it? God, that's fantastic!" He had the presence of mind to acknowledge, "I know it's not something you particularly enjoy, tramping through fields and forests and all that. But if you're really serious—well, all I can say is it—it's terrific of you. When can we start?"

"Tomorrow, if you like. I'm free all day." His enthusiasm was making her tired in advance. "To be honest, I'm not that busy."

In fact, with Christophe's gallery on hold, she was close to twiddling her thumbs.

16

Mara had never seen Julian so exuberant. He rapped at her door early the following morning, embraced her energetically, and helped her climb into his van even though she was perfectly capable of stepping up unaided. Jazz jumped in to join Bismuth in the back, where both dogs settled down for the ride among the tools and flowerpots.

"So. Are you ready for this?"

He whistled as he drove.

They did not approach Aurillac in the normal way, from the valley floor, but instead came at it from the east, along another network of roads because, as Julian had said, the back of the property was where he thought they should concentrate their search.

"I've gone over every square centimeter of the gardens," he told her by way of a briefing. "I don't just mean around the house. Originally, the gardens were much more extensive than they are now. I know because I've uncovered traces of the old grounds going well beyond what you see today. If Christophe had just been willing to stick with the project, we could have reclaimed it all. I mean, in some parts it would have been as easy as rolling up the overlying turf like a carpet."

"Christophe's enthusiasms wax and wane," Mara said, with a sense of foreboding about the future of his—her—gallery, "like the moon."

"Then I moved on to the woods at the front and sides of the property. Again nothing."

"That leaves everything else." Mara thought she saw where this was leading. Aurillac was a huge estate. The house perched on the spine of the ridge. Much of the terrain sloped steeply away from it. "I hope you don't expect—"

He forestalled her. "Ah, but that's my point. I doubt Cécile would have been clambering down ravines or scaling cliffs. So I thought we'd focus on places where the terrain is relatively level and open. This means the rest of the property I haven't searched, all the land behind the house that extends into woods and meadows. It narrows our search considerably. I worked it out, using the Série bleue maps."

"Oh," said Mara, only somewhat relieved. The maps, she knew, showed every topographical feature on a scale of one to twenty-five thousand, including type of ground cover, but they did not pinpoint orchid colonies, let alone specific plants.

They were passing through open woodland along a road so narrow that at one point they had to pull over and stop when they met an oncoming Deux Chevaux. The other car stopped as well. Two men and a spaniel were in it. Hunters, from the look of them. One of them held a shotgun between his knees. The driver leaned out the open window.

"*Salut*. Just thought I'd let you know. There's been another possible sighting of the Beast near here. A group of us have been combing the woods for it since dawn. You haven't seen anything, have you?"

"No," said Julian.

"Well, keep your eyes open. Are you armed? Too bad. If you plan on hanging around these parts, you'll want to be careful. The accursed thing is moving around in broad daylight now."

The driver raised a hand in farewell and edged forward. The car was soon lost to sight.

"Why the hell do they insist on calling it 'the Beast'," Julian said in disgust as he put the van in gear, "when everyone knows it's nothing more than a feral dog?"

"Tell that to the man who was killed. Or the woman who got mauled."

"In both cases it was protecting its kill."

"So what are you saying? Don't bother it when it's eating? Quite honestly, Julian, do you think this is a good idea? That man said the thing was spotted around here this morning."

"Miles away by now, with all those hunters after it. Anyway, you've got me and Jazz to protect you."

"It eats dogs, too."

"Good. Maybe it'll eat Bismuth."

They drove on. Eventually, the road deteriorated to a rutted track. They were now in deep forest. Julian stopped and consulted a Série bleue map. He drove slowly, hanging his head out of the van window, for another couple of hundred meters before he spotted what he was looking for: a trailhead. They parked the van opposite it and got out. Julian checked his equipment: camera, binoculars, map, botanist's loupe, provisions, water bottle. He slung his backpack over one shoulder, and they started out on foot, making their way along a path that led at an incline toward the eastern face of Aurillac Ridge. Along the way, Jazz flushed a rabbit and disappeared in a noisy wake of barking. Bismuth crashed after him but at least held his tongue, a restraint no doubt inherited from his pointer mother. It was one thing about his dog that Julian really did appreciate.

"Too much cover around here for anything of interest," Julian said, meaning orchids. "But we should be coming out of this pretty soon."

Mara, remembering the hunter's warning, did not like the way the trees seemed to crowd in on them. She was relieved when they broke into a large, sloping meadow. At the top of the meadow, more woods ran up to the crest of the escarpment.

"This is the back side of the estate." Julian pointed. "The house is up there, off to the left, although you can't see it through the trees. All this is old pasture. Christophe still rents the land to farmers in the area."

The dogs had arrived before them. Their tails could be seen thrashing above the waving grass.

"So where do we begin?" asked Mara, sensing that this orchid hunt was going to be like no other that she had done with him. Before, they had been looking for a sequence of identifiable flowers. This time it was down to a single plant, if not illusory, at least unknown.

"Right here." He grinned and swung an arm in a wide arc about them. "If *Cypripedium incognitum* needs an environment similar to *Cypripedium calceolus*, it'll do best in mottled shade. This means the transition zone between trees and clearing." He designated the perimeter of the field.

"Why not the field itself?" The grassy expanse looked like much easier walking.

"Because it's been used for grazing. Any orchid that might have grown there wouldn't stand much of a chance of survival. Once destroyed, orchids don't come back that easily because, as I told you, they require years to develop. Lady's Slippers are one of the slowest. They can take more than fifteen years just to put out their first flower. That's why it's such a crime to pick them, let alone dig them up, like you-know-who." He paused, reflecting unhappily on the many grievances he had with Géraud. "My idea is to search in parallel around the field. You take the margin. I'll walk a bit farther into the woods because the tree line will have shifted over the years. The important thing is to go slowly and look carefully either side of you. This flower could be highly localized, and it could be down to a single representative. Oh, and here, I brought along a copy of Iris's sketch if you need it."

Mara knew the orchid in all its sinister beauty by heart, but she studied the sketch all the same. If it had finished blooming, she would have to be on the lookout for anything with similar leaves. Iris's drawing showed three smooth, broad ones with strong parallel veining, narrowing to a point and sheathing a single stem.

"Also," Julian went on, "keep your eyes open for Monkshood." He told her that the bushy plant stood about hip-to-shoulder-high and put out cowl-like purple flowers, hence its name. It wasn't yet in bloom, but the foliage, dark green and sharply toothed, was easily identifiable.

"What happens if we don't find anything?" Mara asked.

"We move on to the next field."

Her eyes narrowed. "What next field?"

"There are—er—three of them, didn't I tell you?"

"No, you didn't."

"Ah. Well, this is the northernmost meadow. The other two are strung out in a line from here across the ridge flank. Don't worry"—he slung an arm cheerfully about her shoulders—"I have a feeling this is going to go really well."

They set off. At first the dogs accompanied them but soon lost interest and went about their own business, reappearing at intervals and disappearing again. Mara had the easier line of search; Julian, moving along to her right, the harder job of working around trees and pushing through undergrowth.

Julian was, Mara decided as she scanned the ground, at his best and worst at such times. On the one hand, his instinct for orchids was almost awe-inspiring. "Orchid Eyes," she called him. It wasn't just that he had an uncanny ability to sense their presence (undoubtedly his botanical knowledge and experience enabled him to make sense of clues like other flowers, soil, moisture, and light conditions). It was his intense way of relating to orchids—in fact, to all growing things. He was sensual, like a lover, when he stroked a flower head; tender as he stooped to right an injured plant; gallant in stepping wide to avoid treading on a humble clump of *Poly-*

gala vulgaris, Common Milkwort to people like her. The tiny flowers, blue and pink, were the kind of thing she walked right over. Emily Dickinson, a poet Mara had once liked (in the days before she became too busy redesigning space to think about poetry), had said it all:

> *To him who keeps an Orchis' heart*
> *The swamps are pink with June*

Julian kept an Orchis' heart, and his world was ablaze with color. It was hard for Mara not to be seduced by his passion. She was only regretful that so little of it found its way to her.

But he could also be cranky. At one point, he had yelled, "For heaven's sake, Mara, watch where you put your feet. You're trampling that *Neottia.*" Unnerved, she had jumped back and sat down painfully in a patch of nettles.

He irritated Mara by constantly encroaching on her territory to point out things that she had overlooked. "Nice stand of *Epipactis* right there. You walked right by it."

And he was insufferably pedantic. He found *Ophrys* and *Orchis,* *Platanthera,* and *Himantoglossum,* all possessing equally unpronounceable last names. But, he warned her as they went along, this was changing because orchid classification, hitherto based on morphological characteristics, was being overturned by DNA analysis. Thus, *Orchis ustulata* was now *Neotinea ustulata,* while *Coeloglossum viride,* the little Frog Orchid, had been folded in with the genus *Dactylorhiza.* It was something, he said with satisfaction, old Géraud was going to have a lot of trouble with, mired up to the eyebrows as he was in the old taxonomy.

Pâté or ham?" Julian asked. It had taken them almost two hours to go around the first field, and they were now sitting side by side on a log, taking a breather and sharing the sandwiches that he had packed. "One down, two to go."

Mara assumed his last statement referred to meadows. "Ham,"

she sighed. Ruefully, she examined her arms, scratched from the embrace of a hawthorn bush.

"You do know, Julian," Mara said after a long silence, "that it's a long shot. If your orchid and Devil's Clog are the same thing, and if people dug it up everywhere, it's probably been wiped out."

The look on his face told her that she had voiced the unthinkable. "It's out there," he said very seriously. "And I'll find it. I'm not just on the trail of something rare and beautiful, Mara, but something botanically tantalizing as well. When I first saw Bedie's photo, I knew it was some kind of Slipper Orchid. The question was, what? Although it was a bit of a stretch, I toyed with the idea that it might be a mutant of *Cypripedium calceolus,* since I knew efforts had been made to establish the plant here. If so, it probably was a one-off because the chances of a mutant reproducing are generally slim. The new characteristics would have to offer some kind of evolutionary advantage, and they would also have to be dominant for them to persist. I expect you know about genes as the basic units of heredity? They come in pairs, one from each parent. A dominant gene will always override a recessive gene, so that a recessive trait can never show up unless you have two paired recessives."

She nodded, vaguely remembering something to that effect from her high-school biology class.

"But the embroidery changes everything. It tells me the plant has a living track record, going back god knows how long. Moreover, the separate lateral sepals, if they're truly representative, put it in a group with your North American Ram's Head Orchid and *Cypripedium plectrochilum,* found in China. But in all other ways, *Cypripedium incognitum* is nothing like those two. So, for now, I have to treat my Mystery Orchid as an entirely distinct and unknown species." He shifted about on the log to look at her with glowing eyes. "I know of no other orchid like *Cypripedium incognitum* anywhere in the world, Mara. You see why I have to find it, don't you? And when I do, it's going to make botanical history, no matter what that *chameau* Géraud says."

O h well," said Julian, trying to boost their spirits. They had finished their circuit around the last pasture, and he was now leading them on an oblique line through the forest. It was the more direct way of making their way back to the road, but it meant a lot of pushing through the dense understory of the trees. "We'll find it. Next time. An orchid hunter always believes in the next time."

Mara, following unenthusiastically, made no reply. Even the dogs lagged behind.

"I forgot to tell you," she said after a while. "Thérèse phoned last night. Christophe is still missing. It's been five days now. I think she should call the police."

"Ridiculous," scoffed Julian. "If I know Christophe, he's tucked up comfortably in a three-star hotel somewhere, waiting until the noise around Baby Blue dies down."

"But Thérèse said Christophe's assistant editor in Bordeaux is also worried because he's had no feedback on the author's proofs for the de Bonfond history he sent over last week. And that's one thing Christophe really cares about."

Julian, climbing over a fallen tree, called back to her, "It's as plain as your nose he planned to go away all along. Otherwise, why would he have delegated you to deal with Lover Boy Fournier? He'll turn up in a couple of days. You'll see."

Mara, detouring around the tree, found herself wading hip-deep through a sea of ferns. "He's your friend. How can you be so dismissive? Oh, damn!" She tripped on a root and went sprawling.

A deep, warning grunt rumbled out of the earth. Something large and dark, like a nightmare, lurched up out of the greenery a short distance in front of her: a massive head covered in dark bristles, two piggy eyes, and a couple of sets of nasty, upward-curving tusks. The wild boar, wakened from its afternoon nap, glared, ears flicking, its nose disk twitching a wet warning.

"Julian!" Mara screamed and scrambled backward on hands and knees faster than she thought possible. Not fast enough. The animal charged. In the same instant, a frenzied barking exploded as Jazz and Bismuth sailed past her right ear. Julian yelled and came running. The boar, beset by the cacophony of noise and two hurtling dogs, checked its attack a meter from Mara's face, wheeled, and thundered away, leaving a broken swath of bracken in its wake.

"Don't let them—" Julian roared, but Jazz and Bismuth were already on its trail. Julian raced after them, shouting.

Mara sank back shakily onto the ground. "Next time?" she yelled up to the trees. "What next time?"

17

Mara was limping. Julian, supporting her while keeping both Jazz and Bismuth on the lead, was describing graphically what an adult boar could do to a dog, the slashing power of its tusks, and so on. Although, he assured her, they rarely attacked people.

"Ha!" said Mara, with very ill humor.

They broke out of the trees onto the road.

"Wait here," Julian said. "I'll get the van and pick you up."

"I am not," Mara declared through gritted teeth, "staying alone in these woods."

So they made their way as a sorry group slowly down the road. They had rounded a bend when a glint of metal buried deep in the foliage off to their right caught Julian's eye.

"Hello," Julian said. "There's a car in there."

It was a gray Citroën that had been driven off the road and parked up a slip trail. Julian left Mara to investigate. He walked around it, trying the doors. It was locked up tight.

"Someone else is out here," he called back, staring about him.

Mara hobbled forward to have a look. "Maybe another hunter. Looking for the Beast." Then she said something that made him almost physically sick. "Doesn't Géraud drive some kind of gray car?"

Julian stared at her, pushing down a sense of panic. He slammed his hand down on the car roof. "I swear, Mara," he said hoarsely, "if that bastard finds the orchid—if he so much as touches it—I'll kill him. I'll choke him with my bare hands!"

She forgot her own discomfort and regarded him with sympathy.

"We need help," she said after a moment. "It's more than two people can do."

"What, organize a search team? I've thought of that, but then Géraud would hear of it. You know he's already been over every nook and cranny of Les Colombes. What are my chances, what are the orchid's chances, if he realizes I've switched my focus to Aurillac? Although," he concluded darkly, "by the look of it, he already has."

"Not a search team," Mara said. "One person who knows the woods and valleys for kilometers around. Someone who prowls the forests like a bear."

"Who?" Julian's face showed his despair.

"Vrac," said Mara.

They first sought Vrac out at his grim farmhouse, situated below Les Colombes, but found no one there. So they drove up the steep, winding road to the château, where Jeanne de Sauvignac was living, according to Iris, under the dubious care of the Rochers.

Les Colombes was more dilapidated than either of them remembered it. Some of the shutters hung at crooked angles, and the windows looked grimy. Julian parked the van in the rear courtyard, where no attempt had been made to curb the weeds growing up between the flagstones. Mara thought with pity that Jeanne's existence in the great house must now be like that of a poor ghost, twittering in shadows. The house looked so still, so abandoned, that they really did not expect anyone to answer their summons. They were startled when the door jerked open before they had even had a chance to knock. A large form stood before them in the dim opening.

"You," growled la Binette. "What do you want?" Her face, with its disfiguring mulberry stain over one eye, was expressionless. The straw-colored wig she wore, which gave rise to her nickname, was tipped slightly askew. She grunted as Jazz and Bismuth slipped past her into the cool depths of the great kitchen.

"Vrac," said Mara.

"Not here."

"Where is he?" Julian asked, hoping desperately that the halfwit had not gone walkabout, for Vrac often was away for days at a time, wandering the woods, sleeping rough, and eating whatever he could catch or steal.

"What business is it of yours?"

"Well, can you give him a message?"

"Maybe."

"Tell him I want to see him."

"Why?" said the mother as the son loomed out of the shadows behind her.

"Ah, Vrac," Julian said, much relieved to see him and trying hard to sound sociable.

"What?" Vrac Rocher coughed out his harsh inquiry. He stepped up beside la Binette. As big as she, he had a large head, hair standing up in tufts, and a misshapen face covered in gray bristle. Although he played the village idiot when it suited him, Mara and Julian knew him to be surprisingly skilled at poaching livestock and beating defunct farm machinery into some kind of working order. He was in his fifties, his mother not much older, for she had borne him young. Together the two kept to themselves in their corner of the world, quietly doing their worst.

Julian held up Iris's sketch.

"There's a hundred euros in it for you if you can find this flower. It may be growing around Les Colombes or in the Sigoulane Valley or up on Aurillac Ridge. But I want you to look for it everywhere you go. And I want it living, mind. Don't pick it, don't step on it, don't dig it up, don't touch it at all. Just find it and lead me to it. And if you do find it, for god's sake don't tell anyone else."

"Two hundred," said la Binette.

"One fifty."

"Two fifty." The woman moved back into the kitchen to drive the dogs forward with a swipe of a booted foot.

"One seventy-five. It's my final offer," Julian said firmly.

"Three hundred or get stuffed," said the woman.

Vrac laughed, a sound like cawing crows.

"All right, three hundred," Julian conceded angrily as the dogs, flat-eared, came running past him. "But you have a damned funny way of bargaining." Then he remembered. The Rochers never did play by the rules.

18

The following morning, Mara watched anxiously for Julian through her front window. She lived in a handsome stone house, one of a handful of dwellings making up the hamlet of Ecoute-la-Pluie (Listen-to-the-Rain, so named because of a mill, dependent on a rain-fed stream, that had once operated there). The room where she stood was her showcase. Literally. Every item in it, except an Aubusson rug of floral design, was potentially for sale, so that the clusters of period sofas, chairs and tables, mirrors and fireplace accessories never remained the same. The Dordogne was filling up with expatriate year-round and summer residents who bought up farmhouses, abandoned mills, fourteenth-century towers, and decaying châteaux. The renovation of some of these structures fell to Mara, who was gradually establishing a reputation as a creative designer and a reliable coordinator of work crews. Work was patchy, however, and necessity rather than inclination led her to the add-on business of procuring the furnishings to fill these residences.

Julian's van pulled up with a groaning of brakes in front of the house. One leg followed the other as Julian himself climbed down. Mara hurried out to meet him.

"Julian, I tried to call you, but you'd already left. You really should get a cell phone. You and Christophe."

"Hate the things. Playing silly tunes and going off all the time. Besides, you're always losing yours."

"Well, I wanted to tell you, we have a problem."

"Problem?"

"Cécile, as it turns out"—her voice was full of implication—"was an avid horsewoman. In fact, apparently she got on better with horses than with people."

He closed his eyes briefly and swore. He had pictured Cécile sticking to footpaths, at best hiking up her skirts and strolling through spring meadows when the grasses were low. On horseback, she could have ridden all over the valley. All over the region, for that matter. And seen the orchid anywhere.

He cursed again. "Couldn't you have told me this before?"

"Well, I didn't *know* before. And please don't glare like that. Jean-Claude just called, and he happened to mention it."

"I'm not glaring. But you realize this changes my entire search strategy. We need to revise."

"Revise how? You don't honestly expect us to continue, do you?"

"Oh?" he said, purposely stupid, but his eyes held a sharp disappointment.

"Julian, I know I said I'd help you, but this is hopeless." She might have added that she had been charged by a *sanglier*, some kind of killer animal was on the loose, and her ankle hurt. "Be reasonable. You've searched the garden and the forests around Aurillac. We've searched around the meadows. This leaves what? The Sigoulane Valley? Most of it is planted over with vines. What hasn't been is sheer rock face or forest. You honestly don't expect us to find anything, do you?"

Unhappily, he took her point.

"So what else did Lover Boy have to say?" he inquired sourly.

"His name's Jean-Claude. There's no need to call him Lover Boy."

"Sorry. I thought you said he tried to seduce you."

She ignored this. "He wants to meet with me again."

"You two seem to be having a lot of meetings lately."

"He's supposed to report daily," she replied, exasperated. "He said he discovered something new. In fact, he sounded quite excited."

Julian looked unimpressed.

"You just don't care, do you," she burst out angrily, offloading at last the grievance she had with him, "about what happened to Baby Blue. For you, he doesn't exist except as something your shawl was wrapped around."

He seemed taken aback. "Of course I care."

"No, you don't. Nothing matters to you but your orchid."

"Oh, I get it. If that's what's bothering you, let me say I'm sorry as hell the kid was killed. But that was a long time ago, Mara. What am I supposed to do? Go into mourning?"

"Please don't be sarcastic."

"Well, please be reasonable. Has it occurred to you that you're agonizing needlessly? You're beating yourself up because you couldn't prevent your sister's death, so you've transferred your sense of guilt to Baby Blue, that sort of thing? There's nothing you could have done to help either of them, you know."

Her head snapped up. "I've never heard anything so ridiculous in my life. If you want to engage in psychoanalysis, Julian, look at yourself. A child was murdered, and all you can think about is your damned *Cypripedium*. Is that normal?"

They glared at each other.

"So where does that leave us?" Julian said finally. "This isn't just about Baby Blue or the orchid, you know. We agreed we'd spend more time together. As in tonight."

She looked him straight in the eye. "I'm sorry, Julian, I can't."

He waited for more. Her face assumed a mulish expression.

"I see," he muttered finally, feeling another of his stress headaches coming on. "Well, in that case, I won't take up any more of your time."

He climbed back into his van, slammed the door with unnecessary violence, and drove off.

Mara spent the rest of the day in her studio, a detached building behind her house, which, unlike her front room, revealed her more natural environment: a clutter of objects salvaged from wrecking sites, old bolts of cloth, client files and accounts stored in sagging cardboard boxes. She was becoming increasingly convinced that Christophe's gallery was doomed to remain unfinished. As a means of forestalling bankruptcy, she had decided to bid on the renovation of an ugly farmhouse near Meyrals. The new project failed to stir her imagination. Or was it that Julian kept intruding on her concentration? After many hours, she stamped out of her studio and returned to the house. She picked up a message on her phone: the stonemason she thought she had lined up for Christophe could not take the job on after all.

"*Merde,*" cried Mara to no one but Jazz, who butted her with his head to tell her it was dinnertime. He had a very hard head.

Dogs, she thought as she fed him, were easy compared with people. They were happy eating the same old thing every day. They were straightforward, took you as you came, and didn't throw tantrums. Hadn't someone once said, "The more I know people, the more I like dogs"?

A clock, an antique *pendule* obtained from a dealer in Monpazier, sounded six. Its harsh, brassy chime was bearable only because it, like everything else, was a temporary acquisition. She headed for the bathroom, where she turned the tub taps on fullbore, pouring in a generous dollop of a product called Bain de Mer that turned your bath an improbable blue. She returned to the kitchen, where she found half a bottle of muscat in the *frigo.* She carried it to the bathroom. She tuned her radio to the classical station, but they were playing a modern opera that made her teeth shiver. She found something that was easier listening. It was only after she had stripped that she discovered she had forgotten a glass, so she made do with her tooth mug, filling it to the brim with cold, sweet wine. This in hand, she sank gratefully into the hot, bubbling ultramarine water.

Minutes later, to the strains of Duke Ellington's "Come Sunday," she lay submerged to the neck, in a drifting state of mindlessness.

She awoke with a start. The cooling bath was no longer pleasant. It was ten to seven.

"Damn," she cried, scrambling up, slipping, and splashing water everywhere. She dried off hastily, using her towel to mop up the floor. In the bedroom she grabbed a change of underwear and yanked clothing out of the closet. Not that. Or that. Briefly she considered a long batik sarong skirt and a low-cut russet silk top that complemented her strong coloring, but settled in the end for a tailored gray shirtwaist. Her wedge sandals were where she had kicked them, one under the dresser, the other in a corner of the room.

She made quick work of her still-damp hair. Luckily, it was short enough that it required little grooming. Jazz. She had to remember to let him in. The last time she'd left him outside, his barking had put the neighbors in a rage. She hurried to the rear door, where he was waiting for her. He trotted into the front room, toenails clicking like castanets on the highly polished walnut floor, and settled happily on the Aubusson. She galloped back to the bathroom to make up her face.

Moments later, she surveyed herself in the cheval glass, adjusted her collar, and twitched her hem straight. Then she searched about for her cell phone, which she eventually found in the kitchen, dropped it into her shoulder bag, and strode out of the house to keep her appointment with Jean-Claude Fournier.

19

wasn't expecting this," Mara said. They were standing by the low stone parapet of his terrace, admiring a fiery orange western sky. The earth dropped away below them, the ravine bottom already deep in shadow. A drinks trolley nearby held glasses, bottles, and a tray of cold shrimp hors d'oeuvres. She was sipping a Kir Royal, a blend of champagne and cassis. "When you said dinner, I naturally thought—"

Jean-Claude laughed. "That we'd meet here for drinks and then go to some restaurant—a good one, of course, but out. Why not here? I can offer you"—his eyes glowed over the rim of his glass, or perhaps it was just that in that moment they reflected the setting sun—"all the comforts of home."

She found herself laughing, too, and once more caught the whiff of his sexy, musky odor. He was dressed this time in burgundy slacks to match his Gucci loafers and a gray ribbed silk pullover. His yellow hair, falling either side of a central parting, gave him an almost Renaissance look.

They had dinner in his front room. He seated her at a table set with old silver, antique Sèvres dishes, and hand-cut crystalware. Mara sniffed the air appreciatively. It carried an intricacy of smells: the richness of oven-baked pastry, the enticing odor of pan-fried garlic. Against a background of flowers, soft music, and discreet lighting, he brought out the steaming first course: aromatic wedges of *saumon en croûte*.

"Délicieux," Mara murmured around her first bite, a flaky casing

that crumbled exquisitely away from a core of salmon in a creamy caper sauce. "I mean, fabulous. I'm tremendously impressed."

"Why so? All the great chefs of the world are men, you know." He gazed archly across the table at her.

"Debatable."

"All right, name me one really famous woman chef. I'm not speaking about collectors of other people's recipes, writers of cookbooks. I mean true culinary geniuses."

"*Ma mère.* It's true. She's a knockout cook. Comes from a little place called Saint-Louis-du-Ha! Ha!, near the Quebec–New Brunswick border. You should taste her six-pastry chicken pie, to say nothing of her moose steak."

It was Jean-Claude's turn to laugh.

She waved her fork over her plate. "But how did you learn to do this?"

Jean-Claude shrugged. "*My* mother—god rest her soul—was an unmentionably bad cook."

Mara, in sympathy with Madame Fournier, shifted self-consciously in her chair.

"Consequently," he went on, "I insist on eating well. At least dining well. I don't mind plain meals during the rest of the day as long as I can look forward to a really good *dîner.* A beautiful companion makes it all the more enjoyable."

"Jean-Claude, this is supposed to be a business affair."

"At least you admit the possibility of an affair?" He leaned forward, insinuating.

"Not in the sense I think you mean. Really, I'm impressed all to hell, but hadn't we better focus on Baby Blue? You said you've found out something more about the family. What?"

"Ah." He gave her a sly smile and rose from the table. "But first, the *plat principal.* One should always satisfy the appetites of the flesh before other things, don't you think?"

He had prepared his version of a Dordogne speciality, *magret de canard,* grilled duck breast, in a port-and-pepper sauce with a pear compote. Watching him as he served up, Mara thought he had the air—she swept her mind for fitting aphorisms—of the cat who'd swallowed the cream. Or maybe it was that butter wouldn't melt in his mouth? At any rate, his first course had been replete with both butter and cream, and he really looked as if he'd licked the spoon.

"I am very fond of breast," said Jean-Claude as he put an artistically assembled plate before her. "Of duck, I mean. It's the best part because it's covered with a delicate layer of fat that melts in the cooking. That's what makes the meat so tender."

There were side platters of baked endive and *pommes de terre sarladaises.* Mara felt a guilty twinge at the sight of the last. It was Julian's favorite dish, garlicky potatoes lightly sautéed in goose fat and sprinkled with parsley. The main course was followed by salad, local cheeses, and a plum tart purchased from the Boulangerie Méliès in Brames, which turned out some of the best *pâtisserie* in the region. They talked very little during the meal, both too absorbed in plying fork and knife.

"*Superbe,*" Mara sighed at last, laying her napkin beside her coffee cup.

He regarded her with satisfaction. "Then let me propose an exchange. The results of my research, which I think you'll find interesting, for a great deal more of your company."

"I'm not your client, Jean-Claude," Mara told him firmly but with a smile. The excellence of the meal had put her in a mellow mood. "Christophe is."

He gave an exaggerated sigh. "My efforts go for naught. With you Americans—"

"Canadian."

"Canadians, it's always *le business* first. Very well, I shall lay before you my findings to date with no strings attached. I need a smoke. Shall we go out on the terrace?"

It had grown dark by then, but the warmth of the day lingered. Crickets chirped softly in the ravine below. He opened a packet of Davidoffs, tapped out a mini-cigar, lit up, and tossed the packet onto a wooden bench set into the terrace wall.

"I have been forced," he began, "to review my conclusions about the de Bonfonds. Thanks"—he swept her a small bow—"entirely to you."

"Me?"

"*Mais oui.* You pointed out the inconsistency in the family *devise.* It set me thinking. I've already described to you the de Bonfonds in their unembellished state. But until now I had no idea how really nasty they were." He exhaled smoke that hung about his head on the still night air. "After you pointed out the spelling discrepancy in the family motto, I did a little more research. Well, quite a lot, to be honest. First of all, I should say that I was able to determine that the painted motto on the scroll came first. The portrait was done in Xavier's lifetime, probably sometime in the 1780s. However, the mantelpiece was purchased and carved after Xavier's death—in 1831, according to the bill of sale I found. This led me to ask why the spelling was changed. Was it simply an error? Or a cover-up?"

Mara's eyebrows lifted. "A cover-up for what?"

"Blood *And* My Right. Blood *Is* My Right. As you said, there's a difference. In this case, a big difference. The more I probed, the more I began to wonder if the de Bonfonds didn't have something even more horrific to add to their reputation." He regarded her thoughtfully. "What do you know about *loups-garous,* Mara?"

"Werewolves?" She laughed outright. "Only that they go hairy and bite people at the full moon."

"Don't make light of it. France has a long history of *loups-garous* and a formidable record of werewolf executions."

"Ignorant superstition and mass hysteria," she scoffed. "Like burning people at the stake for being witches."

He said, almost severely, "Everything has its strand of truth. Supposing I told you that I'm convinced that many of the legends surrounding *loups-garous* are exactly what they purport to be: accounts of werewolf sightings and attacks." Seeing her obvious disbelief, he ground out his cigar and strode swiftly into the house. He returned moments later, a long straplike object draped over both hands.

"Here." He held it out to her. "Since you're so skeptical. This is a wolf belt. It was given to me by an old woman a number of years ago, when I was compiling material for my book on Dordogne folktales. Take it."

The thing was made from some kind of animal skin, greenish gray and supple, with a simple brass buckle. The stitching along the edges was frayed and worn. For some reason Mara felt unwilling to touch it. With a brief laugh she stepped away. "Is this supposed to be some kind of protection against werewolves?"

He shook his head gravely. "Far from it. According to local beliefs, a wolf belt condemns the wearer to become a werewolf at each full moon for a period of seven years. The old woman claimed her grandmother bought it from an itinerant vendor. Against her family's warning, she wore it to a festivity. The next full moon, she changed into a she-wolf and ran snarling from the house. She was found two days later, hiding in the bushes. Her hair was matted with dirt and leaves, and her nightdress was covered in dried blood. Nearby was a dead sheep. She had killed it by biting its throat out and had fed on the carcass. Go on, since you're so sure this is nonsense, put it on. Nothing will happen to you if it's just superstitious rubbish." He pushed it into her hand, but she recoiled and threw it down. The feel of it made her skin crawl.

"You see." His eyes were mocking. "You claim to doubt what I've said, but when it comes down to it, you won't even touch it."

"Jean-Claude, what does all this have to do with the de Bonfonds?" Mara asked angrily, but she was angrier at herself than at him for being so inexplicably shaken.

With a smile—he had made his point—he picked up the wolf belt, rolled it up carefully, and set it on the drinks trolley. "Not a good idea to leave this lying around. These things have lives of their own." He reached for the packet of Davidoffs and tapped out another cigar. "What does this have to do with the de Bonfonds? Quite a bit, as it turns out. You've certainly heard of the Sigoulane Beast. The media are full of it. But have you ever heard"—his face was suddenly illuminated by the flare of a match—"of the Beast of Le Gévaudan?"

Mara regarded him warily. "No, I have not."

"Then let me tell you." He drew the cigar to life. It's fiery tip glowed like an angry eye in the darkness. "Between 1764 and 1767, some kind of creature roamed the hills of Le Gévaudan, which, if you don't know it, is a mountainous region at the foot of the Massif Central. For three years it left a trail of mutilated bodies. Those who saw it said it was a large, wolflike creature. Some said it had the ability to go on two legs like a man. Others claimed to have met it in human form as a hairy stranger who tried to lure them into the woods. Many believed it was a werewolf.

"The thing was killed. Twice. In both cases, its carcass was displayed to quiet the fears of the local population. The attacks ceased after 1767. The records of these events have been preserved, and nearly two dozen books have been written trying to explain the mystery of the Beast. None, to my mind, satisfactorily." He paused. "Did the Beast die? Or did it simply change territory?"

"What are you saying, Jean-Claude?" Mara's chin went up skeptically.

"Just this. Xavier de Bonfond came from Le Gévaudan, from the village of Paulhac, in the very area where the attacks were concentrated. At the time of the Beast, he would have been in his thirties. Apart from that and the fact that he served as a *gabelou*, we know little else about his early life. He first appeared in the Sigoulane Valley in 1770, three years after the Gévaudan Beast was allegedly killed. Parish records in the Sigoulane Valley show that in 1772 some kind of savage creature began killing a large number of sheep. In 1775 the first human attacks began. People who saw the thing claimed it was not a wolf, although wolves roamed the forests in those days, but a hairy wolflike creature that had the ability to walk upright. The first references to the Sigoulane Beast date from that time. The attacks in the valley peaked in 1787, tapered off in the late 1790s, and stopped entirely after Xavier's death in 1810. For the next forty-nine years, there were no more sightings of the 'thing that went on two legs.'

"Xavier did well for himself after he came to Sigoulane, although he was feared more than respected. Not only did he have a reputation for violence, he also had a spooky knack of disappearing from one place and reappearing somewhere else with almost supernatural speed. Still, as I told you, he married into a good family and acquired the trappings of social respectability. But I think the one thing he could not, or would not, obscure was his true nature." Jean-Claude moved to stand uncomfortably close to Mara. "I think the motto as you spotted it on Xavier's portrait is the right one. The carving on the mantel, *Sang E Mon Drech*, Blood And My Right, is a later version that was altered by the simple suppression of the letter 's' for the sake of appearances, as was the creation of the fake family tree. The real motto is *Sang Es Mon Drech*. Blood *Is* My Right. You understand the meaning of it now, don't you?"

Mara took a deep breath. "You want me to believe the Gévaudan Beast and the Sigoulane Beast were one, and that Xavier de Bonfond was a werewolf? I think I've heard quite enough." She turned to walk away. He caught her arm.

"Wait. I'm not finished. We have to fast-forward to 1859,

when Xavier's great-grandson Hugo was in his twenties. Another rash of 'happenings' began about that time. Again, it's all documented in parish records. Over the next thirteen years, several children went missing and two other children and an old woman were found with their throats bitten out. Hugo died in 1872. The attacks ceased after that date."

"Unless you count the *maquisard sans tête*," Mara said, seizing on anything to jam a stick in the smoothly turning spokes of his narrative. "Thérèse seems to think it was the work of the Beast as well. Hugo was long gone by then."

Jean-Claude shook his head. "That was a wartime atrocity." He spoke with certainty. "The man was decapitated by a human agent, not a werewolf. Which brings us to the present." He paused, tipping his face up to contemplate the sky, where the moon, just on the wane, rode high above the treetops. "Things seem to be starting up again."

Mara stepped back, incredulous. "Are you talking about the feral dog? Oh, come on, Jean-Claude."

He leaned in. His eyes were serious in the light from the open terrace door. "Is it a dog? There are many who believe that werewolfism is a heritable condition, Mara. Not necessarily passed from parent to child, because there are quiescent periods which suggest the condition skips generations. Xavier was Hugo's great-grandfather. Hugo is Christophe's great-grandfather."

"Are you suggesting Christophe is behind these recent attacks?"

Jean-Claude took a last drag on his cigar, stubbed the butt out on the parapet, and flipped it over the side. "You said it, not I."

"But you certainly implied it!"

He raised both hands. "Hear me out. While I was working with Christophe on his book, I became aware of something odd in his behavior. Every now and then he shut himself in his room, wouldn't talk to people, or simply left without warning. Thérèse always put it down to 'one of his moods.' Yesterday I went back through my old work diaries. Over the period of twenty-five months, there were at least half a dozen times when he canceled meetings with me owing to 'indisposition.' "

"He could have been sick. It happens, you know."

"Each instance occurred a few days before the full moon. He always remained unavailable for a week or so, and then everything returned to normal. Last month, when that man was killed by the so-called feral dog, the moon was full. Last week, when Christophe locked himself in his room, the moon was again full. Doesn't it seem strange to you that he delegated you to see me when he could have very easily done so himself? Is it coincidence that the very night he went missing something broke into a hen-house and attacked the Dupuy woman?"

"I'm finding this in very bad taste, Jean-Claude."

"Very well. If you don't believe me, ask Thérèse. She knows Christophe better than anyone. Ask her if what I've said isn't true."

"Good idea." Mara dug her cell phone out of her bag. "Let's call her right now. You can tell her your crazy—" She broke off, thinking she saw his lips twitch. "Now, look," she shouted and slapped the phone down. "If this is your idea of a joke, I am not amused."

He threw up his hands. "I swear to you, Mara, this is no joke." He seemed in earnest, but were his eyes slightly mocking? "Everything I said is absolutely true. The dates and events all mesh. Christophe does go into seclusion at the full moon. Something is out there that's killing and mauling people. Would I joke about something as serious as this?"

"I think"—Mara glared at him in disgust—"you'd do anything to make a point." She almost said "score a hit." He had given her the impression that he had discovered something important about the de Bonfonds. This load of rubbish was nothing more than a flimsy excuse for an intimate dinner *à deux,* intended to lead no doubt to other things. "And Baby Blue?" she inquired coldly. "Without the werewolf sideshow, if you don't mind."

He shrugged, weathering her disbelief. "As I said. Cécile's bastard. She killed him. Or someone in the family did. Whatever, it really doesn't matter."

He was right. Mara subsided, thinking of the sad little bundle of dried-out flesh, the manner of its death. For Baby Blue, it really didn't matter.

Gently, he traced the prominence of her collarbone, leaving his finger to rest lightly on the pulse point of her throat. "You know, I find it strange that such a desirable woman as yourself is unattached. Why don't we forget about Baby Blue and the de Bonfonds and focus on more interesting things? Us, for example."

"No thanks." She pushed away from him, sick of his constant foreplay, his innuendo, his physical encroachments. "I've had just about all the focus I can take. *Merci* for dinner and the entertainment. I'm afraid I have to be on my way."

"But you can't go. It's early yet." He sounded deeply offended.

"You forget. I'm a working girl." She hooked her bag over her shoulder, waggled her fingers at him, and turned to leave.

His attack was swift and brutal. He grabbed her roughly from behind, spun her around, and jerked her in close.

"Come on, Mara." His voice rang harshly in her ear; his breath was fumy with alcohol and tobacco. "Quit the teasing. I don't like women who play hard to get." His mouth came down on hers so forcefully that his teeth cut her lower lip. His free hand groped her breast. Mara gave a muffled cry against the invasion of his probing tongue and did the only thing she could—kneed him hard, aiming for the groin. He took the blow on the inside of the thigh. She broke free and slapped him across the face.

"You bastard!" she screamed.

"Admit it, you like it rough. Most women do." He came at her again, his face ugly with intent.

Using her purse as a weapon, Mara swung it at him. The blow caught him on the side of the head. She followed up with an almighty shove, sending him reeling, arms flailing, backward into the drinks trolley. Amid the sound of crashing bottles, she fled through his house, out his front door, and to her car. With shaking hands she started the motor, killed it in her haste, started it up again, and shot backward down the driveway.

A yell brought her foot down hard on the brake. A figure surged forward out of the darkness: an elderly man with a dog.

"Oh god, I'm so sorry," she cried, rolling down her window. Her voice sounded unnaturally high to her own ears.

Outraged, the man told her what he thought of her and her driving. He was still hurling insults at her as she gained the road and swung her car around, heading for home.

That night Mara e-mailed Patsy:

>*Patsy, "Hands" Fournier has proven himself an all-out, giant-sized prick. I'm not speaking anatomically. Tonight the bastard actually assaulted me . . .*

She paused. Had she led him on? She was quite certain she had not.

. . . It seems Christophe has badly misjudged his man. Far from clearing the de Bonfonds, Jean-Claude makes them sound like the family from hell. Not only are they bloodthirsty, grasping, and not noble, two of them were werewolves, one of them the actual Beast of Le Gévaudan, would you believe, who made himself over as the Sigoulane Beast when he moved to the Dordogne. More-

over, the condition runs in the family because the feral dog I told you about isn't a dog at all, according to Jean-Claude, but Christophe, who is the most recent de Bonfond to terrorize the Sigoulane Valley. As for Baby Blue, he was probably the illegitimate kid of Christophe's great-great-aunt Cécile, who smothered him, or someone in the family did.

Christophe is still missing. I'm now inclined to agree with Julian that the little twerp is probably happily perched in a three-star hotel somewhere while I do his dirty work. Well, he can deal direct with Jean-Claude from now on. I no longer care if I lose the Aurillac project. In fact, I've decided to send a letter of resignation to the house (since I don't know how else to communicate with Christophe) and return his deposit. My only other problem, apart from the fact that I'm very low on funds, is that I think I left my cell phone at Jean-Claude's, and I really don't want to go back there to collect it. Unfortunately, I've had a bit of a misunderstanding with Julian, otherwise I'd ask him to get it for me, and I can't ask Prudence because she'd want to know why. I can't exist without my portable, so I suppose I'll just have to march up to Jean-Claude's door and demand it back. I'll take Jazz with me this time. Baying at the moon,

Mara

P.S. What do you know about werewolves?<

20

Julian stood in the open doorway of his kitchen, downing a double dose of headache tablets with hot, sweet tea. Glumly, he stared out onto his garden. The grass was wet, and a thin mist hung over everything. A pale morning light struggled to filter through the trees.

He had woken with one of his thumpers, the result of too much wine the night before. The ground all about him was covered in patches of worm-turned soil. His brain felt like that, heaved up, dark, and soggy. Of course, it wasn't just the wine. It had been Denise, too. Reeling from what he could only call the snap end of the elastic, he had turned to Denise and got what he'd asked for: a monumental one-night stand during which Denise had laid him, not the other way around, at least three times. He had found her lean, muscular body extremely sensuous and a little intimidating. Shuddering, he remembered strong legs clamping around his middle with such force that he'd had difficulty drawing breath. It had been like making love to a python.

In between bouts, for it had also been a bit like wrestling, Denise had told him about the many other men she had laid, just so he wouldn't get ideas about a long-term relationship. If her count was right, she'd had it on with practically every eligible male in the Dordogne. He in turn had complained to her about this fellow Jean-Claude Fournier, suggesting that the man was a phony, reeling Mara in with the bait of further revelations on Baby Blue.

While he talked, Denise had run circles with her finger on his chest, making it clear that she was interested in other things.

Sometime in the night, she had left him. He wasn't sure when, because after the third round he had simply lost consciousness. He had come to in the morning with a sore back, a bad head, and a pressing need to urinate.

Damn Mara. True, he hadn't made Sunday night with her a firm date, but you'd think, after their understanding—at least, he thought they had one—it would have gone without saying. Instead, she had stood him up for that prat Jean-Claude, he was sure of it. All of this made their future look about as hopeful as a bomb crater.

The bushes by the side of the house parted. Bismuth emerged. Absently, Julian fondled the dog's head, seeking the comforting, silky roll of his floppy ears. The shrubberies rustled again. Edith, Bismuth's mother, also appeared. Both dogs looked at him, pleading for breakfast. Momentarily, Julian considered ignoring their needs since he was quite sure they had already cadged successfully from every farm along the road. His tea, however, was cooling, and he needed a top-up.

"All right, you two," he sighed, and went for the can-opener.

The man with the dog stared hard at Mara as she turned into Jean-Claude's driveway.

"He's not home," he called out. "I've just been there."

No doubt to complain about dangerous drivers in the night, she thought, climbing out of her car. The man, now that she could see him in daylight, was small, with a fussy-looking toothbrush mustache under a pointed nose. His dog, a fat black spaniel, barked furiously at Jazz, who ignored it and went to cock his leg copiously against a corner of the house. After which he disappeared into the bushes. So much for canine protection, she thought.

But Toothbrush Mustache—a nosy neighbor, she assumed—was right. Jean-Claude did not answer her knock. The neighbor watched her suspiciously as she went around to the back of the house.

There was a chance that her phone might still be outside on the terrace where she thought she had left it. With any luck, she could take it and go. It wasn't. But the drinks trolley was. It lay overturned, broken glass everywhere. A crow that had been pecking at a leftover shrimp hors d'oeuvre flapped ponderously away. The mess, Mara thought, seemed disturbingly uncharacteristic of a man who wore designer clothes and Gucci shoes. She turned troubled eyes to the French doors leading into the house. They stood partly ajar. Reluctantly, she put her head in. The table was as they had left it—cups with the dregs of last night's coffee, rumpled napkins lying where they had been tossed. The lamps were still on, glowing anemically in the corners of the room. The flowers looked tired.

"Jean-Claude?"

The silence in the house was broken only by the persistent thudding of a hornet against a windowpane. He had not answered her knock or, presumably, the neighbor's. So, obviously, he really was not there. But there was the wreckage on the terrace. And the open doors.

Had he been taken ill? She stepped fully into the room.

"Jean-Claude?"

In the kitchen, soiled dishes were stacked on the counter. The bathroom off the entry hall was tidy and clean. And empty. The adjoining WC was also unoccupied.

She stopped at the bottom of the stairs, gazing with apprehension into the darkness of the narrow stairwell that led to the upper story of the house.

Jazz's barking outside aroused her. Really, she should not be there after what had happened the night before. She turned and almost fled back into the sunlight of the terrace. A flock of crows circled overhead, cawing harshly. They settled with a great deal of flapping in the trees. The barking, urgent, sharp, sounded somewhere below her. She went to the parapet and looked down. Jazz was at the bottom of the ravine, some ten meters below, hidden by shrubbery. Only his tail, extending in a rigid line from his rump, was visible, then his head, as he moved backward, whining now. Mara looked around for a way to reach him. At the edge of the terrace, stone slabs set into the hillside formed rough steps. She descended, hanging on to a rickety wooden railing.

The bottom of the ravine was heavily overgrown. A thin droning, as if someone were humming, came from behind a screen of bushes. She pushed through the branches. What she saw made her mind go numb. Then she gave a choked cry, lurched back, crashed into Jazz, who was nosing about uneasily behind her, and sat down hard on the stony ground. The jarring did something to restore her senses. She got to her feet and ran, stumbling up the steps, hauling herself up by the rotten wooden railing that twice came away in pieces in her hand. When she reached the terrace, she doubled over and vomited.

Jean-Claude lay on his back on a bed of broken vegetation. His right arm, flung out to the side, ended in a bloodied stump. His blackened throat and abdomen seemed to writhe. Disturbed by Mara's intrusion, the whining swarm of flies that covered the gaping parts of his body rose in a cloud. Iridescent, they roiled and hovered, then settled down again to their busy feasting.

Adjudant Jacques Compagnon of the Brames Gendarmerie was a big man with pockmarked skin, carroty hair, and bulging eyes which he kept fixed on Mara. She sat hunched on the wooden bench on the terrace while he loomed over her, rocking rhythmically, heel to toe. Nearby a stocky gendarme, Sergeant Albert

Batailler, his foot propped on the stone parapet, took notes on a pad balanced on his knee. Members of the Criminal Brigade moved about methodically at the ravine bottom and inside the house.

"I had dinner with Jean-Claude last night," Mara said woodenly. "I left my cell phone on the terrace. I came back today for it."

"Dinner," said the adjutant. "Do I take it you were on intimate terms with Monsieur Fournier?" His glance swept over the remains of last night's entertainment.

"No, I was not." Minimally she explained Christophe's commission regarding Baby Blue and her role as go-between. "Jean-Claude was supposed to report to me on a daily basis. And that's what he did. Dinner was his idea." He had invited her for seven-thirty, but she had arrived late, and had left maybe around eleven. Half past at the latest. Her host had been well and alive at that time.

"How did the drinks trolley come to be overturned?"

"I don't know," she lied. Or was she lying? She remembered Jean-Claude stumbling backward into the trolley, the sound of glass breaking, but not its actually going over. "I left him out here on the terrace. Maybe he knocked it over later."

Compagnon regarded her skeptically. She stared back. He reminded her of someone she didn't like. Or maybe it was his increasingly aggressive tone that she found offensive.

"You left him on the terrace? He didn't bother to see you out?"

"N-no," she said, sensing quicksand. "Something came up. I— I had to leave in a hurry."

He arched thick orange eyebrows. "So, when you returned today, you saw signs of violence, smashed glass all over the terrace, the doors left open. It was very brave of you to go into the house. Or were you still looking for your phone?"

"Yes. No. I mean, it wasn't just the phone. I didn't even know for sure where I'd left it. I'm always misplacing it. I—I thought something might be wrong. Jean-Claude might be sick. But he— wasn't there." He was at the bottom of the ravine.

"*Mon adjudant*," a familiar voice spoke behind her. Turning, she saw the round face and big ears of Laurent Naudet. His wrists, as usual, protruded from the sleeves of his navy *pull*. He gave her a worried glance of recognition. This time he did not shake her hand. He addressed his chief. "I've just talked with one of the neighbors, sir. A Monsieur Imbert. He insists on seeing you. Says he has important information."

"What?" Compagnon wheeled around. "Bring him—" But at that point the nosy neighbor burst onto the terrace, jabbing an accusing finger at Mara. "That's the one," he cried. "She was with him last night. They had a flaming row. I heard it all. Left in a hurry, she did. Nearly ran me down!"

Slowly the adjudant turned back to her. A hard light came on in his eyes, which seemed to protrude even more from their sockets. "Is what this man says true? Did you have an argument with Monsieur Fournier last night?"

"No," Mara denied stonily. There had been no flaming row. Only a brief, unpleasant struggle. That much was true, and she had to hold to it. To admit anything more was to open up damning possibilities.

"She's lying. I heard glass breaking." As he spoke, the little man's mustache jerked about on his upper lip, like a caterpillar at the end of a twig. Mara repressed a desperate urge to rip it off his face, anything to shut him up. "She probably hit him on the head with a bottle."

"Madame Dunn." Compagnon's voice was almost a growl. "How did Monsieur Fournier come to fall off the terrace?"

As in a nightmare, Mara saw her exit scene again, Jean-Claude's flailing arms, the collision with the trolley. She stared in panic about her. "I don't know."

Compagnon leaned in. "Did you push him? And then, realizing you had left incriminating evidence behind, did you come back today to get it?"

"No," she cried hoarsely. "No!" Cold doubt swept over her as she confronted an awful possibility. Could Jean-Claude, stumbling backward, have toppled off the terrace as she had run from his house?

21

O f course you didn't do it, sweetie," Prudence murmured. She
sat beside Mara on a small settee in Mara's front room. Paul,
Mado, and Baby Eddie occupied an Empire daybed. Loulou and
Julian perched uncomfortably on a couple of period chairs that
seemed too small for them. Jazz and Bismuth lay on the Aubusson rug.

"But the police think I did."

At the Brames Gendarmerie, Mara had been cautioned and
had sustained three hours of intense interrogation by Adjudant
Compagnon. He had not been impressed by her suggestion that
Jean-Claude had taken her cell phone inside, proving that he was
still alive after she left. Only one *portable* had been found in the
house, and that belonged to Fournier himself. Mara began to
doubt her own theory. It was entirely possible that she had taken
her phone away with her after all, that she would eventually find
it buried under a pile of clothing or between the seats of her car.
She considered legal counsel, but, because she didn't have a lawyer,
in the end made her permitted call to Loulou.

The ex-cop had carried the day, or so he told her: "I put it to
Compagnon. 'Look,' I said, 'if she had pushed this Fournier fellow
over, why would she return, climb down into the ravine to discover
the body, and then stay around to call the police?' " (To which
Compagnon had replied, *"Le diable chie toujours au même endroit"*—
The devil always shits in the same place—another way of saying,
"A criminal always returns to the scene of the crime," but Loulou

didn't tell Mara that.) As a result, she had been allowed to walk out, very shakily, on condition that she make herself available for further questioning.

"Not us," Prudence reassured her. "We know you're innocent. Tell her, everyone."

"Of course she's innocent," Julian said energetically, their angry exchange on Sunday entirely forgotten.

Paul grunted his assent. Mado, round-eyed, nodded over her baby's fuzzy head.

"No doubt about it," Loulou agreed. Ever the Job's comforter, he added, "Although you have to admit you make a good prime suspect. You had the means—a good, hard shove—and opportunity. You were with the deceased during the critical time. The *médecin légiste*—I have this unofficially, by the way—estimates time of death as somewhere between eleven last night and four this morning. It's hard to be more precise because the body was in terrible condition. Moreover, there's a witness. The neighbor said he heard you fighting with the victim." He paused. "You didn't have a motive, too, did you?"

"No, I did not!" Mara shouted. "I told you. He tried to feed me that garbage about the de Bonfonds, and Christophe being a descendant of werewolves. I was annoyed. So would you have been. I told him off and left. I didn't push him over and I didn't r-rip his throat out!" She needed desperately to believe that Jean-Claude had been alive when she had left him. Her story ought to have improved with each telling, but she didn't feel any more confident of her version of events now than when she had made her statement to Adjudant Compagnon.

"That's good," the ex-*flic* responded cheerfully. "It's always better to be clear on these little details."

"Well, if you didn't do it," said Paul, "someone did. Made a damned sorry mess of his insides as well—" He broke off as Mado shoved him with her elbow.

Loulou tipped his head from side to side. "Provisionally, the cause of death was a broken neck, presumably sustained from the fall. The mess, as Paul calls it"—even he grimaced—"was caused by the depredations of animals. They identified the bite marks of foxes, *sangliers*—"

"*Sangliers?*" echoed Prudence, dumbfounded.

"They scavenge anything," grunted Julian.

"But," continued Loulou with meaning, "most of the initial damage was done by some kind of large canid, a very big dog or a wolf . . ."

Mutely, they all stared at him.

"The Beast," whispered Mado, clutching Eddie tightly. "*Mon dieu.* You don't suppose that's what got him?"

There was another moment of silence while all eyes swiveled to her.

Julian was the first to recover. "You think it attacked him and knocked him off the terrace, then went down and ate him?" He looked doubtful. "Pretty bold to go for a person so close to the house. More likely an accident. Jean-Claude tripped on the trolley and catapulted over. That's the trouble with these cantilevered terraces. They're damned dangerous, to say nothing of impossible to landscape."

"What about robbery?" suggested Prudence. "Jean-Claude surprised the thief, there was a struggle—"

"Compagnon ruled out robbery," Loulou cut in. "Nothing was disturbed."

"Blackmail, then," said Paul. "Jean-Claude threatened Christophe that if he didn't cough up he'd unmask him as the Sigoulane Beast."

"Did you tell Adjudant Compagnon about this werewolf nonsense?" Julian asked Mara.

She gave him a scandalized look. "Of course not. I was in enough trouble as it was without sounding like a fruit basket. I just said I'd had dinner with Jean-Claude, he reported on some further findings, and I—I left."

"I mean"—the bistro owner sat forward on the daybed, warming to his idea—"most people would be pretty upset to be accused of being a werewolf, let alone be told it runs in the family. Maybe Christophe didn't mean to kill him, just lost control and—*paf!*—over he goes."

"*Quelle merde,*" Julian objected. "There's no way Christophe would have taken Jean-Claude seriously. It's ridiculous. Besides, Christophe's simply not the type of person to knock people over walls. He hates violence."

"Unless it's a full moon," Paul suggested with relish.

This time Mado slapped him.

"Anyway, he's not the only de Bonfond," Prudence observed. "There's Antoine and his lot as well. Besides, if Jean-Claude had just figured out his werewolf theory, how would he have had a chance to blackmail Christophe? The man's been missing almost a week."

"Christophe made me his go-between," said Mara, "but I wouldn't put it past him to have been in contact with Jean-Claude all along. It's just the kind of thing he would do."

"Thérèse thinks something's happened to him," Julian said.

"My eye," Mara retorted angrily. "He's hiding out somewhere. Even if he's completely innocent, I think it's damned cowardly of him. He got me into this, and his disappearance has put me in a horrible position. The police have only my word that he engaged me to deal with Jean-Claude. Adjudant Compagnon would like nothing better than to hang a murder charge on me."

It was interesting, Julian thought, how their positions had changed. Mara had gone from fretting about Christophe's well-being only a few days ago to treating his disappearance as a material inconvenience, not that one could blame her. Julian, on the other hand, was beginning to worry seriously, for he no longer believed that Christophe was simply lying low because of Baby Blue.

"But look, Mara," Julian continued to defend his friend, "according to you, Jean-Claude had already told Christophe plenty of unflattering things about his family. For pity's sake, what can be more humiliating than the fact that the so-called de Bonfond title is bogus? He's known that for some time. Why kill him now, and for such a fantastic reason?"

Loulou cocked his head. "Nevertheless, the blackmail idea has possibilities. As a genealogist, our Monsieur Fournier must have uncovered a lot of family skeletons. Maybe he made a routine practice of selective *chantage*."

"He certainly lived well enough," Mara put in.

Loulou tugged thoughtfully at a loose lobe of neck flesh. "I think I'll have a word—diplomatically, of course—with our good adjudant about checking into Jean-Claude's client list."

"Well, thank god someone's finally making sense," said Julian. "That must be it. Jean-Claude was blackmailing someone else. That person got tired of paying through the nose. He or she turned up after Mara left. There was a struggle, and Jean-Claude either fell or was thrown off the terrace."

"He was also a womanizer," added Prudence. "Maybe a jilted lover killed him."

"*Cherchez la femme, eh?*" snorted Paul.

"I'm serious," said Prudence. "He's had affairs with women from Bordeaux to Bretenoux. They all talk about him. The perfect gentleman at first but kinky in bed. Some like it that way, apparently. He had a landmark relationship with what's-her-name of Coteaux de Bonfond, Christophe's niece, not long ago."

"You mean Denise?" Julian asked, taken aback.

"That's right. It ended like it started, fast and hard."

Julian fell silent. He could see Denise as a killer. But did she have a motive? Besides, he recalled, she had been with him last night. Or most of it. And then he remembered that, of the many past lovers she had told him about, Denise had not once mentioned Jean-Claude Fournier.

"I'm still for the *loup-garou* thing," said Paul. "Look, if this Jean-Claude made a hobby of collecting werewolf stories, he probably believed in them himself. What's wrong with him really thinking he'd solved the Le Gévaudan Beast mystery?"

"For heaven's sake!" Julian exclaimed. "He was having Mara on. He promised her new information, so he had to deliver."

But Mara broke in. "Paul may be right. I know it sounds crazy, and I thought he was putting me on at the time as well. But I wonder now if Jean-Claude mightn't have been serious. You should see his house. Full of occult objects. And then there's his book. You've read it, Prudence. He believed those folktales were based on actual events. I think he was genuinely excited about making the connection between the Beast of Le Gévaudan, the Sigoulane Beast, and Xavier de Bonfond. Imagine what it would have meant to him to come up with the solution to a baffling mystery *and* a live descendant responsible for the awful things that have been happening."

"Bollocks," Julian objected. "That Piquet fellow was killed by an animal. They know from the bite marks. Ditto for the woman who was attacked in Les Ronces. So, unless you seriously think Christophe turns into a werewolf, how the hell could he—or any human being—have been responsible?"

"I don't know," Mara admitted unhappily.

"Besides, even if that was what Jean-Claude tried to blackmail Christophe about, assuming he was crazy enough to do it, why would he have told you? Wouldn't that be like giving away his line of credit?"

She said doggedly, "He needed to brag. At the same time, there was no risk. He knew I wouldn't believe him."

"Then neither would anyone else. Jean-Claude could never have gone public with such a daft theory. Or blackmailed Christophe with it."

Loulou cleared his throat. "Ah, but the threat of publicity might have been enough. That kind of daft theory, as you say, is just the sort of thing that would go down well in certain circles, with very embarrassing consequences for Christophe. He could have found himself the focus of an international cult. I think our Jean-Claude knew very well what he was doing."

"Right, then." Paul slapped his thigh. "All the *flics* have to do is find Christophe. They'll sort out soon enough whether or not he really is the Sigoulane Beast."

"Then hope to god they get him fast," said Mado, looking very worried. "Before someone else gets eaten."

The others had gone. Only Julian remained. He reached out to draw her to him.

"Look, Mara," he murmured into her hair. "The police can't really think you did it. You were simply in the wrong place at the wrong time." Her body felt small and unresponsive. She mumbled something into his shirtfront. He bent his head. "What's that?"

"I said I couldn't admit it in front of the others." She looked him in the eye, but with difficulty. "And I was afraid to tell that awful adjudant. Jean-Claude tried to make a pass at me, Julian. Well, more than a pass. He came on in a very nasty way. I slapped him."

"Damn right," Julian said indignantly.

"You don't understand. We struggled. And I—" She broke off and glanced away. Gently, Julian hooked his finger under her chin, turning her face back.

"You what?"

"I pushed him. Oh, Julian, I pushed him. Really hard."

He stood still, taking this in. "Are you saying you shoved him over the terrace wall?"

"No!" She shook her head vehemently, and then muttered with

less conviction, "I don't know. I didn't think we were that near the edge. The thing is, he stumbled backward into the drinks trolley. I didn't hang around to see what happened next. All I wanted to do was get out of there."

"Okay," he whispered, pulling her in to him again. "It's okay." But as he tried to reassure her, he wondered. Could Mara have unintentionally sent Jean-Claude sailing over the parapet after all?

Mara's hypersensitive antennae immediately picked up Julian's doubt. She stiffened.

"You don't believe me."

"Of course I do. Look, if anything, it was an accident. He assaulted you, there was a struggle. No one can blame you for running—"

The monstrosity of what he was saying hit her hard. She broke sharply from him.

"You think I did it!" Her voice rose in volume with every word. "You really think I knocked him over and then *left* him down there? That I would be capa-bu-ble of just *leaving* him for—for animals to eat?" She was close to tears. To her, that was his far greater offense: not just his suspicion that there had been more to the push than she remembered or wanted to admit, but that he thought her base enough to run away, knowing that Jean-Claude was lying, injured or dying, at the bottom of the ravine.

"No." He tried to frame another denial. "That's not what I meant."

But she shouted him down. "You bastard! You really think I did it. Oh, leave me alone. Just leave me alone!"

If there had been a ledge handy, Mara really thought she would have shoved Julian off it.

Mara sat at her kitchen table, head in her hands. It was one of life's bitterest ironies that the people you trusted most did not, when the chips were down, trust you. Julian had gone, protesting ineffectually. He, Loulou, Prudence, Mado, and Paul—all of them were secretly convinced of her guilt. And her cowardice. They were just too polite, or unwilling, to say so. She blew her nose. Miserably, she acknowledged that they, Julian included, were probably reflecting her own terrible self-doubts which, as the night wore on, grew increasingly greater. Over and over, she played through the scene: the struggle, the push, Jean-Claude staggering backward. It now seemed to her that she really had caused him to fall over the parapet. *But she had not knowingly left him to die.* Of that she was certain. Could she get off on a claim of self-defense? Or would she spend the rest of her life in a French prison? And then there was the mess the animals had made of him, eating him as he lay at the bottom of the ravine. The thought made her physically ill.

Jazz, sensing her despair, moved in to sit beside her. Also, he wanted his dinner. He ventured a low sigh. Then a sharp bark. She filled his feed dish and watched him woodenly as he gobbled his food. She herself had no appetite.

Well, at least she had the measure of him. Julian, that was. Not there in the crunch. Also, she was sure she'd surprised a guilty look on his face when Prudence had mentioned Denise. How hollow his protestations about permanence now seemed. Maybe it was her fate to get entangled with men with short shelf-lives. If she had thought of Julian as turning in circles, going nowhere, she now saw herself for what she was: a log in high water on which all manner of undesirable debris snagged and clung.

What she needed was a long, stiff drink, but she only had a bottle of supermarket Sauvignon Blanc in the house. She uncorked it and drank it at room temperature since she had forgotten to chill it in the *frigo*. It tasted sour, and it went straight to her head. By the time she had finished the bottle, it was nearly midnight and she was feeling slightly sick. She was tired to the bone, but knew she would not sleep. With a sigh, she rose and stumbled out to her studio. Her garden was filled with dark shapes, shrubbery in need of trimming and oversized statues (Patsy's) from the time when sculpturing had been her friend's second avocation. May as well get it over with, she thought, flipping on the studio light and zigzagging through the obstacle course of litter on her way to the computer.

Patsy's reply to her last message was waiting for her, cheerful and unperturbed by the latest developments:

>*Hey, kid, you're doing the right thing. Dump the project, dump de Bonfond, and especially dump Hands Fournier, who sounds like a date rape waiting to happen. If you have to retrieve your cell phone, make it up with Julian and take him as backup. In fact, make it up with him anyway. He may be kooky about orchids, but deep down he's a sweetie.*

What do I know about werewolves? Apart from the fact that they go all snouty with teeth at the full moon and are tougher to deal with than vampires because they handle sunlight fine and don't have to sleep all day in a coffin, not much. Although I'm told one way of spotting a werewolf is that their pee is purple, assuming you can get close enough to check. Is this what you wanted to know? Or are you talking about the other kind of werewolf?

By the way, I really hope you dealt with Jean-Claude, as in smashed the bastard's balls. I mean, hard enough to give him a permanently funny walk.<

With wooden fingers, Mara typed:

>*I did, in a matter of speaking. In fact, I think I killed him . . .*

It took her forty minutes to complete her message. She almost forgot to ask, and therefore had to append as a postscript, the question that Patsy's e-mail had raised:

P.S. What other kinds of werewolves are there?<

22

Rain thundered on the roof of the car. Like a frantic heart, the wipers beat their rhythm across the windshield, thudding at the bottom of their arc, squealing on the return. Christophe slowed. It had just gone six in the morning, but it was as dark as night and almost impossible to see. His headlights illuminated dancing puddles in the road immediately before him but scarcely penetrated the heavy sheets of rain that drifted diagonally across his view. Finally, he pulled onto the shoulder and cut the engine. He sat for a moment, staring out into the moving wall of water. Fumbling above his head, he flicked on the interior light of the car. A newspaper lay on the passenger seat, folded to expose the morning's headlines: *Beast Strikes Again?* He opened the paper and scanned the front page to read again the part that had so disturbed him: ". . . An unidentified Canadian woman who was with the deceased prior to his death was questioned and released . . . dined with Fournier and discussed a business matter, claimed to have left him alive and well . . . treating the case as a suspicious death . . ."

With a rush of anxiety that made him almost nauseated, Christophe crumpled the paper into a ball. If he had foreseen the ghastly way things would turn out, he would never have involved Mara, would never have engaged that cunning bastard Jean-Claude. But now, even if Jean-Claude was no longer in a position to talk, Mara had seen him prior to his death, had discussed with him a "business matter." Which meant that the two of them had probably been in it together. Or at least that there was a risk that Jean-Claude had told her everything.

You can't be sure of that, a voice in his head reasoned. *But can you take the chance?* another voice, the voice of the eye, argued. If Mara had the information, what would she do with it? What could she *not* do with it? Christophe stared into the rearview mirror. His left eye, the yellow one, looked slyly back at him. *You must,* both voices rang out at once, *stop her from talking.* With a groan, he plunged his face into hands that he no longer recognized as his own.

23

If France ever held a contest for Most Glamorous *Boulangère,* Marie-Sylvette, née Méliès, of the Boulangerie Méliès in Brames, would have won hands-down. She was an imposing woman in her fifties who wore her hair swept up at the sides in two silver wings. She had a neat chin, full lips, dark, lustrous eyes, and exquisitely plucked eyebrows that expressed with the slightest twitch an impressive range of emotions. Her bosom thrust like a ship's prow beyond a tightly controlled tummy, for she never appeared without a girdle, and the whole of her moved grandly about on slim legs that ended in small feet shod in smart mid-heeled shoes.

Marie-Sylvette handled the shop front. Her husband, an enormously fat man named Thierry, did the baking. Thierry had started out as Madame's father's apprentice and had been a part of the establishment so long that most people forgot that his surname was not Méliès but Potdevin. Thierry rose at three every morning to make the day's pastries in a big electric oven: gâteaux and fruit tarts and colorful macaroons. He baked his bread—his speciality was a sourdough loaf that people from the surrounding area queued up to buy—in a great, traditional wood *four,* using as his fuel of preference walnut hulls, which imparted, according to him, a special flavor.

The lineup of patrons at the Boulangerie Méliès was larger than normal on that rainy Tuesday morning. Everyone wanted to talk about the ghastly murder. Also, everyone knew that Laurent Naudet, who was a distant cousin of Madame Méliès, came in first thing from the Gendarmerie where he was quartered to buy his breakfast croissants.

"I can't talk about it," the young man said, looking flustered as people crowded around him.

"They're saying he was killed by the Beast," a little man in carpet slippers shrilled. "They say it tore him open and ate his heart and liver. Just like it did that Piquet fellow."

"Dieu du ciel!" exclaimed a woman in a housecoat. She crossed herself, nearly letting slip the baguettes she held clamped under her arm.

Other voices chimed in:

"Ringuet's old spaniel has been missing for weeks, and Chabanas lost a lamb last week."

"It's the Sigoulane Beast, I tell you. We're not safe in our beds!"

"Non, non, et non!" Laurent cried loudly, throwing up his hands. "This is all nonsense. There is no Beast."

"So you say," boomed a deep voice. "Our lives could be in danger. And what are you lot doing about it? That's what I'd like to know."

"I assure you, Madame Barrage"—Laurent found himself sweating, although the morning was cool—"there's absolutely no danger to you." Madame Barrage, big, with arms like a logger, was more than a match for any beast.

"Oh, do leave the boy in peace," interceded Madame Méliès, taking pity on her young kinsman. "He has his job to do like the rest of us. Now, who's next? *Un demi-pain au levain,* did you say, Madame Vignot?"

Later that morning, Adjudant Compagnon looked up from his desk to see Laurent hovering in the doorway. The gendarme held some typed sheets in his hand.

"What is it, Naudet?" Compagnon barked. He had been up most of the night, had not shaved, and exuded a bitter smell of sweat and frustration. On top of having to assign personnel to help rout out this damned animal that was running amuck, he now had a murder on his hands. Also, the Police Judiciaire from Bergerac were breathing down his neck. The last thing he wanted was interference from that lot on his patch.

"*Procès-verbal* on our interview with Madame Tardieux, *mon adjudant.*" Laurent put the report on Compagnon's desk. The previous evening, he and Albert Batailler had been dispatched to Aurillac Manor to take a statement from Christophe de Bonfond because of his association with the dead man. The housekeeper had informed them that her employer was away. "She said he left last Tuesday, sir. She doesn't know where he is or when he's coming back. She said he often takes off without telling her."

Compagnon frowned. "What do you make of it?" He indicated a chair. Laurent sat down. The chair as usual was too low for him. He did not like to sprawl in the presence of his superior officer, so he perched on the edge of it with his knees rising up before him like two bony peaks.

"He could be off on business. He runs a publishing house. Editions Arobas. But I think it has more to do with the baby. De Bonfond locked himself in his room after they found it"—Laurent prudently omitted to say how he knew this—"and he may have just gone away to avoid the publicity."

"Well, I want to talk to him, Naudet. Get on to Editions Arobas. If he's really off on business, somebody's bound to know where he went. He was one of Fournier's clients, and that uncle of yours"—Compagnon said it grudgingly—"suggested we look into the possibility of blackmail. I think it's a bit premature myself, at least until I'm sure this Dunn woman isn't at the bottom of everything, but it doesn't do to leave stones unturned."

"People are awfully nervous about this death," Laurent thought it necessary to say. "Because of what happened to the body."

"No thanks to the media!" Compagnon shoved a copy of the morning paper—*Beast Strikes Again?*—across the desk.

Laurent shared his superior officer's sentiments. He believed in the feral-dog theory. Most people of sense did. He couldn't imagine Stéphanie, for example, going along with any of the other rubbish. But there were always those, like the patrons of the Boulangerie Méliès that morning, who were genuinely convinced that something worse was out there. Irresponsible journalism like this didn't help.

Laurent cleared his throat. "I also came to tell you, sir, that hunters are taking it on themselves to patrol the woods. There are groups of them operating in the Sigoulane Forest and Aurillac Ridge. They're practically tripping over each other." He made a rolling gesture with his hands to describe the willy-nilly nature of their activities.

"*Putain!*" groaned Compagnon. "That's all we need. Those morons pose more of a threat to public safety than any damned Beast."

The rain had stopped. Julian and Bernard were debating the placement of the electrical cable for the water pump when Denise and Antoine came down from the pavilion to inspect the work. It was the first time Julian had seen Denise since their recent strenuous coupling, and he greeted her with a certain amount of constraint. With her, however, it was business as usual. Sunday night might never have been.

"I thought this thing was supposed to be a waterfall," she snapped, taking in Bernard's efforts. "It looks like a mud puddle to me."

"This is the basin," Julian explained patiently. "Where the water collects to be recycled. The pump will be installed here and will drive the water up through rocks that we'll set in place to create the impression of a natural spring." He glanced at the father.

Antoine's quick eyes took in everything. "When will this be up and running?"

"End of the week. No problem."

"*Bon*," said the winemaker. He gave a jerk of the head that passed for a nod and strode off toward the parking area. A moment later, he drove off in the Twingo.

Denise, looking unconvinced, headed back to the pavilion. Julian took the opportunity to walk with her.

"Terrible thing, this Fournier business," he remarked. "Who do you think would have wanted him dead?"

"Lots of people, I expect. Your *petite amie*, for one." Denise said it without breaking stride. "I take it she's the Canadian woman who was with him the night he died?"

Julian was still stinging from Mara's anger of the night before, but he rose to her defense. "That doesn't mean she killed him. In fact, if I know Mara, she's probably doing everything she can to find out who did."

"Beating the gendarmes at their own game?"

"Maybe. She thinks the answer is somehow tied up with something Jean-Claude found out about Baby Blue."

Denise seemed amused. "They *say* she pushed him off the terrace in a lovers' quarrel."

He parried, "Was Jean-Claude the kind of person one had lovers' quarrels with?"

"I wouldn't know."

"Oh? I heard you were pretty friendly with him yourself at one time."

"You shouldn't believe everything you hear." Denise's cold, flat eyes gave nothing away. "Anyway, I was with you the night he died, if you recall."

Julian steeled himself. "But not all night. Where did you go, Denise, after you left my house?"

She faced him coolly. "Home," she said. "I have to start my day early, and I prefer to do it from my own bed."

As Denise walked away, Julian realized that, with eyes like hers, it was hard to know if she was lying or telling the truth.

24

Mara got out of bed, still swamped by the depressing thought that she really had been responsible for Jean-Claude's death. The sleeping pill she had taken the night before hadn't helped her sleep, it had simply made her brain fuzzy. She walked unsteadily into the kitchen, filled the coffeemaker, spooned grounds into a cone filter, and flipped the switch to "On." She leaned against the counter in a kind of stupor, staring unseeing as the dark liquid trickled into the receptacle. Gradually, she became aware of the coldness of the flagstone floor on her bare feet and the fact that the phone was ringing. It was Prudence, asking how she was. Awful, she told her truthfully, and, no, she didn't want company. She just needed to be alone. To put her life, which had been blown apart in the last twenty-four hours, back in order.

The coffee, hot and bitter, made her feel somewhat better. She poured herself a refill and drank it while she dressed. She slipped on a pair of rubber clogs and ran out over the wet grass to her studio. Patsy's reply, waiting for her when she switched on her computer, gave her a much-needed morale boost:

>My god, Mara. Of course you didn't kill the bastard. Did you hear him scream? Most people do when they fall from a height, you know. So if you didn't hear him scream, you didn't push him off. Period. Don't even consider a case of self-defense. It didn't happen like that. If the cops thought it had, they'd have you in custody. So keep your lid on, kid. A lot could have happened to

Jean-Claude between your leaving and his hitting the bottom of the ravine. I'll call you tomorrow. This needs voice-to-voice. Or, if you want hands-on, say so. I'll get on a plane and be there.

Patsy's commonsense assurance—Jean-Claude had *not* screamed—and unconditional offer of support was as good for the soul as chocolate cake, as comforting to the heart as hot pancakes in maple syrup on a frosty morning. Patsy went on:

As far as the other kind of werewolves are concerned, I'm talking about lycanthropes. These are real people who believe they trans-form into wolves. This means they see themselves as wolves and act like wolves, including howling, biting, and predation. The condition, called lycanthropy, is a clinically recognized psychi-atric disorder. If you want to know more, get in touch with Dr. Nathalie Thibaud at the psychiatric hospital near Cahors. She's France's leading authority on the subject. I've met her at a couple of conferences, and I'm sure she'll be willing to talk to you if you mention my name. She can tell you everything you ever wanted to know about the breed. Meantime, hang in there, kid. Don't let the gendarmes grind you down.
Hugs, Patsy.<

Mara wrote back:

>Patsy, thanks for the offer, but no need to hop a plane. I'm fine. Really. However, I wish I could be as sure as you about the cops. I was there, and I was seen leaving Jean-Claude's house in a hurry at the critical moment. I've got to be their prime suspect. If they haven't manacled me yet, it's only because Adjudant Com-pagnon, an awful man with bad skin and pop-eyes, is building his case. To be honest, you're the only one who doesn't believe I

killed Jean-Claude—or at least pushed him off the terrace and left him to be eaten by animals—and that includes Julian.

Mara thought with renewed bitterness about Julian's defection. There was no other word for it. He had blatantly shown her that he could not be relied on.

But if I didn't do it, who did? And why? So try this on for size. I told you about Jean-Claude's Gévaudan/Sigoulane Beast theory, as well as Paul's idea that our genial genealogist might have been trying his hand at blackmail. Supposing Jean-Claude, in threatening to reveal a werewolf, unwittingly hit on a lycanthrope?

Again she paused, reading on-screen the words she had just entered. She knew her hypothesis sounded far-fetched. But was it? She was convinced that Jean-Claude had believed in his werewolf idea, at least enough to try to profit from it. And Christophe, with his extreme family pride and horror of scandal, might well have reacted violently, especially if his antecedents were not as faultless as he liked to make out. Once again, she put her fingers to the keyboard:

Okay. I know exactly what you're going to say: before I begin criticizing the de Bonfond bloodline or concluding that Christophe killed Jean-Claude to keep him from revealing his lycanthropic alter-ego, I'm going to need proof. So what have I got? Unfortunately, nothing, apart from what Jean-Claude told me about the Gévaudan and Sigoulane Beasts and the de Bonfonds. However, who knows what I'll turn up with a bit of digging? In any case, it's better than sitting here feeling sorry for myself. Leave it to the gendarmes, you say? Since they think I did it, I

can hardly count on them to get me off the hook. And that's the other thing. The only way I can see to clear my name, let alone continue to make a living out here, is to find out what really happened. I mean, who wants to hire a suspected murderer to redesign their kitchen? Werewolf or not, I think the answer is somehow bound up with Christophe. Wherever he is, he must have heard about Jean-Claude's death by now. So why hasn't he come forward? What's he hiding, or more to the point, why *is he* hiding? *But, as you're sure to point out, I'm going to need a lot more evidence than I have before I go public with accusations. I suppose that's where I'll have to start. Getting the evidence.*
Wish me luck,
Mara<

Mara got to the public library in Le Buisson at half past one. Even in the short walk from *le parking* to the entrance, she was sure she caught the odd sideways glance, saw heads come together as she passed. Really, the media might as well have named her outright as the person questioned in regard to Jean-Claude's death. She was generally known in these parts as *la canadienne*. There weren't that many other Canadian women in the region. She kept her sunglasses on while she moved furtively among the bookshelves.

On leaving the library, she remembered that she needed food. She slipped into a mini-mart she normally never used a few minutes before closing. The produce bins contained only the wilted leftovers no one else would buy, and the single staff person, a youth with spiky hair, was unconcernedly flipping off banks of lights, so that she had to finish her shopping almost in the dark. Dark was fine by her. She was glad, as she hurried out to her car, that it had begun to rain again. Bad weather obscured things.

When she returned home, she picked up a phone message from Patsy:

"Listen, Mara, I'm not saying don't get your evidence. But if you're thinking about chasing down a real live lycanthrope, think again. These folks are potentially dangerous. My advice to you is to stay out of it and let the cops do their job. Stay right out of it, do you hear?"

The sharp concern in Patsy's voice brought a grim smile of determination to Mara's lips. She did not call Patsy back, knowing she would only get more of the same. She heated up the remains of the morning's coffee and drank it off. Then she sat down to read. She read until eight o'clock, when she prepared a package of instant vegetable soup. While she sipped it, she watched, with a kind of mindless, fatalistic fascination, the evening news coverage of Jean-Claude's death.

"Accident? Murder? Or something more horrific?" a woman reporter cried shrilly into the camera. She stood in the little square in Sigoulane against a backdrop of houses. Had the same animal that had killed André Piquet and attacked Clémentine Dupuy also fed on Jean-Claude Fournier's cadaver? Or had the thing leaped at him, causing him to fall to his death, before devouring his body?

Mara sat up. It was Paul's theory, and, journalistic hyperbole or not, she liked hearing it broadcast for general consumption. Let the Sigoulane Beast or whatever it was take the blame.

The reporter went on, conveniently blurring the line between animal attacks and murder: "This death represents the latest in a string of macabre and terrifying incidents that have rocked not only the region, but all of France." She noted that Colline Basse, Les Ronces, and the other places where the animal had been active were clustered near the heavily forested north end of the valley. However, Tirac, where Jean-Claude Fournier's house was situated, was some seventeen kilometers away to the east. Was the thing shifting its area of operation? The Sigoulane Forest was linked to other forests of the region by wooded corridors through which a predator could easily move. Residents in surrounding areas were warned to take precautions. The reporter also pointed out, with ominous overtones, that the Colline Basse and Les Ronces attacks had occurred at or around the full moon.

She wrapped up: "Here in the valley, where werewolves have a certain track record, people are talking openly about the return of the Sigoulane Beast, a legendary werewolf that terrorized the area during the 1700s and 1800s. Gendarmes are urging calm, but that's unlikely to happen until they trap the thing responsible and, more important, find out what *really* happened to Jean-Claude Fournier."

Mara laughed bitterly.

The *pendule* struck eleven. Its harsh chime, reverberating unpleasantly through the house, jarred her nerves. Mara made the decision then and there to sell the clock off as quickly as possible, even at a loss. She pulled off her glasses and leaned back in her chair. Jazz had long ago retired for the night. Around her, spread across her dining-room table, were books from which she had gleaned the basic facts about her subject.

In the course of three years between 1764 and 1767, 230 Beast attacks were recorded in Le Gévaudan, of which 121 were fatal. The majority of the victims were women and children, whom the Beast in some cases stripped of their clothing. In one instance, with a kind of horrific coquetry, the Beast left a woman propped up against a tree, her hat placed jauntily on her head. The Beast partially ate many of the bodies, often selecting the internal organs. It also seemed to delight in mutilating its victims. Some were decapitated, their heads deposited at a distance from the bodies. The Beast seemed invulnerable to guns, spears, pitchforks, and all other kinds of weapons. Some witnesses claimed it wore protective armor. Others remarked on the uncanny intelligence with which it managed to elude every trap set for it, spurning poisoned bait and avoiding the parties of beaters and hunters who tried to flush it out. Finally, it appeared to be able to cover great distances with supernatural speed.

All of the books sought to unravel the true nature of the Beast, which to this day remained a mystery. Eyewitness reports (the murderous career of the Beast was documented in parish records and written statements) described it as an animal resembling a huge wolf or dog, reddish with black markings. This did not prevent subsequent theorists from suggesting that it was a scourge of God; a pack of wolves (a notion supported by the fact that the attacks occurred over roughly 150 square kilometers of mountainous, forested terrain, a big area for a lone animal to cover); a giant wolverine; a hyena escaped from a menagerie; or one or several madmen dressed in wolf skins. Related to this, Mara had also found frequent reference to a deeply rooted popular belief that the Beast was a werewolf, an idea that drew strength from contemporary accounts of a wild-looking, hairy stranger seen in places where attacks had subsequently occurred.

A smaller group of writers espoused the idea that the Beast was a canid of some sort that had been trained to kill by a sadistic human owner. She considered this theory seriously, turning over its possibilities. Several sources inculpated members of the feared Chastel family, working together or alone, perhaps with the complicity of the decadent Count de Morangiès, with whom the Chastels were associated. Well, they were off the hook, Mara concluded, if what Jean-Claude had said about Xavier de Bonfond was true.

In fact, it was Jean Chastel who dispatched the Beast with a silver bullet on 19 June 1767. It had to be remembered, however, that the Beast had also purportedly been killed by the King's gunbearer, Antoine de Beauterne, twenty-one months previously. Was the animal that Jean Chastel shot really the Beast? All that Mara could determine with any certainty was that the attacks had ceased after that date.

And had begun five years later over three hundred kilometers away, in the Sigoulane Valley. Initially, livestock had been the main targets. Wolves might have accounted for all of the depredations, but for the fact that frightened shepherds and farmers claimed that the thing, a large wolflike creature, rose up monstrously on two legs when confronted. Soon people were in no doubt that a werewolf was at work. Attacks on humans began in 1775, although at a much less murderous rate than in Le Gévaudan: four children and two women over the next two decades. The attacks ceased in 1810. Peace returned to the valley for forty-nine years.

Then, in the fall of 1859, the terror recommenced. Three children disappeared, believed to have been taken by the Beast. Their bodies were never recovered. Then a fourteen-year-old boy was found with his throat ripped out. An old washerwoman known as la Claudine was killed on the road between Buffevent and L'Espeyre, with her throat so savagely bitten that her head was nearly severed from her body. Then, three weeks before Christmas 1871, the naked body of a seven-year-old girl was discovered in the woods below Aurillac Manor. Her throat, too, had been torn open. The main difference between the new attacks and the earlier ones was that no definitive sightings of a wolflike animal were reported. The thing had struck, leaving no witnesses and no trace of its presence.

All of this Mara had read in a thin monograph recounting the career of the Sigoulane Beast. The work, based on parish records and published in 1995, had been written by Jean-Claude Fournier. Was a single creature of supernatural longevity responsible? Or had the Sigoulane Valley been plagued by two separate Beasts? The author had favored the latter idea. He had not, at that point, made the connection with the de Bonfonds.

The phone rang. Mara, pulled out of her thoughts, checked her watch. At this time of night, it was surely not Patsy, who was aware of the six-hour lag between France and New York.

"Hello?"

There was a live presence at the other end of the line, that much she knew, but no response.

"Patsy, is that you? Julian?" The sudden, steady note of the dial tone sounded in her ear. Mara replaced the receiver, feeling disappointed and annoyed. She had been the target of either a prank or a wrong number. Obscene callers usually breathed heavily or said lewd things.

She was exhausted. She went into the bedroom and sat down heavily on the edge of the bed. Jazz, stretched lengthwise across it, squinted up at her against the glare of the overhead light. She fondled his big head. He dropped it heavily into her lap.

"I need sleep," she muttered as she pushed him over to one side. "No snoring. No farting. No barfing in the night. Got that?" She kicked away her shoes, pulled off her T-shirt and unbuckled her belt, an expensive item with a heavy ceramic buckle that she'd bought in a trendy boutique just the week before. It dropped with a thud to the floor. She looked at it stupidly.

"My god," she whispered as the realization hit her brain. "The wolf belt."

W hat wolf belt?" Julian mumbled. She had jerked him out of a deep sleep, and he was struggling to surface. It was a bit like swimming through golden syrup.

She went on talking rapidly in his ear. "Jean-Claude showed it to me and then rolled it up and put it on the trolley. But when I went back, it wasn't there."

"Hmm. Maybe you just didn't see it. I mean, you said the terrace was a mess. It would have been easy to miss." Not that long ago, she had ordered him from her house for doubting her. He wondered if he was putting his foot in it again. However, she seemed to have forgotten all about it.

"Not something like that. It really gave me the creeps. Don't you see, Julian, he must have put it away. He was very careful with it. He said it wasn't the kind of thing he wanted to leave lying around. Compagnon didn't believe me about my cell phone. Well, he'll have to listen to me about the belt. If the police find it in the house, it will prove Jean-Claude was still alive after I left him!"

25

Adjudant Compagnon had just returned to brigade headquarters from a meeting called by the company commander. Other heads of brigade from neighboring cantons, an agent from the Ministry of Ecology, and someone from the departmental prefect's office had also been present. Another sighting of the feral dog or wolf or whatever it was had been reported the previous evening, near Rezac. Several brigades would assist in yet another *battue* of the woods between Rezac and Sigoulane. Laurent Naudet intercepted his superior as he entered the building.

"Just took a call from Madame Dunn, *mon adjudant*. She wanted to know if we'd found some kind of belt made out of animal skin at the Fournier house. She called it a wolf belt." Laurent explained with slight embarrassment, "It's supposed to turn the wearer into a werewolf."

Compagnon snorted and kept walking. Laurent followed him into his office.

"She said Fournier brought it out onto the terrace to show it to her on Sunday night. Apparently he was very interested in werewolves. She said she remembers him rolling it up and putting it on the drinks trolley, but she didn't see it anywhere on the terrace when she returned for her phone. She thinks this proves Fournier was alive after she left him because he must have taken it back inside the house. I went through the *procès-verbal*, sir. I found no mention of a belt of that description anywhere on the premises."

Compagnon pulled off his *képi* and tossed it on the desk. His carroty hair stood up on end. "That's because she's lying, Naudet. She's a complicated liar, that one. Tried the same thing with her cell phone, if you recall. And the row the neighbor said he overheard. She says there was no fight, but I sense she slices the truth very fine. Well"—Compagnon unbuttoned his jacket and gave his trousers a hitch—"let her have her head. She'll try one fancy trick too many. We'll have her in the end."

The phone rang. Compagnon scooped up the receiver with a big paw and moved behind his desk to sit down. *"Oui?"* He was silent for a moment, a thundercloud gathering on his face. "Say that again?" he demanded. While he listened, his nostrils flared dangerously. Then, "You're sure? Of course it does," he barked. "Okay, okay. Just keep me informed." He dropped the receiver into its cradle.

"That was Lamartine," he told the sergeant grimly. "He says the fall broke Fournier's neck all right, but that's not what killed him. He didn't spot it right away because the destruction of tissue and bone by whatever ate him was so massive. But something about the way the hyoid was fractured led him to examine the eyes more closely. He found petechiae in the conjunctiva. He thinks Fournier was strangled. Fournier's throat was destroyed, but he found marks on the back of the neck that suggest a straplike object. Madame Dunn could still have done the pushing, but either she or someone else climbed down there afterward and finished the poor *bougre* off."

Naudet took a deep breath. "The wolf belt, sir. Maybe that's what was used to strangle him."

The orange eyebrows leaped. "Get that Dunn woman down here, Naudet," Compagnon bellowed. "I want a statement and an exact description of that belt. Then you and Batailler go back to Fournier's place. Look for it. Search his closets and drawers. It might have been left in among his clothing, where it wouldn't be noticed. Comb the ravine and the area around the house. And talk to the neighbors again. I want a full report on anything that moved in the area Sunday night. Someone's bound to have seen something. We need to make progress with this case. The PJ boys are sniffing around like hungry wolves"—he winced at the unintended allusion—"and I want them to know we have things firmly in hand."

26

'm off now," said Thérèse. "Stéphanie is driving me." The housekeeper stood in the doorway leading from the library into the adjacent grand salon. She carried her coat over one arm, a canvas
valise in the other hand. She was going to her sister's in Gourdon.
She had heard the Wailing Ghost again the night before and refused to stay on any longer alone in the house.

Mara looked up from the library table where she was working
her way through the de Bonfond archives. She was doing it methodically. First the family papers. Then Cécile's diary.

"Thérèse, are you sure you don't know where Christophe is?"
Earlier she had spent an hour giving Laurent Naudet a description
of the wolf belt and its history, and the rest of the morning convincing a twitchy *juge d'instruction* that she would hardly be likely
to raise the matter of the belt if she had used it as a murder
weapon. Christophe's whereabouts was an increasingly pressing
concern for her. The examining magistrate did not believe that she
had gone to see Jean-Claude solely on de Bonfond business. He
thought they had been lovers.

"I already told you. And I told the police. He never says where
he goes, and it's not my place to ask."

"But he's disappeared before?"

"When he's in one of his moods."

"Well, did he do it in April, around the fifth of the month?"

"I don't keep track of him. I have my work to do."

"Yes, but this is important, Thérèse. Please try to remember."

"Why do you want to know?"

"Just answer the question."

The housekeeper looked sulky. "He might have. He was away for a few days around that time. Although what business it is of yours, I can't see." She shifted her grip on the valise. "Well, I can't stand here wasting time. I'll leave you to it. But if you plan on coming back here, you'd better let Didier know. He doesn't like dogs"—she jabbed her chin at Jazz, sleeping beneath the table— "his eyesight's not that good anymore, and"—an oblique look of many meanings—"he has his Babette."

The woman was gone before Mara thought to ask who or what Babette was.

Several hours later, Mara came to the conclusion that, whatever she thought of Jean-Claude, the genealogist had known his stuff and had done his homework. He had undertaken an exhaustive search—verified births, marriages, and deaths against church and parish records; looked up cadastral plans and census and military records; checked facts with library and other archival sources; and searched newspaper files for relevant citations, photographs, and articles. Séverine's family (Bonfonds without the "de") were well-to-do Huguenots whose holdings in the Sigoulane Valley had waxed and waned with the Wars of Religion and the persecution of Protestants in the region. Aurillac, built in 1505, had been the family seat, and in this sense, Christophe was correct—the house had been in the family, at least Séverine's side of it, for five hundred years. Early information on Xavier was scant. The village of Paulhac in Le Gévaudan was given as his birthplace, and there were mentions of a Xavier Lebrun who had worked in the area as an official for *la gabelle,* the infamous salt tax. In 1770, Xavier, le Baron de Bonfond, appeared in Sigoulane. After his marriage to his cousin Séverine, he proved himself to have been a man of ambition and ability, turning the tide of her family's fortunes, then on the brink of disaster, almost single-handedly. Séverine converted to Catholicism before she died of puerperal fever, and Aurillac slowly recovered its former prosperity. Everything was neatly filed by subject and date. There was nothing under werewolves.

One fat folder contained the minutiae of daily life at Aurillac over past centuries: a remedy for goiter; orders to the cook and to the washerwomen who came up from the village; lists of wages; bills of sale; notes of purchase of livestock; accounts of hunts (probably written in Hugo's hand) itemizing the numbers of *sangliers* and *cerfs* killed; seating plans and menus for banquets, including one flagged by Jean-Claude as being the occasion of Hugo's thirty-sixth birthday, the day he was thrown from his horse. According to his funerary notice, Hugo died seventeen days later.

Moving into more recent times, Mara leafed through photocopies of newspaper articles and rotogravures: Dieudonné and Léonie, née Boursicaut, in front of the Bordeaux *mairie* on their wedding day; Dieudonné in 1921 being feted at the Salle Municipale in Brames for his development of the revolutionary inking technique that Jean-Claude had mentioned and that had so advanced the de Bonfond fortunes.

Mara leaned back in her chair and let her focus drift to the middle distance. A livid sunset lit the western windows of the library. So far she had found nothing suspicious in the de Bonfond family archives. Certainly no accounts of howling at the moon or evidence of shape-shifting or uncontrolled growth of bodily hair. With a sigh, she returned to her task, taking up yellowed packets of documents tied with ribbon: notarial acts, for the notary was an integral part of French life then as now. She scanned wills, bequests, and land dispositions. One document related to Dominique de Bonfond's provisions for Odile; another set out Hugo's provisions for Henriette. The terms were similar: the wife, if she bore a surviving male heir, received an annuity and a life interest in the estate, but only on condition that she continued to live at Aurillac in a state of pious widowhood. French succession law then as now was governed by bloodline, and it was only recently that a surviving spouse shared with children an entrenched right to a deceased person's estate.

And finally, there were notes, written in Jean-Claude's flowing script, of names, dates, places, and assertions that he had not been able to verify. They ran backward from 1730, the year of the false baron's birth, and were undoubtedly the source of the genealogist's conclusion that three-quarters of the de Bonfond family tree had been fabricated. She was amused to see the occasional strenuous objection: "Nothing listed in this regard!"; "Impossible! Facts are widely divergent!" It was almost as if the genealogist had taken a perverse satisfaction in finding no substantiation to the de Bonfond claims.

It was now growing dark. Outside, a wind was building up. Mara heard it gusting against the glass panes. She rose to turn on a standing lamp. It filled the library with a comfortable, rosy glow. Jazz moaned his hunger. Dinnertime had come and gone, according to his stomach, but she returned to her reading, too engrossed to care about food. Eventually, Jazz's noises took on a new, more pressing note. She gave in.

"Okay, monster." She stood up, pulled off her glasses, stretched, and let him out. The dog disappeared immediately into the garden. The wind, redolent of impending rain, ruffled her hair as she stood in the doorway that opened directly from the library onto the rear terrace. Below her, the stone dolphin, dribbling into its pool, was a dark, indistinct shape. She gave the dog sufficient time, then whistled him back. Jazz came reluctantly, looking reproachful.

Mara noted with surprise that it was nearly half past eight. She assembled Jean-Claude's notes and replaced them in the cabinet with every intention of packing up for the night. She would come back another time to tackle Cécile's diary. Yet she hesitated. There was one thing she wanted to check before she left.

"Fifteen more minutes," she promised her dog and put her glasses on again.

Cécile's diary was contained in eleven folders, dated by year, running from 1861 to 1871. Skimming through a few, she quickly saw what Jean-Claude had complained about. The diary was more a series of personal notes, with little sense of coherence or chronological order. The genealogist had organized the material as best he could, sequencing the unbound sheets according to the writer's references to verifiable events, religious holidays, birthdays, and seasonal descriptions. As he had said, much of it was guesswork because most of the entries were undated. The handwriting was large and scrawling. "Unformed" was the word that came to Mara's mind. Or "unfulfilled."

In the 1870 folder, which Jean-Claude had shown her, Mara read through dull and unvarying accounts of daily life at Aurillac. The slaughter of a pig merited note as an important event. Mara got the sense of a clumsy, susceptible young woman, the object of perceived or real slights. Cécile had penned, somewhat pathetically:

Maman dismisses me as unimportant, Papa thinks me stupid, the servants treat me as if I do not exist, and Hugo uses me brutally after his fashion. Even Eloïse scorns me. Yesterday she said I sit my horse like a sack of potatoes. The only creature who cares at all for me is Argent, my mare, and her Maman wants to sell to the knacker.

The material also attested to Odile's meanness:

We dined on haunch of mutton this evening. It was the first time these three days that Maman allowed meat to be served. If Hugo did not hunt, we would have nothing to put under the tooth. Maman guards each sou as if her soul depended on it.

Later entries contained what Mara had hoped to find: an account of the summer visit to Paris, undoubtedly a high point in Cécile's life. Hugo and his father had been there since March. Odile, Cécile, and Eloïse had followed in June. "We went," Cécile had written with naïve candor, "only because Maman heard of Papa and Hugo's gaming, which she fears will bankrupt us, but for which I was glad, else I would not have seen Paris. Maman and Eloïse traveled up first-class. I went third with Marie, the maid, to oversee the luggage." Mara cross-checked with the family tree and concluded that more than gaming had been going on. Hugo had married Henriette in August of that year.

Of greatest interest to her were entries on a certain Armand Vigier, one of Hugo's friends and a captain in Napoleon III's army. Cécile's acquaintance with him had been struck while the women were driving in the Bois de Boulogne:

> He bowed as they rode past, and then he and Hugo turned back so that Hugo could make an introduction. I very much admired the way he spurred his horse, a spirited black, to canter round and round our carriage. He has a very fine mustache, and I learned that he comes from Tours. He addressed himself mainly to Maman, but I noticed that he kept his eyes on me, for all that Eloïse simpered at him under her bonnet. He addressed me as no other man has ever done, as if I were not plain.

There were accounts of several meetings with the captain during the space of two months, all in public places and closely chaperoned by Odile or Eloïse. Nevertheless, the captain had managed to get his point across:

> Armand, for he has asked me to call him by his given name, hung back a moment to let Maman and Eloïse go on ahead. Then he took my hand and asked had I an *amant,* to which I said

no. He asked if I could love one such as him. I could hardly speak, the blood rushed so to my face.

But Cécile's romance was doomed from the start. Maman interceded once it became clear that the captain had no money, and the family, except for Hugo, returned to the Dordogne in July. In any case, the captain was mobilized that same month and died soon after fighting the Prussians at Sedan. A grief-stricken Cécile had mourned:

He is taken from me, cruelly and untimely. My grief is past bearing. I have spoken with my sister about taking the veil as she has done. She doubts I have the calling, but if I do not give myself to God, what will I do? I am left with nothing.

Except a swelling belly, Mara thought. Reason enough to enter a convent. For Mara had found the references to the "stealthy visits" that Jean-Claude had read out to her. They were undated, stand-alone pieces that the genealogist had filed with the pages on the Paris summer. Mara decided that the captain, while alive, must have been very resourceful or extremely determined. With all the close surveillance and so little time, it was a wonder that the pair had managed to get it on at all. In one vivid passage, Cécile described what Mara took to be her first, rather horrific sexual encounter with her mustachioed lover:

It was my first. I remember it now as clearly as if it were yesterday. Dear God! The flow of blood! And the pain. I was terrified, for I understood nothing then. I thought my stomach had come apart, and it made me think of the time they bled the pig for the making of *boudin*. He had come to me in the night, stealthily [that word again], as was his wont, and I felt certain that he would not desire me thus. But he pressed his hand over my mouth, saying that he liked it that way, and if I held my tongue, he would be gentle with me. It was the only time that he was so.

The passage made Armand Vigier appear a brute. But it was curiously disjunctive as well, relating, it seemed, to an event from a more distant past. Mara was also puzzled by the implied volume of hymenal blood and the phrase "as was his wont," which suggested more frequent visitations and easier access than Captain Vigier could have enjoyed. Studying the words more closely, she began to see another interpretation, one which Jean-Claude, as a man, might well have overlooked. "It was my first" and "I thought my stomach had come apart" did not have to refer to the rupturing of a maidenhead. Could this not be Cécile's account of her first menstruation? In which case, Jean-Claude had wrongly linked it with Cécile's army captain. Viewed in this light, the passage strongly suggested that the stealthy visitations had begun long before Cécile had gone to Paris and that they had more likely occurred within the precincts of her own home. But who was he who came to her in the night, who "liked it that way" and had promised gentleness, but just the once? One person came to Mara's mind: Hugo, whom Cécile had accused of "using her brutally." Had he been subjecting his youngest sister to systematic rape since childhood?

Frowning, Mara rose and walked over to Cécile's unfortunate portrait. The terrified girl had grown into a dispirited female with a low forehead, her father's eyes, and an undershot jaw. Her olive-green gown framed an uninteresting décolletage, and her hands, encircling a temperamental-looking brindled pug, were large. The sitter, probably then in her mid-twenties, used to a lifetime of abuse and with little hope of marriage, looked resentfully conscious of her unloveliness and slightly mad.

"You bastard," she said aloud to Hugo's painted self, hanging opposite.

Farther down the wall, Xavier drew her with his wolfish glare. She moved to stand squarely before him, glaring back, as if by doing so she was challenging the whole of the unpleasant de Bonfond clan. *"Sang Es Mon Drech."* The scroll declared its bearer's self-proclaimed right to blood. A thought struck her. She scanned the bookshelves and eventually found a French-Occitan dictionary. She opened it and ran her finger down the page for the Occitan equivalent of the word *loup-garou*. It was, she learned, *leberon*. She almost laughed aloud at the irony of it. Despite his unpleasant features, Xavier, it seemed, had a sense of humor. As for Baby Blue—she sighed inwardly—if he was Cécile's bastard, he was not a love child; instead the product of that age-old, sordid family pastime, incest.

Mara suddenly had no desire to read the remaining pages of the 1870 folder. The library with its handsome architectural features felt somehow oppressive and slightly menacing, as if the book-lined walls and hanging portraits had slyly closed in on her as she sat in her lonely pool of light. The rest of the space about her was in shadow. To her left, the doorway leading into the grand salon gaped black and uninviting.

It was then that she heard it—a distant wail that reverberated through the house like a cat in an echo chamber. With a low growl, Jazz lumbered to his feet, hackles rising. Mara rose, too, gripping the edge of the table. She strained her ears to trace the source of the cry. Perhaps it had not come from the house after all but from outside. A night bird, she told herself, and realized that she had been holding her breath. The unexpected proximity of the next sound nearly caused her to scream. It was soft, like a drawn-out sigh, coming from the darkness of the adjoining salon. Slowly, Mara turned terrified eyes to the doorway.

"Thérèse?" she croaked. Had the housekeeper returned unexpectedly?

A sharp crack from another direction caused her to wheel

about. The exterior door of the library flew open. A dark, narrow object wavered about in the opening. It took Mara a second to recognize it for what it was, and the threat it represented. With a scream, she threw herself down behind the table.

"For god's sake, Didier, don't shoot!"

You oughtn't to be here," the gardener shrilled, every bit as frightened as she. "He's gone. She's off to her sister's. I see a light. Babette here doesn't take kindly to strangers in the house." He waved his shotgun, and again Mara ducked.

"I'm sorry, Didier. I should have told you. But I'm not a stranger. You know me."

"Babette doesn't," the old man insisted. "And she doesn't like dogs." During this interchange, Jazz, who was not an attack dog despite his pit-bull ancestry, had approached and was nosing the old man's knee tentatively.

"What do you think you're doing here anyway, in the middle of the night?" Didier's tone was still aggrieved, but he pushed Jazz away with the muzzle of the shotgun before lowering it to the floor. Mara breathed more easily and stood up.

"I'm looking for information on the de Bonfonds," she told him honestly. "Anything that will help clear up Jean-Claude Fournier's murder."

"Him!" The gardener scowled and stepped fully into the room, pulling the door shut behind him since it was raining outside. His jacket was spotted with water. "Always poking his nose where it didn't belong. Asking questions."

"Questions? What kind of questions?"

"Daft things about the family, such as was no business of his. Nor yours, either. Now, if I was you, I'd go home and leave well enough alone. And take this animal with you." Babette's steely snout came up again.

"All right." Mara needed no further urging to put away Cécile's diary and gather up her things. But she made a mental note: one way or another, she was coming back to find out what it was Jean-Claude had been after.

Didier marched her at gunpoint through the salon, innocent of specters now that the light had been turned on. Had she really heard something in there? As he ushered her out the front door, she said: "Didier, I heard a noise just a little while ago. A kind of wailing. Did you hear it?"

Up close she could see stubble on his chin and the milky circles around his irises, smell his odor, an old man's whiff of stale urine.

"Wailing?" he said, giving the word a full measure of contempt. "No wailing around here. Unless it was done by that hound of yours."

27

Le Coquelicot was a ramshackle eatery situated in the humble delta of the Rauze, a minor tributary of the Dordogne. It sold ice creams, drinks, and *frites,* served at little tables set out on a silty beach under the trees. Mara arrived at a little past four. Julian was waiting for her, a canoe, which he had rented from the concession there, already loaded in his van. She left her car in *le parking* and climbed in beside him. They would drive to some point on the main valley road, put the canoe in the water, and paddle downstream. That much she knew.

What she had not realized was that the Rauze drained the Sigoulane Valley, running north-south along the western foot of Aurillac Ridge. Normally a shallow stream sliding sluggishly in a wide bed, it was in full spate at the moment from the recent heavy rains. Julian drove until he found a spot at the north end of the valley where the road came close enough to the stream to let them put directly into the water.

"I wish you'd tell me what this is all about," said Mara as they carried the canoe between them to the bank.

"You'll see."

"But why do we have to go by boat?"

"Because according to Didier, where I want to take you is inaccessible by foot right now."

"Well, at least explain how he comes into it."

"He was the one who told me about it. He's full of odd bits of information, is old Didier."

They pushed off, Julian paddling stern, Mara in the bow. Wisely, they had left the dogs at home. Jazz had never been in a canoe, and Bismuth, according to Julian, would probably try to dig his way out through the bottom.

"Are you supposed to do it like that?" Mara called over her shoulder, referring to something Julian called a J-stroke. She, rummaging deep in her Canadian Girl Guide past, was not so sure.

"Do it like what?"

"Well, flick your oar out of the water quite so hard."

"It's called finishing the stroke." The aluminum craft bonged hollowly each time his paddle struck the side. "The rental fellow showed me how. It's what keeps us going straight."

"We're wobbling."

"We're not. We're dead on course."

"Then how come we point left one minute and right the next?"

"You must be overpulling."

"I'm not."

"Look," said Julian in exasperation, because they were in fact zigzagging, "both of us have to work as an efficient, well-coordinated team."

After that they paddled silently, if somewhat jerkily. Eventually, they realized that the current was strong enough to let them drift at a leisurely pace downstream without any paddling at all.

think it must be around here," Julian said, gazing up at the ridge towering above them, as if looking for markers. "In fact, that may be the spot we're looking for, just up ahead." The canoe slid slowly beneath a great, overhanging cliff.

They beached on a narrow strip of shingle that in a drier season would have been a wide, stony shore. Julian jumped out and began exploring the base of the cliff, wading heedlessly in water up to his knees. He quickly found the opening of a cave, partly obscured by overhanging bushes.

"I'm afraid it's a bit wet," he said. "The stream's riding a lot higher than normal. Hope you don't mind."

"Do I have a choice?"

"Er—no."

In fact, they had to walk through water for only the first few meters of the cave. The floor of it sloped upward, and they were soon standing dry in a dim, circular rock chamber. The air had a heavy, unpleasant smell.

"Julian, why are we here? Are there bats in this cave?"

"According to Didier, this place is called the Wolf Cave because it's where, legend has it, *loups-garous* used to gather when the moon was full. Given you're so into werewolves, I thought you'd be interested in seeing it." He had a flashlight and was sweeping the beam of it across the cave walls.

"I am," she conceded. She looked up. The cave roof seemed to shift. Bats.

"Aha," he said. "Follow me. The thing I really wanted to check out"—he disappeared suddenly, leaving her in semidarkness with nothing but the echo of his voice—"is this tunnel, which apparently runs straight under Aurillac Ridge and directly up into the cellar of Aurillac Manor."

"It does what?" Mara hurried after him, slipping sideways through a narrow opening in the rock. The tunnel, picked out by Julian's flashlight, ran blackly before her, piercing solid limestone.

"That's right. As best as I can make out, it's at least a kilometer and a half long." The flashlight bounced off sloping walls that gleamed with moisture. "During the Occupation, it was a hideout for Resistance fighters. But originally it must have been constructed for some other purpose."

"I think you're right," Mara affirmed, and told Julian of Aurillac's Huguenot origins. "The Bonfonds, as they were called then, must have built it as an escape route. The Wars of Religion during the sixteenth century were pretty bloody, and Protestants generally got the worst of it." She also told him Jean-Claude's tale of the man bathing in the river who transformed into a wolf, and described Xavier's supernatural ability to disappear at will and reappear in other places.

"I wonder if this was how he moved about," she speculated, staying on Julian's heels to keep close to the source of light. She did not like the darkness and the way the tunnel walls leaned in on her. "If someone saw him and that dog of his outside this cave on a moonlit night, you can understand how the idea of a man transforming into a werewolf might have taken hold."

After another minute she said, "Julian, you don't suppose Christophe used this tunnel as well?"

"D'you mean when he disappeared? Not likely. His car's gone. I think he just walked out of the house and drove away. Anyway, if he had, you saw for yourself he'd have needed a boat." Fifty meters farther along he said, "Besides, he couldn't have got past this."

Mara peered over his shoulder. The flashlight illuminated a rock fall. The way was entirely choked off by a wall of debris.

They were shoving off into the stream again when Julian stood up suddenly. The canoe rocked dangerously. Mara gave a small shriek and grabbed both gunnels. Her paddle slid away. She made a lunge for it, causing them to dip even more precariously.

"You made me drop my paddle," she yelled, as she leaned out to retrieve it from the water. "Are you trying to sink us?"

He sat down quickly. "Look." He pointed to something green and leafy growing at the top of the opposite shore. "Aconite. Monkshood."

They were across the stream in a few swift strokes.

"That reminds me—" Mara began, but he was already out of the canoe and scrambling up the rocky bank. Only his legs were visible as he investigated the plant.

"No Devil's Clog." He slithered down again in a shower of

stones. "No orchids of any kind. But Aconite likes stream margins. There may be more around here. I'll come back and have a thorough look around another time. I'll walk the Rauze end to end if I have to."

"I meant to tell you, Julian," Mara resumed as he climbed back in the canoe. "I read something about another kind of Aconite the other day."

"Oh yes?" He resumed his bonging J-stroke. Their craft slid into the main part of the current.

"This one has yellow flowers. *Aconitum vulparia.* Wolfsbane. In French, *aconit tue-loup,* because the plant was used to poison wolves."

He was silent for a moment, letting his paddle trail in the water. "Damn. I wonder if that's what Didier meant. I'll have to ask him. Trouble is, I don't know my Aconite well enough to tell the yellow from the purple without the flowers, and they won't bloom for another month. But if it was Wolfsbane and not Monkshood they planted wherever they found Devil's Clog, that means Didier's old ones must have somehow associated Devil's Clog with wolves." He stared into a waving bed of water weeds slipping away beneath them.

"Maybe wolves liked it," Mara suggested. "In the same way cats go for catnip."

"Hmm. I've been digging through my books, but I didn't see anything like that. I found out that *Cypripediums* can cause a rash in humans. I also learned that they've been used medicinally for centuries to treat everything from neuralgia to cancer. Many species have a narcotic effect similar to opium."

"Do you smoke it?"

"No, you take it as a tincture made from the dried roots. Apparently, it's a powerful sedative, unless you overdose, in which case it can bring on hallucinations."

"Hallucinations?" Now it was Mara's turn to stop paddling.

She craned around. "Julian, what if Xavier and Hugo used your orchid as an hallucinogenic?"

He snorted. "What, to enhance their werewolf transformations?"

She gestured impatiently. "And why not? They could have heard about some kind of high you could get with it. Or they could have experimented with it themselves. Folk medicine is full of this kind of thing."

"But it sounds like a tincture of *Cypripedium* would be more likely to put you to sleep, or into a trance, not drive you to bite people's throats out."

"You don't know that. Maybe *Cypripedium incognitum* acts like LSD. Now, if the Sigoulanese suspected the de Bonfonds were involved in the Beast killings, and if your orchid came to be associated with Xavier and Hugo—say, people caught them picking the plant under a full moon—then there's your explanation for why it came to be called Devil's Clog. It's a pretty sinister-sounding name, when you think of it. *And* that could be your connection with Wolfsbane. It was the locals' way of warding off evil."

Julian took this in. After a moment he said, "But if *Cypripedium incognitum* is Devil's Clog and is associated with werewolves, why did Cécile embroider it on the shawl? I mean, wouldn't it have been like going public with a dark family secret? And anyway, if people really thought the de Bonfonds were linked to the Sigoulane Beast, you'd think they'd have done something about it." His paddle also hung motionless over the gunnel.

"The de Bonfonds were a pretty powerful family, don't forget. And maybe it was nothing more than a vague suspicion. Authorities scoffed at the idea that the Gévaudan Beast was a werewolf. They would have reacted the same way here."

"Somehow," he grumbled, "it always comes back to the de Bonfonds as a bloody pack of *loups-garous,* and that's something I really can't accept."

She gave him a long look. "You might. If they were the right kind of werewolves."

"What's that supposed to mean?"

"I'm not sure," she said, not ready to try her untested theory out on him. "But I'll tell you when I find out."

know what you thought," said Julian. "The other night." They were back at Le Coquelicot, having returned the canoe, and now stood on the beach, looking out over the Dordogne. The sun, low in the sky, gave the water a heavy, undulating appearance, like flowing oil. "But I want you to know I never for one minute believed you had anything to do with Jean-Claude's death. Or that you would have left him to die."

It was a minor lie, Mara judged, although entirely understandable. Julian had only been reflecting back her own uncertainty. She had wanted to forget the unpleasant episode, almost had, in fact. Now she wished he were man enough to speak the truth. Her eyes followed a pair of lovers as they drifted past in a red canoe. It was a romantic sight, two bodies stretched out in the bottom of the craft, heads together against the stern thwart, the woman's arm trailing languidly in the glowing water. The pair seemed caught forever in an enchanted net of gold.

She said, patching over the breach, "It was my fault. I overreacted."

"Well, no," he insisted. "I could have been more supportive."

She strongly felt that was true. Friendships were about solidarity. Friendships ought not to admit doubts. She was very much in need of absolutes at the moment. The stern of the red canoe appeared to be circling about in an interesting pursuit of the bow. She said, "Let's not talk about it."

"All right," said Julian, momentarily distracted by the spectacle of a canoe running broadside to the current. Then, as he watched the frantic efforts of its paddlers to correct its course, he realized that he had not really been forgiven.

The red light on her *répondeur* was flashing when Mara walked into her front room later that evening. She retrieved her phone mail: a message from a severe-sounding administrative secretary saying she had an appointment at one o'clock the following afternoon and to confirm by 9 a.m.; and another from Prudence: "When is that man coming back to do my walls? I'm growing old waiting."

Mara called Prudence back, but she was out. She left a message: "Sorry. I'll get right on it."

She was exhausted, too tired for food or a shower. She fed Jazz, stripped, and fell into bed, lacking even the energy to warn her dog to keep to his side of it. But sleep, that deep, restoring oblivion, did not come. She drifted restlessly in shallow pools of semiconsciousness strung together by ragged dreams. "All legends have their roots in the reality of a people," Jean-Claude had written. Had he known about the Wolf Cave and the tunnel?

The phone rang. She fought her way to consciousness, fumbling for the extension on the bedside table.

"*Oui?*" A split second later, she was fully awake. "Who is this?" she shouted into the silence. "Damn you, don't think you can frighten—" The line went dead.

In a fury, Mara slammed the receiver down. She switched on the light, snatched up the receiver again, and punched in 3131 for caller identification. This was no prank. It was nasty and frightening. It took a moment for the information provided by the automated voice to sink in. When it did, it hit her with an almost sickening force. The originating number of her last caller was *her own cell phone*. Whoever had called her had her *portable*. That person had taken it from Jean-Claude's terrace. That person was very likely Jean-Claude's killer.

She keyed in 17 for the Gendarmerie, but swiftly killed the connection. An anonymous call from her own cell phone? It would be one more thing they wouldn't believe. There had been no actual intimidation. No words had been spoken. But it seemed to her that the silence had been more implicitly menacing than an articulated threat.

Christophe? Was he aware that she was digging for the truth about the de Bonfonds, and was he trying to frighten her, to warn her off? Where the hell was he? Then she realized that with a cell phone her caller could be anywhere. Outside her house at that very moment. She sat rigid in her bed, willing her breathing, her heart to slow to normal pace. Then she roused Jazz and, dragging him with her, went about checking and rechecking all the doors and windows of her house.

28

Shortly before one the following afternoon, Mara parked her car in the visitors' bay outside the high stone wall enclosing the Midi-Pyrénées Psychiatric Hospital for the Criminally Insane. The wall was topped with multiple strands of electrically charged wire and equipped with closed-circuit cameras that tracked her approach. At the security checkpoint she pushed her driver's license through a metal grille. An armed guard on the other side of the grille examined her identification, typed something into a computer, adjusted his telephone headset, and barked into a tiny receiver that wavered about on a stalk in front of his mouth. He stared impassively at her, running his tongue over his upper teeth while waiting for a response. His gaze shifted. He spoke again into the receiver.

"*Oui,*" he said. "*Oui. Oui.*" He dropped her identification into a clear plastic bag and clipped the bag to a wallboard intended for the display of such documents. He slid something out through the grille, a coded visitor's badge that he motioned for her to pin to her clothing. "*Attendez. On vient.*"

She waited as instructed. Another armed guard appeared. The heavy steel gate slid open, and she was allowed to enter the hospital precincts. The guard led her wordlessly along a narrow cement walkway toward a large gray stone building. Its façade had an air of forbidding, institutional massiveness. Mara found it as grim as a bunker and deeply depressing.

In the vestibule, she was again told to wait and left under the observation of a third armed guard. She looked around and saw that she was standing in a dim, echoing rotunda that rose to a shallow dome overhead. At the far side of the rotunda, people in faded green scrubs hurried back and forth, disappearing down hallways. Prison personnel, she wondered, or trusted inmates? Footsteps, coming from her right, rang out sharply. She turned.

"Madame Dunn? Nathalie Thibaud." A tall, slim woman with shoulder-length blond hair approached, hand extended. Mara took the hand in surprise. When she had phoned for an appointment, she had spoken not with the doctor but with the severe-sounding administrative secretary who had left the message. By extension, she had assumed the doctor to be a stern, forbidding, scientific type. This woman had the long look of a runway model.

"I appreciate your seeing me," said Mara.

"I was intrigued by your request." The doctor's French had that rich throatiness that Mara, with her flat Montreal drawl, so much admired. *"Et la chère Patsy Reicher?* How is she?"

"En bonne forme. She sends her best and asked after Bibi."

The doctor grinned. "My grandson."

Up close, Mara realized that Nathalie Thibaud was much older than she had first appeared, the champagne-colored hair shot through with silver, laugh lines deeply grooved, fine skin crinkled like tissue paper around green eyes. A well-preserved late fifties.

The doctor glanced at her watch. "I'm afraid I have limited time this afternoon, but let's make the best of it, shall we?" She led Mara at a brisk pace across the rotunda, down a corridor, up a flight of stairs, down another corridor, and into a cramped office.

"Please. Sit down. It's spartan, I'm afraid, for budgetary as well as security reasons. I can't even offer you a cup of coffee."

Mara shook her head. "No need, but thanks all the same." She lowered herself onto a hard wooden chair placed squarely before a utilitarian desk. A metal filing cabinet, a crane-neck lamp, and a computer unit completed the furnishings. The only personal touch was a photograph of a little boy. Bibi, she assumed.

Dr. Thibaud seated herself behind the desk. "Now," she said, appraising her visitor, "before anything, why do you want to know about lycanthropes?"

Mara was prepared for the question. "I'm interested in the link between lycanthropes and werewolf lore," she said, liberally editing the truth. She added more candidly, "I'd also like to test a theory."

The other smiled. *"Bon.* As long as it's absolutely clear that lycanthropes are real people with real, acute psychiatric problems. They are not werewolves."

"Of course." Mara nodded.

"At the same time, lycanthropes are what might be called delusional werewolves because they actually think they turn into wolves. Hence the term 'lycanthrope,' from the Greek *lykanthropos,* wolfman. It's a rare disorder, although it's been around for centuries, and it's possibly what spawned the belief in werewolves. At one time lycanthropy was regarded as an acute form of melancholia. Nowadays it's considered a form of depersonalization disorder involving a complex cluster of diagnostic entities that include acute schizophrenia, depressive psychosis, dissociative hysterical neurosis, and in some cases psychomotor epilepsy. The frequent involvement of hallucinogenics complicates diagnosis. You being an American—"

"Canadian," Mara corrected.

"Ah, pardon. Nevertheless, you may have heard of a famous study that was written up years ago in the *American Journal of Psychiatry?"*

Mara shook her head.

"It involved a forty-nine-year-old woman who believed herself to change into a wolf. She bit and clawed, experienced compulsive bestial urges, and, most significantly, saw in herself the wolflike features—claws and fangs—of a wild animal who wanted to kill."

"But she didn't actually . . . transform?"

"Certainly not. However, she *saw* herself differently. It's one of the principal presenting characteristics of full-blown lycanthropy. The delusion is so great that patients truly believe they're wolves and see themselves as changing physically—for example, being covered in hair, or having wolf eyes and feet. Their behavior changes, they howl, go on all fours, bite. There are also cases of partial lycanthropy, where the subjects see themselves as taking on wolf features but stop short of thinking they are real wolves."

Mara thought for a moment. "But why wolves? Why not bears or—or lions?"

"That's a very good question. I suspect it's cultural. Elsewhere, the condition may take other forms. I've heard that foxes are the animal of choice in some parts of Asia. The cases I'm familiar with are North American or European, where the wolf historically has been a major predator and where wolf stories are embedded in our culture. Who hasn't heard the story of 'Le Petit Capuchon rouge'?"

Little Red Riding Hood. *Or the Big Bad Wolf,* Mara added mentally. "Are lycanthropes affected by the phases of the moon? I'd also like to know if the condition is hereditary."

Nathalie Thibaud tipped her head from side to side. "Some patients have reported an episodic onset that seems to correspond to the full moon. But that's not surprising. The moon is known to have a powerful effect on our psyches. I have a small private practice apart from my work here where I treat patients with conditions ranging from bipolar disorder to kleptomania, and I'd say a good sixty percent of them claim to be affected by the moon." She cocked an eyebrow at Mara, inviting her to draw her own conclusions. "As far as the question of heredity is concerned, some psychiatric disorders show a definite genetic association. Why not lycanthropy? The difficulty is, so little is known about it. In my view, trauma may play as great a role as genetic predisposition."

Mara thought carefully how to word her next questions. "Dr. Thibaud, I assume you've heard of the Beast of Le Gévaudan?"

"Of course." The doctor grinned. "It's one of France's most enduring mysteries."

"Do you think it's possible that the Beast could actually have been a person who used a trained wolf or wolf-dog cross as his killing machine?"

The eyes crinkled. "Your theory, I presume? Hardly a new one."

Mara nodded. "My theory. And you're right. The idea isn't original, except the books I've read suggest the person was some kind of sadistic madman."

"And you think it was a lycanthrope?" Dr. Thibaud pursed her lips. "The idea has its merits."

"I also have an additional twist. You've probably also heard of the Sigoulane Beast?"

The grin faded. "You're talking about the recent incidents in the Dordogne?"

"Not yet. I'm talking about whatever terrorized the Sigoulane Valley in the last half of the 1700s. You see, I have reason to believe that a lycanthrope was behind *both* the Gévaudan Beast and the Sigoulane Beast."

The green eyes fixed intently on her. "Go on."

"I think the killings in Le Gévaudan didn't end in 1767 because the Beast was destroyed, but because the human 'Beast' escaped to the Dordogne, where he trained up other dogs and resumed his attacks a few years later, becoming known as the Sigoulane Beast." She scanned the doctor's face for any sign of incredulity and saw none. "The modus operandi was identical—attacks by a large wolflike animal, feeding on and mutilation of the bodies, probably with the participation of the human partner. The attacks persisted until 1810. Forty-nine years after that date, there was another rash of attacks, again in Sigoulane. In these cases, although people believed the Beast had returned, no wolflike creature was ever actually seen. I think a descendant of the original Beast, again a lycanthrope, was responsible for the later attacks, but that he murdered his human victims without the agency of dogs." She went on to sketch out briefly, without mentioning names, what she knew about the de Bonfonds, their reputation, and their family motto.

Nathalie Thibaud was silent for a moment. Then she said carefully, "In my opinion, it's entirely possible—in fact, probable—that a human agent was behind the Gévaudan Beast. The idea that this person shifted his killing field from Le Gévaudan to the Dordogne is also possible, if what you say about the similarity in the MO is true. However, you'll have a time proving it. As for your idea that a descendant carried on the tradition at a later date—" She shrugged. "And whether the perpetrators were true lycanthropes or psychopaths is something I'm afraid we'll never know."

"There's more." Mara paused. This was the difficult part. She took a deep breath and plunged. "Dr. Thibaud, I think a present-day descendant of the Beast may be responsible for the murder of a man called Jean-Claude Fournier." At the doctor's startled reaction, she hurried on. "Whether or not this person is also somehow involved in a series of other recent incidents in the Sigoulane Valley, I don't know, but I have reason to believe that he had a very strong motive to kill Fournier."

Nathalie Thibaud said warily, "Are you talking about the death of that genealogist?"

Mara nodded.

"I hope you realize you're making a very serious accusation." The doctor's voice was suddenly harsh. "If you're trying to suggest that a lycanthrope is at work, you'd better have, in addition to solid forensic evidence, a damned good clinical basis for such a claim. Does your suspect have a history of wolflike behavior? Does the person believe he or she transforms into a wolf? Are other, associated symptoms present?"

Mara held her hands up. "That's my problem. I don't know. It's why I'm here. I only know that this person is a direct descendant of the family I mentioned, and that he goes into periodic seclusion. I also know that he disappeared twice recently, the first time coinciding with the fatal attack on a *sanglier*-baiter, the second with the mauling of a woman, and that both instances were around the time of a full moon. Plus, he was missing when Jean-Claude Fournier was killed. Most important, I said he had a strong motive for silencing Fournier. I think Fournier was trying to blackmail him—for being a werewolf. Jean-Claude, you see, was the one who made the link between the Gévaudan and Sigoulane Beasts and this person's family."

Nathalie Thibaud's face was concentrated into a deep frown. When she spoke again, her tone was troubled. "In the thirty years I've been in practice, I've treated or been consulted on a number of instances of complete or partial lycanthropy. In most cases, secrecy was a major issue. It's a terrifying condition that utterly alienates the patient from his or her own identity, from society, as you can imagine. Also, because of the predatory delusions involved, lycanthropes can run afoul of the law, although not all lycanthropes engage in violence. So it's not surprising that lycanthropes, when they're in the throes of their delusion, become reclusive. Secrecy may be their only protection, and such individuals might go to extremes to hide their delusional persona. On the other hand, our annals of criminal justice are full of cases of people who have killed for reasons of self-protection."

"Have you ever dealt with a situation like the one I described?"

Nathalie Thibaud took her time answering. "I personally have treated only five cases of diagnosed lycanthropy. Three were patients who eventually made satisfactory recoveries with medication and psychotherapy. Another was a man who suffered periodic seizures followed by days, sometimes weeks, of delusions that he was a wolf, during which time he was so violent he had to be re-strained. He went to his grave convinced that he was a *loup-garou.*"

"And the fifth?"

The doctor drew a long breath. "He was, in fact, my first case—a young man when he came to me, slim, soft-spoken, withdrawn. I had little experience with lycanthropy at the time, and I'm sorry to say I didn't deal with him as"—she paused—"appropriately as I should have when he told me his symptoms. In the early stages, you see, he merely complained of feelings of disorientation and aggres-sion that caused him to growl and throw red ink at his 'victims.' In-convenient but not life-threatening. I treated it as an expression of suppressed anger, stemming from childhood abuse, because this poor fellow really had a horrific family history. However, seven months into treatment, he reported that he'd begun changing into a fully formed wolf at each turn of the moon. That was when I real-ized what I was dealing with. He also revealed to me that his mother, who had just died, had been a wolf-woman who had repeatedly forced him to couple with her, like a wolf, from his teen years on-ward, and who savagely bit anyone who came near her when the moon was full. Her death, in fact, may have been what triggered his perceived transformations. So there you have two possible instances of lunar effect and, who knows, your genetic link."

"Were you able to cure him?"

The doctor stared into her hands, which she had placed palms-up before her on her desk, as if seeking something there. "No. At least, not in time. A year after he began therapy with me, he at-tacked a woman. A postmistress." She paused and looked up. "It was a frenzied attack."

Mara waited in silence. "What happened?" she ventured at last.

There was a look almost of apology in the green eyes. "He ripped her head from her body, using his teeth, nails, and a hack-saw. When the police found him, he was howling and attempting to eat the body."

Mara felt herself go pale.

"*Pas beau, eh?*"

No, Mara had to agree. It was not pretty. It reminded her too much of Jean-Claude's torn remains.

Then Dr. Thibaud said something totally unexpected: "Would you like to meet him?"

"He's here?" Involuntarily, Mara shifted back in her seat, only to discover that her chair was bolted to the floor. The doctor seemed amused at her look of alarm.

"He was the last time I checked."

His name was Jules Delage, and he was now forty-two years of age. He had been sentenced in 1985 to life imprisonment for the murder of an elderly postmistress in the Auvergne, a woman not generally mourned because she had a nasty habit of prying into other people's affairs. Since that time, Jules had been transferred to three different prisons before ending up at the Midi-Pyrénées institution, where he lived behind a heavy metal door. A barred window cut into the upper half of the door gave a view of Jules's world: a cell equipped with a lidless toilet, a sink, and minimal furnishings.

Mara's first sight of him came as a shock. The slim youth of Dr. Thibaud's description was now a swollen caricature of a human being. Jules was huge. His body ballooned out below a disproportionately small head sparsely covered with fuzzy brown hair, as downy as a baby's. His eyes were lost in pillows of fat. Arms draped in curtains of flesh bulged from a tentlike short-sleeved shirt. The lower half of his body was clothed in a vast pair of cotton trousers. He sat facing them at a table, intent on folding and refolding small squares of pre-cut paper. As he worked, his lips formed into a pout that reminded Mara bizarrely of the sulky moue of a dissatisfied debutante.

"*Ça va, Jules?*" the doctor called cheerfully through the barred window. "I've brought someone to see you. Madame Dunn. From Canada. She's not a shrink, so you can have a normal conversation for a change." In a lower voice she said to Mara, "Our model patient. He enjoys visitors, although he doesn't get any, except for clinicians who want to study him. To be honest, I'm doing this more for him than for you. He needs contact with the outside world."

Mara nodded, watching in fascination as the prisoner's fingers manipulated a piece of paper with surprising delicacy.

"Origami," informed the doctor. "He makes some quite wonderful things." She smiled at Mara's look of amazement. "I'll leave you to chat for a few minutes, shall I? You'll find him quite knowledgeable about current affairs. He reads a lot. But if you don't mind, Madame Dunn"—Nathalie Thibaud lowered her voice even more—"please don't ask him about the murder." She left.

The hacksaw murder of the postmistress, Mara assumed, not Jean-Claude's. She stood in the corridor before Jules's window. Closed-circuit cameras, suspended from the ceiling, recorded her presence. A row of similar barred windows stretched away to her left. Occasional sounds, the moans and murmurs of other unseen inmates, echoed distantly.

"*Bonjour,* Jules," she said, trying to imitate the doctor's brightness. "My name is Mara. What are you making?"

With an effort, he rose from his seat and lumbered toward her, feet clad in carpet slippers, legs splayed, knees locked beneath his great weight. Wordlessly, Jules pushed a small object, pinched between thumb and forefinger, through the barrier. Mara took it gingerly. It was a minutely-fashioned bird.

"It's beautiful." She turned it over, marveling at the cunning creases that formed the beak and body.

"It's a heron." His voice was surprisingly soft. "You may keep it."

"Thank you. Do you like birds?"

"In flight. Origami herons can't fly. Have you come to get me out of here?"

Mara shook her head. "I'm afraid not."

He said more harshly, "Then don't talk to me about birds."

"All right. What would you like to talk about?"

He shrugged, a mountainous movement. "You know why you're here. I suppose you've never met anyone like me before, have you?"

"No," she admitted. "But I haven't come to study you clinically. As Dr. Thibaud said, I'm not a psychiatrist. I expect you've seen enough of them already."

"Then why did you come?"

She decided to put her case simply. "I'm interested in lycanthropy. I want to know what it's like to be a lycanthrope."

He stepped back distrustfully. "You wouldn't understand. It's like nothing you've ever experienced. Or will experience."

She toyed with the tiny heron. "Try me."

Jules's mouth shaped into something that Mara took to be a smile. "All right. If you really want to know. One enters an exalted state. Have you ever felt exalted, Mara Dunn from Canada?"

She told him truthfully, "No. Not in the way I think you mean."

Her admission seemed to please him. "Of course you haven't. Psychiatrists have their own name for it, but they understand nothing. Even the good Dr. Thibaud." He leaned forward confidentially. "Do you know why they call us lycanthropes? Because they feel more comfortable, being able to label us. They fool themselves into thinking they're in control that way, you see. But the truth is, they're afraid to recognize us for what we are: wolves, powerful, mystic, and vengeful."

"You consider yourself a wolf?"

The smile stretched painfully wide, exposing yellow teeth. "Oh yes."

"Why vengeful?"

Jules's mouth snapped back in a grimace of anger. "You can ask? After what your kind has done? You've shot us, trapped us, poisoned us. Driven us from the forests, cut us open, nailed our skins to walls. And you wonder that we seek revenge?"

He was speaking on behalf of real wolves, Mara realized, and at the same time of himself. If wolves in France had been hunted nearly to extinction, his existence was as drastically reduced.

His anger subsided as quickly as it had come. "But let me tell you something. For every wolf one of you kills, one of *me* emerges. The soul of a wolf takes on a human form. You can cage us, drug us, but you will never destroy us. Remember that. There are many more of my kind than you might think. Running free." The smile again, stretched this time to hideous proportions. "Don't rest easy in your bed, Mara Dunn."

Was he telling her something that he truly believed, or was he simply trying to frighten her? Perhaps, Mara thought, it was the only thing he had left: the power to terrify.

"How does it come on you?" Mara asked, struggling to project an air of calm detachment. "This feeling of being a wolf?"

"I *am* a wolf. At all times."

Mara knew this to be untrue. On the way to the cells, Nathalie Thibaud had told her that Jules Delage experienced long periods of abeyance, when he went into an almost somnolent state and no longer thought of his wolfish other self.

As if reading her mind, the lycanthrope went on, "Don't believe what the doctor tells you. She means well, but she hopes to cure me by pumping me full of chemicals, giving me psychotherapy, without understanding that she can't change what I am. That is the objective of their so-called treatment, you know. To keep me and others like me fragmented."

"Fragmented? I don't understand."

"No." He sneered. "You wouldn't. You can't. Integration is power. Wholeness is freedom. And that is what your kind lacks and

can never allow in others. Because your own fears keep you separated from yourselves, you seek to prevent *us* from becoming one
with what we really are. You think as long as you can do that, you're
safe." He shook his small head. "But no matter what you do, we will
always roam the darkness of your minds, we will stalk you down the
corridors of your own worst thoughts. You will never be safe."

"I mean," said Mara, her dogged line of inquiry a feeble coun-
terpoint to his ominous assertion, "what brings your transformation on? Does the moon have an effect on you?"

Jules Delage stepped back and emitted a great, rusty, hacking
laugh. His flesh shook. His sour breath rode out in gusts at her.
"There is no transformation. I am at all times a wolf. As for the
moon, use your eyes." He gestured at the blank walls around him.
"I can't see it. But I can feel it." Lightly, he touched his breast with
his fingertips. "I know its phases like the beating of my own heart."

Mara took a breath and asked, "Is it true your mother was also
a lycanthrope?"

"She-wolf." Anger flashed across his face again.

"Tell me about her. Please."

He said bitterly, "There's very little to tell. One day, my mother
grew whole. In so doing, she became a powerful, beautiful wolf-
woman. I was only a kid at the time, just turned twelve, but I remember her still, her dress in shreds because she'd tried to tear it
off, her hair hanging down her back. Her only desire was to run
free, to hunt to fill her need, to mate with her own kind. Instead,
she was forced to slink in shadows like a dog for fear of what the
villagers would do if they found out about her. They were steeped
in the old superstitions, and they didn't part lightly with their
sheep, those damned herders. For the first few years, Papa tried to
keep her locked in the cellar. Eventually, he left us. He was a cow-
ard. From then on it was up to me to take care of Maman. We
hunted in the forest, ate what we could bring down. Fresh-killed
meat was the only thing that satisfied her hunger."

"But," Mara objected, "how could you have kept something like that secret?" And for so long? Dr. Thibaud had told her that Jules's mother had died when he was in his early twenties. That meant Jules's father, and subsequently, Jules alone, had hidden her condition for possibly ten years, or even longer. "Surely people must have found out about you?"

Jules gave Mara a lingering look. "Just the one." His gaze shifted to fix on a point far beyond her. "After Maman died . . ." His voice trailed off. Seeming to lose interest in their conversation, he made as if to move away.

"Wait," Mara cried, clinging to the tenuous contact she had established with this enormous, frightening man. "Don't go. What happened after your mother died?" The death of the mother, she remembered Dr. Thibaud saying, had triggered the onset of Jules's own delusions.

He turned back, a sly expression slipping over his face. "Do you really want to know?"

"Yes."

"Come nearer, and I'll tell you."

Involuntarily, Mara's left hand closed down on the origami bird she still held. She felt its form crumple sharply against her palm. She shook her head. "I'm sorry. I'm comfortable where I am."

He regarded her scornfully. "For your kind, barriers are never strong enough. You ask questions, but you haven't the courage to hear the answers. Look. How can I hurt you?" By way of demonstration, he thrust his fingers through the close-set bars as far as they would go. They jammed at the third knuckle, where they remained before her, clutching futilely at the air in a gesture that was as much beseeching as transfixing.

"Let me touch you," said Jules Delage. "Just touch."

Slowly, unwillingly, Mara put out her right hand.

"No," he said, bargaining. "Your face."

For the first time Mara looked the prisoner full in the eyes.

They were dark and small, buried in their fatty creases, the eyes of a caged animal, wary and extinguished of hope. She held his gaze as she took another step forward. At that proximity, she could smell the acrid odor rising from his body, see the labored rise and fall of his chest. Her heart was pounding somewhere in the region of her throat. Gently, with infinite care, he extended a forefinger and tremblingly stroked her cheek. The touch lasted no more than a few seconds before Mara pulled back.

"What happened after your mother died, Jules?" she asked.

He put his mouth to the bars and whispered three words. Suddenly, his features seemed to collapse. As if jerked by a string, Jules swung abruptly away from her. Stumbling back to the middle of his cell, the wolf threw back his head in a long, ringing howl of despair. His anguish awoke a responding cacophony of sounds down the length of the prison wing. A guard came running. Now Jules was circling about, as if following the spiraling flight of an enraged hornet. His body began to quiver. Horrified, Mara watched as he transformed before her view into a melee of flailing arms and legs and fell to the ground in an ecstasy of spittle and uncontrolled thrashing.

'm sorry," said Dr. Thibaud. "It's the first seizure he's had in years. Not a pleasant sight for you, I'm afraid."

"I'm really all right," Mara insisted, although she was deeply shaken. "Is he?"

"Oh, he'll recover. They've taken him to the infirmary. I'll keep him under observation for a day or so. He probably needs his meds increased. Incidentally, what was it that set him off?"

Mara hesitated, thinking of Jules, drugged to a stupor, deprived of the only thing he had left—the ability to run free in his mind. She fingered the crumpled paper heron in her pocket.

"He said to ask the postmistress," she said faintly.

29

Ortolan."

"Garden bunting," Julian translated for the benefit of Prudence, who had joined them for their usual Friday evening at Chez Nous.

"Little bird. Not much bigger than that." Loulou measured a distance between thumb and forefinger. "Now, the only way to cook them, in my opinion, is to put half a dozen or so in a pan and roast them whole in their own dripping. It's their fat, you see, that makes them so delicious. A little salt, a little pepper, *et voilà*." He brought his fingertips to his lips. "Melts on the tongue like butter. In fact, a real gastronome covers his head with a cloth while eating ortolan, so as not to lose the wonderful aroma."

"My god." Prudence's perfectly made-up face looked scandalized. "It'd be like having dinner with a spook."

"A real gastronome," said Julian, "covers his head because eating ortolans is messy and he doesn't want people seeing him with grease running down his chin."

"*Balivernes!* Anyway, all this business of stuffing them with foie gras, smothering them with truffles, and flambéing them in Armagnac is so much flummery, as far as I'm concerned. Where ortolan is concerned, simplest is best, I say."

Julian, Prudence, and Loulou sat at a table at the front of the bistro. They were already deep into their meal, which did not consist of ortolan, now a protected species in France, but the evening's special, a fricassee of rabbit served with spring vegetables. Jazz,

Bismuth, and Edith hung about hopefully. At that point, the beaded curtain separating the dining area from the rest of the Brieux enterprise flew apart. Mara, who had phoned ahead to say she would be late, walked in. She sat down with them but ordered only sorrel soup. She looked rumpled. Her air of suppressed excitement, however, suggested that she had news. She saved it until the bistro had emptied of all other customers and Mado and Paul could join them. If Loulou could keep them dangling, so could she.

Poor thing," Prudence said after they had heard Mara's conclusions on Cécile and the parentage of Baby Blue. "You think her brother Hugo was abusing her?"

Mara nodded. "And possibly doing the same thing to his other sister, Catherine. Which could explain why she wound up in a convent. At a guess, he might have tried it on with Eloïse, too, although she would probably have been a willing participant since she was looking to marry him. Of course, Eloïse went back to her family when Hugo married Henriette. But Cécile, being his youngest sister with nowhere to go, was probably his special victim."

"Bastard," cried Mado with feeling, tossing her red mane and crossing Rubenesque arms before a magnificent bosom. "I'd have cut off his *couilles* and fed them to the pigs."

Loulou coughed. "Maybe she did. In a manner of speaking."

"Eh?" Mado queried. Baby Eddie, in his carry cot behind the bar, gurgled. She jumped up to check on him. The dogs, ever hopeful of food, rushed after her. She shooed them away and returned with a bottle of local plum brandy and a clutch of glasses.

Loulou, who had been eyeing the ceiling thoughtfully, followed up. "After all, he came to a sorry end, *n'est-ce pas?*" He paused to watch Mado pour the dark liqueur into the glasses, took a sip from one, and smacked his lips. "Very good, this." He nodded at Mara. "Didn't you say Jean-Claude told you that Hugo died from a fall from a horse when his saddle girth snapped? Maybe Cécile engineered it. She knew about horses."

"*Bigre!*" uttered Paul. "You think she did for him?"

Julian stirred restlessly and addressed Mara. "Was there nothing in the diary about orchids? No mention, say, of Cécile liking embroidery? Or 'I was out riding the other day and saw an unusual flower'? Or even where the woman liked to ride?"

Mara shook her head. "I'm sorry, Julian. I was concentrating on other things, and I only read a small part of her diary. I saw nothing about Lady's Slippers or flowers of any kind. I take it Vrac hasn't been in touch?"

"No."

"And nothing about *loups-garous*?" Paul put in slyly.

"In fact," said Mara, and went on to tell them about her day.

et me get this straight." Paul squinted at her skeptically. "According to you, Christophe isn't a werewolf but a lycanthrope, and he gets it from his great-something-grandfather Xavier, who *was* a werewolf?"

"Lycanthrope," Mara corrected. "I'm saying Xavier suffered from lycanthropy, and he passed the condition on. He really believed he was a wolf, and he took on the behaviors of one. So, yes, in a way, Xavier was a werewolf, and he was the true Gévaudan Beast. But he expressed his sickness in an unusual way. He didn't attack people directly. He used a trained, vicious animal to do his work. It was his alter-ego and his killing machine. It's the only way of reconciling conflicting eyewitness accounts. People described the Beast as some kind of wolflike creature, but others swore it went on two legs. Many said it was invulnerable to injury, and a few claimed the thing wore some kind of leather cuirass that buttoned underneath. A wolf in a protective jacket? Or a man in a wolf suit? Or both, working together? And then there was the way the bodies were left. Clothing was removed—not torn away, as an animal would do it. Heads were severed, not ripped off with tooth and claw. I think the animal carried out the attacks, but the master, maybe dressed in a wolf skin, was on hand to direct its movements and participate in the eating and despoiling of human flesh. This went on for three years. Then, when his beasts were killed— I say beasts because two were shot—and things got too hot for him in Le Gévaudan, Xavier shifted to the Sigoulane Valley, where he trained up other generations of wolves or wolf-dogs. One of them went for him in the end."

"Gee!" exclaimed Prudence.

"Wait a minute," said Julian. "All this evidence simply points to a nutter with an attack dog. Why do you assume Xavier was a lycanthrope?"

"Because of the psychology of the case. The killer chose to hide behind the identity of a wolflike creature. That's significant. You saw the dog in the portrait, Julian. It's painted in such a way that it almost merges with Xavier himself. I think that was how he wanted it. The de Bonfond motto, 'Blood Is My Right,' was probably created by Xavier and sounds like the declaration of someone who saw himself as a predator. A wolf, in fact, because Xavier would have believed himself to be one. He might even have used Julian's orchid as a drug to enhance his delusion, because Julian says that some Lady's Slippers have hallucinogenic properties. But to me the most compelling thing is something I didn't tell Dr. Thibaud. I was afraid she'd think it silly." Mara glanced around her. No one seemed in a laughing mood. "You see, Jean-Claude told me Xavier's title of 'le Baron' was a purposeful corruption of the surname 'Lebrun.' But I found out that the word for werewolf in Occitan is *leberon*. I think 'le Baron' was actually a different play on words. *Leberon*. Lebrun. Le Baron."

Paul whistled. "*Leberon* de Bonfond! The *con* was having everybody on."

"Gee-hee!" uttered Prudence again, the sound this time seeming to emanate from the depths of her Giorgio Armani shoes.

"There's more," Mara went on. "I think Hugo inherited the condition, except he didn't use an animal. But like Xavier, he may also have hopped himself up on a tincture of *Cypripedium incognitum* to heighten the effect of his 'transformations.' He had a reputation for drinking the blood of game he brought down while they were still kicking. He probably did the same with his human prey." She paused. "And then there was Baby Blue." They all turned questioning faces to her. Everyone had forgotten about him. "I don't believe his killer was simply eliminating an embarrassing bastard. I think whoever smothered him was trying to end a tainted bloodline. We have to remember, with Cécile and Hugo as parents, that kid had it in spades."

"Hmm," said Loulou. "Which would account for the secret way he was disposed of. Makes sense. Despite the rosary and the crucifix, if it's as Mara said, there was no way Baby Blue could have been given a Christian burial."

"*Mon dieu,*" said Mado, and poured herself another tot of plum brandy.

"Which brings us to the present," said Mara, "and Christophe."

"Oh, for pity's sake," Julian declared.

"Look, Dr. Thibaud seems to think lycanthropy might be hereditary. There's exactly a three-generation spread between Xavier and Hugo and again between Hugo and Christophe. Maybe it means nothing, but it does seem curious. Also, Thérèse confirmed that Christophe disappears periodically. I had to pull worms from her nose, but I finally got her to admit that he might have been away around the time that man was killed in Colline Basse. We also know he went off the same day the Dupuy woman was hit outside her henhouse. Pretty coincidental, don't you think?"

"There you go again," objected Julian. "What you're suggesting is preposterous. It was an animal that went at those people, not a human being. Unless you seriously think Christophe is able to grow fangs and claws?"

"No, of course I don't. But I feel somehow there's a link. Something I'm missing." She paused. "You don't know if Christophe has a dog, do you? I know he doesn't keep one about the house. I mean a dog or dogs that he kennels elsewhere on the property?"

"No, he doesn't," snapped Julian. "He has an allergy to fur. And Didier doesn't like them. In any case, Jean-Claude wasn't killed by an animal. He was pushed off the terrace and strangled."

"I think by Christophe," said Mara. "As a lycanthrope, Christophe would have taken an accusation of werewolfism seriously because it came too close to the truth. That's why he had to silence Jean-Claude. Who else had as good a motive for murder?"

Julian thought of Denise's flat, black eyes, the way she had coolly dismissed his question about her whereabouts on Sunday night. She was a woman who, he had no doubt, could hate intensely. "Denise," he hazarded. "She had an affair with Jean-Claude, don't forget. Maybe it was a lovers' quarrel after all. They fought, and she pushed him over."

"Hmm." Mara was gratified to hear him suggest it. "That takes care of means and motive"—a nod at Loulou—"but what about opportunity? You'd have to place her at the scene of the crime during the critical time."

"If she did it," Prudence observed, "you can bet she's the kind who would have organized a convincing alibi."

She tried to, Julian thought. *Me.* He couldn't acknowledge the fact openly, and he couldn't prove where she had been during the early hours of Monday morning. But he sure as hell knew where she hadn't been.

"And then," Mara went on, "she would have had to climb down afterward and strangle him with the wolf belt. Can you see her doing it?"

"Yes," said Julian very seriously. "I think I could."

The question of Whose Place was simply decided. Mara drove Julian and their dogs back to his cottage and opted to stay. A light rain was falling by then, and the air was chill and damp. Julian hustled around, opened a bottle of wine, set it aside to breathe, and tried to get a fire going in his front room. It was smoky work. His chimney drew badly, undoubtedly because it was clogged with soot and swallows' nests. He kept forgetting to get it cleaned. Eventually, he achieved a promising flare. The dogs flopped down in front of it, and he pushed the sofa forward to be nearer the warmth that the fire was not yet giving. They sat together in comfortable companionship, the first they had shared in days. Julian poured the wine.

"Nice," Mara said appreciatively, noting the label, a Coteaux de Bonfond Domaine de la Source 2000.

"Their Gold Medal Vintage." He did not mention that Denise had brought over half a case on the occasion of their one-night stand. "Not bad for a small Bergeracois winery." He swirled the liquid slowly in his glass and sniffed, allowing his mind to range through the hyperbolic phrases that wine-promoters indulged in. A serious bouquet, underlain by a darker whiff of—what?—autumn leaves, the gardener in him decided. Wet ones. He took a mouthful, sucking in noisily to let the aeration do its thing and holding it long on his tongue. Very smooth, with a good balance of sweetness, bitterness, and astringency. A lengthy finish that made him think of chocolate and—to his surprise—a hint of well-aged manure. Suspiciously, he held his glass up to the light, studying its color and body. It was a clear ruby-red with good visual texture, measured by the time it took for the glycerine and alcohol in the wine to coalesce into droplets and slide down the interior of the glass. In English they called it legs. He thought of Denise's legs and cleared his throat.

"You know, the more I think about it, the more I'm convinced it's a mistake to leave Denise out of the equation." By then he had reconciled himself to the manure, in fact quite liked it. "I'm not saying this just because Christophe's my friend. I really think the woman's pathologically ambitious and capable of anything, especially where the winery is concerned. Sometimes I wonder who really runs Coteaux de Bonfond, she or Antoine. He's a master winemaker, but she's the one who's positioning them for the bloodletting that's happening in the French wine industry. I think she'd cheerfully eliminate anyone who stood in her way."

Mara considered this. She liked the notion of Denise as murderer, but one thing didn't fit. "I got a threatening, anonymous phone call from someone last night. And maybe the night before as well. Using my cell phone. Trouble is, I'm pretty sure it was Christophe."

"What?" Julian sat up so fast that he almost spilled his wine. "What did he say?"

"Nothing. That was the threatening part."

"Then how do you know it was him?"

"Julian, someone found my *portable* on the terrace and took it, probably after he killed Jean-Claude. Christophe is the only person in the world, apart from you, who doesn't have his own cell phone and who wouldn't know how to key in the block for caller ID."

30

Vrac pushed cautiously through the dripping branches. It had stopped raining sometime in the night, but the world was soaked, and an early-morning mist blanketed the ground so that the trees in the field below him looked as if they were floating. Squinting through the gray light, he assessed the lay of the land. A skilled poacher, Vrac knew sheep firsthand, how to approach a flock and move, despite his bulk, among them. He even smelled like one of them. It was true that his mind, damaged at birth, was barely capable of more than simple thought. In the prison of his skull, ideas sparked on and off like faulty wiring; more complex concepts were condemned to darkness. He operated instead by instinct and well-established action sequences, deeply channeled by repetition into the muddy delta of his brain. Catch sheep, kill sheep, gut sheep, and there you had your evening chops.

The trick, Vrac had learned over time, was never to come up on a sheep directly—it was also better if you didn't look at it—but to close in by moving alongside it at an ever-decreasing angle. This maneuver he called "the shears," because to him it was like bringing the blades of a pair of shears together, slowly, slowly, until the sudden, swift cut.

Moving away from the trees and across the wet, tussocky grass, he held his knife at the ready. Usually he chose a yearling, one resting slightly apart from the others that could be taken unawares and with the minimum of fuss. But this time, in the predawn, when most creatures still slept, the flock seemed restless. From where he stood, he sensed their movement even before he heard them snorting and stamping. Skittish, they were. And that was odd, because he was approaching them downwind. He paused, crouching low. Then he realized that the wind had shifted. They had got his scent, all right. He sat tight. The wind would shift again.

Joseph Chabanas, a sheep-farmer for most of his sixty-two years, awakened with the sense that something was disturbing his flock. They grazed in this season on the eastern flank of the hill adjacent to his farm—not his hill; he rented it from a neighbor. Call it a sixth sense or just a hunch. Without knowing exactly what was wrong, Joseph was out of bed and into his boots, pulling a jacket on over his pajama top, calling for his dog, Voltaire, and his son, André, who, with his wife, slept in another part of the house.

André, who had spent the previous evening at the Astro Bar in Brames playing *belote* with pals and drinking red wine, arose to the summons, looking and feeling bad-tempered. However, one glance at his father loading his shotgun told him the matter was serious. He, too, pulled on his boots, dragged a rubberized poncho over his head, and grabbed his gun.

"Go back to bed," André ordered his wife, Marthe, who had followed him into the kitchen, her hair in pink curlers.

"Mon dieu," muttered Marthe, clutching her housecoat to her throat.

Grimly the two men left the house, the dog racing ahead of them. They drove their truck to the field, encircled by a thin blue ribbon of electrified fencing, where the sheep were pastured. As father and son jumped out of the truck, they sensed immediately the restlessness of the flock. It was hard to see in the misty light, but they could make out movement at the far end of the field. André hoisted the dog over the fence. Voltaire ran off barking. The men followed, stepping over the ribbon, ignoring the prickle of the electric charge, and hurrying in the direction of the flock.

Suddenly Joseph grabbed his son's arm. "There," he cried hoarsely, pointing off to his right. Something, tall as a man, rose up out of the mist. "Shoot, for god's sake. Kill the brute!" He himself let off a wild discharge.

André also fired, and the two began to run through the wet grass.

"Got the son of a bitch!" André, outdistancing his father, yelled. The racing form, barely visible against the background of the trees, seemed to shrink and fall to the ground. But it had only dropped to all fours and was running now with even greater speed toward the cover of the woods. André swore.

"Merde!" Joseph gasped from the rear. "It's getting away." He paused to aim more carefully and fired. There was a howl of pain. The thing swerved sharply and vanished altogether.

"Putain!" André's anguished voice shrilled. "I'm hit!"

Joseph found André writhing on the ground. Blood poured down his face. The older man dropped his gun and nearly fainted. The dog could be heard barking frantically in the distance.

"You stupid old fool! You could have killed me," screamed the son. He clutched the side of his head, where most of his ear had been blown away.

The father waved his arms. "I couldn't see. Oh, god in heaven, how was I to know?"

"You always were a lousy shot." Blood was oozing between André's fingers.

"Me? What about you? You should have had it." Joseph pulled off his jacket and attempted to staunch the bleeding with it.

The mutual recriminations continued for a moment, until both men realized that the dog had gone silent. Joseph helped his son up. The men found Voltaire a few moments later at the top of the field, warily nosing a dead lamb. In the strengthening light, they could see that its throat had been torn out and its belly ripped open.

"*Putain!*" This time it was Joseph who uttered the expletive. It was the second they'd lost in a month.

Vrac, startled by the barking of a dog, froze. Moments later, yelling and an explosion of gunfire caused him to drop to the ground. Raising his head cautiously, he made out hazy shapes at the bottom of the field running toward him. The first shot was followed by a second. That was enough for Vrac. He bolted, sprinting for the cover of the trees. He was surprisingly fast for his size, but he felt himself being overtaken. Something was running at his heels. A third shot boomed in the air. There was a piercing shriek. Vrac swung about in time to see a large gray form sheer off in another direction, leaving behind a feral stench such as Vrac, who was not one of God's sweetest creatures, had never smelled before.

Laurent Naudet hovered in the doorway. Adjudant Compagnon sensed the gendarme's presence but did not look up. Instead, he growled, "What?" and went on initialing expense claims.

"Someone just phoned in with another incident, sir."

"That makes seventeen, if we count missing dogs and cats. Where?"

"Tronac. Fellow named Joseph Chabanas. Said he and his son caught something worrying his sheep early this morning. Fired at it and thinks they may have wounded it, but it got away. It killed a lamb. It's the second he's lost this month. I told him to secure the carcass until we could come out and have a look."

"Tronac," Compagnon muttered thoughtfully. He swiveled about to squint at a map on the wall. Red pins marked the locations of verified "Beast" incidents; green, alleged sightings. "That's thirty kilometers north of Sigoulane. The thing expands its *territoire* every day."

"There's something else, sir. Chabanas says he's positive the creature went on two legs, like a man. He got a good look at it. But when they started shooting, it dropped to all fours and ran off."

Compagnon threw his pen down in disgust. "Why is it no one would ever tell you to your face they believe in werewolves, and yet, given half a chance, they all want to make out it's a *loup-garou*? On top of that, have you seen this?" He tossed a newspaper to the gendarme. The day's headline read: *Save Our Wolves. Animal Rights Activists Protest.* "So now we have to deal with this lot. Speaking of which, what's the situation with those damned self-styled vigilantes?"

Laurent grimaced. "Several loose groups continue to operate in and around Sigoulane. Others are being set up elsewhere. They seem to go out mostly on weekends. Wouldn't be surprised if it isn't just an excuse for some of them to do a little illegal hunting."

"*Bordel,*" said the adjudant, weary down to his boots. "I don't have enough officers to go on combing the forests, run a murder investigation, and keep a lid on those *maudit* hunters. To them it's a game. Wind up potting each other before you know it."

"I think they already have." Laurent grinned. "I also got a report from the doctor on call in Buffevent. That's just down the road from Tronac. She said Chabanas's son called her out at six o'clock this morning. His ear was shot away. Wouldn't say how, but I think we can guess."

31

Julian came to with a pleasant memory of the night before. He and Mara had put the prickles of the past two weeks behind them and had engaged in lovemaking that had been slow and very satisfying. He rolled over, catching a welcome whiff of sandalwood on the pillowcase, in the sheets. It was a clean scent, with just enough complexity to be interesting. He reached out to enfold Mara. His arms closed on nothing. His eyes snapped open. Her side of the bed was cold and empty. He sat up. Then he heard movement in the kitchen. Mara was making tea. He sighed. Her tea, which she somehow never let steep long enough, came out as pale as gnat's piss.

He got up, took a quick shower, and stood a moment examining himself in the blemished, steamy mirror over his bathroom counter. Thatch thinning a bit on top, facial hair in need of trimming, puffy eyes that hinted at last night's excesses. They had taken a second bottle of Domaine de la Source to bed with them and finished it off there. Then he remembered the moment when, postcoital, she had poked him playfully in the stomach: "Getting a bit of a tummy, aren't we?" A minor wound to his amour propre, one he would get over, but he wished she hadn't said it.

Viewed front-on, his chest was lean, his arms long and wiry, ending in typical gardener's hands, what he called pitchfork hands, large, work-worn, and permanently soiled around the nails. Turning sideways, he craned about to squint at the slight pear-shaped profile of a paunch and sucked his stomach in. The mirror cut him off at the hips. Just as well. His naked legs, pale, skinny, and covered in dark hair, were not to his mind his best feature.

He scraped those parts of his face that required shaving, dressed, and wandered into the kitchen. Mara, also dressed, was seated at the table with a mug of tea. She traded pecks with him without looking up from the morning paper. A bag of fresh croissants was on the counter.

"Bless you," he said with feeling.

When they overnighted at his house, it was usually his job to go down to Chez Nous for breakfast and the paper. Among its many functions, the bistro also served as the local *dépot de pain*. In the Dordogne, where villages were steadily dying off unless they were being bought up wholesale by the English, the provision of bread (or not, as it were) served as a rough indicator of the viability of a settlement. Places *avec boulangerie* had a claim to life, unlike those *sans boulangerie*, which were little more than moribund hamlets populated by octogenarians. Towns like Brames, with a whopping 2,507 residents, enjoyed not only the Méliès establishment, but a rival pastry specialist and a plain baker who also roasted and ground coffee *sur place*. Small villages like Grissac, with only a *dépot*, serviced in this case by a long, thin, silent breadman named Lucien Peyrat, occupied a kind of middle ground. Julian bit into a flaky croissant—the first bite was always the best, to his mind—leaving a scattering of crumbs on his beard.

Mara, still deep in her paper, said, "The SPA is campaigning on behalf of the feral dog or rogue wolf or whatever it is. They want it humanely trapped. And the police are now looking for an unidentified man known to have employed Jean-Claude for genealogical research. That would be Christophe. About time."

Julian stopped chewing. It was another way of saying that Christophe was now the focus of a manhunt. Where the hell was he? Had he made those phone calls to Mara? If he was a lycanthrope, as Mara seemed to believe, he was sick. He needed help.

Julian didn't like the idea of his friend being run to earth like an animal. He poured himself a mug of weak tea, spooned in more sugar than he normally took, and added milk.

Mara's voice cut across his thoughts. "You know, Julian, I've been thinking. About Cécile's diary. Why don't we read it together? I'm looking for evidence of lycanthropy. You're looking for a lead on your orchid. Assuming Cécile did the embroidery, even if she doesn't mention the orchid itself, she might have said something about where she rode. I still have the key to the house Christophe gave me when I started work on his *galérie*. We can divide the work between us. It would go much faster."

Julian's mug stopped halfway to his mouth. "That's bloody brilliant." Christophe was forgotten.

"Besides," she added, "I want to talk to Didier. He told me Jean-Claude had been asking him questions. I want to know about what."

"And I," said Julian, "want to find out exactly what kind of Aconite he's talking about."

They left the dogs at the cottage because of Didier's aversion to them. The old man lived on the Aurillac grounds in a stone hut buried in the bushes. An adjacent *potager,* lovingly tended, suggested that Didier put more effort into his vegetables than he did into tending the estate. The *potager* was surrounded by a picket fence that was covered in blackened, gruesome, knobbly objects nailed to the wooden palings: the forefeet of *sangliers* that the gardener, also an enthusiastic hunter, had killed in his lifetime.

They knocked and stood a long time before Didier's door, examining the blistering green paint. The branches overhanging the front were still dripping with last night's rain. After walking around his clearing and calling his name, they gave up. The gardener was clearly not there.

"Maybe we should leave him a note," Mara said. "I wouldn't want him to come rushing in again with that shotgun of his."

ere's another one," Mara said. They had divided the eleven folders of Cécile's diary between them, Julian taking the even and Mara the odd years, so that they could proceed chronologically while staying more or less in tandem. She read aloud, translating into English from the folder marked 1867, when the writer was twenty-three:

> . . . A fine canter through the open field past Rameau's farm. On the return Argent threw a shoe, which was too bad because it made me late back. Stewed rabbit for dinner, but very little left for me. When I complained, Maman said, If you're hungry, eat your fist.

The earlier years, 1861 to 1866, had offered similar accounts of movement on horseback. Julian added another tick next to "Rameau" on a list of place-names he was compiling. That made, he noted, the seventh mention of a ride in that vicinity. With a bit of digging, he was sure he could locate the property. It was even possible that it was still in the hands of Rameau's descendants.

"And another," Julian said a moment later. He held up a page from the 1868 folder:

> . . . I rode out today to see Garnier's bullock slaughtered. The beast struggled so violently while they bled it that three men had to hold it fast . . .

Mara closed her eyes. "My god. She was as bloodthirsty as her brother."

"Well, you said it runs in the family." He read further:

. . . To the spring and back this morning with Eloïse. My cousin complained that Hugo ignores her, for all that they live under the same roof and are affianced . . .

He scratched his beard and leaned back in his chair, stretching his long legs out under the library table. "I wonder if she meant the *source* at the north end of the valley? Trouble is, there could be more than one spring. She had to be using a track or road of some sort. I don't suppose it would be too hard to reconstruct her path."

Mara closed the 1867 folder and reached for 1869. He took up 1870. It contained material that Mara had already told him about: Cécile's account of the Paris visit and her army captain; her grief at his death; and the appended material of her sexual encounters with her stealthy visitor whose *"regard bleu"* had pierced her to the entrails. He was more interested in the writer's accounts of daily activities at Aurillac, especially anything related to rides, canters, and gallopades within the environs of the valley. These were more numerous before the Paris visit. After her return from the capital, Cécile was too overcome by the loss of her captain to take much to the saddle. Or too caught up in family matters, for in the fall of 1870 Hugo brought Henriette, with no warning, as his bride to Aurillac:

. . . She came to us with naught but her Parisian airs and three large trunks. Eloïse went white around the mouth on hearing the news and quit us within the hour. She is wild at being thrown over. Maman is furious and forbids me to speak to my new *belle-soeur—la Blonde Horizontale,* she calls her—and says she is no better than a common whore. Hugo seems very satisfied with himself. Papa is angry that Henriette brings no dowry, but he behaves disgustingly all the same, like an old stallion around a filly in season. He does that with every woman in the valley . . .

Julian also found letters from Eloïse to Cécile, written *après* Henriette, which he shared with Mara:

25 September 1870
My dear cousin,
I received your note. Given your circumstances, I think you had much better follow your sister to the Abbaye des Eaux. In any case, your family's reputation is already ruined. I do not judge Hugo, for I know one day he will face a far sterner judge than I. Had Hugo and I wed, as both our families intended, you as my sister-in-law would have naturally continued to make your home with us. However, from what I have heard of the person whom Hugo now calls wife, I fear you will not find an easy welcome once she is mistress of Aurillac. I thank God for your sake that my aunt, your mother, keeps control of things, for your father, as you know, is a wastrel, and Hugo has put himself beyond the pale . . .

18 October 1870
My dear Cécile,
I will, of course, continue to be your friend, although you must understand that relations between our families are irrevocably altered. I will also endeavor to give such support as I can to my aunt Odile, for I know that she struggles to swim against the tide of social censure. Hugo's disastrous alliance must henceforth bar the de Bonfonds from all decent society, despite my aunt's attempts to buy back lost respectability with her "entertainments." I pity your family, and you particularly, from the bottom of my heart . . .

"Sententious bitch," Mara commented.

"Well, she did get dumped. And at least she dated her letters," said Julian.

Mara took up the 1871 folder. By the summer of that year, Cécile, in her inimitable style, reported that Henriette was with child. Mara read aloud:

> . . . The whore keeps to her bed and complains of feeling ill. The temperature soars, causing her to break out in a prickly heat all over her body. Maman has ordered the cook to serve spicy foods in the hopes it will worsen her discomfort . . .

> . . . Henriette has taken the downstairs servant, Marie, for her personal *femme de chambre.* As a result, Marie gives herself airs and allows herself to be openly courted by the gardener's lad, Jacquot Pujol. Yesterday she actually talked back to Maman, and Maman would have sent her packing but that Henriette complained loudly and persuaded Hugo to forbid it.

"Jacquot Pujol. An ancestor of Didier?" Julian wondered.

Mentions of hot weather gave way to references to a rainy fall. Cécile continued to provide descriptions of domestic scenes in which Dominique behaved disgustingly, Odile sought to make her daughter-in-law's existence a misery, and Henriette, getting bigger by the day, gave as good as she got. Mara began to feel something like an exasperated affection for the writer, who had the knack of telling it like it was. Indeed, Cécile offered the same unadorned treatment to death as to life.

"Oh my god, Julian," Mara said. "Listen to this."

> . . . Today Papa choked on his food in the middle of our Advent luncheon. It happened so quickly that he was dead before anyone could do a thing . . . It was right after the *hure de sanglier* had been served. Everyone was already upset because our *régisseur* had just burst in to tell us that Garneau's little girl, Yvette, had been found in the woods, her throat torn open, like the oth-

ers . . . Maman is prostrate, but I think less for Papa than because she fears for Hugo. Dear God, calamities fall on us like rain, and just when we had all begun to hope that the scourge had passed.

"Julian, three children went missing and three known victims had their throats ripped out during Hugo's lifetime. A teenage boy, Emile Joubert, who was tending his father's cows, an old washerwoman named la Claudine, and Yvette Garneau."

"And Maman Odile was frightened for her son. I wonder why."

"I think we know."

"Does Cécile say more?"

Unfortunately, she did not. That entry was Cécile's last.

32

The luncheon was held on the day of the Feast of Sainte-Barbe. The guests came to Aurillac in closed carriages, the horses steaming and stamping in the cold air. Henriette, big with child, had refused to be confined to her room, as decency demanded. She had put on a loose gown of rose-colored satin and was on hand to greet (and scandalize) the guests with her smile, her unseemly dress, and her swollen belly. Abbé Fortin, wrapped like a mummy against the weather, arrived first, in an ancient black cabriolet. The others who followed were people whom Henriette had also met: Hugo's uncle and aunt; Maître and Madame Caillaud; the Saint-Anselm headmaster; the fat, velveteen-jacketed squire and his wife, a broad-hipped woman with the ruddy cheeks of a milkmaid.

The only stranger to Henriette was Hugo's other sister, Catherine, on exeat *for the holidays from the Abbaye des Eaux. Henriette studied this member of the family with interest. She had little else to divert her. The tall, pale* religieuse, *with her otherworldly air, seemed indifferent to her surroundings and oblivious of her pregnant sister-in-law. She kept herself entirely to a long, murmured conversation with the old abbot, who huddled in a high-backed chair near the fire.*

Odile sat with the women guests on sofas in the middle of the grand salon. Henriette sat in the same area but somewhat apart. Cécile slouched ungainly in a bergère *next to the piano that no one played. On his feet for a change, Dominique stood in another part of the room with the* notaire *and the headmaster, making desultory talk. Hugo, who had gone hunting that morning, had not yet returned. Odile expressed her* annoyance, or perhaps her anxiety, by looking frequently for him to arrive through the double doors of the salon. They remained shut.

Eventually, unable to contain herself any longer, Odile rose and approached Henriette, who was positioned too far away for her to address without raising her voice.

"Shameless! This is your fault," hissed the mother. "But for you, he would be here. He tires of you already."

Henriette's riposte was swift. With a terrible sweetness, she responded loudly enough for the aunt, Madame Velveteen Jacket, and Madame Caillaud to hear, "Oh, belle-mère, you know he stays away only because of you. He has often complained to me that you keep such a poor table that he must hunt daily to keep us all in meat."

Odile went rigid with rage and returned to her chair. Henriette's words were partly true. The family and household staff numbered fifteen, including three outdoor servants, all of whom had to be fed. Except for her social entertainments, when it was necessary to make a good impression, Odile was notoriously mean with her fare.

Henriette nodded archly at the open-mouthed female guests and rose. Her porcelain exterior hid the facts that she felt unwell and that she was now furious. Furious with Odile, with Hugo for not being there. She therefore sought a victim in Cécile, who immediately struggled out of her armchair to move away the moment she saw her sister-in-law approaching the spot where she sheltered.

"Don't go." Henriette followed the large young woman across the room, cornering her in a window bay. "I want to talk to you."

"What about?" Cécile looked warily at her belle-soeur. Henriette only ever spoke to her to make wounding comments.

"Is it true you leave for the nunnery in the new year?"

"None of your business," said Cécile, sensing a trap.

"Oh, la! Am I about to uncover more nasty family secrets? Are they making you do it, ma pauvre? Surely you're not in the family way? Or is it simply that no man will have you? It will be good for the family coffers, you know, because you will be made, like your sister, to give up your rights to the estate, and there's little enough left to go around as it is. Poor sacrificial goat, your father's excesses make it necessary to bury you alive in that god-hole. No more riding for you."

Cécile maintained a mulish silence.

"Very well," said Henriette cheerfully. She was feeling better already. "Tell me about your sister." Henriette gestured at the religieuse, deep in her tête-à-tête with the abbot. "Was she also forced to take the veil?"

"I don't know what you mean. You shouldn't talk like that. She gave herself to God."

"Cats more likely, else why take the name Sister Gertrude?"

"What's wrong with that?"

"Oh, you are such a ninny, Cécile. Gertrude is the patron saint of cats."

Cécile, who did not know how to answer this, said the only thing that came into her head: "You think you've made such a good marriage, don't you. But you don't know Hugo."

"Indeed?" Henriette for once was intrigued. And vaguely troubled. She did not, in fact, know her husband well at all, except that he was a heavy man, heavy in bed, hard of hand—but, then, weren't all men?—who spoke little except to talk about the hunt, and who brought with him the smell of damp woods and horses and earth.

Cécile, having captured Henriette's attention, was unable to sustain it, however. In answer to her sister-in-law's inquiring look, she responded weakly, "He—he does things."

Henriette continued to stare at her mockingly.

"He drinks the blood of animals he kills," Cécile blurted out in desperation. It was something she had never told a soul. "I've—I've seen him."

"Oh, ma chère," said Henriette, destroying any element of shock Cécile's revelation might have had. "I've known that for ages!"

In the end they were thirteen to table—Hugo unpardonably had still not made an appearance—an inauspicious number sitting down to a *ponderous meal unleavened by wit, news, or repartee. The one spot of color was Henriette (in her shameless pink gown), whom Dominique had insisted on placing to his right, thus offending protocol and Madame Caillaud. The menu consisted of six courses, beginning with a thin leek soup, followed by a cheese soufflé. They had just finished a rather tough ragout of goose, and the table was being prepared for the fourth course, when the de Bonfonds' steward rushed in to inform the company of a terrible piece of news: the naked body of the youngest daughter of a neighboring farmer had just been found in a field. The child's throat had been torn open.*

"Mon dieu!" shrieked Madame Caillaud, clutching her napkin to her breast. "The Beast again!"

A group of hunters was combing the woods in the hope of catching the thing that had done it, and the steward wished to know if he could dispatch all available menservants to join the effort.

"Certainly not," snapped Odile from the other end of the table. "The child is dead. Nothing more can be done for her. It will have to wait until the boar's head has been served."

She referred to the pièce de résistance, and, Beast or no Beast, she was not being entirely unreasonable, for the head was set out on an immense platter that required two serving men to carry it in. Hugo had killed the boar, of course, and the stripping of the skull, together with the preparation of the forcemeat and the salpicon of chicken, bacon, nuts, and pigs' tongues with which the head skin was stuffed, had taken two days.

But the horrific news had cast a pall on the company. They sat in silence as the dish was paraded around the table for all to admire, and then placed before Dominique to be served. Eventually, the abbot spoke. In his reedy voice, he told the party of a time some fifty years ago when, as a young curé *newly arrived in Sigoulane, he had been given to understand that he had come to a place where something very evil lived. His rambling recollections did nothing to lighten the mood.*

It was one of the boar's ears that did Dominique de Bonfond in.

They had been cut off earlier and simmered in a jelly stock, then skew-ered back in place and coated with a cold brown sauce. The host had been eating one of the ears while telling an off-color story (about a sex-ton who had lost his trousers) in an attempt to enliven the party. For-tunately, Abbé Fortin, because of his deafness, heard very little of the lengthy tale. He sat bemused and thoughtful throughout the account. Sister Gertrude, to his right, bowed over her plate. Her lips moved, as if in prayer. Dominique had just delivered the punch line and had thrown his head back to roar with laughter, when a piece of the ear lodged in his throat. He coughed, gagged, reared out of his chair, clawed at his neck, turned purple, and finally pitched forward onto the pièce de résistance with a sickening thud and a spectacular splattering of forcemeats.

It was at this point that the doors to the terrace flew open, admit-ting a cold blast of air. Hugo entered, a dazed expression on his face. His boots were muddy, and his neckcloth and the front of his hunting jacket were covered in blood. He must have made some attempt to wash himself, however, for most of his face was clean, except for some faint smears around his mouth and under his chin. His hands were also moderately clean, although the nails were rimmed in red. The horrified company stared speechless from the father, lying in the ruins of the boar's head, to the son.

"Heaven save us," gasped Madame Caillaud. "The child—"

Madame Velveteen Jacket crossed herself and began to weep. Odile went pale and gripped the table's edge. Hugo's uncle half rose and sat down again. His wife let out a low moan.

Henriette salvaged the moment and what remained of her hus-band's reputation. "For heaven's sake, Hugo," she said coolly, "come and sit down. What was it this time? A stag or a chevreuil?"

Crazily, Cécile laughed.

33

·

Mara closed the last folder of Cécile's diary and checked her watch. They had been at it over four hours. She pulled off her glasses and rolled her neck. Then, with a puzzled frown, she said:

"You know, Julian, it's really odd. If Cécile did have it on with her army captain in Paris, she should have given birth sometime around February or March of 1871. I don't remember seeing a mention of her pregnancy anywhere, do you?"

He shoved his glasses to the top of his head. "Come to think of it, no."

She scanned the pages of the 1871 folder again. "You'd think she would have written about something as important as that. I mean, the woman's existence was utterly bleak. Apart from seeing animals slaughtered, nothing happened in her life. And of course there's no official record of a birth."

"Well, there wouldn't be, would there? I mean, if she or the family killed the kid. Maybe that applies to the diary, too. Perhaps parts of it are missing."

"Someone destroyed the bits that referred to the baby? I suppose that's what they would have done. The problem is, it's hard to tell if there are gaps because most of the entries aren't dated. The organization of the material is entirely Jean-Claude's guesswork." She took up the 1870 folder from Julian's stack and began riffling through it. "The only hint of Cécile being in a family way is this comment in Eloïse's letter about 'given your circumstances.'

And I'm not even sure about that. The woman sounds so self-righteous, you'd think she'd have delivered a full-blown moral lecture, given the chance."

"I didn't see a thing about my orchid, either." Julian's tone was aggrieved. "In fact, Cécile made no mention of flora of any sort. I'm beginning to wonder if the damned woman had any feeling at all for nature, let alone flowers. I mean, even her horse was called 'Money.' Or I suppose 'Argent' could have meant 'Silver.' Anyway, I doubt if she ever embroidered so much as an initial on a handkerchief, let alone an accurate depiction of a *Cypripedium* on a shawl." He stood up. Hands in his pockets, he strolled slowly past the paintings of the de Bonfond ancestors. Mara had earlier given him the family tour. He paused before Henriette, Odile, and Cécile. "Quite frankly, none of them looks like a flower-lover or an embroiderer."

"No," Mara agreed. "They don't."

She joined him in a second circuit around the room.

"Nasty-looking beast," Julian commented, stopping before Xavier's portrait. He meant the dog. "I could see it as a man-killer."

Mara, scowling up at the baron's features, sucked her breath in sharply. "Julian, I just realized who Adjudant Compagnon reminds me of. Xavier de Bonfond. He has the same red eyebrows and sticking-out eyes."

"Hmm. Well, seigneurial rights and all that, you know. And his grandson Dominique seemed to have been a skirt-chaser in his own right. Maybe they both spread the family genes about a bit."

Then Mara said, "You know, maybe we're not getting the full picture. If Eloïse wrote to Cécile, then surely Cécile must have written to Eloïse. Jean-Claude said something about the Verdier family papers."

"You think we should pay a visit to Christophe's Verdier cousins and find out if they have any of Cécile's letters?"

"Right. Come to think of it, I suspect that's exactly what Jean-

Claude did. Even though he promised not to deal with them, I think he talked his way into the Verdier archives and discovered something that got him killed."

The house was a large stone structure located just off the square in Sigoulane Village. Guy and Mariette Verdier received them with a mixture of wariness and affability. Both knew that Mara was working in some capacity for Christophe, and that Julian was landscaping the Coteaux de Bonfond pavilion. Both seemed to regard their visitors as emissaries of the enemy who could be persuaded, with the right treatment, to switch allegiances. Julian found himself staring at the wife. He could have sworn Mariette had been a brunette when he last saw her. Her hair was now a brassy blond. Maybe she had dyed it to go with the banana-skin-yellow spandex halter top she wore.

"You're lucky you caught me in." Guy waved the visitors over to a fake zebra-hide sofa. "I usually golf on Saturday afternoons."

"And Sundays," Mariette mouthed to Julian. "I'm a weekend widow." Julian half suspected she would have dug her elbow into his side if he had been within digging distance.

The plump, pink-faced lawyer gave a whinnying laugh to show that he knew his wife to be a great kidder. Mara caught a glint of gold in one of his back molars.

"It's really your father we came to see, Maître Verdier," said Mara, careful to use his title. The pair lived with Michel Verdier, or perhaps it was the other way around. "We really don't want to trouble you."

"Oh, I'm sure I can answer any questions you may have about the de Bonfonds just as well." He obviously preferred it that way. "Anyway, Papa is out with the vines right now. Now, how about some coffee?"

Mariette laid on the works: a silver tray with a silver pot, porcelain demitasses and saucers, a plate of pastel-colored macaroons.

Since she assumed they were there to talk about Baby Blue, she launched right into the matter as she poured. *"C'est une très mauvaise affaire.* The villagers are very upset about it. You were there that morning"—a nod in Julian's direction—"you saw how worked up they were. Why, if it hadn't been for my husband, I think they would have torn Antoine and Denise apart."

"That may be putting it a little strong," said Guy in the careful manner of his profession. "At any rate, it's been most distressing. For us, too. We Verdiers, you see, are related by marriage to the de Bonfonds through my four-times-great-aunt Odile. An infanticide in the family. Well, you can imagine. Naturally, we want to find out the truth."

"So do we," said Mara in a tone that made the husband pause momentarily to look at her.

"Our concern, of course," Guy went on, "is that the de Bonfonds will attempt to sweep things under the carpet."

"Christophe would much rather Baby Blue had nothing to do with his family," Mara conceded. "But then, since you're related, I suppose you feel the same?"

"Pas du tout. Crime must out," cried Mariette, smug in the knowledge that it was someone else's crime. "You do know he's gay, don't you?"

"What's that got to do with it?" Julian objected. In fact, the little man had somehow always struck him as asexual.

"Oh," she said, "not that *we* care. It's nobody's business, is it? But it just shows the kind of person he is."

Julian found himself disliking the nouvelle-blonde.

Guy made a noise, a judicial clearing of the throat. "All we're saying is, the child was obviously murdered, and it would be best for all concerned—I speak for everyone in Sigoulane—if the child were identified once and for all as a de Bonfond—"

"—bastard," inserted Mariette.

"—and the matter laid to rest."

"Of course, it will blacken the family's reputation around here even more, if that's possible." Mariette leaned across confidentially toward Julian, offering deep cleavage. "You saw how much the villagers hate them."

"I saw that someone broke a window and had a go with spray paint. It all seemed a bit over the top to me."

"Ah"—the lawyer wagged a finger in the air—"that's because you don't understand the underlying dynamics."

"I understand the other winegrowers in the valley, your father included, wanted the de Bonfonds to expand their *chai* to give them local processing and storage, and the de Bonfonds turned them down."

A gruff voice spoke behind them. "It was a reasonable offer." Guy's father, Michel, had come quietly into the room. Julian remembered him as the wiry old fellow he had seen talking to Antoine in front of the pavilion. He was wearing the same clothes: dungarees, a plaid shirt, and a floppy black beret which he now took off and tossed onto a table. "We said we'd help build the addition and pay a lower fee for use, or they could build it and we'd pay a higher usage fee. They were expanding anyway. Would have been worth their while to add a few square meters."

"Except that Pierre and that sister of his wanted it all their way," said Guy with feeling. "They wanted the growers to contribute to capital costs *and* pay the higher fee. It's their way of squeezing people out because they want the land."

It wasn't what Denise had told him. Julian wondered which was the true story.

"For some people, land—*le terroir*—is a commodity," Michel said. There was anger in his voice. "Especially Denise. She has no feeling for it, no respect. The character of a wine comes from the soil. She thinks with the right tinkering she can produce something the land was never meant to give. Antoine understands *terroir*, but he's not the way of the future. Nor am I," the winegrower added with an overlay of bitterness. It was the age-old conflict between nature and technology, in which some survived and others got buried.

Introductions were made. Michel Verdier shook hands with Mara and Julian without any real show of friendliness. He helped himself to coffee, preferring a mug to a demitasse, and sat down in a rocking chair by the window.

"It seems to me," Julian said bluntly, "that no love is lost between the Verdiers and the de Bonfonds, however you view it."

Guy, looking cagey, opened his mouth, but Mariette upstaged him. "The de Bonfonds have done despicable things." She fairly bounced with outrage. "Land-grabbers, all of them. Tell them, Guy."

Michel cut in. "*A quoi bon?* Why rake over old history?" The rockers of his chair grated harshly on the floorboards.

The lawyer said, "What my wife said is true. The treachery of the de Bonfonds goes back a long way. You see, in the 1800s, because of a reversal of fortune, the Verdiers came to owe the de Bonfonds a large amount of money. When Tante Odile married Dominique de Bonfond, the de Bonfonds agreed to settle both the debt and the dowry in return for the Verdier house, although we retained the lease on the property. Stiff terms, but still acceptable to our family, if only the de Bonfonds had kept to the agreement."

"Ha!" scoffed Mariette.

"The agreement was that Odile and Dominique's eldest son would marry one of his Verdier cousins—Hugo and Eloïse, as it turned out."

"They were engaged until that *putain* Henriette entered the scene," Mariette cut in.

Guy shot her a severe look. "Had they married, *their* children would have inherited both properties. It would have brought the two families and the estates together in a very satisfactory way."

Thereby getting back for the Verdiers what went out with Odile, Julian thought. It was somehow always about land and property.

"Our family brought an action against the de Bonfonds for breach of promise, but the ruling went against us. We always suspected that Dominique de Bonfond bribed the court. Tante Odile was on our side of course, but by then Hugo had already married Henriette, there was nothing she could do, and a settlement at that point would have meant money out of hand for the de Bonfonds."

"But that's not all," interrupted Mariette. "Tell them about the *tontine.*"

"Water under the bridge." Michel favored his daughter-in-law with a look of distaste.

"At least let me put the record straight, Father," Guy said. "You see, before the war, my grandfather Guillaume Verdier and Hérault de Bonfond, Antoine's father, bought a parcel of land together. Twelve hectares—"

"On the west side of the valley, which just so happens to be the most productive part of the Coteaux de Bonfond *vignoble* today," put in Mariette with a sniff.

"They bought it *en tontine,* which, if you're unfamiliar with the term, is a simple arrangement whereby the property, on the death of one party, goes to the survivor. During the war, both fought in the Resistance. My grandfather was caught trying to blow up a German supply depot. He was sent to a detainment camp in Périgueux and reportedly shot in March 1943, so the land went to Antoine's father as the survivor. Then Hérault was killed in a skirmish outside Allas-les-Mines nine months later, in December. However, the next year we got word that my grandfather had not been shot. He had been deported but had managed to escape and was still alive."

"Listen to him. Not even born, and he tells it like he was there." Michel's voice was laced with the bitter irony of a man so long used to drawing the short straw that he had come to see the faintly funny side of it. He rose stiffly and refilled his mug.

"That meant," went on the irrepressible Guy, "that my grandfather had survived Hérault, which of course reversed the *tontine*. My grandmother approached the de Bonfonds on the matter—"

"She just wanted some kind of *redressement*." Michel stirred in sugar. "A half-share, not the whole parcel. After all, both families had suffered enough."

"Those grasping *avares* wouldn't give up so much as a sou!" Mariette was unable to contain herself any longer. "Not them! 'Land is land,' they said. 'It can be bought or inherited. Not given.' 'If Guillaume is still alive,' they said, 'let him come forth to make his claim.' "

"And did he?" asked Mara.

"No," replied Michel. His tone was hollow. "He was one of many who never returned."

"But he was a hero of the Resistance, let me assure you." Guy went over to a table and returned with a photograph framed in silver. "This is him. Taken before the war. Ask anyone in the valley who knew my grandfather. A man of courage. A man who risked his life for others. Did you know there's a special plaque dedicated to him in the square? That, at least, is something those de Bonfonds can't take away from us."

Mara and Julian saw a stout young man in his thirties. The round face, topped by curly, sandy hair, was the less fleshy precursor to Guy's, except that it was distinguished by a broken nose that tilted comically to one side.

Guy said, "Well, you said you wanted information on the de Bonfonds. There you have it. Land-hungry and shameless. As for Baby Blue, Christophe will have a job accounting for the child in his family history"—he looked intensely gratified at the prospect—"but, then, I'm sure he employs minions to deal with that kind of thing." He smiled blandly at Mara.

The implication caused Mara to prickle immediately. "Not me. You've got it wrong." She was nobody's minion. Not anymore. She rose and replaced Guillaume's photograph on the table.

"But you were acting on his behalf vis-à-vis that Fournier fellow, were you not? And when you said you wanted information on the de Bonfonds, naturally I assumed . . ." Guy broke off, puzzled. "Then, if you're not working for Christophe, why are you here?"

Mara hesitated. The only answer she could give him was that she was a prime suspect trying to avoid a murder charge by uncovering Jean-Claude's killer, or at least the motive behind his death. She doubted that would go over well with a lawyer.

"Because, in addition to information on Baby Blue, I'm looking for a flower," Julian stepped in. "I've only seen an embroidered representation of it, on the shawl Baby Blue was wrapped in, as a matter of fact, and I want to trace the real thing." He addressed the lawyer directly. "Christophe's great-great-aunt Cécile corresponded for several years with *your* great-great-great-aunt Eloïse Verdier. We'd like to know if you have any of Cécile's letters. If Cécile did the embroidery, she may have written to your aunt about it, saying where she'd seen the actual flower or how she came to make a likeness of it."

"Not Cécile," Mariette surprised him by saying. "Eloïse. She was the needlewoman. There's an example of her work just over there." She wriggled out of her chair and led Julian to a large frame hanging on the wall at the far end of the room. Mounted within it was an antique square of silk, heavily embroidered with flowers. Julian was no judge of stitchery, but he could see that here was the same minute attention to botanical detail, the same subtle shading of tone as distinguished the embroidery on Baby Blue's shawl. He promptly dismissed the impression of sour piety conveyed by Eloïse's letters. Her needlework took his breath away.

"*C'est magnifique,*" he murmured. The flowers were life-sized, almost as fresh as those growing in meadows and hedgerows on a spring morning: *Rosa rugosa,* the simple wild rose; the many-pronged blossom of wild honeysuckle, what the French called *chèvrefeuille;* bright-yellow cowslip, nested in a bed of puckered leaves fashioned with cunning skill; and *Aquilegia vulgaris,* the deep-blue spurred cap of columbine. There were no orchids.

"The Verdiers have always been people of refinement," Mariette simpered. "The appreciation of nature was in Eloïse's blood."

"Unfortunately, I don't see the flower I'm looking for. You haven't anything else like this?" Julian asked as he followed Mariette back to their seats.

Mariette shook her head.

"That's too bad," said Mara. "Then I'm afraid it really is down to any evidence we can unearth through other material. Such as letters." She put the suggestion out hopefully.

Guy harrumphed. "You're asking for access to personal family papers?" He glanced at his father, who sat watchfully in his chair, the rockers still for the moment. "I'm afraid, madame, the Verdier archives contain things of a highly sensitive nature, to say nothing of their inestimable historical value. For example, the documents in our possession chart the disposition of lands and buildings in Verdier hands for over four centuries. Moreover, our archives don't just concern ourselves. They touch on the affairs of over a dozen local related families. I have an obligation to others."

He shook his head, getting into his stride. "You as strangers don't appreciate the intricacies of French succession law. Inheritance follows blood ties and is based on a priority system of entrenched heirs. Children before everyone. Barring issue, it goes to siblings and back *up* the line to surviving parents, grandparents, and so forth. Spouses didn't count until only recently. Under such circumstances there very naturally have arisen disputes that were settled by particular arrangements from time to time. Such material is therefore highly confidential. You appreciate, of course, that we can't allow just anyone—"

"I assume Jean-Claude Fournier also came to see you about this?" Mara interposed.

Guy turned coy. "I'm afraid I'm not at liberty to say."

She took that as a yes. "Do you mind my asking what he was interested in?"

"Really, madame, excuse my candor, but it's none of your business."

"He's been murdered," she told him. "Your archives might have a bearing on his death. Did you inform the police that he'd been to see you?"

She could see from their reactions that they had not. Guy's mouth opened but no sound came out. The watchfulness in Michel's eyes turned hostile. Mariette's mind was working, and whatever it was working on made her expression tight with fear.

Michel was the first to recover. "Why should we have? There was no connection."

"Look," Mara conciliated, "we don't want to cause problems. As Julian said, we're mainly interested in the exchange of letters between Cécile and Eloïse. But I'd also like to see anything else you have pertaining to the de Bonfonds, and especially anything you showed to Jean-Claude Fournier. We're not asking a lot. Co-operate with us, and I assure you we'll be very respectful of your privacy." She left the alternative scenario to their imaginations.

The situation had suddenly become tense. Father and son exchanged a quick glance. Mariette writhed in her spandex. "Oh, what does it matter?" she cried out. "Show it to them, for god's sake. We don't want the gendarmes on our doorstep. What is it anyway? Just some miserable bits of paper—"

"Mariette!" thundered Guy.

"Pas question." Michel put an end to the discussion. He did not raise his voice, yet the authority in it was undeniable. "If the police think there's something in our family papers, let them come for them. Until then, what's private stays private." He rose, set his mug on the tray with a force that made the china rattle, hooked his beret from the table with a gnarled finger, and strode out of the house. They heard the back door slam. Seconds later, a car started up.

Guy and Mariette stared coldly at their visitors, clearly wanting them to go. But Julian ignored the sudden drop in ambient temperature. He had realized that it was not Cécile who would lead him to his *Cypripedium*. It was Eloïse. Her needlework was as distinctive as an artist's brushstroke. He needed no further confirmation of who had embroidered Baby Blue's shawl. He needed instead to know everything possible about Eloïse herself, where she had lived, walked, and ridden, for she, like Cécile, had also gone on horseback. However, in answer to his questions, the only thing Guy could, or would, tell him was that she had never married and that she had lived out her life on the old Verdier estate. But that was no longer in the family, hadn't been for 169 years.

"Where is it?" Julian asked.

Mariette stared at him as if he were stupid. "In the valley, of course. Antoine has it. It used to be called 'Les Verdiers.' *They* renamed it 'Les Chardonnerets,' but to us it will always be 'Les Verdiers.' " It was a nasty play on words. A kind of avian one-upmanship. *Chardonneret* meant "goldfinch." *Verdier* meant plain old "greenfinch."

For Julian, it was the worst possible news. He knew the house all right. Les Chardonnerets stood in the middle of a vineyard. Any orchid that might have once grown there had long since given up the ghost.

They didn't want us poking around in their papers," Mara observed as they drove out of Sigoulane Village. "But they were willing to let Jean-Claude have a look. I wonder if that means he found something in those archives that now has the Verdiers running scared."

Julian gave her a sideways glance before downshifting. "You think Christophe may not be the only one Jean-Claude tried to blackmail?"

"I think he made a practice of it."

34

The little man was breathing hard. The normally rosy O of his mouth was gray and drawn back sharply against his teeth. Unused to exertion, he struggled up the rugged slope, fighting his way through the heavy undergrowth, running as fast as his short, plump legs would carry him. The sounds of pursuit spread out noisily through the woods below him, men yelling, crashing through the trees, the frantic barking of a dog.

"Get it! Get it!"

"Over here!"

"Merde!"

Damn his luck! With so much forest all around, why did he have to run into those savages just here? Thank god there was only one dog, an awful liver-and-white Brittany spaniel. But the howling it had set up when it had scented him was bloodcurdling and sounded like a pack in full bay.

The explosion of a shotgun caused him to utter a shriek of terror. Dear god, now they were shooting at him. He knew from his boyhood hunting days what a shotgun could do. At close range, the shot entered as a solid mass, leaving a crater big enough to put your fist into. From a distance, the shot rained out, peppering the target with bloody holes. Rifles were infinitely more elegant.

He ran, clambering over roots, dodging branches, tripping, pushing himself to his feet, and continuing to scramble as best he could up the steep, forested incline. Just as he thought he could go no farther, another explosion drove him on. At last his legs gave way beneath him. Christophe fell heavily to the ground, his lungs burning, his breath squeezing painfully out of him in broken sobs. Eventually, he managed to drag himself under the branches of a broadly spreading pine.

The irony of it was that *they* were on *his* land! As he lay recovering, he was briefly tempted to stand his ground, to order those morons off his property. But he knew he could not do that. He could keep his hands in his pockets, but his eye, his yellow, slanting eye, would certainly raise suspicion. His only safety lay in going to ground and remaining hidden until the situation changed.

The dog had ceased barking. Everything was oddly quiet. Had he succeeded in throwing the hunters off his trail? He sat up shakily. Peering through foliage, he found that he had a view of the clearing at the bottom of the slope. What he saw astonished him. Another group of people, women among them, had converged on the hunters, one of whom held the dog in check by the collar. However, instead of joining forces and coming after him, it seemed that they were having an argument. Some of the newcomers were waving their arms, and one carried a placard. SAVE—he squinted to make out the large, hand-painted letters—SAVE OUR WOLVES. Christophe almost burst out laughing. Not lingering to question his change of luck, he got to his feet and hurried away.

He had to get to Didier before it was too late, and he had very little time.

Mara heard the distant gunfire as she made her way down the path toward Didier's hut. Was the old man off hunting with his Babette? she wondered. If so, he was definitely out of season. To her surprise, the door with the blistered green paint swung back just as her knuckles made contact with it.

"Ah, bonjour, Didier." She jumped slightly as the gardener materialized, troll-like, out of the gloom. *"Vous êtes ici."*

" 'Course I'm here." His patois was heavily drawn out, everything ending in "mm" and "ng." "There's a bell." He pointed with a blackened forefinger to the side of the door. Buried in the ivy to her right Mara saw an old brass bell, green with age, riveted to the stonework. Neither she nor Julian had noticed it when they were there before. "What do you want?"

"Well, I was hoping I could speak with you. It's important. It concerns Christophe." She invoked his employer's name for effect. Beyond the old man, Mara glimpsed a cavelike room, a fireplace, and a chair. She could make out nothing more of his living environment. Did he have indoor plumbing, electricity, a television?

Didier considered her suspiciously for a moment. "Wait here," he said and ducked away. He returned a minute later with a plastic sack. "Come on." He pushed past her, pulling the door to behind him. In the way of many country people, he never bothered to lock up. Folks in the valley went about their business as they should. They didn't have time to steal your belongings or pester you with useless questions.

Mara hurried after him. For an old man, he was surprisingly agile and walked at a terrific pace.

"Where are you going?" she barely had time to ask before he cut abruptly off through the trees, onto a faint trail probably known only to himself. She scrambled after him.

"Morels," he said cryptically.

The morel was a favorite spring mushroom that made its sudden appearance after a rain. An ungainly-looking fungus with a wrinkled head that reminded Mara of brains, it was highly prized by locals for its mild, smooth flavor. Didier was off to gather a bag of them. That he so readily allowed her to accompany him told Mara two things: first, he didn't regard her as competition, for mushroom-hunters were notoriously secretive about their favorite sites; and, second, he had somehow correctly surmised that even if she were given a morel she wouldn't know what to do with it.

Mara trotted after his retreating back. "Didier," she said a little breathlessly, "you told me Jean-Claude Fournier was asking you questions. You know that Christophe has made me responsible for this Baby Blue thing. That is, I commissioned Jean-Claude for Christophe to find out who the baby was. Therefore"—she dodged in time as a branch, pulled forward by Didier's passage, snapped back into her face—"I really do need to know what Jean-Claude talked to you about."

They were now descending the back slope of the Aurillac estate, Didier bobbing down the trail like an elderly but sure-footed chamois.

"It could be important," she called after him, running now because he was fast disappearing through the brush. In the next minute, she nearly fell over him. He was bent, nose to ground, over a ring of morels growing in a small clearing.

"Good crop, this." He cackled.

"I said it could be important." Mara found herself almost shouting into his rather dirty left ear. Was the man deaf or purposely ignoring her? "Didier, you know Jean-Claude was killed. I think someone murdered him because of something he found out about the de Bonfonds. And the baby. Surely you see that you've got to tell me what he asked you. It could be the clue to everything."

"It was none of his business, and none of yours," muttered the old man. He was now harvesting mushrooms with a small wide-bladed knife and popping them into his sack.

She decided to take a firm hand with him. "I think you'd better let me be the judge of that." And when this produced no response, she said, "Didier, how do you think Christophe will take it if I tell him you refused to cooperate with me?"

"He's not here to say, is he?"

A thought occurred to Mara. "Do you know where he is?"

The gardener slid an eye in her direction. "No, I don't. He don't confide in me. Anyway," he added, "this is family matters that's best not spoke of by you nor me."

"That's where you're wrong. This thing has gone beyond the family, Didier. Let me tell you what I think. I think Baby Blue was the child of Christophe's great-great-aunt Cécile by her own brother. I think Cécile killed her baby not just because he was the product of incest but because she also believed that werewolves ran in the family! You're from here, Didier. Your family has worked on this estate for generations. You know the old stories, so you must know that people really did believe in werewolves at one time. And that's what Jean-Claude came to ask you about, wasn't it? He wanted proof that the de Bonfonds were behind the creature known as the Sigoulane Beast, proof that Christophe has inherited the strain, and that he's the one who's responsible for the recent attacks in the valley."

The old man straightened up to stare at her, knife in hand. He looked angry, but that might have been because his face was flushed from bending over.

She pressed ahead. "Now, what if we try a slightly different take on that story? What if Christophe isn't a werewolf but suffers from an illness that makes him act like a wolf? It's called lycanthropy, Didier. It's a real condition, and it's treatable, or at least controllable with drugs. Christophe goes into hiding with every full moon, doesn't he? You and Thérèse have always covered up for him because until now you've been able to control him. What do you do, tie him down? Lock him up? Except that he's learned to give you the slip. You can't shield him anymore, you know. Christophe may have been relatively harmless before, but this time he's turned violent. I think Jean-Claude tried to blackmail Christophe because he's a lycanthrope, and Christophe threw him from the terrace and finished him off by strangling him and maybe even biting his throat out."

Didier continued to stare at her. A droplet of mucus had formed on the end of his nose and now snailed onto his upper lip. He wiped it away with his sleeve. "I've got nothing to say," he muttered finally, "bar one thing." He shuffled off, glaring back at her over his shoulder. "I never heard of no whatever-you-call-it, and you're *folle*. You've lost your senses."

"Listen, you stubborn old man," Mara shouted in frustration, catching up to him. "You don't have to believe me, but there's one thing you have to understand. Jean-Claude was murdered, and you're probably the only person who knows why. Can't you get it through your head that there's a killer on the loose? Forget your loyalties, Didier. You can't let Christophe go on—"

The sudden explosion came from behind her and to her right. Didier spun around with a look of bewilderment on his weathered face. Confusedly, Mara remembered the shooting she had heard earlier. Was some careless hunter firing nearby? The old man was standing at a funny angle, tipping awkwardly to one side, knees slightly bent, his left arm dangling loosely. She realized that he had been hit when she saw blood dripping from his fingertips. Then she screamed as another shot rang out, leaving a spattered image of scarlet and the dead certainty that whoever was shooting at them had made no mistake.

They both struck the ground together. That was because she had thrown herself on the old man. Didier lay under her, sprawled on his back, staring up at the sky with the same puzzled expression. Blood was pumping out of him at an alarming rate. Out of her, too, she realized. She felt suddenly sick and light-headed. A searing pain spread through her right shoulder. She watched with amazement as dark, wet patches blossomed vividly on Didier's chest, on her own clothing, soaked into the earth.

They were at the edge of the clearing, in plain view, with no cover at hand. Even if there was, their assailant had only to circle around and come at them from their unprotected side. Their only defense was Didier's little knife. It lay beyond her reach among a scattering of cut morels that had spilled from the sack when the gardener had fallen. Play dead, the functioning part of her brain ordered. Very shortly they might not have to pretend. She pressed herself down against the old man. Didier's breathing, at first raspy, had now trailed away to a light, rapid squeak. His eyes were closed; his skin was ashen. Where was the shooter? Her ears strained to pick up the soft swish of grass, the sounds of a killer's approach. At any moment she expected to feel the barrel of a rifle jammed into the back of her neck, imagined her brain exploding with the devastation of the bullet.

Didier made a gurgling noise. His mouth was filling up with blood. She had to do something or he would choke. Carefully, she turned his head to the side and pulled down the corner of his mouth to let the blood drain. He struggled weakly, trying to speak.

"Stay still," she whispered urgently.

" 'coutez."

"Oui? I'm listening. Just don't move."

"Should've told you."

Yes, you should have, you pigheaded old coot, she raged inwardly. Whatever he had to say, it was now too late.

His speech was heavily slurred, but she made it out well enough. "More than one."

"More than one? Didier, more than one what?"

Blood had welled up again in his mouth. His lips pushed together in the effort of forming a single word.

"Baby." He choked. His final words before they both lost consciousness were "Cut off his head."

Laurent, who had just come on duty, took the call. A minute later, he ran down the hall and burst into his superior's office.

"There's been another shooting, sir," he shouted. "This one sounds serious."

35

S he's conscious."

Mara turned her head in the direction of the voice. A face came near her. Glasses reflecting twin orbs of light, the eyes behind them invisible, the rest of the features blurred. She wondered if she was still in the little clearing. However, the air had a different quality, a kind of denseness. There was a smell, too, sharp, sour. Then she made out a white ceiling, a green curtain, the corner of a stainless-steel cart. She tried to move and found that her right arm was immobilized.

"You're in hospital," said the face. The voice was feminine. "I'm Dr. Villotte."

"Why—?"

"You were shot. Fortunately, it's a flesh wound. The bullet passed directly through the deltoid without doing any serious damage. You've lost blood, but you should be out of here in a few days."

"Didier?" Mara asked, remembering.

"Intensive Care and well looked after."

The truth of the matter was that it was doubtful Didier would make it. A bullet had been removed from his left lung. The surgeon gave him a thirty-seventy chance. His granddaughter had been there earlier, crying her heart out in the visitors' bay. Sergeant Naudet had questioned Stéphanie closely, pressing her to think of anyone who might have wanted to harm her grandfather. Sobbing, she had shaken her head, her pigtails dangling like sad little sheaves of corn over her breasts. Breathing hard, the kindly gendarme had taken her hand and promised solemnly that he would do everything in his power to ensure that the assailant was apprehended.

Dr. Villotte conferred with someone—*"Très bien.* She's heavily sedated. Fifteen minutes"—and withdrew. The pockmarked features of Adjudant Compagnon came into view. Behind him Mara glimpsed Laurent's gangling form.

"Alors, madame," said Compagnon, pulling a chair up to the bedside. He sat down heavily. His tone was unusually gentle. "You had a lucky break. A group of hunters and their dog found you. Their appearance probably interrupted whoever did this. Do you have any idea who might have wanted to kill you?"

"Not me," Mara murmured. "Didier. Stop him talking."

"Stop him talking about what?"

Mara's lids drooped against the eyebrows that hovered above her like orange wings. "It has to do," she whispered, "with werewolves."

To his credit, Compagnon listened to her without interruption. Only when she reached the part about lycanthropes and the modern Sigoulane Beast did his face contract into a scowl so violent that it looked as if it were being squeezed sideways in a duck press. Behind him, Laurent scribbled rapidly on his pad.

Compagnon pinched the bridge of his nose and took a deep breath. "All right. Let's say your theory is right. Jean-Claude Fournier tried to blackmail Christophe de Bonfond for being a lycanthrope or whatever, and de Bonfond felt sufficiently threatened to eliminate him. Why shoot the gardener?"

"He knows something." Mara's voice was barely audible, and both gendarmes had to strain to catch her words. "His family's been with the de Bonfonds for generations."

"Then why wait a whole week to silence him? Fournier was killed on the ninth. Today's the sixteenth. Why not eliminate the old fellow straight away as well?"

In the absence of any response from the woman in the bed, Laurent suggested, "Maybe de Bonfond thought he could trust Didier to hold his tongue, sir. Loyal family retainer, that kind of thing. Until Madame Dunn went to see him. Maybe de Bonfond was afraid this time Didier would talk. He could have seen her questioning the old man and realized it was too risky to let either of them live."

Compagnon stared at the gendarme and then turned back to Mara. "Madame Dunn, have you been in contact with Christophe de Bonfond?"

A shake of the head. "Not him." Mara was beginning to drift into space again. "Dr. Thibaud. Midi-Pyrénées Psychiatric Hospital . . . Ask her. If you don't believe me, ask her."

Laurent noted this down.

The adjudant pursued: "Did you happen to mention your plans to see Monsieur Pujol today to anyone, or were you aware of anyone following you en route to Aurillac?"

She felt herself floating above the hospital bed, out the window, back to the grassy clearing. Once again she heard the gardener's labored breathing, saw the blood spilling out of his mouth. And then it came back to her.

"Didier." She gestured feebly with her free hand. "Told me. Ba—ba—" Mara's tongue felt like an alien thing over which she had little control.

"Baba?" Compagnon had to lean in again to catch her words.

"Baby. Another baby."

Compagnon snapped up like a jack-in-the-box. "Are you saying there's another dead baby in the wall?"

Laurent jumped, too. "Maybe it was twins, sir."

She was hovering high in the air now, blowing like a leaf over a dark forest. But she managed to mumble before she lost consciousness, "Cut its head off. Ask Didier. Knows where Christophe is. Probably in contact with him all the time."

"Christophe de Bonfond." The adjudant eyed Mara speculatively as she slipped from him into a drugged sleep. "Even if this werewolf-lycanthrope business is all nonsense, which I think it is, if he's our assailant, we'll get him." He lumbered to his feet. "Stay with her, Naudet. Batailler's with Pujol. She and the gardener are off limits to everyone except medical personnel. Get identification and contact information from all visitors, and detain anyone fitting de Bonfond's description. As soon as she's awake, get as much out of her as you can. I'm going to have another word with de Bonfond's housekeeper."

"What about the second baby, sir?" Laurent called after his superior as the man strode away.

"*Putain!* All I need is another kid. Headless at that!"

Sergeant Naudet. I've just heard about Didier Pujol and Madame Dunn."

Laurent, recognizing the tall bearded man who came hurrying up to him in the hospital corridor, stood up. The two men shook hands.

"Do you have some identification, monsieur?"

"Identification?" Julian stared, unbelieving. "What's going on? You know me. I was there when they found the baby, when you and your uncle Loulou La Pouge turned up."

"So was Christophe de Bonfond," Laurent said woodenly. "I need to see some ID, please."

"All right, for pity's sake." Julian dug out his wallet. "Is she all right? Is it serious? Who the hell would want to shoot her?" He craned around Laurent to glimpse the motionless form on the bed, his voice strident with worry.

Laurent, scanning Julian's driver's license, relented. "It's just a flesh wound, monsieur, and it may be that Pujol was the intended victim."

"Didier? But why? I heard there were hunters about. Weren't they shot by accident?"

Laurent shook his head. "Madame Dunn and Monsieur Pujol were shot with a rifle. The hunters carried shotguns." Realizing that he had probably already divulged too much, the gendarme turned official. "I'm sorry, monsieur, I can't say anything more. Even what I've told you is confidential, strictly speaking."

"Incroyable!" Julian exclaimed, throwing up his arms. "All right. Keep your mouth buttoned, if you must. However, as one of France's Bravest and Best, perhaps you're not above receiving information? You might even find what I have to say of interest."

36

WEDNESDAY, 19 MAY

The hospital room was crowded. Julian sat at a little table wedged into a corner. Mara, cranked up to a sitting position, her right arm in a sling, worked on a portable bed desk. Both surfaces were covered with papers. Cartons filled with documents stood on the floor between them. One long uniformed leg, belonging to Laurent Naudet, on duty in the corridor, was just visible through the open doorway.

Guy Verdier had been furious when Compagnon had turned up to subpoena his family archives. Julian had not only convinced both the adjudant and Mara's twitchy *juge d'instruction* that the motive for Jean-Claude's death might lie in those archives, he had persuaded both men (after an official perusal of the material had turned up nothing) that he and Mara were the best people to pick out the critical material. Unable to deny them access, Guy sought to obstruct: although several gendarmes had already pawed through the material, he had insisted that Mara and Julian wear gloves while handling the documents. They were fragile. He said that Jean-Claude had worn white cotton gloves.

"Quelle merde," Mara had snorted. The genealogist had not worn any kind of protective gear when he had flipped through Cécile's diary.

Mara found Cécile's letters to Eloïse right away. There were sixteen of them, bundled together in a packet tied with a faded red ribbon. They covered the period between Eloïse's departure from Aurillac in the fall of 1870 and June 1879 (fortunately, the writer was better about dating her correspondence than her diary) and confirmed Cécile's talent for plain writing:

27 October 1870
Dear Eloïse,
I write to tell you that you should not worry overmuch for my family's reputation or take the matter so much to heart yourself, for all that Hugo left you in the lurch. No one really seems to care that Hugo did not marry you. They're far too taken up with gossiping about Henriette's décolletage . . .

A moment later, Mara called out excitedly, "Julian, come here. This is it. It's the proof you're looking for."

He leaned in to read with her:

4 November 1870
Dear Eloïse,
I cannot return the shawl as you asked because, even though you did the embroidery, I supplied the silk. You made it for my birthday last year, and I think it is too bad of you to demand it back. Besides, Henriette wants it for herself. She likes the color blue. Maman says for that reason I am to wear it as often as possible . . .

"Brilliant," said Julian, hungrily scanning the letter, as if Cécile's ungainly scrawl would tell him more. It didn't, and he realized with a sense of disappointment that it only confirmed what he already knew. However, the letter did raise an important point. Eloïse had made the shawl for Cécile in 1869. Was the orchid her idea or Cécile's? He revisited the question he had asked coming away from the Wolf Cave: why choose that particular flower? If it had the werewolf associations that Mara suspected, and since the shawl had been specifically intended for Cécile, did it point to a lycanthropic side to Hugo's sister that they had not suspected? She was, after all, a de Bonfond. Or was Eloïse making a nasty statement about the de Bonfonds in general? But no, she had done the needlework while she still had hopes of marrying Hugo. She would not have wanted to impugn the reputation of her future husband's family. He shook his head. The soundest conclusion seemed to be that *Cypripedium incognitum* was simply an unusual flower that had attracted the embroiderer's eye.

He pulled his chair over to read the rest of the letters with Mara. The next one, dated 5 December 1871, informed Eloïse of the death by choking of Dominique. It was written with Cécile's hallmark candor but provided no more insight into the death of little Yvette Garneau than had her diary entry on the subject. Another announced the birth of Henriette and Hugo's son on 4 January 1872. The baby was named Dieudonné-Dominique-Christophe de Bonfond.

Then, on 7 February 1872, Cécile penned:

Dear Eloïse,

I write to tell you that Hugo fell from his horse today and lies dying. His saddle girth snapped mid-gallop and he went over, dragging Beltrain fully down on him. The poor beast broke a leg and had to be shot. They say Hugo's back is broken, for he can move nothing but his eyes. Maman heard the news while she was overseeing the preparations for Hugo's thirty-sixth-birthday celebration. She set up a wailing like a bagpipe, and walks through the house like a blind person, wailing still, but I wonder now if it isn't as much for the wasted food and expense as for Hugo. Our steward, who saw the fall, says the girth was frayed but looked also to have been partly cut across the underside . . .

"Blimey," said Julian. "Maybe Loulou was right. Maybe Cécile did for him. To get back for all the years of abuse."

"Or Eloïse," said Mara. "Hell hath no fury, and so on. She knew about horses, too."

15 February 1872

My dear cousin,

Maman told me that you have been twice to Aurillac these past eight days without once troubling to see me. Henriette says you come to gloat over our misfortunes. First Papa, now Hugo. It cannot be to console Maman, for, as I have delayed the commencement of my novitiate to be with her, she does not need you, and Hugo, who grows weaker by the day, has no wish to see you, either, I'm sure. In any case, Henriette lets no one near him or her child, so really you needn't come at all, unless it be to keep company with me.

"Hugo died"—Mara referred to a page of notes she had made on key de Bonfond dates—"on the twenty-third of February. It took him seventeen days to do it."

The last few letters were thinly spaced out over the next seven years. Or perhaps they were the only ones that had survived. Cécile never entered the Abbaye des Eaux but remained at Aurillac, growing, as Jean-Claude had said, old, ill, and mad. A letter dated June 1879 informed her cousin that she had been

. . . sick these last weeks, eating nothing but bread and broth. Today was the first time that I felt able to leave my bed. I spent it sitting by my window, watching water run from the dolphin's mouth. It is like my life, draining away . . . Henriette's brat constantly disturbs my rest. "God-given" he is named, but he is the devil's own spawn, with a look as black as his nature. Today he had the effrontery to address me as *tu*, though he is only seven. Maman plots daily to drive Henriette from Aurillac, but I fear the whore has the whip hand of her . . .

The final letter bore the date November 1879 and was written in an almost undecipherable hand:

Dear cousin,

Why do you not come to see me? I cannot come [illegible words] have tied me to my bed. The servants watch me constantly [illegible words] poison my food. Maman cares nothing for my suffering [illegible words] unable to fight back. I think of throwing myself from my window to end my misery. Eloïse, can you not help me?

Mara leaned back against the bed, shaken by this final cri de coeur.

"Bloody hell," said Julian, thinking of the toxic brew that must have been created by those three women, Odile, Henriette, and Cécile, living and hating under the same roof. It was no wonder Cécile went insane.

Wearily, Mara bundled the letters together and tied them up. Her right arm ached. It was ten past two. Fifty minutes before the nurse would come with her next painkiller. Julian returned to his corner. Ten minutes later, he said, "Ha!" and began ferreting about in a box. He pulled out, one after another, yellowed slips of paper which he laid out on the table.

"Hello?" she called after watching him for a time.

"Right!" Triumphantly he turned to her, holding up a clutch of the slips, like a handful of trump cards. "These are bills of sale, Mara, dating from 1815 through to 1833. Between those dates the Verdiers made outlays of cash for the construction of several cast-iron frames fitted out with leaded glass. Here's a bill for a lean-to, and another for a bigger, free-standing structure. There are bills for the purchase of stoves and replacement glass "to be affixed with glazing putty." They ordered cork, sphagnum, and peat, as well as charcoal and woven baskets on a regular basis. And in 1827, someone invested in the installation of a piped hot-water heating system. All told, they spent a tidy sum, in *anciens francs* of course. Now, what does all this suggest?"

He gave her time to work it out. When she did not, he said, "Hothouses, Mara. Someone in the Verdier family took a keen interest in them. And people grew orchids in hothouses."

"Oh, I *see* . . . But wait a minute. They also grew other things. Oranges, for example. Big French estates often had an *orangerie.*"

"Ah, but here's the clincher." He waved a bill at her. "This one's dated 1830 and is for three large, made-to-order *boîtes en verre.*"

"What's so special about that?"

"These, I suspect, were no ordinary glass boxes. If my hunch is right, they were probably the Dordogne equivalent of a Wardian case, a sealed glass container developed by a chap named Nathaniel Ward for transporting live plant material. You see, orchid mania in the nineteenth century was a hobby only the rich could afford. You had to have a hothouse for your plants. And you had to have the plants themselves. That was the harder part. You couldn't just go out and buy your orchids from a nursery or order them by air express. You generally had to send someone out to the far ends of the earth to get them, because the orchids people wanted were tropical exotics, and they wanted ones no one else had yet brought back. Rich fanciers spent fortunes sending collectors around the world in search of new species. The collecting methods were generally disastrous, ecologically speaking, and the transportation conditions even worse. That's where the Wardian case came in. Until the Wardian case was developed, most plants never made it back to Europe alive. Nor did a lot of the collectors, for that matter."

"What happened to them?"

"Oh, they drowned, or died of fever, or were shot. Who knows? Maybe some were even cooked and eaten. It was a dangerous occupation. Still is in some ways." He reflected for a moment. "I think one of the Verdier ancestors was an orchid-fancier who either went himself or hired professional hunters to bring back orchids for his collection. Come to think of it, maybe that's why the Verdiers went into hock. The hothouses were expensive enough to build and maintain, but it was getting the plants to go in them that probably drained the coffers. In Victorian England, fortunes were squandered on the acquisition and propagation of orchids. The same could have happened here."

"Wait a minute," said Mara. "If your orchid was an import, then that solves the problem of where Eloïse saw it. In a hothouse."

Julian blew out a lungful of air. "Possibly. Although, we have to remember it also grew in the wild. So it's either a naturally occurring plant, or a hothouse escapee. Either way, if *Cypripedium incognitum* developed a bad reputation as Devil's Clog, I figure it did so only *after* Eloïse made her embroidery in 1869. She wouldn't knowingly have put something discreditable on the shawl at a time when she was still planning to become a de Bonfond."

Mara considered this. "Then the plant couldn't have been associated with werewolves in Xavier's day. But it might have come to be toward the end of Hugo's life. According to Cécile's diary, little Yvette Garneau had her throat torn out in December 1871. Cécile implied her mother was afraid Hugo had done it. Well, if Odile was having her suspicions, maybe other people were, too." Mara repositioned her shoulder, which was becoming painful. "You know, Hugo's tie with *Cypripedium incognitum* makes sense on another level. If he didn't use a killer dog, he might have relied on a drug to give his lycanthropic delusions an extra kick."

"If Hugo was taking *Cypripedium incognitum* as an hallucinogenic," Julian muttered doubtfully, "he'd have needed a lot of the stuff."

"Then that's it!" Mara exclaimed. "He cultivated it."

"I doubt it. You can't grow orchids like Brussels sprouts, Mara."

"Well, then, he paid people to find it for him. And that could be where Didier got the idea that the old ones dug it up."

Julian remained skeptical. Nevertheless, he blenched at the thought of his orchid being harvested wholesale. "And the Wolfsbane?"

"After people began to suspect that Hugo was a werewolf, they started calling it Devil's Clog and tried to eradicate the plant. Putting Wolfsbane in its place was their way of making sure."

Julian sighed. It was all speculative, but it made a kind of terrible sense. He refolded the bills carefully along their original creases and put them back in the box. "Anyway, getting back to hothouses, there isn't one at Les Chardonnerets. At least, nothing you can see from the road."

"It's probably been destroyed by now, to make way for all those vines."

"That's the trouble," Julian complained bitterly. "It's vines everywhere you look "

"Well, it *is* a vineyard."

t's really disappointing." Mara tossed her glasses down irritably. "We've been at this for hours, and we haven't come across anything that could have given Jean-Claude a reason to try blackmailing Christophe. Or anyone else, for that matter. Compagnon and that *juge d'instruction* are going to think we're frauds." She peered around her. "I'd like to have a look at Cécile's letters again. Bring me that box, will you?"

Julian did so.

"That's funny," said Mara a few minutes later.

"What?" He swiveled about in his chair.

"Do you remember when Cécile complained to Eloïse about being ill? I've got the letter here. She talks about sitting at her window. Listen again to what she says: '. . . *watching water run from the dolphin's mouth. It is like my life, draining away.'* "

"So?"

"Don't you get it, Julian? Baby Blue was put in the wall by someone who had the upstairs end room in the north wing. Or at least by someone who could control access to the room. It would have taken time to pry the stone out through the back of the armoire, and that person couldn't have people coming in at will. But that room can't have been Cécile's room."

His eyebrows curled like question marks. "Why not?"

"Because she had a view of the fountain. There *is* no view of the fountain from the room where Baby Blue was put in the wall. It's at the front of the house."

"Maybe he was put in from the other side of the wall in the next room down. You'd be able to see the fountain from there, wouldn't you?"

"But that's not where the armoire was. Thérèse said the armoire was in the end room. Anyway, the most important thing is that Cécile wrote about seeing the dolphin's mouth. The only way Cécile could have had a view of the dolphin's *mouth* is if her room was in the *south* wing."

"But that's on the other side of the house. If her room was in the south wing, then she—"

"—wasn't the one who put Baby Blue in the wall," Mara finished for him. "Which explains why we haven't been able to find any mention of Cécile's pregnancy or proof of a birth. She never had a baby. Or, if she did, it wasn't Baby Blue. This means we're back to square one. We don't know who Baby Blue was, and we don't know why he was killed."

Julian sat down heavily on the bed, causing Mara to wince.

"Okay," he said. "Then it's a process of elimination. Baby Blue died sometime between 1860 and 1914. If it wasn't Cécile, the only other woman of childbearing age living at Aurillac at that time was Henriette, at least until 1901, when Dieudonné married Léonie. So it's down to those two." Julian frowned, reconsidering. "Or maybe neither. Didn't you say Henriette's bedroom was on the ground floor, off the terrace in the main part of the house? And didn't Thérèse tell you that the roof of the north wing leaked, so that the family has lived in the south wing for generations? That eliminates both Henriette and Léonie. So who had that end room in the north wing? Are we back to a maidservant with a bastard?"

Thoughts were going off in Mara's head like firecrackers. "No, we're not. Christophe did say that his grandmother had the room off the terrace, the one that's now called *le petit salon*. But I think that wasn't until much later on. It's one of the finest in the house, Julian. You should see the *boiserie*. You tell me: what are the chances that Henriette, when she first came to Aurillac, would have been given the best room in the house? Zilch, if Odile had anything to do with it. Much more likely that she and Hugo would have been given adjoining chambers elsewhere. Like in the north wing, under a leaky roof and up a narrow flight of stairs, so she could fall down and break her neck."

Julian pondered for a moment. "All right. What about this? After Hugo's death, Henriette took a lover, got pregnant, and had to dispose of the kid because her annuity depended on her living in a state of exemplary widowhood. That's got to be it. Why the hell didn't we think of it sooner?"

Mara remembered Jean-Claude's dismissal of this theory when she had aired it. "It would have had to be after Odile died. There's no way Henriette could have carried an illegitimate child to term, much less given birth, without Odile knowing, and Odile would have used anything like that as a means of dispossessing Henriette." She referred to her notes. "Odile lived until 1899. Henriette would have been fifty-four by then. Pretty old to start having bastards. And don't forget, we still have a second, headless baby to account for."

"Didier's the only one who can tell us about that," said Julian, sobered by the thought that Didier, with half his lung blown away and fighting for his life, might soon be beyond telling them anything.

37

⸱

S mokey the Greek prized the stone loose.

"Attention!" A soggy Gitane twitched on his lip as he called the warning to his brother below. Theo watched the stone drop with a thud onto the floor very near his left foot.

"Please be more careful!" Mara jumped aside, protecting her injured shoulder. Her wound was mending well, her sling had come off days ago, and the stone had not landed anywhere near her, but she was nervous of everything the brothers did.

The Serafims, press-ganged by the combined muscle of the French Gendarmerie and the state prosecutor's office, had resumed their ill-fated demolition, under the joint supervision of Mara and Laurent Naudet. The logic of the prevailing powers was as follows: Mara had been hired to build a *galérie;* although Christophe was still missing, there was no reason for her not to proceed with her contract. It had taken several days to locate the brothers and several more to get them back on the job.

Mara profoundly resented the high-handedness of the adjudant and the twitchy *juge d'instruction,* who had ordered the work to go forward. In the end, she had agreed to oversee the dismantling only of the wall where Baby Blue had been found, arguing (not untruthfully) that to do anything more could compromise the stability of the structure. With the Serafims, one never knew. Since neither Compagnon nor the examining magistrate wanted to answer for twenty tons of collapsed roof, they had grudgingly compromised.

With every stone that Smokey removed—he was now handing them down to Theo, on Mara's strict orders—she dreaded the discovery of yet another mummified infant, this one sans head. One Baby Blue, intact, was enough for her. For want of anything better to do, Laurent tried to interest her in his theory of twins. She ignored him. As an extension of Adjudant Compagnon, whom Mara thoroughly disliked, he was owed no civility. Hurt, Laurent stood uncomfortably to one side, watching the stones come down.

I hope you're satisfied," she said to the gendarme at the end of the day. The middle section of the wall had been dismantled, leaving only a fringe of masonry on either side that would be reinforced to form the arch abutments to support the roof. The effort had yielded nothing more interesting than dead space. Smokey and Theo had packed up their tools and decamped. They had misgivings about lingering in a house where walls gave up dead babies.

Laurent overlooked, or genuinely did not see, the glint of scornful resentment in her dark eyes.

"It only means the second baby is somewhere else." He glanced speculatively through the gap at the far wall of the next room.

"Oh no," she objected. "If you want anything more taken down, you do it without my cooperation and on your own time. Anyway, all Didier said was that there was another baby. He didn't say where. It could be buried on the grounds. Probably is. Did your clever boss think of that?"

Laurent stiffened. "Of course he did. But he figured, if one baby was put into the wall, there was a good chance the other was, too. Why stick them in different places?"

"Then we should have found them together."

"He thought they *were* placed together, originally. But one of them slipped down farther into the wall cavity."

"Well, he was wrong, wasn't he."

Laurent took a deep breath and turned slightly pink.

"Look, Laurent." Mara relented. The gendarme was such a decent young man it was hard for her to continue being rude to him. "Even if your twin theory is right, even if you find another baby—or five—it doesn't change anything. Jean-Claude is dead and Didier is as good as dead. Your adjutant still counts me a suspect, and you haven't found Christophe."

"We're closing in. We have a number of leads . . ." Laurent left the rest unsaid.

Mara shrugged. "Bordeaux. Paris. He could be holed up anywhere." She fastened the window through which the Serafims had been lowering rubble to the ground and checked around for anything left undone. Earlier she had been through the entire house, securing all of the downstairs shutters. She asked, as she and the gendarme quit the room together, making for the stairs, "Did your boss get anything out of Thérèse?"

"Not much. He feels she's holding back something, though."

Like the truth about Christophe, Mara thought grimly. "What about Dr. Thibaud? Did he talk to her?"

Laurent grinned. "Don't tell him I said so, but I have the feeling he thinks maybe this lycanthrope idea has something to it after all. I mean, once it was explained to him by a scientific type."

"Oh, naturally," said Mara, feeling nasty again.

Laurent said, as they walked around the north wing to the front of the house, "I still think you should have accepted personal protection. You don't know for sure you were shot by accident. And you might not be so lucky next time."

"Look on the bright side. If I turn up dead, there'll be one less person for your boss to suspect. In your trade, it's called the process of elimination." Mara softened, seeing the young man's expression of chagrin. "Don't worry. Whoever it was knows by now I've told you fellows everything I know. There's nothing to be gained by killing me."

"I wouldn't be too sure about that," said the gendarme.

Pierre required regular updates on the landscaping project. Julian provided them willingly enough. It gave him a chance to rub in the fact that his plan was going ahead without most of the Crotte's cost-cutting alterations. Unfortunately, his report this morning was not upbeat. He sat in Pierre's newly completed office at the back of the pavilion, taking in the beige walls, the fluorescent lighting, and the smell of paint. Pierre's environment, like the man himself, was dull, grudging, and guaranteed to give Julian a headache.

Pierre began: "You've been working on that so-called water feature for almost a week. Why isn't it functioning?"

"It is. There's just a spot of trouble with the return. It may have to do with the angle of the pump. I'm planning to have it out today to reset it."

A moist, flabby sound told Julian that the Mouth-Breather had sucked air.

"I was against the idea of it from the start. Waste of good money. I suppose it's how you fellows line your pockets, throwing in expensive add-ons. I don't need to remind you our first delegation of local buyers will be coming through on Wednesday. Sixty-five percent of our sales are to restaurants in the area, so this is an important show. We've never received them on the premises before en masse, and I'm only too aware of the money this circus of Denise's is going to burn. It had better pay off, or we're in deep trouble. Our cost overruns for your landscaping services alone are unconscionable. Now you tell me the pump doesn't work. I hesitate to inquire about the status of the overall project!"

"It does work," Julian retorted irritably. "It just needs adjusting. And the overall project is doing just fine. We're on schedule, the planting is done, the rockery is nearly finished, and, if I say so myself, the approach looks terrific—"

"Naturally you'd say that." Pierre inhaled again, with a shiny display of gums.

Antoine appeared in the doorway. *"Ah, vous voilà,"* he addressed Julian. "Your lad needs help."

Julian jumped up, glad of any opportunity to end the interview.

"And that's another thing," Pierre called after him. "That man of yours. Spends most of his time leaning on his shovel. I object to paying—"

By then Julian was out of earshot, hurrying after Antoine's quickly disappearing back. He was surprised to find that the vintner had stopped to wait for him outside the pavilion. He was even more surprised when Antoine said:

"Pierre's all right. Just doing his job, which is keeping track of the euros. It's what he's best at."

"And I suppose marketing is what Denise is best at?" Julian asked.

"That, and she has a good head for business." Antoine paused, gazing out over the valley. "I'll step down one of these days, and the issue of succession will be difficult. Pierre is older and understands money. Denise is a risk-taker. She could move Coteaux de Bonfond in the direction it needs to go, or she could ruin us. I believe firmly that a body can have only one head."

It was a significant admission that perhaps explained the animosity between brother and sister. Julian had no doubt that control of the winery was something Denise would kill for, ambitious as she was. However, it gave her more of a motive for bumping off her brother than Jean-Claude.

Fearing that Antoine had overheard the talk about the water feature, Julian tried to head off trouble. "Look, I know your first delegation is due next week. I can absolutely assure you that everything will be finished on time."

"I count on it," said Antoine. Typically brief, he knew what he wanted, got straight to the point, and didn't try to do your job. He also made his expectations clear in a way that left you in no doubt that you'd better come up with the goods. Somehow Julian felt that Antoine had always been like that. He could not, for example, imagine him as a whingeing child or a spotty, lovesick youth.

"I heard," said Antoine, positively hanging around to chat, "about old Didier. And that Canadian woman. She's a friend of yours, isn't she? What was she doing out there with Didier anyway?"

"Trying to get information," Julian said, purposely vague.

"Hmm. Police still think she had something to do with Fournier's death?"

"Not anymore. They're going after Christophe, from what I hear."

Antoine frowned. Then he said, almost angrily, "Damned fool. Running off like that. Never had any sense."

"Were you and he close?" Julian profited from Antoine's unusual garrulity to ask. "Growing up as cousins, I mean?"

Antoine stuck out his lower lip. His shoulders lifted slightly. "There are a dozen years between us. To me, he was always just a spoiled little kid. Anyway, his side was too posh for us. My father liked land, the feel of earth between his fingers. Christophe's father liked buildings. That was the difference."

"But you've known him all his life," Julian fished. "Do you really think he's capable of killing anyone?"

This time, Antoine gave a full Gallic shrug. "Who isn't? If the stakes are high enough."

At the end of the lane, Bernard had downed tools. Antoine had said he needed help. What he needed was rescuing. The winery runabout was parked nearby with the driver's door hanging open. Denise was standing in front of the human bulldozer, gesticulating emphatically. She saw Julian and turned on him.

"If it's about the water feature—" he began.

"Screw the fountain!" Her slim body writhed with anger and her dark eyes sparked dangerously, reminding Julian of a spitting live wire. He shuddered to think that he had bedded—or been bedded by—her not that long ago. "I want to know what you're going to do about those *foutu* potholes. *C'est scandaleux!* They're as big as bomb craters. I don't want my buyers breaking their heads."

Julian put up both hands, more as a shield than a gesture of placation. "Look, I'm sorry, but you have to expect a bit of gouging when you shift a ton of stone plus heavy equipment over a dirt road. I'll have a grader here at the beginning of the week to level everything out. It'll be as smooth as a billiard table, promise." How he was going to organize a grader before Wednesday was one more thing he now had to worry about. Another was who was going to pay for it.

"It had better be. As for your fountain, I don't want to know. Just get it working, *entendu?*" Denise scrambled into the car, slammed the door, and shot off toward the pavilion in a cloud of dust.

Julian turned on Bernard. "What the hell did you do to upset her so much?"

"Nothing! I swear it. She just drove up and came at me, shooting black looks like bullets and going for my guts. *Bordel!* If you ask me, I think she hit a pothole on the way up here and cracked her nut." Bernard picked up his shovel. "So did you tell Pierre you have to replace the pump?"

"What?" said Julian. Something Bernard had just said about Denise caused a series of disconnected thoughts to rattle about in his brain like a sudden hailstorm. He stood for a moment, his jaw slack. *Bloody hell. Why hadn't he thought of it before?* "Er—no," he said absently to his assistant. "Look, just get on with it, will you?"

The *faucheuse* blocked three-quarters of the narrow roadway, its cutting arm scything the tall grass on the right-hand verge. Julian seethed with impatience. There was no way past it, and leaning on the horn, he knew from experience, would get him nowhere. Those fellows took a lot of abuse from motorists and were quick to turn touchy.

A kilometer or so down the road, where the road widened, more through happenstance than planning, the driver decided to be obliging. He raised the sawlike arm and pulled the big, bouncing machine slightly to the side, giving Julian just enough room to squeeze past. With a wave of the hand, he shot forward and sped away toward the turnoff to Aurillac.

He reached it too late. Mara, Laurent, and the Serafims had gone. With Didier still in hospital and Thérèse at her sister's, there was no one there to let him in. The place had a blank, unfriendly look. He ran around the sides and back of the house, searching for a way in. All of the wooden shutters of the ground floor had been fastened, except one, which flapped loose against a small window at the rear. Needs must, he thought, and found a flat stone. With a muttered apology to the housekeeper, he smashed the window, using an edge of the stone to clear the jagged shards from the frame. There was barely enough room for him to squeeze through. He went in legs-first, scratching his arms and hands in the process, and dropping down with a crunch onto broken glass.

He was in the kitchen. He ran up three stone steps—the kitchen was built at a slightly lower level than the rest of the structure—into the main part of the house, through the long dining room and the grand salon, to the library. He went straight to the windows, opening them and throwing the shutters back. For what he had to do, he needed full illumination.

Light poured into the room. It fell in long rectangles on the tiled floor and struck a corner of the large table whereon Christophe's family tree was displayed in all its bogus glory. Slowly, Julian took in the many generations of de Bonfonds displayed upon the walls. He paused before Hugo, before Henriette, studied attentively the portrait of Dieudonné the child and, farther down the wall, the photograph of Dieudonné the man, smug and flush with the patina of prosperity.

Julian stepped back and took a deep breath.

"Right, you lot," he said aloud to the host of listening portraits.

Perhaps it was a trick of the light. Xavier de Bonfond seemed to greet his declaration with a ghastly grin.

38

This had better be worth it." Paul wiped his hands on his apron. The restaurant had cleared. He looked beat. He drew a chair up to the table and sat down heavily.

Julian tossed his napkin aside and swept his eye around the circle of faces. "Bernard put me onto it."

"What's Bernard got to do with it?" demanded Mado, looking around for their weekend waiter, but he had vanished outside for a smoke.

Julian grinned. "Denise nearly had the hide off him this afternoon, but we won't go into that. The point is, when he was telling me about it, he described her as 'shooting black looks like bullets.' Now, I don't know if you remember, Mara, but in one of her letters, Cécile also said something about Dieudonné's 'black looks.' "

"I took it as a turn of phrase," Mara said vaguely. She wore a T-shirt that declared: *Everyone is born right-handed. Only the gifted overcome it.*

"No, I think they were both describing what they saw. In Denise's case, I have a pretty good idea what Bernard meant. She has these black eyes that really gun you down."

"And in Dieudonné's case?"

"That's what I went back to Aurillac to check. I had to have another look at those portraits."

"Well?" they all asked.

"There were two babies."

"We know that." Prudence drummed a set of enameled finger-nails on the table.

"Only one was put in the wall."

Loulou pointed out, "We know that, too. Or at least they weren't put in the same wall."

Julian was enjoying himself. "Look, let's start from the beginning, shall we? You remember, Mara, when I was telling you about recessive and dominant traits in orchids? Well, the same principle applies to all living things. It's what makes us what we are. Now, if you look at Hugo's and Henriette's portraits, although the exact eye coloring is hard to determine, both of them are shown as having light eyes. Blue, we know in the case of Henriette, because Christophe told us she was famous for her *Myosotis* eyes. And almost certainly blue for Hugo. Cécile described the man who came to her in the night, the one we think was Hugo, as having a *'regard bleu'*—a blue look."

"Where's this taking us?" Paul crossed large arms over a massive chest.

"To Dieudonné. It was impossible for me to determine the color of Dieudonné's eyes from his photo because everything is reduced to brownish tints. However, the painting of Dieudonné as a boy told me what I needed to know." He turned again to Mara. "You're following me now, aren't you?"

Mara struggled to remember her high-school biology. "Blue eyes are recessive. Two blue-eyed parents can produce only blue-eyed children."

"Well"—Julian waggled his head—"it's actually a bit more complicated than that because eye color is polygenic, but, yes, it would be extremely unusual for blue-eyed parents to have a brown-eyed child. The fact that Hugo's parents were both light-eyed stacks the odds against it even more."

So what color, Mara tried to recall, were the eyes of Hugo's and

Henriette's son? Her memory worked up a round-faced child with dark, curling hair and dark eyes. In fact, a "black look."

"I suppose what you're trying to tell us is that if Dieudonné had dark eyes he couldn't have been Hugo and Henriette's child," she said finally.

"Right. Or at least it would be very unlikely."

"Then who the devil was he?" demanded Loulou.

"That," admitted Julian, "I don't know. But I'm pretty sure who he wasn't. He was not a de Bonfond."

"And the baby in the wall?" asked Prudence.

"Was."

"Cécile and Hugo's?" Mara proposed doubtfully. Were they back to that?

"No. Hugo and Henriette's."

"*Bigre!*" exclaimed Paul, flinging himself back. His chair creaked ominously.

"It was the only explanation I could come up with. I think that's what Didier meant when he said there was another baby, and he's in a position to know because his family has worked for the de Bonfonds for generations."

Prudence said slowly, "So—the person who grew up as Dieudonné wasn't Hugo and Henriette's child. But Baby Blue was, and he was the one who was killed. Why?"

"Think about it. Shortly after Henriette gave birth, Hugo was badly injured in a hunting accident. He was dying. Henriette's annuity, her right to remain at Aurillac, depended on her producing a male heir to survive Hugo."

"Well, then, she'd have had a good reason to make sure her baby lived," Mado pointed out.

"Ah," said Julian, allowing himself to look wise. "But it would have been in other people's interests, particularly those who hated her, to make sure the baby predeceased the father."

They all stared at him.

"I'm beginning to understand," Mara said after a moment. "Someone smothered Henriette's baby as a way of getting rid of Henriette?"

"Exactly."

"And this," said Loulou, plucking at the wattle under his chin, "is where the second baby came in, I suppose?"

"Right," said Julian. "Henriette was one step ahead of the killer. I think she anticipated that someone would try to kill her child—maybe there had already been attempts—and she was smart enough to realize that if anything was going to happen it had to be before her husband died."

"Then all she had to do was make sure no one got to her kid until Hugo snuffed it," declared Paul. "Guard him round the clock."

"Sounds simple, but she couldn't be with him every second—she had to sleep, eat, and also nurse Hugo. Trouble is, he lasted seventeen days. And, from the sound of it, except for the maid Marie, she didn't have many friends in that house. She might have even been afraid they'd drug her food. She did the only thing she could do." He paused for effect, looking around at five expectant faces. "As a contingency plan, she lined up a substitute baby that she could pass off as her own in the event her child was murdered."

"*Ça alors!*" uttered Paul. "She was a cool customer."

"She was desperate," said Julian. "She probably loved her baby like any mother would, but she was facing not only a determined killer but the prospect of a life of poverty. She did everything she could to protect her baby, and at the same time she did what she had to do to survive."

Prudence looked doubtful. "Where would she have gotten the second baby? Kids don't grow on trees, you know."

Julian rubbed his beard. "A foundling? An unwanted bastard? In those days, it might not have been that hard. The critical thing is that one very young baby looks pretty much like another. All the same, it would have been tricky. The transfer had to be seamless, and I'm sure she had very little time to work with."

"I don't see why she didn't just bundle the dead baby up and go outside with it as if she wanted to get some air," reasoned Paul. "Make the switch away from the house. Whoever provided the substitute could have taken the kid away and buried it somewhere. Why stick it in a wall?"

Julian shook his head. "Too risky. She would have been watched by Odile and Cécile and all the inside and outside servants. Supposing she was stopped? The moment her dead baby was discovered, it would have been game over. Also, it would have looked suspicious if she'd been caught trying to take it away. She might even have been accused of killing the child herself."

"So that's why she secretly prepared a hole in the wall through the back of the armoire," Mara mused. "She wasn't a stonemason's daughter for nothing. You're saying that, as soon as she found her own baby dead, she put it in the wall and somehow managed the substitution?"

Julian nodded.

"Someone must have helped her," put in Mado. "No way she could've carried off a thing like that alone. That maid you mentioned, Julian, maybe she was willing to do it for a price."

Prudence objected, "She still couldn't have gotten away with it. The killer, if nobody else, would have known it wasn't the same baby."

Julian had the answer ready. "Ah, but how to expose Henriette without self-exposure? The substitution was something the killer couldn't have anticipated. Where was the body? There couldn't have been a case without a body. That was the beauty of concealing it in the wall. And who could prove the second baby wasn't the real Dieudonné? As I said, one very young infant looks pretty much like another. Henriette would, of course, have sworn it was her baby, and a mother should know her own child. The question is"—his gaze traveled around the table—"which one of them did it? It had to be someone who had access to the baby, and that means Odile or Cécile."

There was a long silence.

"Cécile," Mara said eventually. "It may explain why she eventually went mad. Imagine having to live with someone you smothered in infancy, so to speak."

Julian shook his head. "I think it was Odile."

Everyone debated the merits of each case. Cécile hated her sister-in-law, Mara said. Despite Hugo's abuse, she was probably insanely jealous of Henriette for stealing Hugo's affections, such as they were. The clincher was that Henriette had used Cécile's shawl to wrap her baby in, an accusation in itself.

Julian countered that Odile hated Henriette even more. The Horizontal Blonde had taken her only son. But, more important, the family estate was at stake. "Don't forget," he pointed out, "at the time that Hugo lay dying, Cécile was about to waive her inheritance rights and enter a convent. Because of the way French succession law follows bloodline, if Hugo had died childless, and with Cécile out of the picture, his sole heir would have been his *mother*. The entire estate would have passed from him to her."

"Ha!" declared Loulou. "Look to whom the crime profits. It always boils down to land or money in the end."

It was interesting how the vote split. The women agreed with Mara, preferring Cécile and the psychological motive. Besides, Mara pointed out, even if Odile had hated Henriette, Baby Blue was still her grandson. What woman would kill her own grandchild, even for money? The men, perhaps feeling more comfortable with murder for profit, felt Odile was up to it. Cécile, on the other hand, stood nothing to gain by Baby Blue's death.

"It also," said Loulou, adding a brick to the blockhouse of the male argument, "could have been Maman Odile's way of ensuring that the Verdiers got their own back. Don't forget: the Verdiers' hopes of uniting the two estates were crushed when Hugo dropped Eloïse to marry Henriette. But with Baby Blue out of the way, everything Odile inherited from Hugo would have passed across to the Verdiers on her death."

"The substitute changed all that." Julian clasped his hands behind his neck and leaned back in his chair. "It's ironic. As I said, the killer couldn't even denounce the false Dieudonné without giving herself away. Henriette had her cornered. As far as everyone knew, Hugo died leaving a surviving heir. Henriette had fulfilled her part of the contract. She got her annuity plus a life interest in the estate, and the fake Dieudonné inherited from Hugo. You have to hand it to her. She outsmarted them all." Mentally he swept a bow to the Horizontal Blonde.

"Then that's it!" Prudence, who had been following the back-and-forth discussion like a tennis match, suddenly exclaimed. In her excitement a strand of hair came loose from the black casque of her coiffure. "That was what Jean-Claude tried to blackmail Christophe about. He figured out Baby Blue's real identity. As a genealogist, he would have known about things like genetics, and he must have run into other cases of identity fraud. He threatened to tell the Verdiers about the substitution, which would mean *they* were the rightful heirs."

"In fact," said Mara ruefully, "I pointed out the differences in family features to him. Only I wasn't thinking about eye color."

"Well, then, he would have been quick to figure it out. Christophe is rolling in money. Jean-Claude's prospects for blackmail would have been huge."

Loulou raised a hand. "*Un petit moment* . . . As a hypothesis it's very compelling. Unfortunately, you're forgetting one important thing."

"What?" Prudence's slim-line eyes dared him to upset her theory.

"Time. All this happened a long time ago. The Verdiers, if they took the matter to court, would undoubtedly face some kind of statute of limitations."

"He's right," said Julian. "The case would be dead in the water. Guy's a lawyer. He'd know that straight away. So would Jean-Claude and Christophe."

Loulou nodded. "There's also something called *'la théorie de l'apparence.'* The false Dieudonné was to all intents and purposes the apparent heir of his father. Moreover, he inherited in good faith, since Henriette wouldn't have been likely to tell him the truth. If he and *his* heirs held the de Bonfond property continuously and legally since the time of the substitution, and especially if their labors enhanced the estate, your Verdiers would have a poor chance of making a claim today. And Guy, as you say, is a lawyer. He'd know that."

Prudence sighed. "Well, it was a good idea while it lasted."

Julian held up a hand. "But I have a better one, and since you like psychological motives, Mara, this should suit you. Christophe learns he's not a de Bonfond. His world is turned upside down. You know how the family name defines him. Plus, his neck is on the line professionally. Editions Arobas is about to publish a book on the glorious history of the de Bonfonds, for Christ's sake! I'm sure the book already suppresses the facts that the de Bonfond ancestral tree is bogus and the family was never ennobled, and I suspect Jean-Claude already got a consideration in return for keeping quiet about that. But Baby Blue is harder to suppress. Everyone wants to know who the kid was and why he was killed. So let's say this time Jean-Claude ups the ante: Pay out and I'll concoct some kind of cover story that'll satisfy the public. Otherwise, I'll let the world know not only that your book is a farce, but that the de Bonfonds are baby-killers and frauds. Moreover, you're the biggest fraud of all. How would Christophe have felt to learn that he's not even related to the people he's worshiped all his life? That he's nothing more than the descendant of some maidservant's brat?

Supposing the Verdiers pushed for a DNA test and were able to show that they, but not Christophe, are related to Baby Blue? He'd be a laughingstock on all fronts. It might have been enough to send him over the edge. Or, more accurately, to make him send Jean-Claude over the parapet."

Julian paused and said apologetically to Mara. "I'm sorry. I realize this buries your lycanthrope theory. But surely you must see that if Christophe isn't a de Bonfond he couldn't have inherited a tendency to lycanthropy from Xavier. And if Jean-Claude had figured out that Christophe's grandfather wasn't Hugo and Henriette's child, he would never have tried to blackmail Christophe for his werewolf connections."

They were all looking at her. She gave way with as much grace as she could manage. "All right. Congratulations. You've solved the mystery of Baby Blue. And Jean-Claude. But you still haven't explained away Xavier and his link with the Gévaudan and Sigoulane Beasts. Also, something out there right now is terrifying people in the valley. If Christophe's not behind it, what is? And since both Baby Blue and Dieudonné weren't missing any body parts, who cut off whose head?"

39

Despite everything I said, I still can't see Christophe as a killer," Julian said unhappily. He was standing in the doorway of Mara's kitchen. It was a model kitchen that integrated good layout and the latest European designer appliances with a pleasingly rustic decor. Mara rarely put it to its intended use. Living in a country that boasted some of world's finest gastronomy, she avoided whenever possible tackling what others could do much better than she.

The microwave beeped. Mara pulled out two mugs of steaming milk to which she added generous spoonfuls of Horlicks, purchased from what Paul called *le rayon anglais*, the English section, in that part of Chez Nous that served Grissac as a general store.

Mara handed Julian his drink and a spoon. "How well do you know him?"

Julian shrugged. "We go back a long way. I count him as a friend."

"All right, then, is he gay?"

"Oh, for Christ's sake." Julian stirred irritably. The contents of his mug turned a pale-dun color. "You sound like Mariette. What does it matter—"

She cut in, also stirring. "It doesn't. I'm just proving that you can't answer the question. You don't know Christophe as well as you think."

"Does anyone really ever know another person? He's—how should I put it?—multilayered. Friendly and generous on the surface, very private underneath. I've never asked about his sexual orientation, and he's never volunteered the information. But one thing I do know about him is that he's genuine. I mean, he acts from the heart. If he's in a flamboyant mood, he's all grand gestures and largesse. If he feels petulant, he sulks. He can be difficult at times, but, damn it, I like him."

Mara moved into the front room. Julian followed. They sat down together on an Art Deco settee, a new piece that Mara had recently acquired from a private sale. Jazz and Bismuth were already sprawled on the Aubusson.

"He has lots of friends, you know," Julian went on, "of both genders, in case you wondered. In fact, he told me not long ago that he was coming to look on you as a friend."

Mara chose to ignore this and blew instead on her drink. Frowning at its wrinkled surface, she stuck her finger in and lifted out the skin, which she offered to the dogs. Jazz rose, sniffed, and turned it down. Bismuth pushed forward and ate it. Out of the corner of her eye, she watched as Julian sipped his drink, oblivious of a similar pale membrane clinging to his mustache. She fished a tissue from her pocket and wiped it off. He glanced at her absently, and picked a piece of fluff from her collar. Was this what their relationship was coming to? she wondered. Hot-milk drinks before bedtime and mutual grooming?

Restlessly Julian reclined against the settee back, found its unforgiving angles uncomfortable, and sat up again. "There's someone else we don't know a lot about. Jean-Claude."

"We know he was a womanizer and probably a blackmailer. Also a genealogist, a cultural historian, and an author."

"A man of many parts," Julian said cynically.

"He wasn't a bad writer. See for yourself." Mara leaned across to pull Jean-Claude's books across the coffee table toward them. Julian took them up and glanced through them. His interest was caught by *Le Visage de la Résistance en Dordogne*.

Jean-Claude's text told in simple words the stories of men and women living in so-called Free France, but always under the crush of the Nazi heel. His selection of photographs portrayed the faces of a people fighting a dogged, clandestine war of resistance between the years 1940 and 1944. Many were of *maquisards*, posed singly or in groups, some grim, others cocky, a few of the younger men laughing, unaware or perhaps unheeding of the horror to come. Some photos were of prisoners of war, captured by the Germans and posed before execution or deportation for Nazi propaganda purposes. Others were simply dead, lying in broken heaps, impervious to the forward rush of events. Julian turned to the acknowledgments section to learn that Jean-Claude had gathered his material from municipal, regional, and national archives, newspapers, junk-dealers, family albums, and even Gestapo files. He soon found himself so engrossed that he took the book to bed with him. He was deep in it when Mara came out of the bathroom, smelling of sandalwood and toothpaste. The mattress dipped with her weight as she climbed in beside him.

"Good?"

"Mmm."

"Learn anything more about our murder victim?"

"Mmm."

"I take it Vrac still hasn't found your orchid?"

"What? No. At least, I haven't heard from him if he has."

She sighed, slid more deeply under the covers, and closed her eyes.

"Mara, have a look at this." Julian's voice jerked her back from the first landing of sleep. "Who does this look like?"

She raised her head from the pillow and propped herself on her elbows to squint at the spot on the page indicated by his forefinger. It was the same curly mop of hair, the same round face, thinner perhaps. Definitely the same distinctively broken nose. But not laughing. The man in the photograph was walking, shoulders slumped in an attitude of defeat, in a line of several other men. Prisoners of war. The date, according to the caption, was April 1944.

"Guillaume Verdier." Mara twisted around to sit up. "Antoine's father, Hérault de Bonfond, died in 1943."

Julian nodded. "Which means that Guy was right. Guillaume survived Hérault."

In her dream, they were standing, she and Julian, in a wood. Julian was talking urgently while she stared at something hidden in the trees. *Why here?* she asked, and jerked awake. The digital clock at her bedside read 4:03.

"Julian." She shook him by the shoulder. "Wake up."

"Hmm? What is it?"

"I think I know where Christophe is."

Julian groaned and rolled over on his side. She was already out of bed and heading for the bathroom.

"What did you say?"

40

M aybe you should slow down."

Mara ignored him. The headlights of the Renault did not cut through the swirling mist so much as bounce back at them as a diffuse and eerie light. Black forest rose up on either side. Every now and then a pothole sent them flying. To save his head, Julian braced both hands against the car roof. They were coming to a bend in the road that he vaguely remembered. Mara took it too fast. The car went into a gouging skid. Julian shut his eyes as they slid sideways toward an immense pine. She regained control of the car just in time to avoid it.

"For Christ's sake, Mara!"

To his relief, she slowed to a crawl. He thought the close call had made her cautious. Then he realized that she was merely getting her bearings.

"I thought it was around here somewhere," she said.

"Farther ahead, I think. There." Julian pointed to a slip trail running off to the right.

Mara eased the car onto it, and they bounced along for fifteen meters or so. When the trail ended in a wall of heavy brush, she cut the engine. They got out. Julian played a flashlight in a wide arc around them. The beam swept across low-hanging branches and mottled tree trunks before hitting a flash of metal. They scrambled through the undergrowth toward it. The gray car, well hidden, had been parked and reparked several times, judging from the numerous tracks and expanse of broken ferns around it.

"It's the one we saw before," said Mara. "The one you thought was Géraud's."

"Well, it can't be his. The man loves orchids, but he wouldn't be hunting them in the dark. You think it's Christophe's?"

"Whose else could it be?"

"Cunning bastard. I wonder if he's been there all the time."

They left Mara's Renault on the roadside near the trailhead and trekked through the trees up the back side of Aurillac Ridge, the beam of Julian's flashlight cutting like a blade through the blackness. The forest at night presented itself as a palpable obscurity made up of large, unseen things and ghostly mist that twined silently about their legs. The bottoms of Mara's jeans became quickly soaked as they pushed through wet bracken. In the silence, their muffled footfalls sounded heavy. Julian called out occasional warnings: "Watch it. Bloody great hole here."

Gradually, Mara became aware of another sound. Not a small animal scurrying for safety. Something larger, she sensed, accompanying them, quietly, patiently. Then, as a breeze struck her face, she smelled it, a feral odor that aroused in her an atavistic surge of fear. She pulled Julian to a halt.

"Julian. There's something out there."

He did not argue. He had been hearing it for some minutes: the soft rustle of foliage, keeping pace with them, somewhere off to their left. He trained the flashlight in that direction. It served only to bring to life the trunks of trees that soared above them into a vast, cathedral gloom. Then he, too, caught its scent, riding on the damp air.

"Come on." He pushed Mara sharply forward.

"This was stupid," she said as she trotted rapidly beside him.

"Damned right. We should have brought a gun."

"I don't have a gun. I don't like them."

"Neither do I."

She was falling behind. He seized her hand and dragged her along with him.

They broke with relief into a clearing. Julian turned to sweep the flashlight beam behind them in a wide arc, as if its rays had some power of protection. It picked up gray forms that lumbered off into the misty darkness. The feral odor was replaced by the comforting, familiar smell of wool fat on the wind.

"Whatever it was, it's gone," said Julian, more confidently than he felt.

They were in the southernmost meadow that they had searched three weeks previously. Since that time, sheep had been moved into it. They hurried on through the wet grass, through low-lying, drifting patches of mist. Then they were into cover again as they plunged into the woods at the top of the ridge. After some stumbling about, they picked out another path, twisting away among the trees. Mara thought it might have been the one she had come down with Didier. Even while her mind dwelled on what had been tracking them, she wondered how the morels were doing and if some enterprising poacher had discovered the gardener's private crop. When they came out of the trees again, Aurillac Manor rose up as a black mass above them against a predawn sky.

They approached the back of the house by way of the garden. Julian guided them along one of many gravel paths running between the geometric configurations of boxwood hedges. Ahead, they heard the dreary splash of water. Then their light caught the stone dolphin, forever mid-leap. Suddenly Julian stopped, snatched at Mara's arm, and shoved her behind him. Something in the shadows behind the fountain had moved. He was sure of it. He played the flashlight in that direction. His only thought, as a long shape detached itself slowly from the shadows, was that the thing, with frightening intelligence, had gone ahead to lie in wait for them.

"Arrêtez," said a deep voice. "Stop right there."

A man stood in the wedge of light, holding a rifle level with Julian's chest.

"Nom de dieu!" Julian cried out in relief. "Point that thing somewhere else, will you?"

The man considered this briefly before allowing the nose of the rifle to droop a little. "Who's with you?"

Julian answered, "Mara Dunn." He said to Mara over his shoulder, "Antoine de Bonfond."

"La canadienne," the winegrower grunted. "What are you doing here?"

"Looking for Christophe," Mara answered before Julian could stop her. "We think he's been hiding out in the house all along. You know he's wanted by the police."

"That's rich, coming from you." Antoine's voice had an edge to it.

Julian said, "We might ask you the same question. Why are you here?" He pointed to the weapon. "With that."

Antoine took his time answering. "Maybe for the same reason." Typically, the man was sparing with his words, giving little away. He jerked his head. *"Allons."* He led them to a door giving access to the south wing of the house. "Light," he commanded Julian as he bent to insert a key into the lock. "If he's in there, he'll be asleep. Better to take him unawares."

So, Mara thought, Antoine had figured it out, too. She followed the two men into the still, dark house. The vintner flipped a switch, illuminating a long corridor. He stopped before a door—Mara recognized it as the one Christophe had hidden behind during her last, peculiar conversation with him—and turned the handle. The door swung silently inward.

Another switch brought the room to life: old-fashioned furniture, heavy curtains drawn across the windows. The vintner strode to the bed and jabbed the muzzle of his rifle into the middle of it. A lumpy form stirred, uttered a sharp cry, and sat up.

"*Quoi? Qui? Ah! C'est toi, Antoine.*"

"And us." Mara stepped forward, pulling Julian with her.

A low moan issued from the bed. Christophe, clutching the covers to his chin, stared back at them, like a hedgehog caught in a sweep of high beams. "How did you know?"

"We saw your car in the woods."

"Oh." The little man sighed. "Well, I suppose that's that." He gave them a defiant glare.

"The police are looking for you," Mara said. "And I've been looking for this." She snatched her cell phone from the top of a little cabinet beside the bed. "You took it from Jean-Claude's terrace. After you killed him."

"I did no such thing," Christophe denied, but whether he was referring to the phone or to the genealogist was unclear.

"You've been hiding out here all the time."

"Not at all. Only on and off."

"You made nasty, threatening, dead-air phone calls to me—"

"I couldn't have you spreading lies. Anyway, I never threatened you. Quite frankly, I didn't know what to say. I'm not in the habit of warning people off—"

"You also frightened Thérèse with your impersonation of the Wailing Ghost to get her out of the house, and tried to scare me off the night I was in the library."

Now he giggled. "All I had to do was moan into the heating ducts. The sound carries quite a way. I used to do it as a boy."

"Very funny. And clever. Aurillac is so big no one knew you were here, as long as you kept out of sight. Until, of course, Didier saw you. Is that why you had to shoot him? And me, into the bargain?"

Christophe looked genuinely shocked. "It wasn't me! It was

those damned hunters. Antoine said he saw them hanging around when the ambulance took you away."

"Wait." Julian turned to the winegrower. "You were here that day?"

"Of course he was," said Christophe. "He also gave me the phone. He said he needed a way of keeping in touch with me. How was I to know it was yours?" The little man bristled at Mara.

"That's enough," Antoine snapped. He waved the rifle at Christophe. "Get up. Get dressed."

Christophe blinked doubtfully at his cousin. "Why? Where are we going?"

"Just hurry it up. You two"—the rifle swung around on Mara and Julian—"against the wall."

"What's going on?" Mara demanded uneasily.

Julian said, "Do what he said." Step by step they retreated to the wall.

"Antoine, I swear to you, this is all some dreadful mistake," Christophe babbled as he got out of bed. His round, soft body was clad only in a pair of candy-green boxer shorts. "You surely don't believe this nonsense. For heaven's sake. Tell her." He hopped into his trousers. "Didier was born on the estate. And his father and grandfather before him." He pulled a shirt on, buttoning it awry. "I didn't want him talking, but why would I have shot him? Or her, for that matter?"

Julian took a deep breath. "You didn't."

"If not him, then who?" Mara turned to Julian.

"Antoine."

Mara's astonishment at Julian's reply was mirrored in Christophe's face. The little man gaped at his cousin. "You? But why?"

"Shut up," the vintner barked. "Get your shoes on."

Julian said, "Because Didier saw what he did to Guillaume Verdier."

"Guillaume?" Christophe squeaked, pulling on his sandals. "What's he got to do with it?"

"Guillaume was the *maquisard sans tête*. He escaped from the Germans and made it back to the valley—to safety, he thought." Julian addressed Antoine. "You came across him in the woods, didn't you? You were only—what?—thirteen? fourteen? But old enough to know what was at stake. How did you do it? Bash him on the head with a rock?"

"Why would I kill Guillaume Verdier?" Antoine sneered. "He was a hero of the Resistance."

"Land," said Julian. "With you people, it always comes down to that—land or money. Yours was the only family in the valley that stood to lose if Guillaume resurfaced. And you were the only one who had a reason to cut off his head. If Guillaume's body had been identified, the survivorship of the *tontine* would have been reversed. Christophe said you and Didier brought the body out of the woods together. Did Didier see you do it? Or maybe he just suspected you had. And he's undoubtedly held his tongue all these years because you are a de Bonfond."

Antoine's harsh laugh rang out. "Good luck proving it. Even if you could, the statute of limitations is well past. So why would I want to shoot Didier for something the law can't get me for?"

"Two reasons. First, the law may not be able to get you, but the people of Sigoulane can. As you said, Guillaume Verdier was a hero of the Resistance. You think you have labor problems now. If Didier talked, if Guy Verdier got hold of this information, you'd never get another person in the Dordogne, let alone the valley, to work for you again. You'd be shut out of every restaurant in the region. That's sixty-five percent of your sales right there. You'd be ruined. And, second, Didier was a danger to you because he could link you to a much more recent crime, one that will get you life. Jean-Claude Fournier."

"Jean-Claude?" Christophe cried. *"Mon dieu!"* He broke off to appeal to Mara and Julian. "Antoine said he'd take care of it. I never expected him to kill the man. In fact, he said *you* did it." He waved a hand at Mara.

"Tais-toi, imbécile!" Antoine roared.

But Christophe was irrepressible. "Although I don't say that *crapaud* didn't deserve what he got. The *lies* he manufactured about that damned baby! And he actually tried to demand *money* of me. Fifty thousand euros to hold his tongue. Naturally, I told Antoine about it. After all, he's a de Bonfond, too."

"Antoine didn't kill Jean-Claude to help you out," Julian assured Christophe. "He did it to protect himself. You just provided the cover. After all, you've just admitted Jean-Claude was trying to blackmail you about Baby Blue—"

"Which gives him"—Antoine jerked his head in Christophe's direction—"the perfect motive for silencing him."

Julian turned to the vintner. "Which was a godsend to you because Jean-Claude had you over a barrel. Let me tell you what I think happened. Christophe hired Jean-Claude to put together the de Bonfond family history. Despite everything, the man was a good genealogical researcher. It bothered him that he couldn't verify a lot of the claims—"

"He was a rank amateur," declared Christophe, his face pink with annoyance. "You should have heard some of the things he came up with."

"So he did what any conscientious genealogist would do. He searched out alternative sources of information on the family, one of which was the Verdier archives. And that was when he saw the photograph of Guillaume Verdier. Guy told him the story of the *tontine*, of course. Jean-Claude had just published his book on the Resistance—"

"I kick myself," Christophe cried. "I gave that crook a thousand-euro advance."

"Enough," bellowed Antoine. "Shut it."

But Julian persisted. "He matched up the photo in his book with the Verdiers' photo of Guillaume and concluded that Guillaume had indeed survived your father. But he needed corroboration. He went to see Didier and somehow ferreted out the truth, or enough of it to realize that he'd just stumbled on a lifelong line of credit with Coteaux de Bonfond." Julian turned to address Antoine directly. "And that's when Jean-Claude put the squeeze on you."

"What if he did? I didn't pay up. That's what counts."

"No. You eliminated him. Then you went for Didier because he was a weak link. Mara, too, because she was asking awkward questions. And I expect you came tonight to dispose of another weak link."

"You!" Christophe rounded on his cousin. "You told me to lie low. You said you'd take care of everything. I should never have listened to you."

"Don't waste my time," Antoine snarled. "Get over there with them." He gave Christophe a shove that sent him reeling across the room. He ordered Julian: "The flashlight. On the floor. Slowly."

Julian did not put the flashlight down. He whipped it—backhand—as hard as he could, aiming for the vintner's head. It clipped him on the eyebrow. The rifle went off, bringing down a rain of plaster from the ceiling. With a flying tackle, Julian was on the other man. The rifle spun across the floor. Mara flung herself at it. Antoine, with surprising strength and agility for a man of his age, threw Julian over, scrambled free, scooped up the flashlight, and raced from the room. They heard his footsteps pounding down the corridor.

Julian grabbed the rifle from Mara and went in pursuit. Mara and Christophe ran after him. The chase took them down to the end of the wing and into the main part of the house. With the shutters closed, the darkness there was complete.

"Wait," gasped Christophe. He fumbled along a wall and activated a bank of switches, lighting the entire progression of rooms. Ahead of them they heard Antoine's feet clattering on the stone steps leading down into the kitchen.

"Careful," Christophe panted from the rear. "There—are— meat-cleavers and things in there."

"Terrific," Julian murmured, hoping the vintner was not adept at knife-throwing. He descended the three shallow steps, pressing himself tightly to the wall. Cold air flowed in through the window he had broken the day before. Groping along the inside wall, he found another bank of electrical switches and flipped them on. The space, suddenly illuminated, was empty of any human occupant.

"The cellar!" hissed Christophe, pointing to a door at the back of the room.

More stone steps, these narrow and steep. The way was weakly lit by naked bulbs, dangling by their wires from the ceiling. Julian went part of the way down and stopped. The cellar, he saw, was vast and poorly illuminated. From where he stood, he made out alcoves filled with bottles, venerable with dust. A progression of low arches trailed off to a vanishing point of darkness. Even with the advantage of a gun, he did not fancy flushing Antoine out in such conditions. Then he realized he didn't have to. The cellar was a true *cave*. The man was trapped down there. He turned back.

"Call the gendarmes, Christophe. He's stuck down there. We have him."

"No, we don't," said Christophe. "The tunnel." He pointed to a low door, partly ajar, set into the far-side cellar wall. "He's gone for the tunnel."

Julian laughed. "It's blocked off. We saw it ourselves a couple of weeks ago. There's no way he can get out."

"You don't understand," Christophe shrilled. "The tunnel

branches. About fifty meters down. The right fork leads to another opening in a field below the house. It—it's how I've been coming and going."

"Merde!" Julian clattered down the steps. "Mara," he yelled over his shoulder, "stay here. Get on to Compagnon."

"In a pig's eye," she shouted.

Christophe snatched a battery lantern from a hook at the top of the stairwell and clattered after them. "You'll need this. I'll—I'll show you the way."

The tunnel was faced with rough-hewn stone for about the first ten meters. Then it became a passage crudely cut into bare rock that ran on a slight downward slope before them. The air was damp and cold, smelling of earth and wet stone. Christophe went first, the light from the lantern bouncing crazily from wall to wall as he hurried along. Julian followed, holding the rifle erect. Mara came last. Their pace, at first rapid, slowed to a trot, then to a stagger. At last, the little man collapsed winded against the tunnel wall. His breathing echoed like bat squeaks in the enclosed space.

"I can't . . . You go." He extended the lantern to Mara, who pushed forward past Julian to take it from him. "Fork—just up ahead. Right branch."

The lantern illuminated two dark voids that yawned uninvitingly before them. They sprinted down the right arm of the tunnel, Mara lighting their way. She glanced back. Christophe was trailing behind. The second time she looked back, she no longer saw him.

"I just thought of something." Julian's voice echoed brokenly behind her. "Antoine—devious bastard. Supposing he's hiding in the other tunnel—waiting to double back up into the house—escape that way?"

Mara stopped, her sides heaving, her injured shoulder throbbing with the exertion of the chase. "Bit late to think about that now."

"Yes, but Christophe is back there. Unarmed and in the dark. I expect," he added, "this was where Antoine intended him to disappear. Permanently."

"Well, let's hope Christophe has the sense not to move. So what do we do?"

They ran on.

The quality of the air changed. Mara felt it flowing past her, carrying with it a perceptible freshness. The tunnel floor began to slope upward, so that soon she had to stoop and then crawl on hands and knees, pushing the lantern before her, up to the surface of the earth. The opening was heavily overhung with shrubbery. She thrust her head and shoulders through a curtain of vines, set the lantern outside, stabilizing it on a flat spot, and slid out into a brightening world with its complex mix of smells: wet earth, vegetation, and sheep.

Moments later, Julian emerged from the tunnel, sliding out on his knees and elbows, shoving the rifle ahead of him. A boot came down painfully on his right hand.

"Leave it."

In the morning light, Julian did not need the lantern to make out the boning knife, or the man who held it, neatly tucked up against Mara's throat. The fingers of Julian's free hand froze, centimeters from the gun. The boot followed up with a brutal kick to his jaw that caused an explosion to go off in his head. With a grunt, Julian slumped to the ground, half in, half out of the tunnel.

Antoine threw Mara from him. She landed, with a yelp of pain, on her injured shoulder. However, she had the presence of mind to grab the only weapon to hand: the lantern. With all the force she could muster, she smashed it up into the vintner's face as he bent to retrieve the rifle. He staggered back, blood spurting from his nose. However, he had the gun. He turned it on her, fired point-blank, and ran.

He ran straight into it.

Mara, stunned and unable to believe that the shot had missed her, heard the shout first. Then she saw it, rising out of the tall grass directly before the vintner, bigger than any wolf or dog she had ever seen and covered in coarse gray hair that seemed to give an added, diabolical dimension to its form. Its ears were flattened against a large head, its muzzle, wet with the blood of the sheep it had been devouring, rucked into a ferocious snarl. Antoine had time to give a choked shout of fear, to swerve and start back along the line he had come, before the thing was on him.

The beast drove him to the ground. The vintner fell screaming a short way from Mara, the rifle beneath him. He went on screaming as he fought the thing off, but the sounds coming from him were pitched unnaturally high. Each time Antoine rolled away from the gun, Mara snatched at it, only to be driven back by the shifting, frenzied struggle between man and animal. Again and again she grabbed for it and was defeated by kicking legs, a lashing tail, or powerful, pivoting hindquarters. At last, as Antoine's cries trailed off to a wailing plea, her hand closed on the gun barrel, and she pulled it free.

The animal, correctly sensing its new adversary, whirled about. It left Antoine's bleeding body and began to circle Mara, wrapping her with its awful smell. It went slowly at first, then at increasing speed, practicing its killing art in almost complete silence, its yellow eyes never leaving her face, its upper lip fully retracted to expose enormous fangs. She turned with it, knowing instinctively that she must not let it get behind her. It seemed almost to play with her, darting back and forth in a series of rushes and feints. She fended it off with the rifle, gripping it as she had picked it up, by the barrel, using it like a club. But she was already dizzy from spinning about and knew with a mounting sense of terror that she could not outlast the animal's deadly persistence.

Suddenly a shape appeared outside the whirling circle. Julian had joined the macabre dance. Crouching, swaying with the movement, seeking his chance, he held the boning knife extended before him like an offering. He made two tentative stabs at the powerfully bunched haunches, but the animal, aware of him, was too swift. And smart. It swung wide to include Julian in the epicenter of its attack, driving him and Mara together, swirling about them like a devilish storm. Julian stumbled and fell to one knee. With a roar, the beast lunged. In that moment, as it bore down on him, Julian drove the blade in deep.

A wild shriek shattered the early morning stillness. In a frenzy of snapping and snarling, the beast spun about on itself, seeking the source of its agony. Mara had the rifle the right way round by now, her finger on the curvature of the trigger. She squeezed. In the explosion that followed, the animal seemed to rise gigantic in the air. Behind it, the fiery edge of the sun, nudging above the horizon, gave demonic illumination to its death.

41

Mara wrote to Patsy:

>*. . . The Beast, of course, is the current nine-day wonder, nearly eighty centimeters at the shoulder, one and a half meters long, nose to tail, and fifty-five kilos in weight. Some kind of wolfhound-mastiff cross, they think. Someone set this monster loose, probably because it was so vicious they couldn't control it. Or maybe because it smelled so awful. Compagnon and his boys are now trying to track down the bastard responsible. There's no doubt it's what's created havoc in the valley. Antoine is in hospital being stitched back together. He admits nothing, but the gendarmes found soil in his car that matched samples taken from the spot where Jean-Claude's body landed, and the bullet they recovered from Didier's lung as well as the one that went through my shoulder came from his rifle, so they've charged him with murder and two counts of attempted murder. Considering his antecedents, it's easy to see where he gets his propensity for violence. Wild wolves and werewolves are off the hook, and so am I.*

Didier, amazingly, is mending. He's a tough old bird and is being nursed at Aurillac by Thérèse and Stéphanie. They've put him in the big house, so Christophe is around, too, fussing like a hen. Laurent Naudet also spends his spare time there, making a nuisance of himself. Stéphanie, however, doesn't seem to mind.

I should also tell you that Nathalie Thibaud likes my lycanthrope explanation for the Gévaudan-Sigoulane Beast and plans

to develop it into a book, when she has time. As for the wolf belt,
until Antoine decides to talk, we won't know where he dumped it.
But I don't like the thought of that thing lying around. Like
Jean-Claude said, those things have a life of their own.

Christophe has decided to go ahead with the gallery, thank
god. As for how he's doing, well, let me just say he's not a de Bon-
fond. Which creates a curious situation . . .

Her last conversation with the little man had left her shaken.

"You shut yourself in your room. You disappear mysteriously.
You stay away without letting anyone know where you are. You say
it's none of my business. Well, you made it my business. You involved me, and then you left me holding the bag. I deserve some
answers, Christophe. So where exactly do you go, when you're not
hiding out at Aurillac?"

Christophe had turned pale. He fidgeted in his chair, eyes
swiveling left and right. "Oh, very well," he gave in irritably.

"I'm waiting."

"It's just that it's terribly sensitive."

"Go on."

"I-I'm under treatment for a rather rare condition. Let's just
call it a form of hysterical neurosis. It's triggered by stress as well
as the lunar cycle, which brings on quite frightening physical man-
ifestations: hairiness and—ah—other inconvenient characteristics.
It's all in my head, of course, but it seems terribly real. Whenever
I feel the symptoms coming on, I lock myself in my room. Or I go
to stay for a few days at a clinic. That's why I asked you to deal
with Jean-Claude for me. I was in no position to see anyone."

Mara stared at him. "Are you telling me you really are a lycanthrope?"

"Heavens!" uttered the little man, dismayed. "Only partially. I
certainly don't *believe* I turn into a wolf or any such thing, and that
makes all the difference. I'm in the care of a wonderful doctor—

she has a small private practice in Cahors—and she assures me I'm making good progress toward recovery. She's absolutely first-rate, one of the world's foremost specialists in the field. Of course, you won't have heard of her—"

"No," Mara cut in. She stood up, suddenly feeling very tired and no longer wanting to know. "You're right. I won't have."

. . . because, although Christophe has no blood tie to the family, he is, in fact, a lycanthrope. Or as he says, a partial lycanthrope. And if he is, he must have come by it independently, since he couldn't have gotten it from Xavier. He's also behaving very badly about Baby Blue . . .

"Pooh," Christophe had countered airily when Mara had confronted him with the lie he was intent on living. "Who does it hurt? And why should it matter?"

"It matters," Mara had answered, "because that child deserves his true identity. One that only you can give him." It was something she felt strongly about. Baby Blue merited better than being consigned to oblivion as a footnote to Christophe's vanity.

"And mine?" Christophe had shrilled. "What about my identity? If he's the real Dieudonné, where does that leave me? Or is that of no account to you?" The anguish on his face was so apparent that Mara almost wavered. Baby Blue had hit him where it most hurt.

"The trouble with you, Mara," he went on, "is that you have no passion. Everyone needs to feel passionate about something. My passion is my family—yes, *my* family—and this house. Julian's is his orchid. What do you really care about? I mean, care about so much it goes right to the core?"

At one time Mara might have answered: "Bedie." But her sister was dead. The pain of not knowing was over. She looked into herself and wondered if nineteen years of searching for her missing twin had somehow sucked her dry, leaving her like an abandoned shell, sounding emptily.

. . . Speaking of Baby Blue, the vote's still split on who killed him. Mado, Prudence, and I think it was Cécile. Julian, Paul, and Loulou back Odile. It's something, I guess, we'll never know. We gave him a quiet little burial last week, no one but Julian, me, Paul, and Mado in attendance. I found it sad, but Julian's over the moon because he finally has his shawl with the embroidered Cypripedium incognitum *on it. And of course he's still looking for the real thing every chance he has.*

The truth is, Patsy, Julian and I have been bumping along pretty rockily of late, and now we've had a serious disagreement that I don't think we can patch over. I mean, how do you deal with someone who has a bungee-cord notion of right and wrong? I can understand why he's prepared to keep quiet about Guillaume Verdier's murder. Even if Didier testified against Antoine, the statute of limitations has passed, and the man will probably spend the rest of his life in prison anyway for the murder of Jean-Claude. But to let Christophe get away with publishing a knowingly fraudulent version of his family's history (among other things, he's passing Baby Blue off as a maidservant's bastard) strikes me as terribly wrong. Christophe says my problem is I lack passion. Maybe I do, and maybe that's why I don't understand those who have it. Write soon. Desperate in the Dordogne, Mara<

Patsy's reply was swift and reassuring. It was why Mara loved her:

>. . . Passion is good. But it shouldn't take the place of truth. And truth is good, but absolute truth can be a tyrant and makes a cold bedfellow. Don't worry, kid. If the fire in your belly is on simmer, it only means you're recharging. After what you've been through

with Bedie, you're entitled to a breather. Relax and smell the or-
chids.

P.S. I don't see why Christophe can't have come by his lycanthropy
honestly. You said yourself Dominique had it on with every will-
ing wench in the valley. If you think one of Adjudant Com-
pagnon's forebears might have been a Dominique by-blow, why
not Christophe's grandfather, the false Dieudonné, as well? Fact
is, it would be true to form for Dominique to have knocked up one
of the Aurillac maidservants and for Henriette to have done a
deal with the girl to take the kid off her hands. Christophe might
be a little bastard, but maybe he's not such a fraud as you think.<

Julian sat on a mossy rock. The evening sunlight hung in the
trees like golden fruit. The only sounds were the intermittent,
ringing call of a cuckoo and the trickle of water. The spring (the
original from which Domaine de la Source got its name) gushed
out of a rocky crevice before him and ran away in a clear stream at
his feet. Tiny ferns grew in abundance along the streambed.

The pavilion project had been abruptly discontinued. He had
managed, only with a lot of arm-twisting, to collect from Pierre
for the work and materials he had put into it. However, he was
now free to spend his days prowling the valley in search of his orchid. Typically, he was methodical and exhaustive, poking about in
every likely habitat. He had walked the banks of the Rauze end to
end, had come across a splendid clump of parasitic Toothwort
growing on a stump in a water meadow, and had even discovered
several plants of *Aconitum vulparia*, Wolfsbane, which he was able
to identify by their yellow buds. Julian had asked Didier if it was
Wolfsbane the old ones had planted in the place of Devil's Clog.
The old gardener, comfortably propped up in his convalescent
bed, had shaken his head. He didn't know. It was before his time.
In his continuing search, Julian had found no *Cypripedium incog-*
nitum.

As he searched, he thought occasionally about Eloïse. He didn't much like the picture he had formed of the woman, but he recognized that he owed her an immense debt. Without her and her needlework, he would never have seen his Mystery Orchid whole, never associated it with Aurillac. Her embroidery and Didier's information on Devil's Clog had given him a shadowy history of the flower he sought, but he was still left with more questions than answers.

It had taken seventy-seven stitches to sew Julian up after his encounter with the feral dog, about a tenth the number required for Antoine. His jaw, where the vintner had kicked him, was still extremely painful, the bruising lingering as an ugly purple welt. But these things were nothing compared with what he had been through with Mara. It boiled down to a simple difference in philosophical and ethical perspectives: he was inclined to leave well enough alone, Mara wanted truth to out. Simple things, Julian had come to realize, could be terribly complex.

"*A quoi bon?*" he had asked. To what good? "If we go public with what we suspect about Guillaume Verdier's murder, the public backlash will be so bad the winery will probably go under and take a lot of jobs and innocent people with it."

"Denise? Innocent?" Mara had nearly screamed.

"I didn't say she was *nice.*"

As far as Baby Blue was concerned, again Julian had asked, *A quoi bon?*

At that point, Mara had exploded. "Right and wrong don't matter? Or is that the orchid nerd's philosophy of life? *Orchis, orchis über alles?* In case it slipped your mind," she had thundered on, heedless of the hurt in his eyes—the "orchid nerd" gibe had hit him between the legs, figuratively speaking—"Christophe is about to publish a self-serving, purposely fabricated tissue of lies. It's a question of intellectual honesty."

"No," Julian had retorted angrily. "It's a question of friendship. Something you might want to think about."

"And something you might want to think about, Julian Wood, is why you hide behind a flower you're never going to find. Is it safe because it's unattainable? Does chasing after it let you sidestep reality? Does it let you avoid facing the truth about yourself, that you run from relationships because you're scared to death of failure?"

"For Christ's sake," Julian had yelled. He'd had just about all he could take. "If you're so hung up on truth, why don't you look at yourself? You're inflexible and stubborn and damned judgmental. Worst of all, you just can't let things *be*. You always want to arrange things. You say I can't face reality. Maybe it's just that you don't like my brand of reality. Worst of all, you have one set of rules that you want everyone to play by, as long as it's convenient for you. You expect unquestioning loyalty from your friends, but you sure can't handle it when they give it to someone else. That, as far as I'm concerned, is what your issue of right versus wrong boils down to."

"Ha!"

And that was pretty much the last word he had heard from her, if "ha" could even be considered a word.

However, Julian had one small triumph. In return for keeping quiet about the *maquisard sans tête*, he had wrested from Pierre and Denise a commitment to work out a fair agreement with the other vintners in the valley to enlarge the Coteaux de Bonfond *chai* to accommodate local production. It took a bit of wooing to bring Michel Verdier back to the table, but it was worth the bother just to see the expression on the Crotte's face when he realized that he had no choice, that, in addition to paying Julian what he owed him, he was going to have to spend even more money. Denise, quicker to size up the situation than her brother, had simply snapped, "Do it," sounding eerily like her father as she said it. The look of malice in her black eyes, however, told Julian that he'd better put a lot of space between her and himself for the rest of his life.

But he remained deeply troubled over Mara. The "orchid nerd" taunt and her accusations about his running from reality still stung. Maybe she had a point. He knew she wanted more from him than he had been prepared to give, his pronouncements on permanence notwithstanding. And maybe he really did have to look at this. Or maybe not, because, after their last exchange, things were probably washed up between them anyway.

At this moment in Julian's reflections, Bismuth appeared downstream, splashing across the water and galloping toward him up the path. The dog was wet and muddy as usual, but he looked excited. He scampered around, eyes alight, ears flying.

"Earn your keep," said Julian, with something almost approaching affection. Bit by bit, the dog had dug itself into its master's soft spot. "Find some truffles."

"Too early for them," said a voice he knew. Mara appeared, breaking through the trees on the other side of the stream. Jazz came pushing through the bushes beside her.

Julian stared at her in amazement. "Hello, stranger." He lurched gladly to his feet, then checked himself. "Er—what are you doing here?"

She appeared hesitant, uncertain of her welcome. "Looking for you. I spotted your van parked off the road and figured you'd be around here somewhere." She tried to speak with her normal briskness, but her tone was forced. "Actually, Bismuth found *us*. So. Discovered any rare orchids?"

"Not a single one."

"Didn't think so. Without wanting to sound judgmental, I think you need help."

"Is that an offer?" he asked cautiously.

She paused, giving it serious consideration, her eyes crowded with unspoken questions. "If you ask pretty."

Pretty? He tugged at his beard, wondering how to put it. There were so many things he needed to say to her, and none of them would be easy. May as well get it over with. He opted for the unadorned truth. "All right. The fact is, Mara, we're very different people. You like buildings and moving things around. Tearing down walls just seems damned destructive to me. You have no real feeling for the things I care about—flowers, trees, orchids. All this makes it very hard for us to see eye to eye . . ." He stopped, unable to go on because suddenly he no longer knew what he wanted to say.

" 'To him who keeps an Orchis' heart, the swamps are pink with June.' " The lines from Emily Dickinson came softly and unbidden to Mara's lips.

He regarded her earnestly. A vision of wetlands, ablaze with *Orchis laxiflora*, flashed through his mind. Fancy her knowing that. But he sensed that her words held some far deeper meaning.

"I don't have an Orchis' heart," she said sadly. "But I appreciate beauty in my own way. Who knows? Maybe one day I will see a swamp as a sweep of color rather than a muddy bog . . ." She found that she could not look at him. Instead, she stared into the swiftly running stream between them. A leaf, riding the current, swirled past and was lost to view. "I hope this isn't your way of saying goodbye."

Julian considered this. Very gently he said, "I think it's my way of saying that we should stop trying to make the other into what neither of us is."

Now she looked across at him. "Do we do that?"

"Yes."

"What should we do instead?" Profoundly, Mara realized that this was the knife-edge on which their relationship balanced.

"Build on what we have. On who we really are." He took a deep breath, certain now of his words. "I want to work things out between us, Mara. I want to be with you. Over the long term, through all the seasons." His sudden grin was boyish and self-deprecating. "How's that for pretty?"

A rush of relief followed by a great gladness of heart, radiant with all of nature's colors, swept over Mara.

"It'll do, Julian Wood," she said, her eyes filling with laughter as she looked for a way to cross the water. "It'll do very well."

EPILOGUE

23 FEBRUARY 1872

The beast raised its head, ears alert, its long muzzle freshly bloodied. A pale moon hung huge above a frozen landscape of silvered fields and shadowed forests. The sound drew nearer, the rumble of wheels, the flinty clatter of hooves on a stony roadway. The beast growled low in its throat, crouching over its nocturnal feast. A moment later, the light gig rattled past, swerving off in the direction of the dark mass of a structure, outlined on a rugged prominence against the night sky.

In a downstairs chamber of Aurillac Manor, a woman stood before a dying fire. Her face was pale and expressionless against the somber tones of her dress, her dark hair coiled tightly around her head like a cap. With a crackle, the log in the hearth flared, momentarily catching the whites of her eyes and illuminating features that were small and regular, but without any real beauty. She had been waiting—hours, it seemed—for something, a cry, a rushing of feet, anything to signal the inevitable discovery. She did not hear the arrival of the gig that came to a rocking halt at the rear of the building, or the hurried footsteps of the maidservant who ran gasping up the narrow stone stairway leading to the upper story of the house.

When the first faint wail reached her, the woman raised her head sharply. She tensed. Disbelief replaced incomprehension. Quickly, she moved in the direction of the cry that hung, like a wisp of devilish smoke, in the air. Gathering up her skirts, she ran, stumbling up the dimly lit stairwell, rushed through the antechamber at the top, and burst without knocking into the room.

Henriette was seated beside a table on which burned a single lamp. She looked up, turning scornful blue eyes on the intruder. The woman in the doorway wavered.

"It's you, then," Henriette said. "I wondered which of you it would be."

Eloïse's harsh intake of breath was almost a strangled cry. "It's not possible," she whispered. "Your son is dead. Hugo is now childless—"

"And the Verdiers will take back what belongs to them? Oh, my dear." Henriette smiled like a golden cat. "Once again I must disappoint your hopes. Hugo is already dead. He died half an hour ago. But"—the mother shifted the precious burden in her arms—"as you can see, he leaves an heir. My son, Eloïse, lives and is eager for the breast."

The wolf resumed its feasting, worrying its kill with tooth and claw. In a rush and with a sudden expulsion of air that was as gentle as a sigh, the torn belly yielded up its prize of steaming guts. Eyes rolling to the moon, the wolf threw back its shaggy head in a primeval valedictory over its dead.